BUILDING FROM ASHES

ELIZABETH HUNTER

Building From Ashes
Copyright © 2012
by Elizabeth Hunter
ISBN: 978-1480217843

This is a work of fiction. Names, characters, places, and incidents are the products of the author's imagination, or are used fictitiously. Any resemblance to actual persons, living or dead, business establishments, events, or locales is entirely coincidental.

Cover Design: E. Hunter
Edited by: Amy Eye
Formatted by: Amy Eye

For information about the Elemental Mysteries series, please visit:
www.ElementalMysteries.com

For my sister,
an extraordinary woman

~

And for twenty-one women
who make me brave

Also by Elizabeth Hunter:

The Elemental Mysteries:

A HIDDEN FIRE
THIS SAME EARTH
THE FORCE OF WIND
A FALL OF WATER

The Cambio Springs Series:

LONG RIDE HOME (short story)

Contemporary Romance

THE GENIUS AND THE MUSE

ACKNOWLEDGEMENTS

What to say? There were so many people who made this book possible. It was challenging in ways that most of you cannot imagine. (I hope you never have to.)

Thanks to my pre-readers, Kristy, Caroline, Sarah, Kelli, Paulette, and Lindsay, who are dear friends, as well as some of the smartest women I know.

Thanks to my editing team, who shine things up and make me look less forgetful. Amy and Cassie, you guys rock.

Thanks to my marvelous family, who put up with my distracted behavior.

Thanks, especially, to my son. The light of my life.

And finally, thanks to 'the girls.' You know who you are. You know the ugly stories and the funny ones. Thank you for clapping while I dance naked down Main Street.

He has sent me... to bestow on them
a crown of beauty instead of ashes,
the oil of gladness instead of mourning,
and a garment of praise instead of despair.

Isaiah 61:3

PROLOGUE

Wicklow Mountains, Ireland
June 2010

He emerged from the earth, the acrid smell of smoke hitting his nose as he brushed the loose soil from his face. He could see the flames licking at the houses, and hear the shouts of the humans as they ran, some rushing to safety, others attempting to drown the fire that had already turned the main house to rubble.

His daughter sat at the edge of the garden, staring into the flames, leaning toward the heat as if drawn by some ineffable force.

Carwyn stalked toward her. "Deirdre."

She looked up, her eyes feverish in the moonlight. "I kept everyone away. As soon as I realized… I kept them all away. No one's been hurt."

He pulled her up by the collar of her singed shirt. "What have you done?"

"As soon as I realized… She's still alive. She must be, I think. The flames keep coming, and I feel… I knew as soon as she woke—"

"What have you done?" he roared as the roof of the barn adjacent to the farmhouse started to burn. He glared at her, the blood tears staining her cheeks and her auburn hair wild around her face. His grip on her softened.

"I couldn't…" Deirdre's whisper could barely be heard. "I couldn't lose her, too. Not her." More shouts came from the houses, and somewhere near the dairy barn, a child began to cry.

Carwyn's face fell, and his rage fled. "My daughter"—he groaned —"what have you done?" He let go of her collar, and Deirdre's long legs seemed to crumple under her as she sank back into the cool soil of the summer garden.

He waded through the mass of people running away from the smoking farmhouse. The old building was in ruins, the top having collapsed onto the ground floors. Through the rubble, he could see the black doorway his son had dug into the hill hundreds of years before. What had once been a cozy passageway now gaped like a tomb, and rough stones had fallen in front of it, partially obscuring the entrance.

Carwyn walked toward it, listening for any sounds that escaped the scorched earth. He lifted his hands, forcing out his energy to move the rocks, as he toed off the shoes he'd been wearing. He dug his feet into the earth, letting the hum of elemental energy flow through him as he felt for her. The air hung thick with smoke, but a faint waft of new *amnis*, the immortal energy that animated their bodies, carried the smell of charred hawthorn to his nose, drawing him closer.

As he entered the dark passageway, he heard her; her shallow breaths echoed off the worn walls. He followed the trail of her scent and amnis, trying to keep his heart under control, knowing that any hint of danger could result in a rush of suffocating fire. He opened his mouth to speak, keeping his voice quiet, so as not to startle her.

"Brigid?"

A small hitch in her breath.

"It's me."

The panting picked up speed, and he scoured the past for something that might calm her. The soft refrain of a Welsh lullaby came to him, and he blinked at the memory of a solemn young girl sitting next to his son in the library, her brown eyes rose to Ioan's, frowning to hear the fierce immortal singing a childish tune. Carwyn paused as a rush of grief threatened to overpower him.

Brigid had always been too old for lullabies.

Nevertheless, he began to hum the tune, and he could feel her energy change. At first, it smoothed out, drifting in waves, but then the waves began to sharpen, the peaks and valleys growing as he came closer. Her breathing stopped, and Carwyn could hear her heart give a single, low thump.

"Brigid?" he called again.

Carwyn turned a corner, still humming the soft tune, and brushed away the remnants of a burned oak door, blinking away bloody tears as he entered the chamber.

The furniture had been pushed to the edges of the room by the initial blast. There were still flames teasing the edges of a bookcase and a desk, but the rest of the sturdy oak had been torched. He saw her huddled figure glowing through the smoke.

The small woman sat in the center of the room, curled into herself, utterly still. Her knees were drawn to her forehead, and her arms were wrapped around her legs. No trace of clothing remained on her delicate frame and no hair covered her head. She was naked as the day she had been born into the world, the red-gold flames swirling along her skin having burned away any trace of the human she had once been.

She did not breathe, but her heart began to race. He stopped humming and glanced around the room as he felt the slow draw of air gather around her body. Suddenly, Brigid's head rose and she opened her eyes. Carwyn gasped. Her warm amber eyes had burned to ash-grey around the edge of her irises, and streaks of blood and soot covered her heart-shaped face.

The flames along her arms began to lick up her neck. Carwyn held up both hands.

"Calm, Brigid."

Her face fell in pain and confusion. Then she opened her mouth, fangs gleaming in the firelight, as she let out a feral scream and the fire burst forth.

In the space of a heartbeat, Carwyn lifted his shoulders and pulled the mountain down.

ELIZABETH HUNTER

BOOK ONE: EARTH

Generations come and generations go,
but the Earth remains forever.
Ecclesiastes 1:4

Building From Ashes

Chapter One

Dublin, Ireland
December 1995

Looking back, Brigid Connor would not think it odd how comfortable she'd always been with monsters. The girl had learned at an early age that appearances could be deceiving. Surely her stepfather, with his soft brown hair, calm smile, and open countenance, looked like the picture of fatherly affection and care. Her mother, with her placid face and helping hands, was the ideal of domestic contentment.

So when the monsters burst into her bedroom that cold December night, with her Christmas dress hanging bright and crisp on the closet door and her stepfather bending over her, Brigid should have been horrified. She should have cried out when the dark-haired monster scooped her up in one blurring motion. She should have looked away when the red-haired demon with the burning blue eyes grabbed Richard Kelly by the throat and twisted his neck until she heard the quick pop and he crumbled lifeless to the floor.

But Brigid did none of those things. Because she knew on that cold winter night, as the frost crunched beneath the monsters' shoes and they bundled her into the waiting car, that appearances could be very deceiving.

Her great-aunt's waiting arms were soft and warm, and she was enveloped immediately in their embrace.

"We didn't know, child," the old woman whispered. "As soon as your mum… we didn't know. Why didn't you tell me, Brigid? Don't worry, darling, we're away from here now. You're coming with me and the doctor will take care of everything. Don't worry—"

"I have my Christmas program tomorrow at school."

Brigid remembered a sudden silence and a shifting sound outside the car. Suddenly, a pair of blue eyes met hers over her Aunt Sinead's shoulder. It was the monster who had snapped her stepfather's neck. He stared at her for a moment; then in an inhuman blur, he was gone. Seconds later, she heard the car door open, and her aunt reached out. Sinead spread her Christmas dress next to her on the seat, and Brigid looked back over her shoulder.

The red-haired monster stood in the frigid night air, but no steaming breath puffed from his mouth. He looked at her with solemn eyes. Suddenly, a smile turned up the corner of his mouth. "It's a lovely dress," he said. "You'll look grand in it."

Brigid could only whisper. "Thank you."

The car doors closed. The dark-haired monster with the kind smile slipped into the front seat, and they sped away from the tidy neighborhood in the suburbs of Dublin.

But the red-haired monster stood in front of the house that had been her prison, alone in the freezing night.

Gwynedd, Wales
December 995 AD

"Please." He grasped her cold hand. "Don't."

She only squeezed his fingers and turned back to the fire.

"It is a sin," Carwyn said. "A grave one. To give in to despair—"

"You are my son," Maelona said with a soft smile, "not my priest."

"Mother." Carwyn, son of Bryn, knelt before her, the wind whipping outside the door of the old cottage that fronted the cozy home. Maelona had dug her shelter into the mountain centuries before, forming and twisting the earth to her will as all of her immortal kind did. The elemental energy had sustained her life and protected her for over three hundred years. And the same mountain had sheltered her only child when he had woken twenty-seven years before, transformed by Maelona's immortal blood as the young priest lay on the edge of death.

She had saved him. Loved him as a son. Trained him as a vampire to survive in the harsh world he had entered. Now, the powerful immortal whose energy commanded the very earth beneath him sat hunched in front of the fire, pleading with his sire to live.

"Please, I beg you, do not leave me. Your sister's loss—"

"You know nothing of my loss." Her voice was sharp, but softened when he raised his red-rimmed eyes to meet her gaze. "You are so young. You know only the faint mortal echo of it. Perhaps, one day, you will understand. For three hundred years she was my companion. The only immortal who knew me from my human life. The only one who understood. I told her not to leave. For her to go to the island and be killed by those Northern heathens..." Maelona's eyes tightened in grief. "She was surrounded by water when she died, Carwyn. Her ashes drift alone in the ocean."

Carwyn rose from his knees and sat next to her in front of the crackling fire. "Your sister's death does not have to mean your own."

She closed her eyes and gave him a soft smile. "I am tired of this life. You never abandoned your faith, Carwyn. Do you not believe that my soul will fly to meet hers? Don't you tell me that God does not abandon those touched by our peculiar curse?"

"To willingly meet the day is not a natural death."

She squeezed his hand. "There is nothing natural about this life."

"Perhaps not. But there is much to look forward to." His voice faltered, betraying his own fear. "Many reasons to hope."

"There are for you." She smiled and he remembered her joy from his early years with her. "Do not make my mistake, Carwyn. Do not fear the attachments of family and kin." She reached up and touched his face. "Making you my son has been my greatest joy. I should have had many more children to share my life. Do not make my mistake."

"Mother—"

"You have more love to give than any vampire I have ever known. You should surround yourself with family," she said softly. "You had a wife once. Children. Find a new family in this life as you did in your human one."

He frowned and looked away. "My wife is dead. My children are grown. I am only a faint memory to them. I want no other family."

"No." Maelona grasped his hands in her own. She was slender but tall. Unusually so for a woman of her age, and Carwyn had often wondered whether the Northern blood of the raiders who had killed her sister had not touched her own family as well. His sire was a strong woman but had been melancholy for too long. "Do not abandon love. Love is the foundation of strength. What we build on and hold to. Find a new family to share your love. Find them from those who need healing. The weak who need help. Find a mate and surround yourself with joy. This life is too lonely to travel alone."

He shook his head. "I desire no mate. Perhaps—"

"Then return to the church." He shook his head, but Maelona continued. "Surely there are those who would understand. You have so much to give."

"The church I knew has changed. Perhaps… I will consider it." He knew there were other priests who knew about his kind. He knew he could be of use, but Maelona's despair haunted his thoughts. "If you would only stay—"

"I'm leaving tomorrow evening." A dreamy look fell over her face. "I will walk toward the West, I think."

Cold fear gripped his gut and his blood surged hot. "Do not let your ashes fly to the sea. At least stay in the mountains. I beg you."

A trace of her old humor returned. "I do not think I will get as far as the water. The sun will take me before then."

Carwyn choked back a cry and embraced her. "Is there anything I can do to change your mind?" He knew, even as he asked, there was not. For seven years, she had mourned her sister's death. She was weary of the constant struggle against bloodlust. Tired of hiding from the sun. Burdened by the loneliness of centuries. He knew Maelona would meet her end gladly.

"I have had over three hundred years of life, Carwyn. Three hundred years. Who could ask for more?"

I can.

Even as his heart broke at the thought of her death, Carwyn recognized the burning fire of survival had not lessened in him. Lost in the storm, he had dragged himself toward the smoke of Maelona's fire twenty-seven years before, broken, freezing, and weak from days of wandering in the mountains. He had only one thought that urged him on.

He had wanted to live.

Carwyn had struggled for years over his desire. To live. To thrive. To drink up earthly life in all its rich majesty and splendor.

"Is it my own failing," he asked, "that I do not want to join you?"

Maelona looked horrified. "No! This end is not for you."

He blinked back tears and looked into her eyes. "Is it my own fear? Do I not have faith in God's love? I would see Efa again. My two children taken to heaven as babes. Is it a failing that I am greedy for life?"

She stroked a hand through the shaggy auburn hair that covered his head before she rose to walk to her day chamber. She turned back at the dark hall. "You have many years to live. You possess a rare kind of joy, Carwyn. Treasure it and know that there are many paths to take. Someday, long in the future, we will meet again."

Carwyn stared at her, knowing that by the time he rose the next night, she would be gone. It would be the last time he saw her in this world. He straightened his shoulders and stood, his presence filling the small room. Giving her, in her last moments, the confidence of his strength.

"I love you, *Mam*."

Maelona closed her eyes, and a peaceful smile spread over her face. "I love you, too."

County Wicklow, Ireland
December 1996

She rarely slept lying down. There was a shivering kind of weakness that enveloped her bones at the idea of being prone. She was indulged in her aunt's home, surrounded by strange beings who never grew older; Brigid had come to understand the pleasant-faced monsters were both frightening and kind. Her Aunt Sinead, after whisking her away from her childhood home, never spoke of her mother or stepfather again.

Brigid had only faint memories of her aunt from her younger years. A visit for tea. A stuffed rabbit that had been put on a shelf out of her reach. Promises of visits in the country that Brigid knew her stepfather would never allow. After Brigid was taken from Dublin, no one mentioned her past life again. And Brigid did not ask. It was as if she had been reborn in the mountains the morning she woke curled into her aunt's side.

But still, she could not rest peacefully.

So, the small girl with the dark hair and the haunted eyes took refuge in the library where the doctor worked. She curled into a corner by the fire, and the kind monster, whom she came to know as her protector, smiled at her and turned back to his books. He never approached her when she drifted in the warm room; he brushed away those who tried to take her to the bed she would not sleep in.

For the first year, she lived at Ioan and Deirdre's home in the mountains. Brigid slept in a corner of the library couch, leaning upright in the small alcove, ready to wake at the slightest sense of alarm.

"What do you like to read?"

She looked up, blinking. The doctor was kneeling in front of her by the fire, and she wondered how he had managed to approach her without her senses alerting her to his presence.

"What am I allowed to read?"

Ioan, son of Carwyn, sat back on his heels and frowned a little. "Well, that's an excellent question. I suppose I have things in the library that are not suitable for a child, so—"

"Like what?" She sat up straighter, not realizing she had interrupted one of the most powerful earth vampires in the Western world.

Ioan's eyes twinkled with delight. "Oh, I have… dangerous books here."

"What kind of dangerous books?" Brigid bit her lip and leaned forward.

"Well, there are tales of gods and rebellions. Nothing suitable for a little girl, I don't suppose. There are some fairy tales—"

"I don't like princess stories."

He shrugged. "I'm not a fan of them, either. But I'm not talking about princesses."

She scooted forward. "Well, I want to read them."

Ioan sighed. "I don't know. They're quite dangerous."

Brigid straightened her back and looked at him. "I'm very brave, you know. I never cry."

Ioan looked down into the face of the wounded child who never knew she was a child. She only understood years later the shadow that fell over his eyes.

"I know, Brigid. I know you're very brave."

BUILDING FROM ASHES

So Brigid Connor was introduced to myths and legends, dark fairytales and stories of fantasy. While her aunt might have clucked at the Grimm, Carroll, and MacDonald he gave her, the Poe and Tolkien she devoured, Ioan brushed them away. Ever her protector, the doctor understood the slim girl needed the dark and twisted stories that made her feel quite not as alone when she read them. And it was into these stories that Brigid would fall, over and over again, as she grew into a young woman in the house dug into the mountains of Wicklow.

And yet, despite the loving acceptance she found in her protector's library, despite the warm embrace of her aunt and the gentle guidance of the immortal family she grew to love, Brigid came to understand the shadow in Ioan's eyes that never seemed to leave. Brigid understood, because it mirrored her own.

Wicklow, Ireland
October 1999

Ioan stared at the doorway. "The child is so troubled, Carwyn. I don't know what to do about it."

They spoke in Welsh, seeking what anonymity they could in the crowded house while Ioan's wife, Deirdre, Sinead, and the girl had a shouting match down the hall.

Carwyn shrugged. "Part of your problem is calling her a child. She isn't one. She hasn't been in a long time."

"She is a child. Just a wounded one."

"Surely you've had experience with victims of abuse? You've practiced medicine for over three hundred years, Ioan."

Carwyn watched his son in the library of his home. Ioan was troubled and, for the first time in many years, Carwyn was at a loss to help him. With eleven immortal children of his own, he knew the pain of seeing a family member struggle. The girl, as a member of Ioan's household, had fallen under vampire aegis as soon as she had entered. In the immortal world, that meant Ioan was responsible for her, both for her actions and her safety. But Carwyn knew the girl was also precious to his oldest son, and there was no greater challenge than to see a loved one struggle with no way to help.

Just then, he heard her, the girl's voice dripping with adolescent condescension. Ioan winced and Carwyn tried not to laugh. "Behavior problems?"

"Well, obviously. But she's anxious. She hardly sleeps. Doesn't like to be touched by anyone."

A low, burning rage filled his chest. Carwyn would never forget seeing the monster hovering over the girl in her bedroom. His fingers dug into the oak chair at the memories even years later. He could feel the energy of the mountain humming around him. The library sat at the back of the farmhouse, dug into the side of the hill and sheltered completely from the dangerous sun.

"What ever happened to the mother?"

"You're generous to use that title, considering."

When Sinead had learned of the abuse from the girl's mother, drunk and desperate, Ioan and his mate, Deirdre, had taken immediate action. Carwyn had only happened to be visiting at the time from his home in Wales. They had taken the girl and tried to take the mother.

"Sinead tried to convince her, but she wouldn't leave. I used amnis to alter her memories. She's never come looking for the girl."

Carwyn shook his head, disgusted with those who foolishly threw away the treasure of kin. The shouting between the women grew as the argument moved through the farmhouse. Apparently, the choice of paint in the girl's bedroom was at issue.

Ioan sighed. "The problem is not in her body. There is no sickness I can cure. Her wounds are emotional, not physical." He paused. "What would the church say?"

"Not enough," Carwyn murmured bitterly, well aware of the failings of his hierarchy in dealing with its own demons.

"Would you talk with her? Father Jacob is a fine man, but his wisdom is limited."

"I don't think she needs a priest, Ioan. To tell the truth, I'd not be able to minister to her anyway."

"Why not?"

A crashing came from overhead, along with an impressive string of insults about the color yellow. Carwyn stifled a smile. "I killed her stepfather in front of her, Ioan. Hardly the one to help her when I was partly the cause of her trauma. Even now when I visit, I see the guarded way she looks at me. I don't blame the girl, but it's not my place to be her confessor."

"I think you mistake her feelings. Brigid knows that we protected her. She has no regret for Richard Kelly's death. She's—"

Ioan broke off when Deirdre's voice rose from the kitchen. Carwyn snorted. It sounded like Deirdre may have met her match in the young human.

"Well, she certainly doesn't seem to be the timid type."

"Quite the vicious little thing, to be honest," Ioan muttered. "She can be rather cruel when she wants to wound."

The two vampires paused to listen to the women shouting, and Ioan couldn't contain the smirk at the girl's sharp retort to his wife and his housekeeper. Carwyn reluctantly admired the imaginative nature of the curses. She'd go to confession for them, he'd bet, but she wouldn't really repent.

Ioan said, "She's very intelligent. Frighteningly so at times. She's stifled here, but I can't persuade Sinead to let her go to school. And, to be honest, I understand her reluctance. Without our guidance, I have a feeling the girl would go quite wild."

"You can't keep her here forever. Well, some of our kind might, but not our family."

"She's only fourteen. We have time."

"Not much."

"I know."

"Have you tried to use amnis? To take the edge off the worst of the memories?"

"She's… resistant to any mental manipulation. Our best guess is from about age eight or so. So two years of abuse at the hands of her stepfather? I doubt amnis would be able to touch anything but the surface. I've been able to relieve the worst of her anxiety so she can function, but it's not enough."

Carwyn straightened in his chair and reached over to pat his son's shoulder. "Get the girl the help she needs. Call Anne if you need to; she'll be discreet. I know you don't want to appear weak with a human under your aegis, but there's no shame in seeking help when you don't have the answers."

"I know." Ioan nodded. "I will. I promise."

"Good." Carwyn smiled as he looked at his softhearted child. As long as Ioan had existed, there was still not a human he encountered he didn't want to help in some way. It was his gift and his burden. "Brigid may not be a child of your blood, but she is the child of your heart. You'll find a way to help her; I know it."

"Thanks for the vote of confidence, *Tad*."

Carwyn chuckled to hear the childish endearment. "Oh, it's always easier to put confidence in others instead of yourself."

"True. When are you off to America?"

Carwyn grinned. The vampire was still a priest for his small village in Wales, along with being the head of one of the largest clans of earth vampires on the globe. Though most of his children remained in Britain, his influence and counsel was sought through much of Europe and the Americas on a regular basis. A true vacation for the busy vampire was long overdue.

"I'll leave in November and stay for a few months. I haven't had a proper visit with Giovanni in years."

"Where is he now?"

"Atlanta, Georgia." He imitated a drawl so bad that Ioan turned red in the face from laughter. "But he's talking about moving to Texas."

"Texas?" Ioan said. "I'm having a hard time picturing the Italian in a cowboy hat."

"I'm not. It's been good for a laugh more than once."

"You'll enjoy the warm weather. Take things a bit easier. You've too many responsibilities here."

Carwyn stood. "The joy and headache of children, my son. But I'm definitely looking forward to a bit of a break."

"You're packing all your hideous Hawaiian shirts, aren't you?"

"Absolutely. I've even bought some new ones especially for the visit."

Ioan winced. "Try not to get into too much trouble."

"Who, me? Never."

"That's what you always say."

"And I'm right… fifty percent of the time."

Ioan squinted. "Closer to twenty-five."

"Pessimist."

"Realist."

They turned to leave the library, only to be almost bowled over by the indignant form of Brigid Connor as she rushed in. She glanced at both of them with a curled lip before she rushed over to the bookcase, grabbed a volume, then quickly exited the room, barely sparing them a glance.

Ioan sighed. "Radcliffe. Lovely, she's feeling gothic. Should make for lively dinner conversation."

Carwyn slapped Ioan on the shoulder. "Feel the love, son."

CHAPTER TWO

Dublin, Ireland
September 2004

"Hello?"

Brigid started when she heard the knock on the door of her rooms. Though the bustle of Parliament Street seeped in through the windows, it was the first interruption she'd faced since her Aunt Sinead and Ioan had dropped her off at the secured building in Dublin city center the night before.

"Hello?" The friendly female voice came again, along with another polite knock.

She looked around at the jumble of boxes and hangers that lay around the room before she walked to the door and cracked it open.

"Can I help you?"

A pair of bright blue eyes met her amber-brown ones. The girl's face was open and friendly, a marked contrast to the wary expression Brigid knew she habitually wore. She looked to be the same age as Brigid, but wore bright colors and her light brown hair was pulled into a cheerful ponytail. The girl stuck out her hand.

"I'm Emily. I'm your neighbor next door."

"Oh." Brigid looked down at the offered hand for a moment, tucking a chunk of dark purple hair behind her ear, before she quashed the instinctive leap of anxiety and held out her own. "Brigid Connor. I'm—"

"From Wicklow, I heard." Emily smiled some more and looked at the door that Brigid was guarding. She bit the inside of her lip and forced a smile at the friendly girl. "I have to say, you don't look like your average country girl. But that's cool."

"Right. Um… thanks?"

Natural, safe interactions, Brigid. The comforting voice of her counselor whispered at the back of her mind. *Safe interactions in a comfortable environment. On your terms. Always your terms. You are in control.*

Brigid took a deep breath and opened the door. The human girl was no threat. As she stepped through the door, Brigid noticed her soft appearance and relaxed demeanor. Just a girl. A friendly girl. This was why she had forced herself away from the comfort of the mountains and into the city for school.

"I like your flat! This is one of the biggest in the building, you know?"

She didn't know, but she wasn't surprised. Ioan and Deirdre never failed to give her whatever she asked for, and she'd wanted as much privacy as possible in the crowded apartment building. "I didn't. But, I like my own space, so my—um, family indulges my weirdness."

Emily cleared a pile of hangars from a chair and sat down. "It's okay. Everyone here has their own vampires, so you don't have to hide anything."

Finally, a small smile lifted the corner of her mouth. "I'd heard."

"The whole building. That's why we're all together. They say it's for our own security as humans under vampire aegis, blah, blah, blah, but really"—Emily winked—"it's so they can keep an eye on us. This floor is all students, and the one above us, too. The lower floors are mostly Murphy's people. Very secure, which thrills Mum and Dad."

As Emily chattered on, Brigid returned to unpacking. Emily mentioned Murphy again, with the fluttering awe that Brigid had come to expect from any of the girls who knew of him. Patrick Murphy was a water vampire and the unchallenged immortal leader of Dublin. Though he was fairly young, he had an excellent reputation and a healthy respect for Deirdre and Ioan's power, which was the only reason they'd allowed Brigid to come to Dublin. Brigid had met Murphy on more than one occasion when he came to Wicklow to consult with her family on some matter. When Brigid was ready for school, Dublin was the only place any of them even considered.

Because of the city's popularity with young people, Murphy had set up a safe house of sorts for humans in the city center. Human members of vampire clans came from all over the world to attend school or live there, safe in the knowledge that they could be among peers they wouldn't have to hide from. The house on Parliament Street, though it looked like an old hotel from the outside, was centrally located to the city center, within easy walking distance of most public transport, and very, very secure.

Brigid cleared her throat. "So, are you... do you...?" Though all of Ioan and Deirdre's clan drank animal blood as a habit, Brigid knew how it worked. Murphy would keep healthy, paid blood donors somewhere in the building to feed his staff and others whom he was responsible for. That was how civilized vampires all over the world ran their households. Or so she'd been taught. But how did one go about asking that question politely?

Emily smiled. "My mum and dad both work for Murphy—have my whole life—so this was the only option for me. But I think we're to share a car for school."

"Oh?"

"Most of the students here attend Trinity." She rolled her eyes. "Tradition, tradition. But I'm for UCD like you. I love the campus there. It's so new."

University College Dublin had always been Brigid's goal, but she knew it was more common for humans under aegis to go to Trinity. The handsome buildings and historic traditions of the oldest university in Ireland appealed to the age and character of most vampires, so their humans were encouraged to attend the school. There were even a few vampire professors, she had heard.

"So, how about you?"

"Hmm?" Brigid was standing in the middle of the room, holding a hangar in front of her like a shield. She had been pressing and hanging her wardrobe before she'd heard the knock. She carefully set the hangar down on the coffee table and sat across from Emily.

"Why are you going to UCD?" Emily asked. "Sports fan?"

"No, no. I... uh." She smiled stiffly. "I want to study criminal justice and forensic science. I like the program there. That's why I chose it. I'm not really one for much sport."

Emily grinned and her eyes swept over the room. "Now, why don't I find that a surprise?"

Brigid's dark wardrobe and prized collection of vintage concert shirts was piled in one corner. The walls, per her demand, had been painted a comforting dark grey, and Deirdre and Sinead had helped her pick out a black chair and a grey sofa to go in the small sitting area.

Brigid couldn't help but compare her cave with Emily's bright summer clothes and pink-painted fingernails. Her room was probably baby blue or summer yellow.

"So..." Brigid wiped her hands on her knees. She was doing well, she thought. She had a complete stranger—a safe-looking one—in her room, and she was fine. "Do you want some tea? I was just about to grab some."

"Sure! That'd be great."

"Okay." Brigid rose and walked to the small corner opposite where the bedroom door was. A small kitchen was open to the sitting room, and she plugged in the electric kettle she'd been about to start when she decided her shirts just had to be pressed. "So, are you from Dublin, then?"

"Born and raised. You?"

Brigid had been born and raised for the first ten years in Dublin, but she didn't count that part. "Wicklow. My whole life."

"Ah. Earth vampires?"

"Yes." She focused on preparing two cups of tea. Two mugs. Two teabags from the box.

"Do you have a boyfriend?"

Brigid was tempted to burst into laughter, but she didn't. "Um... no. Definitely not."

"Oh, do you have a girlfriend, then?" Emily gave her a mischievous wink, and Brigid blushed.

"Uh, no. I like… boys." *In theory.*

"Oh, do you like…" She trailed off, and Brigid looked up to see Emily digging two fingers into her neck like fangs. "I mean, I never have, but I've always wondered. It's supposed to be ama—"

"No!" Brigid could feel her face heat and her temper begin to rise. She looked back at the tea and carefully calmed herself. "I'm not into that, either. I may wear a lot of black, but that doesn't mean I like to… you know."

"Okay." Emily leaned back against the couch and looked around again. "So, Brigid Connor, are you always like this?"

Brigid blinked and looked up. "Like what?"

Emily looked like she was about to laugh, but it didn't seem mocking. "Prickly?"

Brigid let out a breath and set down the mug she was crushing in her hand. "Honestly? Yes."

"Ah."

"But I'm trying very hard not to be."

"If you don't want company—"

"No!" She squeezed her eyes closed and concentrated on breathing for a moment to cool her temper. "No, that's part of why I came here, you know?"

"To school?"

"And to the city. To… meet new people. Get out of my comfort zone a bit. Try new things."

A cautious look of understanding crossed Emily's face, and Brigid relaxed. "Well, that's good. I'd like for us to be friends."

Brigid bit the inside of her lip again and nodded as the kettle started to whistle. She quickly poured the water and looked back up to Emily with a smile. "I'd like that, too."

January 2005

"Come on, Brig! End of first week. We need to go out."

"No, you go ahead. I'm just going to…"

"What?" Emily lounged on her sofa as Brigid grabbed two drinks from the fridge. An ale for her and a cider for Emily. "What are you going to do, Brigid Connor? I'll tell you what you're going to do. Nothing. It's Friday night, you're a gorgeous twenty-year-old girl who's just celebrated her birthday, and you're going to hide in your cave, listen to depressing music, and read a book. Maybe write some bad poetry."

Brigid rolled her eyes. "Why do I like you?"

"Because I make you go out for fun."

"I just don't feel like being around people right now."

"You never feel like being around people. That's the point of all this, right? Have a drink. Loosen up a bit, then we'll go out to this new club I keep hearing about. It'll be good *craic* and we need some fun. You'll love it."

Brigid sneered. "No I won't."

Emily paused. "Okay, you won't. But it'll be good for you. It's a nice place. Not too crowded. Maybe we can dance a little. Meet some guys."

"Emily..." Brigid tried to keep her temper. Her first week of second term had been brutal. She knew she was pushing herself, but she was finally taking some classes that challenged her. She was exhausted, but invigorated as well. Maybe...

"If I was as pretty as you, I'd have men eating out of my hand. I don't care what crazy color you dye your hair, the hot guys always notice you."

"Right, they just don't touch. And at least you have breasts."

"And a huge butt. And chubby thighs. And—"

"Piss off. You get plenty of attention, Em."

Emily whined. "I won't get any attention unless we go out!"

She sighed. The few occasions during first term that Emily had dragged her to the numerous pubs or clubs of the Temple Bar nearby hadn't been all that bad. As long as she could keep some distance from the more crowded clubs where people pressed up against her, she could keep her anxiety from getting out of control. And with the right amount of alcohol, she could almost have fun. She looked at the bottle of beer in her hand and quickly drank it.

"Okay. I'll go."

Emily bolted up with a huge grin. "Really?"

"Really. I've conquered going to classes. Maybe this should be my project this term."

"Yes!" Emily stood and did a little happy dance around the room, pulling her friend up into a quick hug. Brigid tensed instinctively, then deliberately tried to relax. She held her arms around her friend. One second. Two seconds. Three.

"Okay, that's enough."

"That was good! Have a few more beers and eventually you might get laid."

"Shut the feck up, and let's go before I change my mind."

"Oh..." Brigid peered into the flashing lights of the club and began to back away. "Oh no."

She felt Emily's hand on her shoulder. "Come on. Inside."

"Too loud. Too crowded."

"It's Friday night. Of course it's crowded."

She could feel her heart begin to pound. "Emily, this isn't a good idea."

"It is, it is. Let's get you a drink and we'll hang out for a while. It's most crowded on the dance floor, see? We don't have to dance; we'll just get a booth." Emily shoved her inside after giving a wink to the bouncer at the door. Brigid wondered if this was one of Murphy's clubs. Seeing numerous people from Parliament House scattered around, along with a few trolling vampires, made her think it was.

To most people, the elegant immortals wouldn't be obvious. But Brigid had spent the previous ten years of her life living among earth and water vampires, the two most common types. All of the elements, earth, water, wind, and fire—not that she'd ever met a rare fire vampire—shared recognizable characteristics to the eyes of a knowledgeable human. Brigid could spot their preternatural grace and carefully concealed speed. A crackle of energy, their *amnis*, always surrounded them, and they avoided modern technology that would short out if they got too close.

Once upon a time, she was told vampires had lived at ease among oblivious humans, but these days, the surest way of spotting a vampire was asking to borrow their mobile. Want to know whether that cute lad with the devilish grin was really an immortal, blood-drinking monster? Just ask to borrow his phone, then wait for the quick smile and the brush across your skin, wiping any memory of the encounter from your mind.

Most of them kept to themselves. In a way, Brigid was more at home in the vampire world than the human one. She snorted when she saw two clueless girls cozying up to a tall, blond vampire who was eyeing their necks and brushing his fingers along their skin.

"Dinner is served," she muttered, looking around the club for Emily. She spotted her at the bar, chatting with a boy from Parliament House. This was definitely one of Murphy's clubs.

"Hey there!" She heard a friendly voice over the pounding music and looked to her right to see a smiling boy about her own age. He was a little taller and had a slim, runner's build. Brown hair fell over his forehead, and he wore a pair of thick-framed glasses around beautiful dark eyes.

Brigid smiled. "Hi."

"I like your shirt. Have you ever seen them in concert?"

She looked down at her black Buzzcocks T-shirt. "Um, no. I wish."

"Me, too. I'm Mark."

"Brigid."

"Can I get you a drink?"

She looked around. Emily was still at the bar, still talking to their neighbor. "I think my friend's getting me a drink, thanks."

"Cool."

Brigid was standing against the wall, her arms crossed over her chest, wishing she could flirt like Emily. Wishing that the thought of Mark crowding her didn't make her heart race in terror.

"Do you want to dance?"

Yes.

No.

Do you want me to throw up on you? "I'm not really a dancer, but thanks."

Faced with the prospect of a still-as-a-board companion, Mark seemed to lose confidence. "Well... um, it was nice meeting you, Brigid."

She couldn't help but feel the pang of disappointment. "You, too."

He held out his hand, but she just looked at it. In her mind, Brigid imagined reaching out. It would be warm. Mark looked warm and comfortable. Friendly. Safe. In her mind, she reached out her hand to take his, but then his hand squeezed tight. Tighter. Until her knuckles were crushed beneath his strong grip. She could almost feel the phantom pain in her fingers as her throat constricted.

Mark blinked and stepped back, tucking his hand into his pocket and retreating.

"Well, like I said. Nice to meet you. Great shirt."

She nodded and tried to smile, but she was afraid it came out more like she was in pain. The boy left and she stared at his back in longing. Why couldn't she be normal? Then she bit the inside of her lip in disgust. Why did she even bother?

Brigid was standing against a wall, avoiding eye contact with anyone who got too close, when Emily came back with a drink for her. Her friend shoved the pink concoction at her and grinned.

"Try it!"

She glared at the fruity-looking drink. "What is this?"

"It's a new drink that Mike was mixing at the bar. Really, try it." She held up her hand. "See, I've got one, too."

Brigid took a sip. It was incredibly sweet. She hated sweet drinks. "Em, this really isn't—"

"Come on. One drink. Mike's a friend, and it's this new cocktail he just made up. He's trying to get a bunch of people to order it to impress his boss."

Brigid looked over Emily's shoulder to see a boyish-looking young man grinning at them. He waved his hand as his head bobbed along to the music. She sighed. "Okay. But just one. I'm not going to lie, this is disgusting."

"Just finish that one." Emily was still grinning. "Trust me, you'll love it."

They drifted through the crowd, sipping their drinks, until Emily spotted the blond vampire Brigid had noticed before. "Oh my God, that's Axel!"

Brigid frowned and looked around, squinting in the direction Emily was looking. "Who? Tall, blond, and..." *Immortal.* She looked around. "You know. The one in the booth?"

"Yes! I heard he was amazing in bed."

Brigid snorted. "Really? After however many years and who knows how many girls, I'd hope so."

Emily slapped her arm, but for some reason, Brigid didn't flinch. In fact, as she sucked down the last of her drink, she realized she was beginning to feel a little sick. Still, the sound of the music seemed to be more pleasant in her ears, and she was beginning to sway to the rhythm.

"Let's go over and say hi."

"What, to the blond one?"

"Sure! I'll tell him we're friends of Murphy's. If nothing else, maybe he'll let us sit down. My feet are killing me."

"I told you not to wear those shoes." Emily was right, though. All the black leather booths that surrounded the dance floor were filled except Axel's. He had one friend—security of some kind, from the way the human was watching the room—with him, but otherwise, the vampire was alone. Brigid wondered what had happened to the two girls he'd been entertaining earlier.

Maybe they weren't his type.

His blood type, she thought with a giggle.

A giggle?

Emily started toward the booth, and Brigid followed behind her. They came up to Axel, and he smiled.

"You ladies are from Parliament House, yes? Friends of Mike's?"

He had a very slight accent, lilting and pleasant. He really was very handsome, Brigid thought. If he were tan instead of pale, he would have looked like a surfer or a lifeguard. He had been sired young, only a bit older than they were, and his face was boyishly handsome. His eyes were a vivid blue-green that Brigid found herself staring into. She shook her head as Axel held out a hand and motioned them into the booth.

"What do you want to drink? I will get it for you. Anything for girls from Parliament House."

Emily giggled and slid closer to him. "Um… a Cosmopolitan for me?"

Axel grinned at Emily, then turned his eyes to Brigid. "And for you?"

"Nothing for me, thanks. Maybe just a bottle of water."

He shrugged in a careless way. "I told you, whatever you want. Valon?" The security guy turned to Axel and they exchanged quick words in some unknown language. Emily and Axel began flirting. Emily was telling the vampire about a holiday she had taken to Sweden a few summers before, and Axel was laughing along as if she was the most fascinating girl he'd ever met.

Brigid had to hand it to him; the blond immortal certainly wasn't lacking in charm. She nodded in thanks when the burly security guard returned with her bottle of water and another fruity cocktail for Emily. Axel, she noticed, was drinking nothing. But he was definitely staring at Emily's neck.

She tried not to be judgmental. It wasn't as if Deirdre and Ioan had warned her off vampires, but she knew her Aunt Sinead wanted her to meet a nice, human boy her own age. Brigid thought anyone besides Cormac Riley would be an improvement. He was the only boy who had ever attempted kissing her, and according to Ioan, his arm had suffered permanent nerve damage as a result.

She took a deep breath and realized that the nausea still hadn't passed. She tugged on Emily's arm, not wanting to brave the crowd without her friend. Emily looked away from Axel.

"You okay?"

"I don't feel very well. I think that drink was too sweet. Where's the loo in this place?" She smiled an apologetic smile in Axel's direction, trying to be polite. To his credit, the vampire did seem perfectly friendly.

Emily's eyebrows immediately creased in concern, so she stood and guided Brigid through the crowd with one hand on her back. In the back of her mind, Brigid realized that something felt off. Wrong. Then she realized she wasn't flinching.

Emily had a hand on the small of her back, leading her through a crowded dance club, and people were brushing past and bumping into her.

But Brigid wasn't flinching.

In fact, the more they wove through the crowd, the more Brigid realized that the music sounded good. Great even. She blinked and looked around, then turned to Emily.

"Em."

Her friend was looking at her with a guilty expression. "What?"

"What the feck was in that drink?"

The color drained from Emily's face. "You know… just vodka. Some cranberry and lime juice… and some…" Her low mumble was lost in the crowd, but Brigid caught the movement of her lips when her friend admitted the truth.

Ecstasy.

Brigid's jaw dropped. She dragged Emily down the hall, past the bathrooms, realizing that she no longer felt the least bit sick to her stomach. In fact, she felt incredible. She pushed past a group of college boys hanging by the door to the alley and shoved Emily up against the back wall.

"What the *feck*, Emily?"

"Don't overreact. It's just a little—"

"What in God's name would make you do that?"

Emily stomped her foot. "Oh, shut up! Do you realize you just walked through that whole group of boys without cringing? And, for your information, I had Mike put *half* a pill in. That's it, Brig. Don't be so high and mighty! What makes this any different than having a few too many drinks? You do that all the time to loosen up. Do you even feel sick anymore?"

She was livid. "No, but Emily—"

"No different. None! You have a few pints; you take the stick out of your arse. You have half—*half*—a pill, and maybe you do the same. It's not dangerous, you know. You're not going to get addicted or any shite like that. Half this fecking club is taking it right now. It's practically on the menu at the bar."

Her heart was racing. She felt warm, but she couldn't seem to care. "Half the club? Are you?"

"Yes."

That brought Brigid up short. "But…"

"I don't seem any different?"

She blinked and her eyes seemed to clear. "Um… not really, no."

Emily rolled her eyes and grabbed Brigid's arm, linking it with hers while she pulled them back toward the main room where the music pounded. "That's because I take it all the time. Well, not *all* the time, but when I'm going out? Sure! It's really not a big deal, Brig. It's no different from having a few drinks to relax. Now, how do you feel?"

How did she feel? Brigid felt… amazing. A boy passed by and did a quick scan. He caught her eye and smiled, but she didn't feel panicky. In fact, she smiled back.

"I feel… I'm okay, I guess."

A sly smile took over Emily's mouth. "Just okay?"

"I feel…" Brigid took a deep breath and closed her eyes as they approached the dance floor. She felt the music as if it was a physical sensation. The bass stroked along her skin. She opened her eyes and the colored lights that lit the pulsating bodies mesmerized her. Her heart felt as if it beat in time to the music. The dance floor moved in one inviting motion. She let out a slow breath.

"I love it."

Emily was forgotten on the edge of the crowd. She saw the boy from earlier, Mark, dancing in the middle of the floor. She lifted her arms and swayed, moving without a care as she made her way toward him. Each touch that brushed against her felt like a caress. She sidled up to Mark and caught his eye with a smile on her face.

"Hey."

He grinned. "I thought you didn't dance!"

Brigid laughed. "I didn't. But I do now."

He placed his hands on her hips and swayed with her. She had been right; they were warm. Inviting. She threw her head back and moved to the beat as Mark pressed closer. For the first time in her life, a man's touch brought neither panic nor disgust. She was relaxed. Fluid. His fingers trailed up her spine. It didn't bring a rush of fear or a racing heart. The contact felt natural. Incredible.

Brigid let her arms fall over his shoulders. When she met his eyes, she realized what she'd been missing. He was wonderful. This was right. And when his mouth met hers, time seemed to spin out in one long fluid sigh. They moved together, body and breath, and the music and the crowd embraced her.

CHAPTER THREE

Wicklow Mountains, Ireland
May 2005

"So, Paddy and Mick—"

"This is the last joke or you can carve a new room into this mountain and sleep in the dirt, Ioan."

His oldest son grinned and pulled his wife into his lap as Carwyn laughed. "No, my love, you'll like this one. So Paddy and Mick are driving to Cork City, and they need to answer the call of nature. They pull to the side of the road and go into the bushes—"

"A piss joke?" Deirdre rolled her eyes and tried to stand, but Ioan pinched her lips together as Carwyn took another drink of his beer.

"They both start pissin' and Mick looks over to Paddy. 'Paddy,' he says, 'I wish I was as well-hung as you are, my friend. I can see that you're using four fingers to hold yerself.' And Paddy says to Mick, 'Ah, Mick, yer fine, lad. And I see you're using four as well.' And Mick says, 'Aye, Paddy, but I'm pissin' on three of 'em.'"

Carwyn and Ioan both burst into laughter as Deirdre snorted. Ioan patted her bottom and held her trapped in his lap. "See, my love, aren't you happy that you married a Welshman?"

"I'm currently feeling the need to visit Gemma in London."

Carwyn hooted. "Ioan, if she's willing to subject herself to shopping with Gemma, you'd better learn some manners."

"I need a long vacation from my own husband."

"She would never..." Ioan tugged at a lock of Deirdre's long red hair and pulled her face down to his. He pursed his lips for a kiss, but she only sneered at him. Undeterred, he chuckled and kissed along her neck, slowly inching his way toward her mouth. "See?" he said between kisses. "She loves me madly."

Deirdre said, "No, I don't."

"Couldn't live without me."

"Obnoxious Welshman."

Carwyn shook his head. "When does the newlywed stage wear off? You've been married for four hundred years."

Ioan finally managed to press his lips to Deirdre's; then he grinned in triumph. "Never! We'll always be as obnoxious as we are now and scare the children."

"And your sire, as well."

Ioan just winked at Deirdre and continued to pin her to his lap. "You're just jealous, Father. Get your own woman."

"Eh." He shrugged. "Too much trouble."

"Carwyn," Deirdre said, "what about this American girl? You said you're going to visit her in Los Angeles. No interest at all? She's just a friend?"

"Who, Beatrice?" Carwyn shook his head. "No. Just a friend. She's meant for Giovanni."

"You'd travel that far—in a boat—for a 'just a friend?'"

Carwyn could see the skeptical looks on the faces of his oldest son and his wife, who were truly more friends than children. "She is. I travel far longer to see Isabel and Gustavo."

Deirdre frowned. "But they're family."

"Who knows?" Carwyn grinned. "Maybe she will be, as well. Gio's like a brother to me, after all." He was frustrated with his friend, certain the stubborn fire vampire loved the young American woman, but equally convinced that Giovanni couldn't see what was standing in front of his face. Beatrice De Novo was no wilting flower. And if the stubborn Giovanni Vecchio didn't show up and claim her, he doubted the girl would wait long for him. Fool.

Ioan's eyes lit in understanding. "Is that so? So the pragmatic Dr. Vecchio has finally fallen to a woman's charms? A human, for that matter?"

Carwyn shrugged again. "You'll have to ask him. He's buried himself in books again, crisscrossing the globe and avoiding my letters. But I don't expect to see him in female company other than Beatrice's. Put it that way." Carwyn sighed. "All my bachelor friends seem to be abandoning me. Caspar is happily domesticated in Houston. Giovanni and Beatrice are… whatever they are. I suppose they'll figure it out."

Deirdre chuckled. "Poor old man. You really do need to find your own woman, Father."

Ioan leaned forward, a serious expression crossing his face. "You've been alone for a thousand years, Carwyn. Is it the church? Because you know my opinion—"

"I know your opinion. No need to state it again."

Deirdre said, "When you took your vows, you were a married man. And you were mortal. It was the church that changed. Not you."

"I changed, as well," he said quietly.

"Nevertheless," Ioan said, "you have devoted a thousand years to them. A thousand years to your family and your faith. I'm only saying that if there was anyone who deserved to be happy—"

"And who says I'm not?" Carwyn smiled. "Why is it that married people always think their friends can't be happy unless they're shackled as they are? Irritating children, you are. Both of you."

Ioan turned his face up to Deirdre. "Shackle me, my love."

Deirdre only rolled her eyes. "Oh, for heaven's sake."

"Best torture in the world, to be shackled to a beautiful woman who drives you crazy," he continued. "Sign me up again. Sign me up for another four hundred years, Father!"

Carwyn cleared his throat. "Well, if the conversation has turned to shackles, I think that's my cue to retire."

Ioan laughed, and Deirdre punched her husband's arm. "Enough, both of you. And, Ioan, Carwyn will do whatever makes him happy. Besides, when has he ever taken our advice about anything?"

"There was that time in the 1780s—"

"Carwyn," Deirdre interrupted with a laugh, "is your ship leaving out of Dublin or Waterford?"

"Terry has a boat leaving Dublin, going to New York. O'Brian is storing my bike for me, so I'll drive cross-country from there. I'll ring you both when I'm in Los Angeles with B. She says she has a safe place for me to stay. Otherwise, I'll work something out with Alvarez. He owes me, anyway. Why do you ask?"

For once, Deirdre looked unsure. "I was wondering if you'd have time to check on Brigid Connor when you were in town. She's staying at Parliament House this summer, and I just wanted—"

"Deirdre." Ioan's voice was a quiet warning.

"What?" Carwyn saw her temper spike. "Sinead says she thinks something seemed wrong the last time she talked to Brigid. And with her staying in Dublin all summer—"

"She's going for summer term. She's very serious about her studies. You two worry too much."

"This is her first summer away from home."

Ioan huffed. "She's a grown woman."

"She's twenty!"

Ioan's eyebrows lifted. "Oh? I had no idea. May I point out, technically, so are you?"

"It's not the same, and you know it. All my sisters were married by the time they were sixteen. I was a grown woman at twenty when I turned."

"You're right. And your childhood was blessedly uneventful. Brigid's gone through far more than you ever did, Deirdre."

"Exactly. I have every right to be worried."

"But not every right to treat her like a child. Have some faith in—"

Carwyn broke into the growing argument. "Why don't I just meet her for a drink when I'm in town?" Ioan and Deirdre both stopped and looked at him. "I'll meet her for a drink. No interrogation. I know I don't know the girl all that well, but I'm happy to say hello and check if anything seems unusual."

Deirdre smiled. "Thanks. I appreciate it. Sinead and I—"

"Worry too much," Ioan muttered, but he nodded at Carwyn. "Still, good of you to meet her and it's good to remind Murphy whose aegis she's under, just in case he's interested."

Carwyn chuckled. "Now who's worrying?"

Ioan said, "Are you joking? You know how much he'd like to form some kind of tie to Deirdre's and my clan. I can't blame him; it would be an excellent political move."

"We don't have any single daughters," Deirdre said. "But he knows that Brigid is family."

"You think Murphy might be interested in Brigid?" Carwyn shrugged. "Wouldn't be the worst thing in the world. As long as she liked him, I suppose."

It was Deirdre who smiled. "And what woman wants to be desired for her connections? You old men. She deserves to have someone who's crazy for her. Mad in love. That's what a woman wants."

Carwyn turned puppy dog eyes on Deirdre. "And that is why I shall remain the eternal bachelor. For what woman could truly appreciate my stunning good looks?"

"Not again," Deirdre said.

Ioan nodded. "And your Hawaiian shirt collection."

"My noble devotion to beer and professional wrestling."

"And your dogs," Ioan added. "Don't forget your dogs."

Deirdre sighed. "Why do I ever try to have a serious conversation with the two of you?"

Dublin, Ireland
June 2005

Carwyn leaned against the grimy walls of the Ha'Penny Bridge Inn, waiting for Brigid Connor to show. He'd stopped by Parliament House the evening before and left a note with the guards in front telling her to meet him at the old pub near the river. Much of the older part of Dublin had been updated in the previous years, but the Ha'Penny had stayed relatively old-fashioned and didn't cater to as many tourists as most of the bars in the city center. Though it was only June, the buzz and bustle of the summer crowds were already filling the evening streets, even on a Wednesday night.

He saw her as soon as she turned the corner, but then, she was hard to miss. Brigid Connor had always been a tiny thing, with a stride that warned people off, despite her small frame. She was pale-skinned, with a scattering of freckles dotting her cheeks, and her garishly dyed hair was chopped short and lay in irregular chunks around a pixie face. Her large eyes were the color of amber ale and her chin came to a sharp point under a bow-shaped mouth.

Carwyn thought she looked like an extremely pissed off fairy, which amused him greatly. He grinned when he saw her bark at a boy who approached her. Then his eyebrows lifted when she reached out and took his hand. So, little Brigid had a boyfriend? Her expression as she approached was a mask of studied nonchalance.

He opened his senses to feel for the boy. Though he was in the city, and the earth beneath him was long buried, he could scent the young man, watch the subtle angles of his body language, and listen for his pulse, which was hammering with nerves, instinctively reacting to the presence of the predator he was. *Good.* Brigid's heartbeat, however, was steady as a low drum. The smell of the river masked their scents as they approached.

She came to a stop in front of him and looked up with a haughty expression. "So, you're here to check up on me?"

The boy awkwardly looked between Brigid and Carwyn. "Um... Brig—"

"It's fine, Mark. He's an old... family friend," she said with a sneer. "Go ahead and I'll meet you at the club later."

"Are you sure?"

Carwyn gave the boy a cheerful smile and held out his hand to shake. The boy grabbed it, and Carwyn let his amnis crawl up to the boy's mind. As the energy flooded the human's cerebral cortex, Carwyn spoke to him. "Hello, Mark. Nice to meet you. You're not going to remember much of me. Now piss off and leave us alone. She'll meet you later."

"Okay."

He could see Brigid roll her eyes, but Mark turned and quickly walked back the way they had come.

"Why did you want to come to this old place? They haven't hung new curtains since before I was born." She walked past him and pulled open the door to the pub.

Carwyn looked after her and called, "Lovely to see you, as well, Brigid. I can see that your sunny demeanor has only blossomed in adulthood."

He walked inside and took the seat opposite her in the old booth. "So, is that your natural hair color, or were you attacked by eggplant-wielding terrorists on the way out of your flat?"

She cocked a haughty eyebrow. "They were protesting at the market, actually. Maybe I should stick to blood like you and Ioan. Might be less dangerous."

"I'd consider it, if I were you."

"Do you really watch American professional wrestling? Been meaning to ask you. I don't believe my aunt. No one actually watches that. It's idiotic."

Carwyn grinned. "What do you think?"

"I'm not sure yet. The older I get, the stranger you seem."

He smirked. "Well, that's not surprising. I am strange. What do you want from the bar?"

"A whiskey, I guess."

"How about a beer?"

"How about a whiskey?"

He stood. "Guinness it is, then."

"Hey!" She called out, but he ignored her. The girl certainly had the same acid tongue that he remembered from her childhood. To tell the truth, he'd never known her well. Like most of Ioan and Deirdre's humans, he kept his distance. Though they remained close with their human clan, he was more circumspect in his mortal connections. He supposed that, after a thousand years, it was easier to remain unattached.

Still, there was always something about the girl that had amused him. He glanced over his shoulder as the barmen built their pints. Brigid stood slumped in her seat, the very picture of adolescent rebellion. She was smart. That had always interested him. And he loved that she threw Deirdre off balance. His redheaded daughter had always been the most stubborn in their family, taking after his oldest daughter Gemma more than anyone else. Carwyn had a feeling that Brigid and Gemma would get on just fine.

He grabbed their drinks, walked back to the table, and slid in across from her. She looked up with a droll expression. "Thanks ever so much for the whiskey."

Carwyn grinned. "You're very welcome. How's life?"

She shrugged. "Busy. Classes. Friends. Lots going on."

"Who's the boyfriend?"

"Just a lad I met out with friends."

"Is it serious? Going to take him home to meet..." He caught himself before he said 'mum and dad.' Carwyn cleared his throat and smiled at the cool eyebrow she raised in his direction. "Take him home to meet your aunt?"

"Sinead? Probably not. I'm not that serious about him."

"So why waste your time?"

She just blinked at him, and for the first time since he'd seen her, Carwyn caught the vulnerability in her eyes. In that moment, he remembered the small girl at the mercy of a monster, and his heart softened. "None of my business, Brigid," he said in a softer voice. "He seems like a nice enough boy."

The hard shell fell over her face again. "He's fine. He doesn't interfere with school."

He grinned. "Well, that's good. So, you're going to be in the *Garda*, are you?"

She shrugged. "Maybe Irish police. Maybe something international. Always wanted to travel."

"You have?" From what he'd remembered Ioan telling him, the girl had trouble leaving the house to attend the village school.

She curled her lip. "Yeah. I have."

"Well, good luck."

"Thanks. Are we done talking now?"

He pointed to her pint. "Drink up. It won't bite."

"Unlike some things at the table."

He laughed. "Well, that's true, I suppose."

Brigid rolled her eyes again, and Carwyn wondered if there was some sort of human medical procedure to keep her from repeating the annoying gesture.

"So—"

"You really don't have to do this."

"What?"

"Check up on me for them. I'm fine, Father."

For some inexplicable reason, Brigid calling him "Father" annoyed him. Perhaps because she said it with such clear disdain. He lowered his glass and leaned across the table. "Look here, Brigid Connor. Get rid of the attitude." He reached out and wrapped a hand around her tiny wrist, but softened it when he felt the flinch. He rubbed one thumb over her knuckles. "You and I both know that I could make you tell me anything I wanted if I used my amnis. I'm trying to be pleasant. I'm trying to do a favor for Ioan and Deirdre and your Aunt Sinead, who I happen to like more than most humans. So why don't you—?"

He broke off when the door opened and a gust of wind blew in. The cool air slid into the room and slipped over Brigid's neck, drifting to his keen nose. His eyes narrowed, and his grip on her wrist tightened slightly. The fangs grew long in his mouth and his heart began to pound.

What the hell?

He brought her hand up to his nose and inhaled the sweet scent of her blood. Thick, rich, human blood along with a hint of something distinctly chemical. Carwyn slid out of the booth and tugged the girl out of the pub and down the street, finding a quiet alley to shove her into before he released her and began to pace.

"What the hell?" he muttered. "The hell, girl." He turned on her. "What are you doing?"

He caught a hint of fear before a disdainful mask fell over her face. "What are you talking about?"

"You know exactly what I'm talking about."

"No, I don't."

He could tell by the look on her face that she did, but she had mastered the arrogance of youth. Carwyn shook his head. "Ioan said to have faith in you. To trust that you were a smart girl. He told everyone not to worry so much."

"I *am* smart. I know what I'm doing."

"Really?" He stalked toward her, boxing her against the wall with his thick arms. The girl looked up defiantly. "Why don't you fill me in, then? Why don't you tell me what you're doing?"

"I'm taking care of things. I'm making myself better."

"What the hell are you talking about, you idiot? I'm asking what drugs you're using! I can smell more than one, and you'd better tell me."

"Read my lips, Carwyn. It is none of your business. I'm not under your aegis, and I never will be. I don't answer to you or anyone else, so piss off and mind your own—"

She broke off when he slapped his hand over her mouth. Her eyes widened in fury, but he ignored her. "It is my business because Ioan and Deirdre are my business, and they love you. You know either of them would tear off their own arm for you, so knowing you're putting poison in your body would absolutely kill them."

Brigid narrowed her eyes and opened her mouth, sinking her little human teeth into the heel of his hand. Despite the seriousness of the situation, Carwyn had to stifle a laugh. He pulled his hand away and blinked when he realized she had drawn blood.

"Careful now," he said. "Drinking vampire blood will make you sick."

She rolled her eyes again and Carwyn ground his fangs. Why did she keep doing that?

"Listen," she said in an utterly reasonable voice. "What I'm doing is nothing more than what people do when they go to the doctor and get medications to deal with their problems. I have symptoms. I know how to help myself now. If I was taking prescription medications, you wouldn't —"

"Say anything? No, because you'd be under the care of a physician, Brigid. That's a bit different than doping yourself up to deal with things, isn't it?"

She only glared at him. "You're not my father or my priest… *Father*."

"No, but I thought I could be a friend. Obviously, I gave you too much credit." He wiped the smear of blood on his jeans and glanced at her from the corner of his eye when she didn't think he was looking. The girl looked young and scared. She may have talked big, but Brigid didn't know what she was doing. His heart broke just a little in that moment.

"Brigid—"

"Are you going to tell them?" Her voice had lost its disdainful tone, and she was staring at the cobblestones in the alley.

"I'm on a boat tomorrow night for New York. I'll be ten days; then I'll call them when I get to America, Brigid. Tell them first. This isn't going to be our secret."

"Fine." She nodded and started toward the mouth of the alley.

"Brigid?" he called. She stopped but didn't turn around. "Take care of yourself."

Carwyn thought he heard a rueful laugh before she turned the corner, disappearing into the bustle of the city.

Malibu, California
July 2005

"Brilliant tradition. Excellent use of explosives."

He and Beatrice were leaning against a pile of rocks he'd formed to create a kind of shelter from the wind that whipped down the California coast. They were roasting marshmallows on the deserted beach, enjoying the bonfire, and watching the distant fireworks that marked American Independence Day.

Beatrice said, "It is fitting, isn't it? We do like our violent celebrations."

"You do. Is this better than the fireworks in Houston?"

"Oh yeah. Rich people put on a great show."

Carwyn snorted, enjoying the fact his friend didn't lump herself in with the rich, despite the rather massive fortune she'd stolen the year before from a vicious water vampire who had kidnapped her. Lorenzo was the estranged son of his friend, Giovanni, and a villain at the core. Carwyn, Giovanni, and their friend Tenzin had attacked his compound in Greece and rescued Beatrice the year before, driving Lorenzo underground—or underwater, as the case may have been—but Carwyn knew he was still lurking. He also knew that, since helping his friends, he had become a target.

It didn't concern him. Another hundred years, another enemy to watch out for. When you lived as long as he did, it was inevitable.

He saw Beatrice glancing at the ocean as the tide came in. Few would notice how the waves still made her tense, but she deliberately turned back to the fire and ignored them.

"Too much?" he asked, catching her eye and gesturing toward the ocean. "We can always take the bike farther up the coast. Plenty of dark left. We can just keep riding if you don't want to listen to the water."

She shook her head. "No, this is good. I'm good. I need to get over it, you know? Otherwise…"

"What?"

She smiled at him. "Sometimes, life hands you things you think you won't survive. You probably know that better than me."

He shrugged. "Despite my years, sometimes I feel as if I've lived a very charmed life. My family, for the most part, has been safe."

"But still, things happen. There's no such thing as complete safety."

He thought of a dark room and a helpless little girl. "Yes, I suppose you're right."

"So when life breaks, you pick up the pieces and keep moving. Otherwise, you stay broken. And instead of being a survivor, you're always a victim." Beatrice leaned toward the fire and crossed her arms over her chest. "And I don't want to be known for what happened to me. I want to be known for me."

"Look at you, wise girl." He winked at her. "You can handle anything, can't you?"

"A good friend. A warm fire. I can't handle everything, but I can handle the waves for a bit."

He smiled. "Just let me know when you want to go."

"I will."

"B?"

"Yeah?"

His thoughts drifted back to a frightened young woman in Dublin, and the mingled bravery and fear he'd seen in her eyes. "I know when your dad first showed up again, after he'd turned and you didn't know..." He paused. "Gio didn't tell me much, but I know you thought... that you thought—"

"I was crazy?" He looked up, and Beatrice was smiling at him.

He chuckled a little. "Yes."

"Well... yeah. Dad dies only to show up years later looking like an emaciated monster? You could say that messed with my head."

"Did you ever—when things were bad—did you ever try drugs? Not the prescription kind."

She cocked her head at him. "Should I ask why you're wondering?"

"You don't have to answer."

Beatrice said, "It's all right. And no. I drank some. Okay, a lot sometimes, but to tell the truth, drugs always scared the shit out of me. Plus, I just knew my grandma and grandpa would find out. There are some things you can't hide."

"I know."

"Can I ask?"

He shook his head and thought of the difficult call he'd had to make to Ioan when he'd arrived in New York. "Just a friend. She had a rough childhood. I'm sure you can relate."

"Not really." He looked up in surprise, and Beatrice shrugged. "I mean, I lost my dad, and I had a really bad time when I was a teenager, but basically, I had it pretty good. I always knew my family loved me. And that's the most important thing."

"Me, too. I had a wonderful family."

"Really?" She grinned. "Your human family? You hardly ever talk about them."

"Oh, my parents were wonderful. And my sisters. I had four sisters. It was a very close family. Extended family, as well. When Efa and I married —our parents were dear friends, so it was arranged. Pure chance we loved each other. But it was a very close community." He nodded. "That's what saved me after I turned. I knew my children would be looked after, even though I couldn't see them and their mother was gone."

"You never talk about her."

"Who, Efa?" Carwyn smiled when he thought about his gentle young wife. He'd been crazy in love with the demure girl. He could still remember their wedding night. Both of them young, fumbling. So eager and overwhelmed with love and excitement. Losing her years later had pierced Carwyn's heart with a pain he hadn't thought he'd be able to live through. But he had. And he'd survived without her for over a thousand years. "She was a very loving girl. I wonder, sometimes, if we would have fallen in love if we hadn't been meant for each other. We were very different."

"What would she think of you now? Do you ever wonder?"

He frowned. "Not really. It was so long ago. I think she would appreciate my faith and devotion to my family. Family was very important to both of us. But I was much more serious when I was young."

"Really?" Beatrice laughed. "Isn't it usually the opposite?"

"Not if you live long enough." A sudden pain swept over him. "After about five hundred years or so, you have to laugh at yourself or you'd go mad." He looked into the fire again, contemplating his human love, who had become such a faint memory. "Efa was a beautiful wife. Wonderful mother. Quiet. I wonder if she'd even recognize me now."

"Quiet, huh?" Beatrice grinned at him. "That's probably only because she couldn't get a word in around you, blabbermouth."

Carwyn's sudden melancholy lifted and his laugh filled the quiet beach. "You're probably right! I can only imagine."

"When you were gone, she probably had plenty to say."

"Tales of putting up with my obnoxious young self. Poor thing." He smiled again and threw an arm over Beatrice's shoulders.

"Why haven't you ever married again? You're a good-looking guy. And you have one of the biggest hearts I've ever known."

He winked. "Besides the obvious, collar-type reasons?"

"I don't think God would get pissed off at this point. You've worked for him for a long time."

"And I'll work for him until the day I leave this earth." He squeezed her shoulders. "I don't know. Just never found the right woman, I suppose."

"Ah."

"And who would put up with me, honestly?"

"You can be pretty charming when you want to be."

He looked down and wiggled his eyebrows at her. "Oh, really?"

Beatrice burst into laughter and tugged at the collar of his garish Hawaiian shirt. "Yep, you're a regular knight in flowered armor. You just need to find your damsel."

"Oh," he groaned. "I don't know. I've never really seen the appeal of the 'damsel-in-distress,' to be totally honest. I'm not really the damsel type."

"Well, maybe you need to find a knight, then."

He grimaced. "*Definitely* never seen the appeal of those."

Beatrice leaned into his shoulder. "You'll find the right one someday. I have faith."

Carwyn smiled and leaned over to kiss her forehead as the rainbow pyrotechnics flashed in the distance. "Well, I'm glad one of us does."

Chapter Four

Dublin, Ireland
July 2005

Brigid sat stoically in the antiseptic air of the doctor's office, only half-listening to the understanding voice of the physician.

"So, the combination of the MDMA, or Ecstasy, along with the intermittent heroin use was creating in your brain the false feeling of contentment and depressing your symptoms of social anxiety through manipulation of serotonin levels. Though the short-term benefits of the drugs would mimic prescription medications for the disorder, long term use…"

Blah.

Blah.

Blah.

The grey-haired physician droned on. She finally lifted her eyes to Ioan's as he sat watching from across the small exam room. He was furious. Disappointed. But the emotion that pierced her heart, the one that had convinced her to follow him to the grey building in the city suburbs, was fear.

Her protector couldn't be afraid. He was too strong. Too sure.

Brigid could never think of Ioan as a father. She had no father, and even the hint of one was enough to make her stomach churn. Ioan was the older brother she'd always wished for. The one who would defend her. And her protector was staring at her with dark, fearful eyes.

Brigid blinked back tears and looked away.

Ioan interrupted softly, "Dr. McTierney, I think that's enough. Thank you. Brigid's health appears normal?"

"Brigid?" The doctor spoke to her softly, his tone asking permission. She just shrugged, and the doctor turned back to Ioan. "All her blood tests came back normal except for the drugs in her system. The levels match the use she described in her interview."

The doctor sat down on the chair across from her. Brigid curled into herself and stared at his hands and the small, dark hairs that sprinkled the back of them. Thick veins crossed the top of hands that he folded in studied, professional concern. "Brigid, I'm a physician, but I am familiar with social anxiety and depression. There are prescription medications that can help you. Your symptoms and history are classic—"

"Piss off and leave me alone." Her voice was soft, but clear. She had nothing to say to the human. She wanted to be left alone.

"Brenden, if you could give us some privacy, I'd appreciate it."

The doctor rose and shook Ioan's hand before he left the small examination room, leaving Brigid and Ioan alone. Ioan often worked in the city doing clinics for the underprivileged. The doctor was a friend who helped and had agreed to perform the lab work confidentially during hours that Ioan could accompany her. She could hear Ioan heave a deep sigh, and she closed her eyes.

"Christ, Brigid, when I think how bad this could have been—"

"Are you going to make me quit school?"

She was still doing well in school. After her first experience at the club, she researched Ecstasy. Illegal drugs weren't something she had ever considered taking, but the effects of the MDMA had been so soothing she had to learn more. She paced herself. She was careful to only use them in social situations, and never too often. And when the MDMA had stopped being quite as effective, a small dose of heroin did the trick. Never too much. She was still in control.

That's what she told herself.

And if her use toward the end of term had increased, that was just because of stress, wasn't it? Her grades had slipped a little, but not enough that it had affected her standing with the university. But if Ioan made her stop taking classes—

"Of course you're quitting school, you idiot! You're quitting school. You're quitting your friends in town. Most importantly, you're quitting drugs. Enough, Brigid. We're lucky to catch this after only a few months. You're entering a program and you're—"

Her head shot up. "I'm not going to any fecking rehab."

"Yes, you are." He glared at her. "It's not open for debate. You're going. You're getting help for the addictions, and you're—"

"You can't force me into one."

"Oh, yes, I can."

"You can't!"

Ioan rose from his seat and stalked toward her. He pulled her up by the collar of her jacket and his voice was a low growl. "You forget yourself, Brigid Connor. Do you forget who I am? Do you forget who Deirdre is? Under piddling Irish law I may not be able to force you into a program, but we're not talking about Irish law, are we?"

He paused, and she forced herself to look up, despite the burning in her eyes.

"Never forget what it means to be under my aegis, Brigid. I am responsible for you. For your actions. When you risk yourself like this, you risk exposing all of us to the mortal world. You will go to treatment if I have to use amnis to put you there. It is not an option."

Her defiance crumbled. She knew he was right. Rebellion had never truly been an option. She had known that from the time she was a girl. Her shoulders slumped, and she curled back into her chair. Ioan sat next to her and gently put an arm around her thin shoulders. Ioan had always been one of the few people she could handle being near. The priest had been another one.

"Fecking Carwyn."

"Don't blame him. How long do you really think you would have been able to hide this from us?"

"I'll never be in the *Garda*," she whispered. "I'll never be able to pass the psychological evaluations, and I'll have a history of prescription drug use for social anxiety. I'll never—"

"Ah, Brig." He groaned. "Girl, how did you think you were going to pass the drug test? The *Garda* was never going to be an option if you were taking drugs."

She took a shaky breath and inched closer to him. "I thought... I thought if I just took them long enough. Maybe I could conquer it. I could get better, and I'd be able to be normal."

"We were wrong, Deirdre and me. Me, most of all. We helped you treat the symptoms, Brig, but we never treated the wound."

Her heart sped and she pulled away. "What are you talking about?"

"You know what I'm talking about."

"I—I don't want to." Her heart began to race.

"You have to."

"No."

"Brigid, there's a doctor. One of us. She's a healer, but one that focuses on the mind."

She scoffed and stood, crossing her arms across her body. "What? So, you want me to go to a—a vampire shrink or some mad thing?"

"She lives in Galway, and she's a very old friend of Deirdre's. Anne is a friend, Brigid. Not an enemy. She specializes in addiction and—"

"I am not an addict!"

"Yes, you are!" he bellowed, rising to his feet. "You were using them every day. You admitted that you couldn't go out socially without them. That you couldn't even be with your boyfriend—"

"He told you that?" She stared at the door in horror, wishing she could hunt down the doctor and kill him. And maybe, just maybe put an end to her own humiliation, as well. "How could he—?"

Ioan stepped toward her and raised his hands to her shoulders, but backed away when he saw her flinch. He lowered his voice. "You're missing the point. And be mad at me. I'm the one who used amnis to make him tell me the details of your interview."

She gasped in horror. He knew everything? That she used before classes and every night out? That she needed to take a heavy dose in order to be intimate with Mark? Brigid collapsed into the chair again. "How could you? How could you, Ioan? I told him... He said it would be confidential."

He knelt in front of her. "You scared me to death. I don't know that I have ever been more frightened. Do you know how dear you are to me? To Deirdre? To your aunt? The thought of you harming yourself *kills* me."

She sat in silence for a few moments. Finally, she sniffed and rolled her eyes. "You can't die, stupid."

He let out a strangled laugh. She finally looked up and for the first time in her life, she saw tears threatening Ioan's eyes. "You have to get help. You have to, Brigid. For everything. God knows, I've tried, but I can't protect you from yourself."

She couldn't seem to move. And the small bag of white powder hidden in the lining of her handbag called to her, promising happiness and peace. She closed her eyes, imagined the easy thrill of the pills, and the deep, pure peace of the heroin. In her mind's eye, she saw the furious glint in a pair of blue eyes, and a hastily tossed-out command.

"Take care of yourself."

She'd always taken care of herself. No one else had ever volunteered. From the earliest time she could remember, even before her mother married Richard, she had always taken care of herself. And though her heart fought against it, Brigid knew what she needed to do.

She took a deep breath. "I'll go."

Kinvara, Co. Galway
September 2005

The dark night wrapped around her like a blanket, and the sea air carried the scent of salt and seaweed from the south shore of Galway Bay. Brigid stood at the open window and resisted the urge to flee down the small road that led to town. Even if Anne didn't stop her, where would she go?

Brigid had sweated out the worst of her physical withdrawal in her aunt's house in Wicklow. She'd wanted to die. Even though she had been careful with her heroin use, her body had come to depend on it far more than she realized. She'd never been as sick as she had those first weeks. At one point, she'd begged Deirdre to kill her. She hadn't, thankfully, but when Brigid thought about her first "talk" with Anne that she was supposed to have that night, she reconsidered the idea.

"The road or the bay?"

Brigid turned. The silent water vampire had entered the glass-enclosed room behind her and was already sitting in an overstuffed chair.

She couldn't help but smile. "The road. I'm not a very good swimmer."

Anne smiled. "Well, definitely don't take the watery escape route, then."

Brigid shook her head and moved to the other chair. "I'll keep that in mind."

The two women, one mortal and one vampire, both stared out the windows that surrounded them. The study was a small room that faced the water. In the morning, the light would stream in, and it was a pleasant place to drink a cup of tea or read a book. At night, the glass-enclosed room was surrounded by stars and the scattered lights that lined the western Irish shore. It was full of bookcases and stacked tables. Deep comfortable chairs and warm, woolen blankets. It didn't look at all like a doctor's office, but that's what it was.

Anne said, "So, a man goes to see a psychologist. 'Doctor,' he says, 'you have to help me. My wife says I'm obsessed with sex.' The doctor sits down and gets out some ink blots and shows them to the man. 'What do you see here?' the doctor asks. 'A couple on a bed, having sex.' The doctor nods and shows him another one. 'And this one?' 'A man and a woman on a couch, having sex.' 'Interesting,' the doctor says. 'And how about this one?' The man squints and says, 'That's a picture of a man and a woman having sex on a boat.' The doctor finally says, 'Well, you do have a problem. It appears you're definitely obsessed with sex.' The man stands up, outraged. 'What do you mean *I'm* obsessed with sex? *You're* the one showing me all the dirty pictures!'"

Despite herself, Brigid snorted.

Anne spoke again. "How are a hooker and a psychiatrist the same?"

Brigid remained silent for a moment, then decided to play along. "How?"

"They both turn to each other after an hour together and say, 'That'll be two hundred, please.'"

Brigid fought back another snort. "So, are psychiatrists like lawyers? Lots of jokes about their noble profession?"

"I don't know. I think my secretary finds them on the internet. I get a new one every night on my desk."

"And I'm supposed to take this process seriously? Now I'm just going to be imagining you in fishnet stockings, saying, 'Looking for a good time, big boy?'"

Anne threw her head back and laughed. "Oh, Brigid, it's nice that you have a sense of humor. Humor is important."

"Is it now?"

"Yes." The counselor turned to her with a wide smile. "It's very important. Truth is important, but so is laughter. Never be afraid to laugh, even when you're crying. Sometimes the two go together."

"Well, I'm trying to think of some junkie jokes, but I'm coming up short. Heard any good ones lately?"

Anne settled into her chair, looking back out the windows. "I'm afraid not. Should I have my secretary look tomorrow?"

"Sure, why not?"

"Do you think you were a junkie?"

She started to say "No," but halted. Did she? "I'm not a junkie, but I was weak."

"Why do you think you were weak? From what your friends and family say about you, you're one of the strongest people they've ever known."

"They..." She took a deep breath, and her voice came out like a whisper. "They don't know me."

"Does anyone know you?"

Her mind flashed through the faces of her friends. Her family. Ioan. Deirdre. Sinead. Emily. Mark. "Probably not." The last image was a pair of vivid blue eyes, but she shoved it away.

"Do you want to be known?"

A sick, oily feeling twisted in her gut. Shame. Even after so many years. Shame piled on top of shame, because she was ashamed to even feel the emotion itself. She bit the inside of her lip and muttered, "Probably not."

"Well, I'd like to know you."

"Because you want your two hundred in the morning?"

"Of course." Brigid's head jerked up, and a smile lifted the corner of Anne's mouth. "I like strong, interesting people, too. And I think you are. Interesting. And strong. Very strong."

"I'm not strong. If I was strong, I wouldn't have had to use drugs."

Anne paused. "Tell me about your father."

Brigid slid down into her chair and looked out the windows. "He died when I was five."

"Tell me about your step-father, then."

Brigid stared out the windows. The shadow of a large bird swooped down in front of them. An owl? She heard a sharp squeak and knew that some tiny creature had just become dinner. "My step-father died when I was ten."

"He was killed. In front of you."

Brigid still stared into the dark night, imagining the razor-sharp talons of the owl tearing into the tiny mole or mouse. "Unfortunately."

"Why unfortunately? If he were in front of me now, I'd kill him." Brigid looked up in surprise, but Anne only shrugged. "Human shrinks aren't allowed to say things like that, but then, I'm not human, am I?"

"I suppose not."

Anne waited for her to speak again, but she didn't know what to say, except that this session wasn't turning out the way she thought it might.

"You said, 'unfortunately,'" Anne continued. "It's not unusual in cases of long-term abuse for a child to confuse abuse and love. It's very common and nothing to be ashamed of. From a young age, you were conditioned—"

"I had no love for Richard. I never did. I hated him. I always knew what he did was wrong. I knew by the look on my mother's face when she found him in my room the first time. I know he was a sick bastard. I know that I wasn't at fault, so don't think that I regret he's dead."

Anne fell silent, and Brigid could hear the wind whistling around the old house on the edge of the sea.

Finally, Anne said, "Then why—?"

"I said 'unfortunately' because I'm still angry he killed him." Brigid's head ached as she sifted through the tucked away childhood memories. The dread of the creaking door and the place she went in her mind when she heard it. It was the same. The same every night he came. Then, one night… it wasn't. Lights pouring in. No place to hide. Unexpected footsteps and her mother's soft sobs. A shock of auburn hair and a small pop as Richard crumbled to the ground in front of her.

"Why then, Brigid? Why were you angry he died?"

"Not angry he died." She turned to Anne. "I only wish he hadn't killed him, because I wanted to do it."

CHAPTER FIVE

Snowdonia, Wales
September 2006

Carwyn murmured the last of his prayers, made the ancient sign of the cross, then rose from his knees. He walked to the closet where he kept his vestments to dress before left the house and went to the small church he'd tended for hundreds of years. It was Friday evening, and in the small town in North Wales, that meant that the Father would be there to hear confession if he was in town. Carwyn didn't know if it was the silence and peace of the tiny church in the mountains, or the safe cloak of darkness, but Friday nights were often his busiest nights when he was home.

Well, if you could call three or four parishioners "busy."

He looked in the mirror to make sure his collar was straight, then hastily brushed back his thick red mop of hair. Sister Maggie would say he needed a haircut, but the nights were growing colder, and Carwyn had never much cared for hats. He grabbed a coat and walked down the hall.

Maggie was baking in the kitchen and looked up. "Down to the church, then?"

"Yes."

"Friday night. Do you think you'll be long?"

"Last week there were four parishioners, Sister." He chuckled. "The week before, there were two. What do you think?"

She gave him a rueful smile. "I'll have dinner waiting, then."

"No, don't bother. I'm in the mood for a hunt later." A hard run in the hills was just what he needed to burn off energy.

"Fine then. No stew for you."

He gave the old nun a quick squeeze around the shoulders and headed out the door. "I'll see you later, Maggie."

"Bye now."

Carwyn sped out the door and down the mountain, enjoying the whip of wind around his face as he moved effortlessly through the hills. Their ancient energy fed his own, and he had to resist the temptation to take off his shoes and dig his feet into the living soil that called him. He could have stayed lost in the mountains for hours, recharging his amnis and taking comfort in his element, but that was not his purpose that night. His purpose was to offer comfort, not take it.

The small town nestled in the isolated valley had been his tiny province for over five hundred years. Like Deirdre and Ioan's people, the villagers never asked any questions, knowing that something otherworldly dwelled among them. They offered seclusion and secrecy and, in turn, Carwyn took care of them. The father who lost a job found another in a nearby town. The child whose parents couldn't afford braces received them. It was a fair trade, in Carwyn's opinion. They were his people, as small as the community might be. He had watched families form and break apart, much to his sorrow. He christened and buried the faithful. He celebrated the weddings and mourned the lost. The town was his, but as the years passed, even Carwyn had to admit things were changing. His parish was slowly shrinking. More and more young people left the town and stayed in the city. Fewer and fewer children were born.

It was the way of things, he supposed, even if the thought filled him with sorrow at times.

When he entered the sanctuary, his keen, immortal eyes spied only two women. One was as faithful as the clock in his library. The other, though, was a surprise.

"Lynne, are you all right?" He placed a soft hand on the young woman's shoulders. He had married the girl and her young husband five years before, and they had christened two children in the church. "Nothing wrong with David, is there?"

Tear-filled eyes blinked up at him. "Do you have time to hear my confession, Father?"

"Of course. Give me a moment."

She nodded and went back to praying while Carwyn entered the small, wooden confessional and took a seat on the bench.

Father God, if you'd like me to be more patient hearing your lambs, put it on Sister Maggie's heart to get me a cushion for this wretched bench.

He settled in and soon heard the other door open. He slid back the tiny screen and listened to the familiar refrain.

"Bless me, Father, for I have sinned. It's been two months since my last confession, and I accuse myself of the following sins…"

The poor girl was pregnant again. And though her heart loved the child, her husband had lost his job and she despaired of how they would manage to pay their bills when they could barely afford to pay their way with two small mouths. Carwyn's heart hurt for the girl, whose husband was a proud, but good, man who wouldn't accept charity. He heard the girl's confession of anger and resentment toward her husband. Her guilt over not feeling joy at the coming new life. Her sharp words to her older children.

By the time she had finished, his heart was heavy, and he knew he'd be seeing another family leave the town. He could find a job for the young man, who he knew was a steady worker, but it wouldn't be in the valley. The jobs were all leaving, along with the people.

"Go in peace, Lynne," he told the young woman after they had prayed together.

"Thank you, Father. It always helps to talk to you."

He saw her cross herself, stand, and leave. Shortly after, a middle-aged man slipped into the booth. He must have come in after Carwyn had started with Lynne.

"Bless me, Father, for I have sinned. It's been six months since my last confession, and these are the sins I have committed…"

I've been drinking again.

I was unfaithful to my husband.

I've had lustful thoughts.

I spoke hateful words to my children.

I lied to my wife.

I beat a man who angered me.

Though the world changed, humanity did not. The sins he had heard in the days of carts and horses were the same committed in the time of computers and automobiles. Life flowed around him. The town grew, then died. Sin and anger, love and life remained the same. As powerful as he was, there was so much Carwyn knew he could not control. Oftentimes, he was helpless to make things right. But he could comfort. He could advise. And as his beloved sire had admonished him a thousand years before, he could have a purpose.

But Carwyn was beginning to wonder if his purpose needed to change. The community he had shepherded through so much was crumbling. It was inevitable.

Shortly after the man had received absolution, the door opened again. He recognized the step and smiled.

"You the last one, Davina?"

"I think so. I waited a bit so I wouldn't be a bother."

"You're never a bother, dear."

"You say that, but I know you tire of hearing about my cats."

Carwyn smiled as she sat her old bones in the chair. Davina was one of his oldest parishioners. He had christened her, married her, christened her children, then her grandchildren. Someday, he would give her the last rites before her soul flew to be with her beloved William again. Davina was there every Friday, faithful as the sun.

"Bless me, Father, for I have sinned. It has been one week since my last confession. These are the sins of which I accuse myself…"

He tried to keep a straight face as she detailed her litany of failings.

"And I should have told her that the dress made her backside look like a mule, but I didn't."

"No?"

"I told her it was grand." Davina sighed. "Brenda has many fine qualities, but she's a poor seamstress. She was just so proud, I didn't have the heart to tell her. But it was a lie. Definitely a lie to say 'grand.'"

"You might have to make a pilgrimage of some kind for that one, Vina."

The old woman chuckled. "You're teasing me again."

"Lying to Brenda about her dress is hardly a mortal sin."

"I hope you're not so light with the young people about these things, Father." Her voice held a slight note of disapproval.

"What young people?"

The old woman sighed. "Don't I know it?"

"How's your daughter and her family in Cardiff?"

"Doing well. Very well. She was just telling me about…"

The friendly woman began filling him in on all her children's doings before launching into her grandchildren's. She did every week. Though her family was caring, they were busy, and Davina was quite adamant about not being a bother to them, so their visits were rare.

"Davina?" He finally broke in.

"Yes, Father?"

"Let's finish up and just go get a cup of tea at the house, dear. This chair is not the most comfortable."

"Oh! Well, that would be fine, Father. Is the sister about?"

His hunt would have to wait. Carwyn smiled. "She is, and I believe she was baking a cake."

"Well, that would be lovely, then."

Carwyn smiled, closed his eyes, and began to pray with her.

CHAPTER SIX

Dublin, Ireland
September 2006

It was amazing how much one city could change in a year. But then, as Brigid opened the door to her new flat that faced the river, she thought she might have changed just as much. And just like the modern construction that lined the River Liffey, she felt ready for the future. Her year with Anne had helped her turn a corner. And though shadows of the past still haunted her at times, she'd finally reached a place where they weren't an anchor dragging her down.

In her time away, Patrick Murphy had moved the center of his operations to the newly refurbished building in the heart of Dublin's emerging Docklands. The old building had been razed and a bright, modern structure of glass and steel had been built in its place. Since Brigid considered this move a new start for a new her, she approved of her flat. She never wanted to step foot in Parliament House again.

"Miss Connor?" The building director was still standing in the door. "Will this be acceptable?"

"Thank you, Smith. It's lovely. When my things arrive, please have them brought up."

The older gentleman nodded. He probably could have worked running any one of the world-class hotels in the city, but instead, Smith coordinated the residents in Murphy's new building. The bottom floors hummed with the night and day business of the immortal leader. Shipping. Clubs. Restaurants. Her new landlord was powerful and very, very wealthy.

"May I escort you to Murphy's office for your interview, Miss Connor?"

She dropped her purse on the table in the entry and picked up a small handbag. Smith cleared his throat. "You won't need your bag, miss. I'll be happy to see you back into your rooms, but security does not allow any bags or briefcases into Murphy's office."

"Well, of course not. Thank you, Smith." She picked up her jacket and patted the pockets, looking to Smith with a smile. "Best make sure I don't have any spare pen-knives, matches, or broadswords in here, either."

"Very thoughtful of you."

They walked down the hall to the elevator and took it down to the first floor. Unlike most executives, who would consider the top floor a mark of stature, Patrick Murphy kept offices on the first. As they walked past the wall of glass that lined the hall, Brigid looked at the lights of the boats floating up and down the river. She noted that the building jutted out over the bank, giving Murphy and any other water vampire immediate river access and what would probably be very strong elemental strength.

They stopped in front of a set of double doors, and Smith paused. He gestured toward a small sitting area with a coffee table and an old rotary phone.

"You may wait here for security to come get you when Murphy is ready for your interview. If you dial fifty-four when you are finished, it will connect directly to my office, Miss Connor. I'll see you directly back to your room, or escort you through the building, if you like."

"Thank you, Smith. But please, call me Brigid."

He smiled. "Of course, Miss."

Brigid held out her hand and gave Smith a firm handshake. Her heart did not race. She was calm, and her palms were not even damp. After months of Anne's unique therapy, which combined traditional counseling with the targeted use of vampire amnis to treat certain symptoms, Brigid finally felt as if she was in control of her reactions for the first time in her life. She no longer felt an instinctive aversion to touch and she was far more comfortable in social situations. She had feared, prior to her return, that being back in Dublin would cause her to relapse, but so far, none had occurred.

She took a seat and started to page through one of the local newspapers that lay neatly on the table, but as soon as she picked up the first one, the door opened.

"Brigid Connor?" The tall vampire had a blank expression as he looked her over. Other than his height, he was very average looking. Average brown hair. Average brown eyes. Pale, unlined skin marked him as an immortal, and his canny eyes scanned her for any detectable threat. She rose quickly.

"I am."

"Murphy is ready for you. Please, come with me."

She walked ahead of him through the doors, but paused before she ran into the second set of doors. The vampire smiled almost imperceptibly.

"All of his offices are light-proof, of course."

"Of course."

The vampire fitted a key in a lock, then drew a stylus from around his neck and punched in a code on a keypad above the lock. He caught her glance and smiled again. "The passcode changes every night. Just in case you were curious."

She blinked. "I—I'm not. I'm just not used to most vampires using electronics and such."

He gave a low chuckle. "The ones who work for Murphy do."

Brigid heard a small buzz, then he pushed the door open and entered. Beyond the door was another office that looked like any rich executive's welcome desk. An efficient-looking human woman worked behind a computer, glancing up with interest. She lifted the half-moon glasses she'd been wearing and tucked a lock of her smooth silver hair behind her ear. "Murphy's ten o'clock?"

"Yes, ma'am." The vampire's voice held a hint of a tease, and Brigid looked up to see humor lighting his face. The secretary scowled.

"*Ma'am* me, you impudent lad. You're a hundred years older than me, and you know it."

"And yet you still call me a lad, Angie. I must be living right."

Angie rolled her eyes at him, but stood and offered Brigid a hand. "I'm Angela McKee, Miss Connor. It's a pleasure to meet you. Ignore Declan. Work here long enough, and he'll start teasing you about your age, too. You'll rue the day your first wrinkle appears, for you'll hear no end of it from these lads."

Brigid thought she might just like working with the older woman, who was, she had to confess, one of the most handsome women she'd ever seen, no matter what Declan teased. She glanced over at the tall vampire, very obviously looking him over. "Well, Ms. McKee. I wouldn't take much heed of him. He's stuck with that unfortunate face for eternity, isn't he? At least we can shove off after eighty or ninety years."

The formerly plain face of her escort broke into a charming grin as he joined Angie laughing. Just then, Brigid heard a door crack open, and she looked over her shoulder.

"You must be Brigid Connor. I was warned about that mouth."

She'd heard a lot about Patrick Murphy in the past ten years, first in Wicklow, but more at school. The girls in Parliament House had treated him with a kind of awe only shown toward movie stars. He was rich, powerful, and appeared to have been frozen in time around thirty years of age. Rumor had it, he still enjoyed a hardy bout of bare-knuckle boxing with his cadre of security guards and employees. And first time Brigid saw him, face-to-face, she thanked God and all the saints that he was a vampire. Because permanently marring that incredible face with a bloody fist would have been a crime against heaven, she was sure of it.

She tried to look cool and calm, but she was fairly sure she was staring. Murphy, to his credit, only smiled politely.

"With insults like that, you'll fit right in here, Miss Connor."

She spoke before she even thought. "Oh, that's nothing. Talk to me after a few pints. They get better."

His blue eyes crinkled in the corners, and his face split open into a mischievous grin. "Is that an invitation?"

Was that her imagination or were his fangs down? Brigid cleared her throat and took a deep breath, trying to stop the flush she could feel creeping up her neck. "I…"

"Oh, for heaven's sake, Patrick," Angie butted in. "Don't pester the girl before she's even started work. She'll run off and I'll be left on my own with you lot again."

Murphy winked at Angie, then opened the door wider and held a hand out for Brigid. "Miss Connor, if you please? We have the formality of an interview to dispense with before I may pester you again."

Brigid smiled and walked into the office. As soon as she entered, she scanned the room.

The walls were solid, with no visible access points, but she had a feeling one of the thick bookshelves against the far wall housed a door of some kind. There was also a slight crease in the center of the area rug that told her a seam of some kind was concealed beneath. River access, if she had to guess.

"Yes," Murphy said quietly, as he walked toward his desk, eyeing her with calculation. "I think this will work. I like the way you just examined this room, Miss Connor."

"Please, call me Brigid."

"Brigid, how many exits do you see?"

She paused, giving the room one last sweep with her eyes. "One."

"And how many do you *not* see?"

"I'd say… one behind the bookcases that leads to whatever room is beyond Ms. McKee's office, and another under the rug where the carpet is worn. That one probably leads to the river somehow."

Murphy walked over and flipped back the rug, revealing bare floor. Brigid frowned in disappointment until he walked to the other side of the room and flipped up another rug, revealing a square door in the floor.

"We rotate them so the wear marks aren't too obvious. The rug you spotted will need to be replaced. I'll remind Angie."

"Or you could keep it. It would make a good distraction for someone not accustomed to your habits."

He cocked an eyebrow at her. "Indeed it could. Excellent suggestion, Brigid."

"Thank you."

"Have a seat."

They walked to the smooth cherry desk in the corner of the room in front of a set of bookcases. Murphy took a seat behind the desk, and Brigid sat across from him.

"I understand you were attending UCD and planning to enter into law enforcement. Then you left school and moved back to your family home. Why?"

Brigid took a deep breath. She had expected the question, but it was still difficult to answer. "I had substance abuse problems that I developed in school. I left to get it taken care of, which I did, but my history and medical record would disqualify me for the *Garda*."

Murphy shrugged. "Records can be expunged. Disappear easily for someone such as Ioan ap Carwyn. Why wouldn't he do that? I know you are a valued member of his aegis."

Records could be expunged, but psychological evaluations could not be avoided, or faked. Brigid had faced the fact that her history of abuse, anxiety, and depression would disqualify her from human law enforcement. But vampire?

"I decided, after some reflection, that I was more suited to private, instead of public, security, Mr. Murphy."

"Call me Murphy. Everyone does." Then he smirked. "Except for a few who don't, but you'll know when you're one of those."

She arched an eyebrow at him. "Is that so?"

Murphy leaned back in his chair and folded his hands in front of himself, the picture of innocence. "Perhaps. I make no assumptions."

"Good idea."

"I have a lot of them."

She couldn't stop the blush that stained her neck. "I'm sure you do."

He had a smart mouth, and Brigid wished she didn't find it quite so appealing. She smoothed the very conservative grey slacks she'd worn and tucked a piece of her hair behind her ear. Gone were the clashing colors and rows of earrings. Her hair was its natural dark brown. Her ears held only two piercings each, and her suit was plain and well tailored, fitting the office, the vampire across from her, and the organization she hoped to work in.

"Almost all the employees in my security department are immortal. Most of them are related to me in some way. I have very few outsiders here, and I'll be quite honest, despite your connections—which are the only reason I'm considering you—I will not trust you until I know you better."

"That's perfectly understandable, sir."

He narrowed his eyes and examined her as she sat across from him, still as a vampire. "As I said, most of my security is vampire, except for Angie. Obviously, this presents some challenges. How proficient are you on the computer?"

"I'm no expert, but I'm very computer-literate, if that's what you're looking for."

"That's all I need. I have my own sources for other kinds of information."

She nodded. "It shouldn't be a problem, then, and I'm a very fast learner."

"Are you?"

"I am."

"Good. And of course, you won't burn up in sunlight, which also has obvious advantages."

She smiled. "True."

He paused for a moment, staring at her intently as his hands steepled on the desk in front of him. "The drugs problem is growing worse in Dublin. To a certain extent, this does not concern me." He must have caught the stiffening of her shoulders. "Not that drug use isn't a concern to all citizens, but for the most part, the mortal authorities are equipped to deal with it. Only rarely does it interfere with those under my aegis or those in my territories."

Her voice was quiet when she asked, "Are you sure about that?"

Murphy arched an eyebrow at her, but continued. "As you may have guessed, the problem of drugs at Parliament House—which *is* in my territories—and the safety of its residents, has been of some concern considering developments over the past year. Further, the import problem does fall under my purview, as well."

"Where is it coming from?"

"In Ireland, Brigid, almost everything arrives by boat. Especially drugs. I am a water vampire and the largest private holder of shipping interests in the country—not that the mortals are aware of it. The import of narcotics, and the criminal activity associated with such, has become something of a problem that overlaps with my own interests. Therefore, I have become involved, no matter how I may have wanted to avoid it."

He fell silent, and Brigid forced herself to meet his eyes. "Why are you telling me this?"

Murphy smiled. "You working for me could be beneficial to us both. You have knowledge about this problem you may not even realize you possess. But that also means you'll have to be in contact with some of the elements you've tried very hard to distance yourself from. Is that something you can manage?"

Brigid thought about her old friends. Thought about the greedy glint in the eye of the boy she'd bought drugs from and the utter terror and pain of heroin withdrawal. Could she willingly put herself into that world again? Would she manage to resist the quick and easy promise of oblivion? If she could really help, she would.

"Depend on it. I'm in." Murphy's face was utterly blank. Brigid could hear the clock on the wall behind her ticking, but there was no electronic hum of a computer or ringing phones to distract her from his examination. She swallowed the lump in her throat. "Did you have any other questions for me?"

He finally smiled and leaned toward her. "Would you like meet the team?"

CHAPTER SEVEN

Snowdonia, Wales
September 2007

"Hello, Father."

Carwyn nodded at the older man who passed him on his way to the small market in town. Sister Maggie had run out of currants and asked him to pick up some more for the scones she was baking in the morning with the ladies at the church. Since the nights were finally getting longer again, he told her he'd enjoy the walk. If he stopped by the small pub in town for a pint… Well, she wasn't baking that night, was she?

"Hello, Father Carwyn." He smiled at the little girl and her mother who passed him.

"*Noswaith dda.*"

"Evening, Father."

"How's Sister Maggie, Father?"

The small village tucked into the hills of Northern Wales was a relic. The majority of his ancestral homeland had long ago abandoned the Roman church, but in the isolated mountain community, his old stone chapel still stood, faithful and enduring, and the people of the town were set in their traditions.

He brushed back the shaggy red hair that fell over his forehead. He still needed that haircut Maggie was pestering him about. A light rain fell and twinkled on the black coat he wore. Though he only wore clerical attire during formal occasions or mass these days, he still kept to a more muted wardrobe when he was home and working.

He stepped into the small market a few minutes before they were set to close. The round face of the young woman at the counter broke into a smile.

"Hello, Father! Can I help with anything this evening?"

He frowned. "Currants for the sister? I'm not sure where they would be."

She waved him over to a row. "I'm not surprised. We keep moving the baking things about the store and I often get lost myself." The clerk handed him a small package of the dry red berries and then started back to the front of the store.

Carwyn frowned. What was her name? Ginny? Jennifer? Her mother's name was Mary, he was sure of that, but the young woman hadn't been to mass in quite some time.

"Thank you..." His embarrassed expression must've given him away. He shot her his most charming grin.

"Jenna."

He smothered the laugh when she blushed. He'd caught her looking for his teeth. They always did. Only the children asked directly, and even then, it was rare. His life, such as it was, was not questioned by the people in the town. He was the Father. They were his people. "Thank you, Jenna."

"You're very welcome. Is there anything else?"

"No, thank you. Tell your mother I said hello."

"I will, Father."

The girl's mother had entertained a furious crush on him when she was younger. It hadn't been the first, nor would it be the last. Far from a deterrent, his vocation was an attraction for a few. It always had been. For some, it was the allure of the forbidden, never mind that he'd been a married man when he was human. For the other, shyer sort, he was considered safe. A man, but not a threat.

He smiled to himself. Except for the teeth. They always forgot about the teeth.

Carwyn whistled as he walked into the pub and waved at the man behind the bar. David had been pouring pints for years in the small, cozy establishment, as his father had before him. Carwyn could see David's son, Dylan, helping another customer as he sat at one of the stools. Father and son working together, following a tradition, year after year and generation after generation. The farmer's son. The teacher's daughter. He thought of his own children. Not a single one in ministry to the church. Of course, a lifelong commitment took on an entirely different tone when you were talking about hundreds of years instead of fifty or sixty.

"What'll you have tonight, Father?"

"What do you have local on tap?"

"I've a new chestnut brown from that brewery in Colwyn Bay."

"I'll take that."

"Nice to see some of the local boys putting their name out, isn't it? Keep some of the younger folk around."

"Nice to see *any* jobs staying."

They passed news back and forth for about an hour, with some of the older men chiming in with stories or jokes. Carwyn laughed and chatted. He shared his own stories—the ones they could relate to, anyway—and jokes. He asked polite questions and tried to remember the details. The village was his home, but he'd come to maintain a careful distance. It was necessary. He couldn't afford to become attached to those he ministered to. They were too short-lived and their lives too ephemeral. But he could help when he could.

That's what he was called to do, after all.

London, England
November 2007

"Does it bother you that they all dislike you?"

Gemma looked up from inspecting the books at the shelter she had started two years before.

"Not at all. I'm here to make sure things are run properly, not be their friend."

"You're not nearly as unpleasant as you pretend to be, Gem."

"And you're not nearly as much of a clown as you pretend to be, but we all put on the masks we need. The children who come to these shelters don't need me to be the director's friend. They need me to make sure they have beds and food to eat. That the lights stay on and the water is warm. They don't care if everyone thinks I'm a raging bitch to get it done."

He walked behind her and squeezed her shoulders as she sat at the desk. "You're a good woman. I'm very proud of what you and Terry are doing here."

His daughter nodded. "He's a good man. A good choice for me."

Ever the pragmatist, Carwyn thought. His oldest daughter may have had humble origins, but she took her responsibilities as the leading woman in London immortal society very seriously. Terry was the jovial cad who ruled with a fist, and Gemma was the elegant lady who assisted with the satin glove. An unlikely a pair as he ever could have imagined, they were a force to be reckoned with when they had formed their partnership.

Gemma's quiet voice drew his attention again. "If you ever grow weary of your disappearing mountain town, we could certainly use your help here. We have plenty of money, not as many people as dedicated to helping."

"And you think any of these children would want to talk to a collar?"

Gemma lifted an eyebrow and scanned his garish red- and blue-flowered shirt. "When was the last time you wore a collar?"

He grinned. "Last Sunday night at mass."

She snorted, but couldn't stop the smile. "You're so ridiculous."

"And proud of it. Too much seriousness in the world as it is. I hardly need to contribute."

"Speaking of seriousness, did you hear that Murphy's finally cracking down on the drug trade in Dublin? I have a feeling Ioan and Deirdre were putting the pressure on. He was just on the phone with Terry about it last night."

"Really?" Carwyn had never paid much attention to Dublin politics. The damn city was always a mess, in his opinion.

"Yes, I think they've become more insistent about it since the trouble with Brigid."

His mind flashed to a pair of golden-brown eyes and a delicate, sneering mouth. "Brigid Connor?"

"What other Brigid is in their clan? Yes, Brigid Connor. She's working for Murphy now."

His head whipped around. "For Murphy?"

Gemma blinked and looked up from her books. "Are you deaf? I didn't know that could happen with our kind. Yes, *Murphy*. Patrick Murphy, head of Dublin. Perhaps that all-animal diet really does dull your senses after a thousand years."

"Shut up and tell me more about Brigid."

Gemma smirked. "She's on his human security team now. According to Ioan, she's quite brilliant at it. Shooting guns. Questioning suspects. He says she loves it."

He felt a smile lift the corner of his mouth. "Is that so? She said she wanted to go into the *Garda*. Good for her."

Gemma shrugged. "Well, she couldn't go into the police with her background, could she? And Murphy was certainly happy to have her."

He frowned, remembering Ioan and Deirdre talking about the man's interest in forming a connection with their clan. "What do you mean about that?"

She smiled. "What do you think? She's a lovely young woman with good connections and obvious intelligence, which Murphy has always valued. Brigid is the opposite of brainless. I imagine he's quite interested in her."

"She's human."

Gemma arched an eyebrow at him. "We all were, once."

Carwyn looked away to study the map of the London Underground that was hanging on the wall. Brigid Connor and Patrick Murphy? He pictured the very proper man in his three-piece suit, then the girl with the brilliant purple streak in her hair who had demanded a whiskey and sneered at a beer. He could certainly see the attraction on Murphy's side, but what would Brigid see in him? For some reason, the idea of the two of them together irritated him.

"None of my business," he muttered.

"What?"

"Nothing."

"Terry wanted me to invite you for Christmas, by the way. You're not going to the States this year, are you?"

"No, Gio's still hopping around the world being mysterious, and I don't want to intrude on Caspar and his family. I thought about going to see Gus and Isabel, but it's too far."

"You're welcome here, if you like."

Carwyn frowned. His thoughts still swirled around a woman in a Dublin pub. "Maybe I'll go to Ireland this year." Gemma was silent behind him, so he turned around. She was looking at him with narrowed eyes. "What?" he asked.

"Ireland?"

"Why not?"

Wicklow Mountains
Christmas 2007

Brigid was so short that Carwyn stared down at the top of her head in the pew at Christmas Eve mass. She was sitting next to him, dressed in a simple black dress, and her hair was her natural dark brown, trimmed into a short, professional bob. Compared to the college girl he'd met two years before, she was hardly recognizable. Her pixie face had taken on the more mature angles of a woman. Her figure was slight and lovely. Luckily, the hard expression in her eyes had softened, and she seemed far more comfortable in her own skin.

She had been formal to him. Polite, but formal. Proper. And more than a little disinterested. He wondered if she was the sort to hold a grudge.

Carwyn found it oddly annoying. He somehow wished she would roll her eyes again. He's be lying to say that he'd not thought of her in the years since he'd seen her outside the pub in Dublin. Something about the young woman had haunted his thoughts. He admired the way she'd struggled through her difficulties. She had finally found success, but for some reason, her very proper clothing and neatly cut hair bothered him.

He whipped out the Christmas program, scribbled a note in the margins, and handed it to her. She looked up at him with disapproval, but took the note, anyway.

'What happened to the purple?'

She mouthed 'Purple?' and looked at him in confusion. He grabbed the note and scribbled again.

'Hair.'

He saw a tiny smile cross her face. An appealing blush came to her cheek, and she grabbed his pen.

'Not exactly office-appropriate.'

He scowled. *'Not the right office, then.'*

Carwyn couldn't stop the grin when he saw her roll her eyes. She took the pen and wrote back.

'What do you know about the right office? According to Ioan, you wear Hawaiian shirts under your vestments. Not to mention your rumored television habits.'

'Lies. All lies. I'm a picture of devotion and obedience. Highly appropriate at all times.'

Irritating children, telling on him like that. Carwyn frowned and poked his son in the shoulder. Ioan and Deirdre were sitting in the pew in front of him. His son looked over his shoulder, then between the two of them and the note Brigid held in her lap.

"Behave, both of you," Ioan whispered. "Brigid, I expect this behavior out of him, but not you. Father Jacob is in the middle of the homily."

"And it's a very boring one," Carwyn whispered back. "Trust me, I've heard a few."

He took perverse pleasure in Brigid's quiet snort. Ioan tried to look disapproving, but he smiled before Deirdre pinched his side and he turned back to the front of the church.

Carwyn took the note and scribbled again. *'Why preach a doom and gloom sermon on Christmas Eve?'*

She wrote back. *'To remind us of our grave sins amidst the worldly revelry.'*

'God loves revelry. He told me.'

Brigid snorted again, and Deirdre turned around, reaching back to snatch the program from them. Carwyn crossed his arms and glared at her as the priest finished the mass. And he may have snuck a few more glances at the intriguing Brigid Connor.

Christmas Eve dinner in Wicklow consisted of a turkey and all the traditional foods Sinead prepared to go along with it. It was the first Christmas Carwyn had spent in Wicklow in over twenty years. He usually went somewhere warmer for the holidays, but Ioan and Deirdre had been pleased to welcome him. Sinead, who had always enjoyed joking with him, was thrilled as well. Several of Ioan and Deirdre's own children had also come with their mates, so the family party included over thirty people.

Ioan caught his eye over the turkey and nodded toward the door. Carwyn nodded back. They would go hunting for something more appetizing after the humans were asleep.

After dinner, they gathered around the fireplace in the family room to open a few gifts, and Carwyn was immediately handed a present from Sinead.

"This is from Brigid and me, Father. I've been wanting to give this to you for years."

Ioan snickered from across the room, and Carwyn tried not to cringe. "Oh, Sinead. That fills me with a grave fear, I cannot lie."

Sinead went back to her seat laughing, and Carwyn looked for Brigid. She was smiling, but she hadn't really laughed all night. He wracked his brain, but he couldn't think of a single time he'd heard the woman laugh. *Really* laugh. Well, that was just like a challenge, wasn't it?

Carwyn shoved the thought from his mind and focused on opening his present. As he lifted away the tissue paper, he roared in laughter. "Sinead! Where did you find it?"

"Brigid had to order it on the internet for me. All the way from Hawaii." The older woman was laughing, tears streaming from her eyes. "I'd say she picked out the best one."

Carwyn held up the shirt for the room to see; it was met with many an agonized groan. In the history of Hawaiian shirts, it was possibly the ugliest he had ever beheld. Florescent green hibiscus flowers dotted bright orange fabric. And along the bottom edge of the shirt, the ugliest hula girls in history danced.

He looked across the room at Brigid. "These are the ugliest hula girls ever. I'm impressed."

Her voice barely carried across the room. "More like hula *men*, I think."

"I think you may be right." He pulled Sinead into a hug and kissed her cheek. "You brilliant women, it's the crown of my collection."

Deirdre said, "Pack it away, Carwyn. It's blinding me."

"Absolutely not. I'm wearing it." He stood and all the humans and vampires around him groaned again. Carwyn glanced at Brigid as he pulled off the very proper Oxford shirt he'd donned for dinner. She still wasn't laughing, but he caught her glancing at his bare chest and had to smother a grin.

She *was* blushing.

"Put your shirt on, Father," Deirdre cried. "No one wants to see your hairy chest."

He winked at Brigid, who was still stealing glances. Her neck was bright red. "I have it on good authority that Sinead has always been fond of my chest hair, Deirdre."

Carwyn buttoned up the truly hideous Hawaiian shirt and pulled Brigid's aunt into another hug.

"You're a bad, bad man, Father." The older woman was blushing as well.

Ioan lifted a glass of whiskey in a toast. "But an excellent vampire, we can all agree."

"Hear, hear." He almost missed it, but Brigid's quiet voice made it to his ears over the din of the party. Carwyn looked over to her, and her beautiful amber eyes met his. For a moment, he saw a hint of the mischief he remembered when she was a girl, and his heart gave a sudden, and completely unexpected, thump. He blinked and looked away, suddenly distracted by Deirdre as she opened a gift from one of her daughters.

When he looked back over to the chair where Brigid had been sitting, she was gone.

"What's going on with you and Brigid?"

Ioan's question caught him by surprise as they walked through the woods, scenting for deer. Carwyn blinked and almost stumbled over a log.

"What are you talking about?"

Ioan narrowed his eyes and smiled, just a little. "You kept looking at her during dinner. Then afterward, as well."

"I wasn't. Really. Not really. I mean, she's looking well. I've worried. Of course. I know how concerned you and Deirdre were over the girl, and she's…" He paused and cleared his throat. "She's looking well, isn't she? It's nice to see, that's all."

Ioan nodded, but Carwyn caught the subtle smirk on his son's face and had to fight back the urge to hit him.

"She is. Security work is a good fit for her. Dublin is having increasing drug problems, and she's quite passionate about it, as I'm sure you can imagine."

"What kind?"

"Heroin, for the most part. Rumors of others, of course. It's bad, and it's becoming more pervasive. Ireland has four times the usage as the rest of Europe now. Murphy's been pleased to have a human on staff who's more in touch with the current environment, and Brigid seems very happy with Murphy."

"*With* Murphy?" The thought brought him up short, and his heart gave another quick beat. He felt his fangs in his mouth. They were partly descended; he must have smelled deer. He kept walking behind Ioan.

"Working with him, I mean. Murphy says she's very good."

"Oh, does he now?" Carwyn muttered.

"Apparently, she's blending in to his organization quite well and has been a huge help on a number of levels. And she loves it. I've never seen her so happy."

Then why isn't she laughing?

He frowned and continued stalking deer. There weren't many of them around during the middle of the winter months. They tended to wander in the lower hills, but there were usually at least some around. That night, there were none. They might have to wander farther. Though Ioan might occasionally drink the donated human blood they kept at the house, Carwyn would not.

The act of drinking human blood triggered too many other hungers he'd struggled for years to conquer. For some reason, the memory of Brigid's blood came to his mind. The hot, sweet smell of it with the faint chemical tinge. The tinge that wouldn't be there anymore. He banished the thought from his mind and continued walking.

"Father, did you want to try farther up the valley?"

Carwyn decided that a run might be just what he needed to clear his head. "I'll race you."

They returned to the farmhouse hours later, as dawn was approaching. They had found a deer to share and Ioan was bringing in the meat for the human workers after they had drained the animal's blood and sated their hunger. Both he and Ioan still preferred the taste of wild game to any domestic animal. A sign of their age, he supposed. Though he had followed a vegetarian diet in his human years, like most in his community and his order, his sire had taught him the value of the hunt as a young vampire. Nothing exerted more physical or mental energy as stalking game. Well… nothing that he let himself indulge in, anyway.

No, the feel of his element beneath bare feet, the wind in his face filled with the myriad scents of the forest, and the rich taste of wild blood—those were the indulgences he allowed himself after a thousand years. And it was enough. It had to be.

He saw a faint puff of smoke as he approached the house and noticed the edge of a familiar scent tinged with tobacco. His eyes narrowed when he caught Brigid's dark bob of hair in the shadows, smoking a cigarette and watching the small flurries of snow that fell that early Christmas morning. She was bundled in a grey wrap that Deirdre had given her, and her whiskey-brown eyes scanned the night. Watching for what, he didn't know. Carwyn observed the girl for a few moments, examining her careful gaze, the ready set of her shoulders, and her tense expression. Even at home, among her people and under the care of the most powerful vampires in Ireland, she was guarded and wary.

Why don't you laugh, Brigid Connor?

An odd wandering thought darted through his mind and he wondered what she would look like when she was sleeping. Would the tension still mark her forehead? Would her mouth still hold a firm, serious line, or would it be soft?

And why am I thinking about your mouth?

He shook his head and approached. The cigarette smoke fluttered from her pursed lips as she stared into the night.

"When did you pick that up?"

Brigid's eyes darted to him, but she didn't move. "Finished drinking Bambi?" She nodded at him. "Made a bit of a mess of yourself, didn't you?"

He looked down at his shirt. There was a smear of blood across his festive green shirt. "Ah, your aunt is going to nag me for that one."

Brigid smirked and took another draw on her cigarette. The smell of it tickled his nose and he held his hand out. "May I?"

She lifted an eyebrow, but handed over the smoke. "I didn't know you indulged."

"Occasionally." His lips closed around the filter. He could feel the faint warmth from her lips. The subtle taste of her that lingered. "Not often. It's a bad habit, or so I'm told."

Brigid rolled her eyes. "There have been moments in the last couple of years when it was a cigarette, a fix, or cutting my own arm off. Smoking seemed like the healthiest of those three options. I'll quit eventually."

He handed it back to her. "Do. No reason to see you to an early grave." But he would. As young as she was now, he'd watch her age. The slight lines around her mouth would grow deeper. The wary gaze would gain wisdom. A strange melancholy filled his chest. "He would change you. If you wanted it."

Her head lifted with a jerk. "Ioan?"

"Yes."

"I know. I don't want it. I never have." She took a deep drag on the cigarette and passed it back to him. He let his fingers brush hers when they touched.

It wasn't unusual. Humans who grew up under immortal aegis often saw the drawbacks to vampire life more clearly than others. Were there benefits? Of course. Carwyn loved being a vampire. It fed his lust for life and his curious nature. But there were drawbacks, as well.

"Why not?" he asked softly. "What are your reasons?"

If he wasn't watching closely, Carwyn would have missed the slice of pain in her eyes. It was quickly smothered as she looked out to the falling snow again.

"Sometimes, it's just good to know that there's an end to things." She must have seen his eyes narrow, because she continued, holding her hand out for the lit cigarette. "I've no death wish. Nothing like that. But... as Father Jacob is fond of reminding us, 'This world is not our home.' Sometimes, that's a comfort to me."

Carwyn ached to see her smile. He wanted the clear ring of her laughter and the joy of watching her face light with amusement. He had the sudden urge to lift her up and tickle her, which was ridiculous. She wasn't a child.

"Far from it," he muttered.

"What?"

"Nothing. I should take shelter. The sun will be up soon."

"Aren't you forgetting something?"

He frowned. "What?"

"Happy Christmas, Carwyn."

He grinned from ear to ear. "Happy Christmas, Brigid. Some priest I am, to almost forget my Lord's own birthday." Her mouth twisted at the corner as she watched him. She was smirking. No, she was smothering a laugh. He winked at her. "Almost."

"I don't know what you're talking about."

"Yes, you do." He started to walk away, but turned back. "There's another verse I like more than Father Jacob's very serious and somber homilies."

"Oh?"

"It's from the book of Jeremiah. 'For I know the thoughts that I think toward you, says the Lord, thoughts of peace and not of evil, to give you a future and a hope.'"

Brigid stared at him, speechless.

Carwyn said, "Have a *hopeful* Christmas, Brigid." He turned and walked into the house just as the sun started to rise.

CHAPTER EIGHT

Dublin, Ireland
April 2008

Brigid emptied the magazine into the target at the end of the range, carefully set down the assault rifle on the bench in front of her, and took a deep breath. Her heart was racing, and she turned when she heard a short chuckle behind her. She grinned at Tom. "That was the most fun I've ever had firing a gun. Ever."

"Wouldn't get to play with those in the *Garda*, would you?"

"Not likely. But then, I wouldn't have been able to touch ninety percent of the weapons you've shown me if I had joined the human police."

"Well, don't get too attached. That's the same rifle the German army uses, and it's not likely Murphy's going to give the okay for you to cart one around town, is he? Though, if you asked, he might make an exception."

She rolled her eyes. "Hush. Not you, too."

Tom picked up the rifle and took it over to the storage counter where one of the employees that worked at Murphy's shooting range would clean and store the weapon.

In the eight months she'd been working for Patrick Murphy, Brigid had come to realize that she held a charmed status among his employees, and not because of her pixie face. No, it was the fact that she was a mortal under Ioan and Deirdre's aegis that made everyone—except Angie and her coworkers—give her special deference. Growing up in Wicklow, she'd never truly understood how powerful or well-respected they were. Here, spending time with immortals from all over the world, it was impossible to escape. She knew the only reason she'd made it onto the security team was because of her family.

Staying on it, however, was entirely up to her.

"Jack says you need to be more diligent with your PT," Tom said as they walked out the door and up the stairs leading toward the first floor of the Docklands Building. Brigid took off her safety glasses, pulled out her earplugs, and tucked both into her bag.

"Do you realize how frustrating it is to train with someone who never gets winded? Never tires out. Never breaks a sweat. Never—"

"Stops teasing you about how slow you are? That's Jack. Get over it and get to work. I'm serious."

Of course Tom was serious. Tom was always serious. They never spoke about it, but Brigid was fairly sure that Murphy and Tom were brothers of some sort. Not biological. Tom Dargin looked nothing like Patrick Murphy. He was far older when he'd been turned, though his waist was still trim and his shoulders un-stooped. His lantern jaw had been broken more than once when he was a human, and he bore heavy facial scars. And yet, despite his brutish appearance, Brigid found his company the easiest of any of the vampires she worked with.

Tom was still talking. "There's no better physical trainer than Jack on the team, and you're still very green. Don't make me put you at the desk. I want you to double your time at the gym."

She curled her lip at the thought of more hours spent with Jack. "Fine."

"And don't give him a bad attitude."

"Fine."

He was glaring down at her. She could practically feel it.

"Do I need to take away your toys?"

Brigid's mouth dropped open. "You wouldn't!"

The corner of his grim mouth turned up. "Double time at the gym or your nine millimeter is mine."

"You're a mean vampire," she muttered, "and I don't like you anymore."

"You never liked me to begin with. You just liked my access to firearms."

"That's not… *completely* true."

They waved at Angie, who was sitting at her desk, as they walked back into the security office that Tom ran with Declan and Jack. Declan was there with his hands, also known as Sean, a young computer programmer who did little besides type what Declan told him to on the computers the water vampire couldn't touch.

A large map of the city spread over the back wall, desks dotted the room, and a full wall was taken up by monitors that covered the building and its perimeter. Jack was paging through a thick file and scanning the monitors. It looked like a small, and very efficient, police station.

And Brigid had a desk there.

"Jack," Tom called, "Murphy around?"

"No." He glanced at Brigid and gave her a devilish grin, as if he knew he'd have her in his clutches for twice as many hours a week. "He's meeting with the Englishman; then he's for France to meet with Desmarais. Brigid, he forgot to send you a kiss, love. Shall I stand in?"

"Piss off, Jack." Brigid set her bag beside her desk and grabbed one of the cloths she kept on the corner to wipe the firing range grime from her skin.

Despite how the boys teased her, there was nothing but polite interaction between Brigid and her employer. She knew Murphy was watching, but so far, he'd kept his distance. Much as she had expected, Brigid was going to have to earn his trust and confidence. When he was around, he was polite, but distant, which was fine by her.

"Connor," Declan barked when he saw her, "what did you say the name of that club was? The one near Parliament House?"

"I don't remember, to be honest. It was Rave… Rage. Something like that. I only went there once. Even when I was using, that place was too rough for me." She saw Sean flinch. It was slight, but it was there when she said the name of the club. She caught Declan's eye and nodded to the young human. "Ask him. He knows."

The young man looked up with a panicked expression. "I—I don't use —"

He was cut off when Declan put a heavy hand on the back of his neck. Beatrice could almost see the creeping amnis as it took hold, flooding his cerebral cortex and opening his mind to the immortal.

Declan said, "What is the name of the club?"

Sean blinked once. "Rage."

"Do you go there regularly?"

"No."

"If you wanted a fix, who would you talk to?"

The young man blinked, and Brigid wondered if Declan was asking the right questions. All Murphy's employees were made to take a drug screen, so if the young man was working in the building, it was likely he wasn't using.

"Sean…" Brigid walked over. "Which of the bartenders had the most business? You know which one had the stuff. They always had the most people asking for them at the bar."

"The girl. Shannon, I think. She always has the most people around, but she's not very pretty."

Brigid looked at Declan. "That could be all he knows. If he's not a user, he probably wouldn't know about the harder stuff. But it's a name. If she doesn't have it, she'll probably know who does, and they might be willing to talk."

Declan scowled and released the young man. Jack walked over from his perch by the television screens and put a hand on the back of Sean's neck as he walked him out to Angie's office. "Look her up tomorrow, Brigid. You've got the best contacts at the clubs. It'll be your job." Declan called out to Jack, "Tell Angie I'll need a new set of hands! Connor, in the meantime, get over here. You can type for me."

She sat at the desk and followed Declan's instructions as Jack came back in and began to speak to Tom in a low murmur.

Declan barked, "Pay attention. This is what I want you to look for…"

Hours later, after her eyes had begun to water from staring at the computer screen as she searched shipping manifests with Declan, Brigid walked to the elevator and hit the button for the fourth floor. It was close to two in the morning and she was exhausted.

She had to admit, part of her loved living where she worked. The other part felt like she mostly never quit working. But that, she decided months ago, was fine. The last thing she needed in Dublin was spare time.

Just as the doors were about to close, a small hand with pink fingernails slipped through and a familiar voice called out, "Hold the lift!"

The young woman was laughing as the doors opened, clearly coming home from a fun night out. But when Emily's eyes rose and met Brigid's, she gasped.

"Brigid Connor?" Emily's mouth spread into a broad, friendly smile and she stepped inside. "You have normal hair now!"

Brigid was at a loss. It was the first time she'd run into any of her old crowd. "Emily… hello. I—I didn't know that you—"

"I can't believe this! I'm so excited. Everyone thought you'd disappeared. No one asked questions, of course, but I had to admit I was worried when you didn't come back to school. And then Mark told us about meeting that vampire—"

"What vampire?"

Emily giggled. "I don't know his name, silly. Mark said… Well, you know how he was. I think he was jealous."

Brigid's mouth dropped open. "Who?" She suddenly remembered that her old boyfriend had been with her that fateful night by the Ha'Penny Bridge Inn when Carwyn had discovered her drug use. "Carwyn? Mark… he never mentioned anything to me. I'd forgotten he even met him."

"So…" Emily's smile turned mischievous. "Is that why you disappeared? Ran away with a handsome vampire, eh? Mark thought you'd had a history with the guy and hadn't told him. Said he was older and—"

"No!" She blushed bright red as she thought about Carwyn at Christmas. The wink he'd shot in her direction as he pulled off his shirt made her feel like a nervous schoolgirl, and her heart raced thinking of the furious crush she'd entertained from a distance when she was young. Then there was their conversation on Christmas morning she still thought about.

Carwyn. Her mind turned too often to the unattainable immortal.

"It's nothing like that." She cleared her throat. "So, Emily, do you work here now?" Brigid straightened her shoulders and faced her old friend, reminding herself she was no longer the awkward girl from Parliament House. Emily had never had a problem with drugs. Not like Brigid. As far as Brigid knew, she'd always toyed around the edges of the scene. Smoking some pot. Taking Ecstasy when she went out. And Brigid had been very good at hiding her use from her friends.

"I'm working in the accounting department." Emily rolled her eyes and pressed the button for the fifth floor. Her eyes saw Brigid's floor and widened. "Fourth floor. Posh! And secure, eh? I suppose your family is still—"

"I'm working here, as well. I'm in security. That's why."

Emily grinned and leaned against the back wall of the lift. "This is so cool. I wondered so many times over the years. How long has it been? What, two—"

"Three years now. It's been almost three years since I was... well, since I quit school."

Emily looked a little confused, but happy, too. "It's so great to see you."

"Have you...?" Brigid shifted. "Have you heard from Mark lately?"

Her old friend gave her a soft smile. "London last I heard. He and Jenny Daly were married last year. Pretty sure they moved to London."

She nodded. "That's nice." Brigid tried to think of anyone else from that time that she cared about asking after. There really wasn't anyone, which made her a little sad. "So, Emily—"

"We should go out to catch up, eh? Just girls?"

Brigid blinked in surprise. "Oh, sure. That'd be fun."

"There's this fun club—" Suddenly, Emily broke off. "Oh, do you like dancing now or not?"

Brigid smiled. Though physical contact and crowded rooms no longer gave her the instinctive anxiety she'd once struggled with, she still wanted to avoid the scene. Besides, going to clubs felt too much like work anymore.

"Not really," she said. "Maybe just lunch or drinks somewhere would be fun."

"Sure." Emily yawned. Her blinks were becoming longer and longer. Brigid realized that the lift had stopped on the fourth floor, but she still hadn't slid the keycard that would open the door. She pushed off from the back wall and got it out, then swiped it and the doors opened with a hiss.

"I better go, Em. I'll—"

"I'm in flat five-ten above, if you want to stop by whenever." Emily was staring at the secured fourth floor with owl-eyes and gave Brigid a sleepy wave before the doors swiftly closed. Brigid spun around and started walking toward her flat.

Well, that was unexpected.

It was two weeks later when Brigid finally decided to ring Emily. She'd accessed her information in the security files. Jack had been relentless in teasing Brigid about her lack of a social life, and Brigid decided to take matters into her own hands. She could have a social life. She could. She already had an old friend to catch up with. If she didn't date much, it just meant the men in Dublin weren't all that interesting.

Much to Brigid's relief, Emily did not insist on a club. She also didn't ask how Brigid had found her number, but then the girl wouldn't. She'd lived around vampires her whole life.

They met at a busy café in Ringsend. The lunch crowd was bustling, but the restaurant wasn't overcrowded. It was one of the newer places in the neighborhood, and Brigid found the whitewashed walls, simple art, and mostly vegetarian menu a nice change from the dark rooms where she spent most of her days. She took a deep breath and smiled across the table.

She could see Emily looking around, as well. "Kind of nice to remind ourselves we can walk amongst the living, isn't it?"

Brigid laughed. "I was just thinking the same thing. I'm very pale, and I have no excuse for it."

"There's not many…" Emily glanced around. "Of *our* kind working in security, are there?"

"No, definitely not."

"I won't ask how you got the job, then, but you like it? The work?"

"I do. I'm very happy with it."

"I remember you wanted to go into the police force. It's much the same, then. So, are you the one behind the cameras? Should I wave the next time I walk down the hall?"

Brigid grinned. "Not me. I mostly…" *Give them information about what I remember from our college days. Try to avoid getting too close to any of the shipments that Murphy intercepts. Avoid thinking about those soothing little pills on my bad days…*

She cleared her throat. "Lots of background checks. Clerical work. Computer work. Things they can't do with their… condition. Stuff like that. Nothing terribly exciting."

"Well, it's still got to be more exciting than all the numbers that swim in my head."

Brigid shook her head. "I never had a brain for those kinds of things. I still need help understanding my bank statement."

Their friendly server brought two steaming plates. Salmon cakes for Brigid and a steak sandwich for Emily. The girl started to devour the sandwich, eating with gusto, which surprised her. Emily had always been the one worried about her figure, not that she needed to be.

Emily must have caught Brigid's look, but she only smiled. "Never mind me. I'm trying to incorporate more red meat into my diet."

"Oh?"

Emily blushed prettily, then swept her collar to the side to reveal two distinct marks that could never be mistaken for anything else.

Brigid's mouth dropped open. "So… you're seeing a—"

"Yes. Haven't said anything to Mum and Dad yet." The blush spread down her neck, sweeping over the marks that lay at the base of her throat. "You're actually the first person I've told. I know… well, you're not as judgmental as most people."

"Who would have a problem with it?"

Emily waved a hand. "You know, so many people are willing to work for… them. It's okay to take the good job and the security and such, but God forbid you actually socialize with them. We've known each other for years, and we've been dating almost six months, but he's still worried about meeting my parents."

Brigid frowned. In her experience, it was usually the other way round. Most vampires kept a polite distance from human staff or casual acquaintances. An understandable habit, as far as she was concerned. She couldn't imagine losing human friends over and over again, but never growing older or aging. It was another aspect of immortal life that she'd never envied and another reason she never wanted to turn. She wondered what kind of vampire Emily was seeing. It couldn't be…

"His name's not Jack, is it?"

Emily blinked. "What, Jack? No."

"He's Irish. Young looking. Curly hair and dimples. Looked like a fecking choir boy, but has the tongue of Satan?" Jack would like Emily. He liked the cute, curvaceous ones that had pulses and didn't ask too many questions.

Emily snorted. "No, I swear, it's not Jack."

"Good. He's an ass."

Emily slapped her hand over her mouth to smother the laugh. She looked around instinctively, even though they were out in broad daylight. "You talk about… them like that? Does he know that you like him so much, Brig?"

"He knows exactly how much I like him."

"I always envied that, you know." Emily took another bite of her sandwich. "You're so bold."

"Ha!" Brigid cleared her throat. "How… Why did you think I was bold? I was never bold."

Emily shrugged. "You had the issues about touching and such—which it looks like you've totally conquered—but you always said whatever you thought. No matter who was listening. I envied that. Still do."

"But you've no reason to be timid about things, Em. You're a smart girl. And obviously pretty special to catch the attention of…" Brigid smiled. "Whoever he is. One of the choosy ones."

"Oh, hush." Emily shook her head, but Brigid could tell the compliment had pleased her.

"So, spill. Are the stories true? Is it really the best sex ever? Fabulous, earth-moving—"

Emily laughed. "Sadly, he's not an earth… type, so there's no earthquakes. Thanks for asking, though."

"You have to give me some details. It wouldn't be fair not to."

Emily just leaned forward across the table and grinned. "The stamina is, I'll admit, impressive. And no need for recovery time."

"Lucky girl."

"Oh"—Emily smiled—"you have no idea."

"And I doubt I ever will." She winked. "No prejudice, just unlikely that any one of them would take a chance pissing off Ioan and Deirdre by asking me out."

"Not even Murphy?" Emily had a wicked gleam in her eye. Brigid couldn't help but smile back. "If the rumors are true… he'd be well worth taking a chance."

"He might be… slightly more bold. But he's my boss, and he acts like it."

"I'm jealous."

"Don't be unless there's a reason. Murphy's very proper with me. So, really, do I know him? I've met most of the people who work for Murphy."

"Oh, he doesn't work for Murphy. But he's been in Dublin for some time. I think you met him once, ages ago."

She frowned. It was possible. She'd met a lot of humans and vampires at one time that she had no memory of the next day, much less three years later. Emily was still talking.

"His name's Axel. Tall, blond. He was at the club. You know, the first night. When you met Mark."

The first night Emily had slipped her drugs. Brigid tried not to be resentful. She'd forgiven Emily years before. It wasn't her fault that what had been a dangerous, but manageable, vice for Emily would spiral out of control for Brigid.

"Axel?" She frowned. "Oh, I do remember him. Scandinavian or something, right?"

Emily grinned. "You know what they say about those handsome Northern raiders."

"Bad girl."

"But a very, very satisfied one." She giggled and started eating again. "He's a water… you know. Does something with shipping. He's old enough to do whatever he wants. We don't really talk about his past much."

"Most of them don't."

He was in shipping? And he worked in Dublin? Why hadn't she heard of him? Murphy *owned* Dublin shipping, and Brigid had come to recognize most of the names of the people he had business with.

"But he's great. Very considerate." Emily paused and smiled. "Honestly, he's the best boyfriend I've ever had. It's kind of odd, if you think about it."

Brigid decided that she worried too much. It was entirely possible that Axel used a different name for business than in his personal life. He wouldn't be the first one.

"You should come with me a couple weeks from now," Emily said. "We're supposed to go meet a friend of his who's visiting from out of the country."

"Oh?"

"Yes, totally posh event. Penthouse in town." Emily mouthed *'water vampires'* and rolled her eyes. "But Axel said it was going to be a big party, and I could bring a friend, since I won't know many people there. Want to come?"

"I'll check my work schedule, but I can probably go."

"Fun! And who knows, you might meet one of his friends that you take a liking to."

That was doubtful, but she smiled anyway. "So, all Axel's friends, huh?"

"Lots of international people. Mostly from Europe, I think."

Brigid took another bite of her lunch. "Sounds fun. Like I said, I'll check my calendar."

Emily paused with a smile on her face. "It's so good to see you again, Brig."

Despite their pasts, Brigid had to agree. It was nice to sit and talk to someone who was just a friend. No vampire politics. No intrigue. Just a regular old human who liked her. "It's good to see you, too."

CHAPTER NINE

Wicklow Mountains
September 2009

Ioan grabbed another reference book from his bookcase and tugged at his hair. Carwyn looked up from the book he'd been reading.

"What are you so frustrated about?"

"I can't…" Ioan muttered. "There's something about all this business that's bothering me."

"I have no idea what you're talking about." He went back to reading his book. "Stop slamming books around."

His son crossed his arms and turned in his chair. "This drugs business in Dublin."

"Well, the whole of it should be bothering you." Carwyn's mind flashed to Brigid's face. "Brigid still working with Murphy on it?"

"Yes, and she asked me a question that's been plaguing me for days now."

Carwyn frowned. "What was it?"

Ioan took a deep breath and leaned back in his chair. "She asked me if there were any drugs that could be intoxicating to immortals."

"Ridiculous question." He closed his book. On the surface, it *was* a ridiculous question. Why was it plaguing Ioan? "Alcohol and drugs do nothing to us. We could shoot ourselves with a lethal dose of heroin, and it wouldn't even make us light-headed. Liquor?" He snorted. "Nothing. Trust me, I've tried."

Ioan was staring into the fire with a preoccupied look on his face.

"It's not possible," Carwyn said again.

"But what if it could be?" Ioan's eyes lit with a familiar curiosity that managed to spark Carwyn's interest. "A drug. Or… a poison of some kind?"

Was it possible? The brightest immortal minds had never truly understood what animated them. Could there be some way to tamper with their health? With their minds?

No, it couldn't be. Carwyn leaned toward Ioan, trying to catch his eye. "In over a thousand years, the only thing I've ever known that is able to harm us is light and losing our heads. Even if we're starving, our bodies shut down and go into a kind of hibernation. Our amnis protects our mind, and as soon as we are fed—"

"Do you remember when we found the old one?"

Carwyn leaned back. "How could I forget?"

"How old do you think he really was?"

"No idea." It had been five hundred years before, in a cave in Cornwall. Carwyn had no idea how old the vampire had been, or even what element he had belonged to. The emaciated figure had been buried in rocks and so thin he'd looked like a mummy. Only the slight hum of amnis had alerted Carwyn and Ioan to his presence. When they poured blood in his mouth, the vampire sprung to life, only to immediately gnash his teeth at their throats. They tried to reason with the vampire. Tried to give him more blood from the deer they had killed, but he was past understanding anything but the bloodlust. In the end, Carwyn twisted his stick-thin neck and ended the creature's misery.

"Have you ever—?"

"Seen one that far gone?" Carwyn shuddered. "No. But we have no idea if he was rational before he was buried, either. Some of the ancients were savages."

"But the idea of a drug…"

He frowned. "I understand why the idea is intriguing, but I still don't think it's possible. Why did Brigid even ask? Did Murphy—?"

"No, if Murphy had the question, he'd ask me himself. No, this is something she's picking up. Something that she's curious about for some reason."

Damn, distracting woman. Carwyn tried opening his book, but closed it almost immediately. "It's ridiculous."

"Everything we understand of our kind says it is not possible." Still, Ioan was biting his lip as he did when he was thinking.

"Agreed."

Then why wouldn't the idea leave Carwyn alone? "I suppose…"

Ioan leaned forward, the scientist in him leaping on the speculation in Carwyn's voice. "What if there were some way to affect our blood, Father? It would have to be our blood, wouldn't it? That's how we sire our children. That's how we bond ourselves to our mates. Our immortality is fed by blood and our power is contained in it. If there were a way to affect our blood—"

"With what? I've been alive for a thousand years, Ioan. I've seen immortals drink every kind of blood you can imagine. Before human beings were so numerous, our kind were forced to drink from any animal we could find if we were hungry. You know this. Humanity, at one point, was a delicacy. Mammal blood. Reptile blood. Even bloods we consider beneath us now can sustain us, if we must. There is no blood that sickens us, or—or intoxicates us—"

"What if there was something that could be added to *human* blood? Something that would affect us. It's possible."

Carwyn was baffled. It was a curious question, and he understood the inquisitive mind of his son, but how the question of tainted human blood affected them, or why it was important to Brigid, he could not fathom.

"Why does she want to know?"

"Brigid?"

"Yes, why was she asking?"

Ioan shrugged. "She's very involved with this push that Murphy's making in Dublin. I know it's annoying to Murphy. All this is being shipped into Ireland somehow, and he's had control of the shipping in and out of this country for a hundred and fifty years. I'm sure it's bothering him that some human has—"

"Are we sure it's a human? Whoever is trafficking the drugs? Do we know?"

Ioan leaned back. "Are we?"

"If it's another immortal, someone infringing on territory under his nose…"

The implications of something like that were far more serious, Carwyn considered. "Something like that could lead to a war, Ioan."

"I know. I've had my suspicions, but on certain matters, I'm sure you can understand why Patrick Murphy is hesitant to involve me."

Carwyn shifted and sat up straighter. "But no problem involving Brigid, eh? No problem involving a defenseless human under your aegis?"

Ioan snorted. "I'd hardly call her defenseless. They've trained her—"

"If this enemy is immortal, no human defenses will suffice! Particularly for a woman."

Ioan cocked an amused eyebrow at him. "Careful, Father. Don't let Deirdre hear you. And don't forget what century we're in. I hardly think Brigid would appreciate your outrage, even if it is on her behalf."

Carwyn sat back in his chair, still frustrated. "I have not forgotten what time we are in." Still, he scowled. He could hear himself; he *sounded* old. And he realized that he had slipped into the language of his past halfway through the conversation with Ioan.

He cleared his throat and made an effort to relax his posture. "Is it wrong to want to protect those weaker than you?"

"Of course not, but I think she's very well protected. If she wasn't, I wouldn't chance her working with him. Or the police. But I know she contributes. She's extremely bright. If she ever…" Ioan trailed off, and he had no doubt his son was considering Brigid's mortality and how much brighter the girl would be with an immortal mind.

He asked quietly, "Has she talked about it? Does she want to be like us?" Why was his heart beating? Was it because he could see the pain in his son's eyes? He knew Ioan and Brigid were very close.

"She says she doesn't want it," Ioan finally said. "I asked, when she was going through withdrawals. I told her... it would cure her of the addiction. That her body would never crave it again. It was unfair of me, to ask her when she was in so much pain, but I cannot deny that I—" Ioan's voice caught. "The idea of losing her is very difficult. It has been many years since I have loved a friend as I love Brigid."

"She is your daughter."

"No!" Ioan shook his head. "No, she isn't. She's never needed or wanted a father. But she is... like a sister, perhaps. I won't deny she's always reminded me of Angharad."

"Your youngest sister?"

"Yes."

Carwyn nodded.

Ioan asked, "You understand?"

"I changed you, didn't I?" He chuckled. "Trust me, I understand sentiment. Your eyes... exactly like Efa's. Exactly. And your grandfather's."

"We're very lucky, Father. We have the comfort of family. We know we are loved."

"Does she?" he murmured. He looked up to see Ioan staring at him with an inexplicable expression on his face. "What?"

His son only smiled and shook his head a little. "Nothing. Lost in my own mind, I suppose. I should get back to working on this research for Brigid. She has a reason for her questions, even though she hasn't told me what it is. It might be something she's not at liberty to talk about. She takes her job very seriously."

"What does she do?" If it had anything to do with violence, Carwyn was putting a stop to it, no matter what Ioan or Murphy thought. Ioan was the most powerful vampire in Ireland, and Carwyn was his sire. His word would not be questioned. If they were too foolish to guard the young woman who had been through so much, then he would step in. It was the only responsible thing to do. After all, she was mortal.

"I know she does a lot of research, but she likes fieldwork as well."

He scowled. "What kind of fieldwork?"

Ioan paused, then burst into laughter. "Am I under investigation, Father? Is there something you're not telling me?" Ioan winked. "Some interest in young Brigid Connor that you haven't told me about?"

Carwyn blinked. "I don't... I am the leader of this clan, Ioan. And she is a human under our aegis. It's my responsibility—"

"Actually," Ioan said, "it's mine. Except for your children, you've always avoided asserting authority over our people, since your vow is to the church. Are you... feeling differently these days?"

Carwyn shut his mouth, which was hanging open, much to his own chagrin. He pushed back the irrational desire to hit the smug-looking vampire across from him. Why was Ioan looking so smug?

Suddenly, Deirdre rushed into the room. "Brigid's on the phone in the kitchen, Ioan. She has a question of some sort."

Ioan shot a quick wink to him and slipped out the door. Carwyn picked up his book and resisted the urge to follow him. Deirdre sat down next to him and looked at his book. "What are you reading?"

"I have no idea," he muttered, then cleared his throat. "What does that woman do in Dublin?"

"Who, Brigid?"

"Yes."

Deirdre shrugged. "I'm not sure of all of it, to be honest. Research. Day-person type of things. And she helps question the humans."

"Why?"

"You know how odd humans are. She understands them better than our sort. Knows the right questions. She's young. Has some experience in the drug world, unfortunately. At least she's putting it to use." He could tell Deirdre was concerned, but trying to hide it. "She likes it. And Murphy knows if she gets hurt, he'll have hell to pay."

Carwyn stared into the fire. Thoughts of dark alleys and vicious, long fangs swirled in his mind. Then, the vision turned, and suddenly it was Brigid's slender neck he saw. But the gasp he imagined was not one of fear. And the mouth that closed over her neck was... He shook his head.

"I'm on my way back home in a few days. I'll catch the boat from Dublin. Maybe I should meet her for a drink. Just to check up on her, you know?"

He could see Deirdre's eyes relax at the corners. "That would be good. I know... I know how responsible she is. And we've never had any hint that she's using again. Still, she's back in that world again, and I worry."

Carwyn threw an arm around her shoulders. "Don't. I'll check on her. I'll make sure everything's safe."

"Thanks, Father."

Dublin, Ireland

There was a wry smile on her face when she entered the Ha'Penny Bridge Inn and slid into the booth across from him.

"Feeling sentimental? Or wanting to remind me of my sordid past?" she asked, but didn't truly seem annoyed.

"I like the beer here."

"You can get Guinness anywhere, Carwyn."

"True, I suppose. Drink?"

"Sure." She shrugged. "Whatever you're having."

He stood and walked to the bar. In truth, he couldn't pass the pub in Dublin anymore without thinking of her. She looked good. Healthy. Her skin was fair, but she looked like she'd been getting some sun. Her hair was still a natural dark brown with no purple streaks in sight, but she was back wearing jeans and an old T-shirt with The Clash on the front instead of her stiff, professional wardrobe.

He ordered two drinks and walked back to the bar, sliding the whiskey toward her. Her eyes lit up, and he caught the smile.

"You're a contrary one, aren't you?" she said.

"I thought you liked whiskey."

Her smile broadened. *Still no laugh.*

"I do. Thanks."

"You're welcome. How's life?"

There was an odd expression in her eyes. "Checking up on me again?"

He frowned. "No. Not... not like that. I was just a bit worried—"

"You were worried about me?"

Yes. "Deirdre and Ioan were worried. And I was, too, of course. Not about the drugs or anything, just life. I know you're doing the security work for Murphy now."

She nodded silently, then took a sip of her drink. An odd smile crossed her face, and he frowned. Humans still boggled his mind at times. What was the woman thinking with that smile on her face? She almost looked disappointed. Did she have other plans that Friday night?

"You had plans, didn't you?" he asked.

Her face reddened immediately, and he felt a quickening in his blood.

"No. No, I didn't. I usually work weekends. That's the most active time for... well, you know. Clubs. Parties. That kind of thing. I usually go with Jack, and we try to identify—"

"Who's Jack?" He was surprised by the harshness of his voice. "Is that someone you work with?"

She curled her lip, and Carwyn felt his heart give a quiet thump.

"Unfortunately. He's a pain in the arse, but he's good protection. And he's good-looking enough that any girls are easy marks for information. As for the men—"

"What men?"

She scowled at him. "Did Ioan and Deirdre say I was being irresponsible? I'm very careful, Carwyn. Very conscious of their position, and what it means to be given this job. I would never be irresponsible or see someone socially that would reflect poorly on them. So if you're worried about that—"

"I'm—they're worried about your safety, that's all." He leaned closer to her. "Ioan seemed to have some suspicion that whoever is responsible for the increase in drug use in Dublin might be immortal."

She leaned across the table, propping her elbows on the edge of the scarred wood. He caught a hint of her scent. Dark, sweet. No hint of chemical remained. He took a deep breath. Then another.

"You know, it's really creepy when your sort do the sniffing thing."

He blinked. "What?"

She rolled her eyes, and his hand lifted immediately to her face. He put his large hand on her cheek and slid a thumb along the delicate ridge under her eyebrow. He could hear her breath catch.

"You know, it's really annoying when your sort do the eye-rolling thing."

Her mouth hung open slightly, and Carwyn stared at her cheek where his hand still rested. "Why the eye-rolling, Brigid?"

"I'm not using drugs anymore; you don't need to sniff me."

"I didn't think you were using drugs." Her cheek was cool under his hand, her skin still chilly from the brisk wind outside.

"Oh."

He frowned a little. Her cheek was heating up. Why was she blushing?

"Why are you blushing?"

"Why is your hand still on my face?"

He blinked and pulled it away. "Your cheek was cold."

"So are my ears, Carwyn. It's cold outside."

He smiled and reached both hands over to cup her ears. "Better?"

The laugh was trying to escape. It was just behind her lips, but Brigid still held it in as he held his hands in the ridiculous pose.

"You're crazy, aren't you?"

He chuckled and lowered his hands. Then he lifted his drink and threw back the whiskey, making a face. "I still don't like that stuff."

She cocked her head at a curious angle, then shook it and looked down at his hands, which were folded on the table in front of him. She took a sip of her whiskey. "Your skin is warm."

He winked. "It's only the water boys who run cold, Brigid. *Our* kind are very warm-blooded."

"And fire, of course."

"Of course."

She finished her whiskey in a few more sips, her tongue catching the edge of her lip to catch the last drop.

"So, what you're working on… it's safe, isn't it?"

Brigid nodded. "Yes, truly. I'm very well protected. And Murphy's very keen to keep me alive."

"Is he?"

She snorted. "Can you imagine Murphy letting Ioan and Deirdre's pet human get in trouble?"

Carwyn scowled. "You're not a pet. You're family."

"It's just an expression."

"Well, it's not one I like. I've never liked it. We're all children of God. Mortal. Immortal. That makes us equal, in my opinion. Always has been."

A smile flickered across her lips. "Good to know, but really, don't worry. I'm quite protected."

"Good."

"Carwyn?"

"Brigid?"

She looked up into his eyes, and his heart thumped. Then it thumped again. She opened her mouth, hesitated, then asked, "Can I ask you something? It's something I've been meaning to ask for a while."

He leaned forward. "Of course."

Her voice was a whisper. "That night... when you and Ioan came for me, did you intend to kill Richard?"

Carwyn's heart crashed in his chest and terrified brown eyes leapt to his memory. In that moment, he felt like the monster he had been that night. Angry. Vengeful. Full of wrath for the man with no thought for the child.

"I—I didn't, Brigid. I know... I shouldn't have done that in front of a child; there's no excuse. I was in a rage when I saw him—"

He broke off when she waved a hand in front of her face. "No, no. You don't have to explain yourself. I'm sorry I asked. I just... I've wondered for years, and Anne said that I should just ask. So I did."

"I'm sorry."

"I'm not sorry he's dead, if that's what you're wondering." He kept silent so she would talk. "I'm rather sorry that I didn't get to do it myself."

He paused. "I understand what you're saying. And I might even be sorry that I took your revenge from you, but..."

"What?"

"The woman may have wanted the vengeance. But I think... I think the child needed to know that she was worth avenging."

Her eyes were glassy when she spoke again. "I'm sorry you had to see that. That you had to be involved."

"I'm not. Why else has God given me this strength if not to protect the innocent?"

She took another sip of her drink. "I'm still sorry."

"Why?"

Brigid's mouth hung open, as if the words struggled to find a voice. "I just am. I don't like thinking about that part of my life."

"It's a part of you."

"Part, yes. But not the whole. Never the whole of me."

He frowned. "Of course it isn't. I know that. Do you?"

"Of course."

Carwyn wondered if she really did, or if some wounds could only be healed with time. Suddenly, his heart thundered with the mad hope that she *would* have time. Far more of it than her human life would allow. He smothered the impulse to embrace her and deliberately turned the conversation to more pleasant topics.

They spoke of friends and family. Amusing stories about her co-workers. Music, which they had surprisingly similar tastes in. And Carwyn almost made her laugh three times, but she was stubborn.

When the pub closed, he could have continued talking to her for hours, but Brigid was yawning, so they decided to call it a night.

"I still don't know who to believe about the wrestling thing. Ioan and Sinead both swear that you watch it."

"Professional wrestling?" he scoffed. "Lies. Who would watch that ridiculous sport?"

"It's not even a sport, really."

"Of course not. They're teasing you." He bit his tongue and glanced at her, catching the exhaustion in her eyes as they walked out. "You're knackered. We're a ways from your building, aren't we? Should I call a cab?"

"I'll walk. I'm a country girl, after all."

Carwyn chuckled. "I'll see you back."

"You don't need to."

He shrugged. "It's no problem."

The walk back to Murphy's building was quiet. The streets were deserted and Brigid's eyes were drooping. She stumbled on the sidewalk more than once.

"Watch yourself. How much did you have to drink, woman?"

"Quiet, vampire."

Carwyn laughed and put a hand on her waist to steady her. Brigid's scent filled his nose. He felt the soft brush of her skin. She leaned into him a little and his heart thumped again.

Shit. He cursed internally at the swift realization.

He was attracted to Brigid.

She squinted up at him. "What?"

Really attracted to her. He shook his head. "Nothing. Are we almost there?"

"Just a few more blocks."

He needed to escape. He had the mad urge to run like hell and plaster himself to her side, all at the same time. Suddenly, every breath Brigid took, every mumbled word tempted him.

Shit.

Though Carwyn had admired beautiful women for over a thousand years, had flirted and played with their attentions, even slipped in his own strict discipline more than once, he kept very careful rein on his own appetites. He enjoyed women as a rule, but was careful, choosing to avoid even a hint of true attraction when he was able.

Shit.

And Brigid wasn't a flirtation in passing. She wasn't a joke or a fancy.

She was Brigid.

Suddenly, the thought of kissing her was the only thing he could think about. Her lips would be soft. Warm. He could hold a hand to her neck and feel her pulse pounding against his skin. He almost cried in relief when Murphy's atrocious glass and metal building appeared. He escorted her to the door and gave her a pat on the shoulder. "Well, bye then."

She frowned at his abrupt good-bye. "Forget something back at the pub, Father?"

His shoulders tensed. "Don't call me 'Father.'"

Brigid blinked with wide, exhausted eyes. "It was just a joke."

Her lips were parted, and her whiskey-colored eyes glowed gold. Her soft body tempted him. The curve of her neck...

Carwyn couldn't hold back. He bent down and brushed his lips along her cheek, pausing only a second to inhale the scent of her skin. He closed his eyes and the sweet smell of her blood rolled over him. He gritted his teeth when his fangs fell down and his throat burned. Then, just as suddenly, he pulled back and began to walk away.

"Hey!"

He paused and turned. The poor woman was confused. Irritated, and with good reason. He knew he was acting like a fickle boy. Her lip curled up in disdain, and for some reason, he took perverse pleasure in her scowl.

"What?" he managed to growl.

She paused, confused. "I... good night."

What must she be thinking of him? "Good night, Brigid. I'll make sure to let Ioan and Deirdre know that you're doing well." He was an ass.

"Right." Brigid took a step forward, then shook her head. "Ioan and Deirdre. Right." She turned back to the door, which the guard was holding for her.

"Brigid."

She turned. "What?"

He tried to talk past the lump in his throat at the thought of leaving her alone in the cold night. "Please, take care of yourself."

Her rueful smile pierced his heart. "I always do."

CHAPTER TEN

Dublin, Ireland
November 2009

The alley behind the pub was deserted at three in the morning, but Brigid kept her hand in her pocket, gripping the handle of her nine millimeter as Jack questioned the dealer. Her thumb rested on the safety, flicking it up and down as voices rose and fell on the city streets. Dublin was a relatively safe city, but no alley was all that safe at three a.m. After all, who would be out except vampires and people looking for trouble?

"Me, apparently," she mumbled.

Jack's head whipped around. "What?"

"Nothing. You done? I'm freezing my arse off."

Jack snorted. "Human."

"Bloodsucker."

She glanced at the dealer. Jack hadn't needed much help to question him. The man had followed her out into the alley with no argument, eager for the promise of sex in exchange for a small bag of heroin. Once there, Jack took over immediately, grabbing him by the neck and questioning him while he manipulated the dealer's mind.

The dealer was an idiot, like most of them. He loved the new, purer drugs he was getting from his supplier, but had no idea where they were coming from. Of course he didn't.

Brigid had become frustrated. She felt like they were constantly putting out small fires and forgetting to look for the source of the ignition. Murphy's security team may have been effective enforcers and damn good at controlling the city, but they were piss poor investigators. Not that the only human on the team was going to tell them that.

A locker at Connolly Station was all the lead they got. The dealer left the money one afternoon; the next night the drugs were there. He had no idea who was supplying them, but at least Jack and Brigid could get the number of the locker.

A few drunk voices started down the alley. Jack turned to her. "Take care of them."

Brigid pulled her hood up, kept her head down, and headed toward the mouth of the alley. As she approached, she could hear the drunks jostling each other while one took a piss against the wall and the other peered down the alley where Jack and the dealer were talking.

"Oy, what's this?" he called out with a grin. "Someone to keep us company tonight?"

She scanned them quickly. Not a threat. Both men were in their late twenties, but she guessed they were boys from the country and not looking for any trouble out of the ordinary sort.

"Hello, lads." She gave them a tight smile as she approached. "Out a bit late, aren't you?"

"Just looking for some fun. Do you have something?"

Brigid shook her head. "No, and you should leave, both of you."

The one pissing on the wall pulled up his pants and swaggered toward her. "Oh? And why's that?"

"Bad sort down this way." She gripped the gun in her pocket and flicked the safety off. "Not a good idea."

The first man looked slightly less scuttered than his friend. His eyes flicked over Brigid's shoulder, squinting into the shadows where the sound of Jack scuffling with the dealer drifted out. Brigid rolled her eyes. Jack just couldn't pass up an easy meal. Particularly an intoxicated one. He said the drugs gave the blood a nice bite.

'How about the hepatitis?'

'Shut up, Brigid.'

The less-drunk one looked back at her cautiously. "Hey, Donal, let's scatter, eh?"

"What are you talking about? She looks fun." The man's breath almost knocked her out as he stumbled toward her.

She was seconds away from drawing her weapon when the first man pulled his friend back. His wary eyes darted from her calm expression, down to the hand in her pocket, then back to the smile she let turn up the corner of her mouth.

"Let's go."

He pulled the drunk from the alley only seconds before she heard Jack speed to her side. The dealer was not with him, and Brigid decided not to ask. Jack's cheeks were flushed, and he was eyeing her with bright eyes and a lusty grin.

"Need any help?"

She rolled her eyes and tugged on his collar, dragging it over to wipe a bit of blood from the corner of his mouth. "Need a napkin?"

"Mmm, messy as always." He chuckled, and Brigid saw his fangs still hanging low in his mouth. It no longer gave her the shivers as it had the first few months they'd worked together.

Typical Jack. She shook her head. "He taken care of?"

Jack patted his flat stomach and grinned. He was a lusty one. He liked his blood, and he liked his women. Luckily, the canny water vampire knew the only workout he'd be getting from Brigid was at the gym.

"Can you check that locker at Connolly tomorrow?"

"Just write down the number for me. I'll go by the station tomorrow, see if anyone's watching it."

"It's not likely that all of the business would be out of one locker."

No, really? "Still worth checking out. I'll have to quit around three, though. I have plans tomorrow night, and I'll need some sleep."

"What's this?" Jack tried throwing a companionable arm over her shoulder, but she shrugged it off. He continued, undeterred. "Does our fair Brigid have a lad?"

"Just a party with friends. Some of your sort, as a fact."

"Who?" He frowned for a moment. "Still the Swedish fellow with Em?"

Brigid snorted. "He's Norwegian."

"They all look the same to me. And why is a fine specimen of Irish womanhood like Emily still wasting time with a foreigner?"

She'd been right. Jack did like Emily. In fact, since the night months before when Jack had seen Brigid and her friend having dinner at the small café in Murphy's building, he'd hardly let a night pass without asking if Emily was available for tasting yet.

"You're such a slag, Jack."

"Now, now. I promise she'd enjoy herself. In fact, that's all I promise." He grinned as they walked back toward the river. "What's her boy at? Forty years immortal? Fifty? A mere babe when it comes to the finer points of pleasing a woman."

"I'm not having this conversation with you."

"Why?"

"Because you're vile!"

"Oh." Brigid could feel him pulling his energy back. "My blood's just running. I think I'll stop at Murphy's and see if anyone's looking for some fun. Come with me?"

She had no desire to go to the after-hours pub Murphy ran for the vampires of Dublin and select humans they invited. "No, thanks. I'll head home."

"Be careful. Use your mobile—"

Brigid cocked her head. "Really, Jack?"

"Fine, my young apprentice. I have trained you well, so I'll be away. Leave me a report on the locker tomorrow. I'll look for it on my desk at first dark."

"It'll be there."

Brigid waved good-bye and cut back to O'Connell, then crossed the bridge to the south side of the river, briskly walking east as she made her way home. Her eyes drooped. While normally she'd enjoy the walk back to her building and the empty streets, she was unusually exhausted.

She passed by a pub and remembered her confusing night out with Carwyn months before. It had been... lovely. Perhaps the most pleasant night out she'd ever had with a man. Not that he saw her that way. Not that he ever would, even if he flirted with her at times. That was just how he was. She'd overcome her silly, romantic notions about Carwyn ap Bryn when she was a teenager. Still... it was nice to feel noticed.

"Take care of yourself."

She did. Though Jack could be a bit loose with her safety, Brigid never felt uneasy walking alone. She was armed and had been trained by the toughest vampires in Ireland. Blinking back her exhaustion, she decided to continue walking. Just a few more blocks to her bed and the sleepy oblivion she craved. That was the key.

If you made yourself tired enough, your mind didn't have the energy to dream.

The following night, after dropping off the extremely unexciting report on a locker that no one visited, Brigid pulled on the dress Emily forced on her.

"Why am I wearing a dress?" she yelled from her room. "I hate dresses. And I don't like you very much right now, either."

"I can't believe you didn't even own one." Emily eyed her with approval when she walked out of the room. "What do you wear to mass when you're at home?"

Axel piped up from the couch, playing with Emily's hair as she sat on his lap in Brigid's small sitting room. "You go to church?"

"When I'm in Wicklow. And I have a few dresses there to appease my aunt. I don't need any in Dublin because I don't like them." She adjusted the hem of her skirt as she walked. "And this dress is too short."

"I like it! You look darling. Axel?"

The blond Adonis-like creature looked up. Axel was extremely good-looking. He was tall, with typically Scandinavian looks and brilliant blue eyes that shone in his pale face. He was lean, but his shoulders were broad and his smile was wide and friendly. He was beautiful. And that, Brigid thought, was probably the reason he'd lasted as long as he had. Because the strangest thing about Axel was, he really wasn't all that sharp for a vampire.

Then he smiled and Brigid was reminded of his teeth. Well, those were sharp anyway.

"You are very beautiful, Brigid. And the dress is not too short. You do not have a man protecting you, but I will take care of you tonight."

Emily cooed and patted his cheek. She liked that alpha-male, "my woman" kind of thing, so Brigid was sure her friend thought Axel's offer was a nice gesture. Brigid just smiled, packed her small, concealed carry gun in her purse, and thought it was an unnecessary one.

"Thanks, Axel. Well, should we be off, then?"

"Sure!" Emily hopped off Axel's lap and plucked her phone out of her purse to call the car downstairs. The three met the dark sedan out front, which would take them to the penthouse where the party was being hosted by some Italian friend of Axel's.

Still mindful of security, Brigid asked, "So, Axel, who is this?"

The blond vampire shrugged. "Just a friend. He and I do some business together. Shipping. He mostly works in Europe."

"He's Italian?" Carwyn's best friend, the fire vampire, was an Italian. But Emily had said that their host was a water vamp. Still, she wondered if this vampire and Carwyn's friend were acquainted. "What's his name?"

"Lorenzo."

"Just Lorenzo?"

Axel smiled. "Yes. Like Madonna. Or Cher."

Brigid snorted. Going by one name wasn't all that uncommon, especially among older vampires, but she still found it pretentious. "Will there be many humans there?"

"There will be a lot of girls." Axel smiled. "He likes women. But there will be some nice men, too, Brigid. And vampires. You should find a good one like me."

Emily's vampire boyfriend was nice, but had the old-fashioned notion —not unusual for middle-aged vampires—that a human woman needed a man. If she was very lucky, she might snag a vampire. In Brigid's experience, the older vampires were smart enough not to underestimate the female sex. Some of the most vicious and ancient immortals were female and had a reputation for being far more dangerous than the males.

"Axel," Emily warned with a giggle. "Stop."

"It's true," he protested. "No man is the equal of a vampire. Emily has learned this."

"Oh, hush." Emily cuddled into his side. Brigid only rolled her eyes. Axel may not have been the brightest immortal she'd ever met, but he did seem to adore her friend. And he was friendly to her, as well. In fact, he was one of the most "human" vampires she'd ever met. But then, Axel was only around fifty years old.

She shook her head and looked out the dark window at the luxurious buildings they passed.

"I'll stay as long as it's fun, but don't try to make me stay all night. I had to work today, so I'm not going to be able to party till dawn."

She glanced over to see Emily and Axel with their tongues down each other's throats.

Great, it's going to be one of those nights.

"Can I get you a drink?"

Brigid turned from her perch in the corner, the automatic refusal on her lips, until she saw who was addressing her. "I… sure. Thanks."

The young vampire smiled and a dimple appeared at the corner of his cheek. He was handsome in a boyish way that reminded her of Jack, but his accent was American and his smile was pleasant, not arrogant. He lifted two passing flutes of champagne and handed one to her.

"I'm Josh."

"You're American."

He laughed, and she could see his fangs gleam in his mouth. They were visible, but not fully extended. He was interested, but not coming on too strong. Nice.

"I am. Guessed that from the accent, did you?"

"Sorry. It's nice to meet you, Josh. I'm Brigid. I don't think I've ever met an American vampire before. I had…" She shook her head with a smile. "I don't know what I was expecting, actually. A cowboy, maybe? Sorry."

He laughed a little. "Well, American vampires mostly keep to themselves. Keep the Wild West safe for damsels. Drink buffalo blood and bed Indian maidens, that kind of thing."

Her eyes widened. "You're joking, right?"

Josh laughed again. "Yes. I'm joking. And I'm from Baltimore, not the Wild West."

"Oh." She could feel herself blushing. "I think I know where that is. On the East Coast?"

"You are correct. And you're from here."

"Guess that from the accent, did you?"

He sipped his champagne. "I did. And it's a lovely one."

"The tourists always think so. Sorry, my aunt loves old western movies from America. So I grew up thinking all American men sounded like John Wayne." Josh burst into laughter and Brigid took a sip of champagne before she continued. "Imagine my surprise when I moved to Dublin and met the tourists."

"I hope we weren't too much of a shock to the young Irish lass."

She frowned. "Did you just call me a lass?"

"I did. And a lovely one, too."

He had kind eyes, she thought, but there was an edge of hunger there that marked him as a young one. She wondered whom he belonged to. He wouldn't be far from his sire, if she was guessing correctly.

"Well, thanks. And who…" She trailed off, hoping he would offer the connection she was curious about.

"I'm in Dublin on business with my sire. He's the host tonight."

"Oh, the Italian fellow?"

Josh nodded. "Yes. I work in his organization."

Well, that was a nice non-answer. What organization was he talking about? Brigid had the feeling that this Lorenzo was trying to keep a low profile for more than personal privacy reasons. She'd have to keep an ear out and see if anything seemed worth reporting to Murphy.

"And you?" Josh asked. "Who did you come with?"

"I came with Axel." She gestured across the room. Axel was standing with his arm around Emily, but was watching Brigid, as well. "The tall one over—"

"Oh, yeah, I know Axel. He's a good guy. Hangs out with me and my friends sometimes."

"You know Axel? How long have you been in Dublin?"

"A few months. He hangs with us at our building over by the river sometimes. It's kind of our after-hours place."

She smiled. "What, like a pub?"

Josh shrugged. "More like a private club. It's no big deal. Humans hang, too. I think the girl he's with, Amelia—"

"Emily," she said. "Her name's Emily. She's a good friend of mine; that's why I came."

"That's cool. Yeah, she's been there. It's fun. We just listen to music. Hang out." Josh's eyes dropped to her neck, and Brigid could see the fangs grow longer in his mouth.

Drink blood from stupid girls you find. She rolled her eyes. "Well, that sounds like a... cool place, Josh."

"The next time Axel and Emily come, you should go along."

Not likely. "Sure, maybe."

Josh put one arm against the wall and leaned closer to her. He sipped his champagne, so she did too. "So what do you do, Brigid? Are you a student?"

Her mouth lifted at the corner in amusement. "No. I work for Murphy."

That surprised him. "Murphy? So..." He laughed a little. "What do you do? Computer work or something?" It was the most common job for a human employed by a vampire. Almost all city leaders kept a staff of humans whose sole responsibility was dealing with the technology the immortals couldn't touch. The technology that was slowly taking over the modern world was completely out of their reach.

"Computer work," she murmured. "Yes, something like that. I do a lot of work on computers."

"That's cool."

It wasn't a secret that Brigid worked for Murphy's security team. In fact, most immortal residents of Dublin were aware of it, along with her relationship to Ioan and Deirdre. But if the young American was ignorant of her connections, it wasn't her job to enlighten him. Josh was just about to say something else when another, slightly older, vampire sped to his side in a blur and grabbed his arm.

Josh looked over with a smile. "Sean, this is Brigid—"

"Lorenzo needs you." The dark-haired Irish vampire with the frigid blue eyes looked her up and down. "Who's this? She looks good."

"Brigid. She's a friend of Axel's." Josh lowered his voice. "And she works for *Murphy*." He turned back to Brigid. "I need to go. It was nice meeting you. You should come with Axel and your friend sometime."

Brigid lifted her glass of champagne. "Nice to meet you, too, Josh." She deliberately ignored the invitation.

The dark-haired vampire named Sean lingered, looking her up and down with a predatory stare. "You look good," he repeated.

Brigid snorted and rolled her eyes. "Learn some manners, vampire." Then she tossed back the rest of her champagne and handed the glass to a passing server before she walked away. Despite her warning, she felt his eyes follow her across the room.

December 2009

"Oh, Brigid will never be satisfied with a mortal, will she now?"

"Shut up, Jack."

They were passing the time going through the security tapes they'd taken from a club one Saturday night. Jack was teasing her mercilessly and had gotten Declan in on it, too. Declan's humor was more tolerable. He had drier sense that matched his personality and closely resembled her own.

Jack said, "It's true. After having a vampire, how would a woman be satisfied with a human again?"

She thought about Axel and Emily teasing her months ago about the same thing. "If I didn't have objections to anemia and insomnia, I might agree with you."

Declan said from across the room. "What makes you think Connor doesn't like the tanned, surfer types, Jack? She hangs out with the ridiculous Swede all the time."

"He's Norwegian!"

Jack frowned. "What's the difference? And Brigid doesn't like surfers. Look how pale she is. And she doesn't even have our excuse."

"What makes you two think I like vampires at all?"

Jack gaped. "Well, surely you've at least tried one out."

Brigid shrugged and continued staring at the television screen. "Never felt the urge. Don't have a biting fetish."

She heard Declan chuckle across the room. "Are you sure about that? It's not just the neck, you know."

"What, never?" Jack said. She glanced at him. He almost looked offended. "Really, Brigid, never?"

"I'm not a virgin or anything. I've just never had a vampire. Is this so shocking?"

Declan said, "As many as you know and are friends with? A little. Most girls are at least curious."

"Well, I'm not." If she was lying about one completely unattainable vampire, well… they didn't need to know that.

Jack spun her around in her chair. "Please, Brigid. Let me help open your eyes." He grinned and his fangs descended. "Consider it part of your training."

Declan snorted. "You're only asking because you're sure she'll say 'no.'"

"Brigid."

Tom's quiet voice called her name and everyone in the room turned. That was the thing about Tom; he never yelled. Everyone just quieted down when he wanted to talk.

She frowned a little at his extra-grim expression. "What's the story, Tom?" He didn't smile, but then Tom rarely did. But there was something in his eyes…

"Murphy'll see you in his office."

"All right."

Her heart began to beat faster. Something was wrong. Murphy never called her to his office. If she'd made a mistake with work, Tom would be the one to correct her. What was going on? Visions of her aunt swam in front of her eyes. Could Sinead have had an accident? Brigid thought she was in good health, but maybe something was wrong. Was it her mother? She hadn't see the woman in fourteen years, and she had no desire to have anything to do with her.

She swallowed back the lump in her throat and tapped on the door.

"Come in."

Brigid opened the door and slipped inside. It was dark. Only one lamp was lit in the corner. Murphy rose behind his desk. His eyes met hers for only a moment before he sped from the room. Brigid blinked in confusion, even more confused than she had been before.

"Brigid."

She spun toward the sound. Carwyn was in the corner, leaning against the wall. "Carwyn?"

Far from his normally affable demeanor, his face was dark. Fierce. He looked like he was on the edge of bursting into a rage.

Brigid's heart raced. "What's going on? Is it my aunt? Is something wrong with Sinead?"

Carwyn walked toward her slowly. "No." He raised his hands, and they hovered over her shoulders, as if he was afraid to touch her.

"What's going on?" she whispered in a shaky voice.

The rage fled from his face, and suddenly, Brigid was enveloped by the crush of his arms. They wrapped around her, enfolding, protecting, as if he was trying to shield her. But she didn't know from what, and her body was racked with violent tremors.

"Please… please tell me."

"We have to find him," Carwyn whispered desperately. "He's been gone too long now. You have to help us. What was he working on, Brigid? He would have told you."

The hot burn of tears threatened the corner of her eyes. "What are you saying?"

Carwyn shook his head. "I'm… Ioan is missing, Brigid. He was in the city, working at one of his clinics."

"I know. We met for a drink Monday night."

"He's gone." His violent whisper tore at her heart. "No one has seen him for days."

"What?" She didn't know where she found the strength, but she pushed away from the solid wall of Carwyn's chest and shoved him back, her fear turning to rage. "What are you talking about? He was just here. He was staying at his place in town and going home on Wednesday after the clinic closed. He can't be missing."

"He is. And he wouldn't just disappear without—"

"He *can't* be missing! Deirdre can find him. They always know where the other is. That's the way it works!"

"Brigid, even with their blood tie, she can't find him if they've kept him away from the earth, love. She's looking. We've all been looking, but he was out of his element, and—"

"Ioan can't be missing," she shouted. "He can't! Where is he?" She stalked over to the rotary phone on Murphy's desk and picked up the handset before Carwyn grasped her arm. She shook him off and dialed.

"He's not at home. He's not at his place here or the clinic. He's missing, Brigid, and he was working on finding something for you. What was he looking for? I need you to tell me."

She just shook her head as the phone rang and rang. Twice. Three times. Four. Why wasn't anyone picking up? She blinked back the tears, but Carwyn was still talking.

"I told you he's not there. What was he working on? He was talking about blood research. Talking about a question you'd asked. Was it related to the drugs business? I know—"

She slammed down the receiver and spun around. "I don't know what he was looking for! I think there's something else going on besides the heroin. There are things that don't… they don't make sense. I was running into too many dead ends. It's not a human. Whatever is going on… I asked him one question, and he seemed to get it in his head that there was something there. I asked him if there were any drugs that affected vampires and that's all! I thought… I thought—I don't know what I thought!"

"There has to be something, Brigid. Think. Has anyone asked after him lately? Or asked about me? It's possible this is because of me or someone else in our clan. Has anyone—?"

"No!" She tore at her hair and paced the room, the panic descending around her. It wasn't safe here. Nowhere was safe. Ioan couldn't be gone. Ioan was her protector. He was the strongest being she had ever known, save for the irate mountain of vampire glaring at her from across the room.

Carwyn was still pacing. "We've run out of ideas, and you're the only one he would have confided in other than Deirdre and me. I need to know whether this is because of me. If this is my fault… Please, Brigid. We need your help."

Her whole body was numb. She shook her head. "I don't know anything, Carwyn. He kept asking me questions. Had I ever seen a vampire taking drugs? Did I know many humans who liked to be bitten? Did *they* take drugs? It was always just a few questions, then he would start muttering…" A gaping hole opened up in her chest and she felt as if her heart caved in. Suddenly, it was as if the life left her legs and she crumbled to the floor. "He would do that muttering thing he does when he gets an idea and he just… I mean, he just…" It was a groan, more than a cry, that wrenched itself out of her mouth.

He couldn't be missing.

He couldn't be gone.

If Ioan was gone then nothing in the world was safe. Brigid felt Carwyn lift her up and carry her to the leather chaise in the corner of the office. He set her down gently and stroked a hand across her cheek, into her hair, his fingers weaving through the thick brown strands until his palm rested warm on the back of her neck. She held on to him like a lifeline.

"Can you think of anything else he mentioned? Anything?"

She couldn't think. Her mind was a whirl of memories, sifting through every image, every conversation, every shared joke she'd ever had with Ioan. She felt Carwyn's lips press down on the top of her head.

"I have to go, love. I have to keep looking. I've called friends to help. This may be related to something I was involved in and I'm calling in a favor. You're not to go anywhere without one of Murphy's men, do you understand?" She felt his hand shake a little where it held her neck. "If someone is targeting my people, they could come after you, too. You're the most—" She heard his voice crack. "The most vulnerable here in the city. Maybe it would be better—"

"I'm not going back home," she muttered. "Not while he's still missing. I'll stay in the city. I can help. I'll do what I can. I have to."

His arms tightened around her. "Brigid, I… we can't lose you, too. Please don't try anything foolish." He held her for a few more moments, then bent down and whispered in her ear. "I have to go."

Her hands reached up and clutched his forearm as it crossed her chest. Her fingers dug into the thick muscle there, keeping his arm close for one more moment before she pushed him away. "Go," she whispered. "Find him, Carwyn."

The search for Ioan was the consuming mission of every member of the Dublin security team for the next week. Every vampire in the city was shocked. Ioan was the most powerful vampire in Ireland and had studiously avoided political struggles for hundreds of years. He was a scientist, a peacemaker. If he was vulnerable, then no one was safe. The city was reeling in shock and no little amount of fear.

Brigid's coworkers spoke in hushed whispers around her and handed her busywork. She wasn't allowed to leave and do anything in the field. She didn't even try to leave the building. She ate and breathed the search, called every contact she had in the human world. Doctors. Nurses. Clergy he'd helped at one point or another. Every former patient of Ioan's in Dublin that she could think of. She hardly slept.

It was the middle of the night when she heard the name. She blinked and her head shot up from the desk where she had fallen asleep for a few minutes. Declan and Jack were muttering nearby in Irish.

"What was that?"

Declan frowned. "I thought you spoke Irish."

"No, that name. What was that name you just said?"

Jack shook his head. "What name? Lorenzo?"

Lorenzo.

Lorenzo, Lorenzo, Lorenzo…

Declan said, "He's an old enemy of Carwyn's. Ioan had no enemies that anyone can think of. It's the only other thing that makes sense. He must have been targeted because of his sire. Lorenzo has had a vendetta against Carwyn and his friend Giovanni Vecchio for years now. He's dangerous, but has stayed out of sight, so he's—"

"In Dublin."

In the blink of an eye, both vampires sped to her and Declan lifted her by the shoulders. His fangs were bared. "Where? When?"

"I didn't know who he was. You didn't tell me his name. No one did." She shook her head. "Why didn't you tell me before? I went to a party with friends. He had a penthouse." She shook off Declan's grip and stalked across the room. "Why the hell didn't you tell me his name?" She pointed to the location on the large map that spread across the back wall. "It was *right here*. Why didn't you tell me before?"

Declan sped out the door, and Jack ran over to her. "I'm sorry, darling. I didn't know… I'm so sorry, Brigid." She saw his fangs descended and he clutched at her shoulders. "Can you think of anything else, Brigid? Anyone you saw. Think! Any locations? Associates who—"

Her heart was racing. She brushed off Jack's hands and the amnis she felt him trying to use to calm her. "He—he had two of his children with him. An American and an Irishman. Both young. And—and there was something…" She scoured her memories.

"…hangs with us at our building over by the river sometimes. It's kind of our after-hours place."

"What, like a pub?"

"More like a private club. It's no big deal…"

She blinked and looked up. "There's a building by the river. One of his children said they had a building by the river where they went sometimes. Like a club. It was on the river."

Near water. Away from the earth. Away from the element Ioan used to draw his strength. A place they could hurt him.

Jack clutched her arms again, but he was rubbing them, trying to warm her. Brigid felt like she'd never be warm again. Declan burst back into the room.

"We already have people going to the house. It was rented under the name of Josh Smith, and—"

"Declan," Jack said. "There's a building by the river. One his boys use. We have to find it."

"Connor!" Tom shouted as he strode into the room. "Get your wits and get on the computer. Let's find that building."

Days later, after more fruitless searching, there was a tapping on her door. Brigid cracked it open. She could see the truth splashed across Murphy's face.

Brigid had found the building. They wouldn't let her search it, but she knew Carwyn and his Italian friend had gone. They had found some vampires there, but none had known anything about Ioan or Lorenzo. In fact, they had found nothing at the warehouse except for too much blood and Ioan's scent everywhere.

Deep in the silent, scared part of her heart, Brigid had known the truth. She took one look at Murphy's grim face and shut the door. Her back slid down the wall as her legs gave out from under her. She forced her fist into her mouth and bit until she tasted her own blood.

"Brigid?" Murphy called. "Brigid, darling, open the door."

She shook her head and dug her small teeth into her hand again as silent tears ran down her cheeks.

"Brigid, please."

She shook her head and continued to sob quietly, remembering the gentle man in the library who had been the rock-solid center of everything that was safe and secure.

"I'm very brave, you know. I never cry."

"I know, Brigid…"

Her protector was gone.

"I know you're very brave."

CHAPTER ELEVEN

Wicklow Mountains
April 2010

Carwyn stared at the pictures on Ioan's desk. His son and Deirdre, smiling at a Christmas dinner. Ioan with Brigid in a playful headlock as they sat in a pub somewhere. Wearing a tuxedo with his sister Gemma at a glamorous party in London. Ioan and him, a candid shot that someone had captured. They were laughing. He didn't remember about what.

Now he knew. Knew the agony of loss his sire had felt when she lost her sister. Knew the creeping despair of losing his most ancient friend.

And in his grief, what had he become?

"Bless me, Father, for I have sinned. I don't remember when my last confession was…"

The whispered words of confession as his son's murderer detailed Ioan's last hours.

The beating. The torture. The quick slice at the neck that had ended nine hundred years of a beautiful life.

"Bless me, Father, for I have sinned…"

Didn't they realize? He offered their prayers up to God, but harbored the memory of their sins for eternity.

"Bless me, Father, for I have sinned…"

Carwyn closed his eyes and heard the quick twist of the boy's neck as Gemma took her vengeance on her brother's murderer. The young vampire paid in the only currency their brutal world understood. And in Carwyn's mind, he realized it wasn't only vengeance. It was a warning. A necessary declaration of power that kept all of them, and all the humans under their aegis, safe from those who intended harm.

"Bless me, Father, for I have sinned…"

But he also knew that he had knelt next to Ioan's killer on the wet deck of a freighter in the English Channel, offered absolution to a sinner, then walked away, knowing he would be killed.

Who had he become? The conflict between his earthly and heavenly obligations had never been so stark.

He brushed the thought aside and shuffled through the correspondence that had built up on Ioan's desk. He'd told Deirdre that he'd sort through it for her, even though he dreaded the task. But life moved on. A passage from Ecclesiastes came to him.

Generations come and generations go, but the Earth remains forever.

He remained. Like the earth that surrounded him in Ioan's library, he remained solid and unchangeable. And life moved on.

The two vampires directly responsible for his son's death were dead. Lorenzo was not. Not yet, anyway. But his close friends, Beatrice and Giovanni, were safe in South America, finding peace and love even in the midst of pain. His clan was shoring up their defenses with an enemy still on the loose. His son, Gus, received word from his twin sister, Carla. Carwyn's child, Luc, had sent a letter from the Netherlands, and Guy had called from his home in Northern France. Tavish and Max had both checked in from Scotland. Gemma was safe in London, secure under the careful guard of her powerful fiancé. She was Carwyn's oldest child now and had already sent men to guard her youngest brother, Daniel, who lived in the Lakes region in England.

Generations came and went. His children rose in power and spread their influence. After a thousand years on earth, Father Carwyn ap Bryn felt the stirring of change in his blood, and the earth surrounding him hummed in awareness.

"Carwyn?" Deirdre called down the hallway. He turned just as she peeked her head into the library. "Are you hungry?"

"No, thank you."

"Is there anything I can help with?"

He saw the hollow grief in her eyes. She had lost half of herself when Ioan was killed. "No. Unless you want something to do."

She nodded, so he pulled a chair next to him and she sat down. He handed her a stack of letters to sort.

Mail from family went in one stack. Letters from medical journals and scientific societies in another. There was correspondence from immortals all over the globe whom Ioan had known professionally and personally. Letters from numerous humans he'd had contact with or helped. Financial statements. Bills. Notices. It was overwhelming.

"This is just from the last four months?"

She nodded. "Well, four and a half, I suppose."

Carwyn shook his head and put another letter in the "family" pile. It was from one of Ioan's children who was considering a move to the United States and needed an introduction. Ioan would have contacted one of his own associates in New York. Or perhaps Seattle or Chicago and consulted with them. Then letters between the two would need to be exchanged. Details of what the business implications of the move were. Why the vampire wanted to relocate. What allegiance or support they could offer. Though the immortal world had no central government, it operated on a feudal system of power, money, allegiance, and personal connections. All things that Ioan, as the oldest of his children, had dealt with in his stead for nine hundred years.

He muttered, "This is ridiculous."

Deirdre looked up with a frown. "What is?"

Carwyn threw up his hands. "All this. He handled all this because I couldn't be bothered with most of it, Deirdre. I had responsibilities and I ignored them."

"You are dedicated to the church. And these were our responsibilities. Our children, not yours."

"They are part of my clan and my connections are the most extensive, so it's something I should have shared. It should never have fallen solely —"

She grabbed his hand. "It didn't. It was shared between all of us. Ioan was just the oldest, so he did the most. And we all understood that you had a calling. You still do. You owe us nothing, Father."

He closed his eyes and leaned back in his chair. "I think it may be time for a change."

"What do you mean?"

"I'm not sure yet."

She was silent as she looked at him, then she turned back to the stack of letters and continued sorting. "He was happy to help. He was always—" Her voice broke, and Carwyn reached across to embrace her.

"Shh." Her shoulders were stiff and he knew she was fighting back tears. Deirdre had always been strong. She was the warrior, never the one to show weakness. "Grieve, daughter. You have the right."

"There are too many depending on me," she whispered. "And you cannot stay here forever. Your church—"

"I've already contacted the bishop. He's sent another priest for the time being. I told him that my family needed me. They know not to argue."

"Carwyn—"

"I am here. For as long as I am needed." He still hadn't made it to Dublin, though his thoughts had turned to Brigid Connor often in the past four months. He wanted to see her. Needed to comfort the girl. Deirdre and Sinead had been, but he'd been so occupied with finding Ioan's murderers, then taking revenge, then sorting through the shattered branches of his family...

He needed to see her.

Deirdre lifted her face, stained with bloody tears. "I need to know that this monster cannot hurt others. I know you will stay here as long as you need, but if Giovanni and Beatrice ask for help finding Lorenzo or any others who took part in this, you must go. I am the mate of Ioan ap Carwyn. I am the leader of this clan. I will guard my people. I do not know to what purpose all this has happened, but there must be some greater good. I will cling to that until I see him again."

Carwyn tugged on a lock of her wild, red hair. "Which will not be for many, many years."

She smiled and lifted a hand to pat his shoulder. "No, Father. I do not despair of this life. I am simply... weary of it at the moment."

He left an arm around her shoulders. "Pray with me?"

"Of course."

Carwyn closed his eyes and felt the ancient mountain surrounding him, the pulse of creation beneath his feet. His soul reached up as he opened his lips to whisper the ancient words. "Give ear to my words, O Lord, consider my meditation. Give heed to the voice of my cry, my King and my God, for to You I will pray. My voice You shall hear in the morning. In the morning, I will direct it to You..."

Deirdre whispered softly, "And I will look up."

Dublin
May 2010

Another day. Another night.

Brigid slung her bag on her desk and picked up the list of tasks Tom had given her. It was too short. She looked up to see Declan watching her with guarded eyes. "This is all?"

He shrugged. "Ask Tom if you want more."

"I have asked. Does he think I'm a weeping mess? I want more to do."

Jack spoke quietly from the other side of the room. "No one thinks you're a weeping mess, but you've been working fourteen-hour nights for the past five months. Perhaps—"

"Perhaps you all should just let me work like I want to and not worry about me."

Jack's mouth turned up at the corner. "Impossible."

Declan said, "Angie said she had some messages for you. Did you check her desk?"

She left the room just as Declan and Jack began one of their wordless conversations that pissed her off. They all pissed her off. Murphy pissed her off with his kid-glove treatment. She hadn't spoken to Emily in months. Axel and his little friends could go to hell. Her family wanted her home, but she had refused to go since Ioan's funeral. Deirdre and Sinead had come to the city the month before. She smiled and nodded and made all the right noises so they would leave her alone. Carwyn... well, he obviously couldn't be bothered.

Another day. Another night.

She picked up a stack of messages from Angie's desk with her name on the top and paged through them. Anne had called again. Fecking doctor.

She didn't need to have a deep heart-to-heart with her therapist. She needed to work and she needed to kill someone.

And once again, Carwyn had already beaten her to it.

Fecking Carwyn.

She walked back in the office and began the manifest searches that Tom had listed for her. The one positive about this whole situation was that Lorenzo had been revealed as the source for the drugs that had been pouring into Dublin. He'd made himself quite rich off her streets, as a matter of fact. They were still trying to get a handle on how extensive his connections had been.

Her boss and colleagues thought they had things well in hand. Thought that the problem would drift away now that Lorenzo had been driven out of Ireland.

"Like the snake he is," she muttered, curling her lip in a dark humor.

Idiots. Despite what Patrick Murphy and the others thought, Brigid knew the murderer hadn't worked alone. He would have needed someone who knew the city better. Who had contacts and knew what clubs to distribute through. There had to be a local. Human? Vampire? It was her mission to find out.

"Connor!"

"What?" She looked up at Tom, annoyed by the interruption.

"Murphy wants to talk to you."

She rolled her eyes. "I'll be right there."

Another day. Another night.

Another phone call from Deirdre that made Murphy hop to attention. Another "friendly chat" to see how she was doing. He'd ask her if she was sleeping well. He'd offer to listen. To give her time off from work so she could go home.

There was nothing and no one she wanted to see at home.

She nodded through her chat with Murphy, worked until Declan and Jack retired for the morning, then she worked a little more. Anything to keep her from the silent rooms where ghosts haunted her and sleep slipped through her grasp.

Another day. Another night.

Finally, she dragged herself up to her room and collapsed on the bed. As soon as her head hit the pillow, images assaulted her—images of Ioan, bloody and tortured in the warehouse by the river. Then images of him from her childhood as they read books in the library. When Brigid finally fell asleep, she dreamed she was beating on a grey metal door, powerless to open it as she heard agonized cries from inside. She dreamt she heard Deirdre weeping, but when she woke, it was her own face that was covered in tears.

Building From Ashes

Carwyn sat up when Deirdre came into the library.

"What do you mean, she's gone?"

Deirdre's eyes were wide with terror. "Murphy said that she didn't come into work tonight. It's the first night she's ever missed work. She never misses work. And he says she hasn't been sleeping. She says she's fine, but she's been working all night and day and—"

Carwyn stood and roared, "What the hell is he doing there? Does he have control of that city or not?" He rushed toward the door. "We're going. Now."

"Wait. She may just be with friends or—"

"Or she may be in trouble!" He spun around. "She may have stumbled onto something about Ioan's murder and run off like a lunatic. She may be…"

Dead.

He couldn't say it. Couldn't even think it. He had known she was traumatized by Ioan's death and he'd avoided her. Avoided her grief and rage like a coward. Had foolishly taken comfort in the regular reports that the girl was coping. This wasn't Murphy's fault; it was his.

Deirdre whispered, "She has to be all right, Carwyn."

"Listen." He took a deep breath and tried to think clearly. "You go to Dublin. You know it better. Murphy—"

"Murphy already has his men searching the city. They all consider her a friend, and they know we'll be searching as well."

"Can you think of anywhere out of Dublin that she might go?"

Deirdre frowned. "Anne, maybe? I know they're close. Anne's been trying to talk to her. Maybe… if Brigid finally broke down, she might have gone to Anne."

Carwyn nodded. "Fine. You go look for her with Murphy's men. I'll call Galway and see if she's there."

"Just go. Travel underground; you'll get there faster. And bring Anne back. Even if Brigid's not there, we'll need her. She'll come. Brigid needs help, and we haven't been there for her."

"You can't blame yourself."

Blame me.

Her eyes were hollow. "She's Ioan's. She was my responsibility."

He swallowed the lump in his throat. "Just go."

Deirdre raised her hand to push in the door of the warehouse. The scent of her husband's blood still lingered, and she held in a sob.

Ioan, have I failed her, too?

Murphy's men had found no trace of Brigid. She had very few places she would go. A pub she liked. A church in Ringsend. The Ha'Penny Bridge at night. She was nowhere. But then Deirdre had found Emily. Had coaxed the awful truth from her, and Deirdre knew with a sinking feeling where she would go.

'She said she only wanted a bit. Just to sleep. She hadn't been sleeping well. I—I told her not to, but she wouldn't listen! I only had a little and I didn't want her getting anything dangerous. I'm sorry. I'm so sorry…'

Deirdre searched the rooms, catching the faint scent in a corner of the basement. She could feel the damp creeping along her skin, but it didn't mask the scent of Brigid or the harsh sweetness of the heroin.

Her breath caught when she saw her.

Ioan's precious girl was lying slumped in the corner and the needle lay next to her leg, still bloody at the tip. The rubber strap lay limp in her other hand. Her eyes were partially open and rolled back in her head. Her heartbeat was faint and erratic.

"No," Deirdre groaned and rushed over. "No, no, no." She brushed the paraphernalia away from the delicate, wounded girl and lifted her up. Brigid's breathing was shallow. Her pulse a mere flutter in her chest.

"Brigid!" she screamed and shook her. "Wake up. Wake up, girl. Please."

She slapped her face; it did nothing. Deirdre slumped to the floor and rocked the small woman in her arms. "No, I can't. I can't lose you, too." She dashed the tears from her eyes as she looked down into the deathly pale face. "I can't, Brigid! He'd never forgive me."

Deirdre screamed and tore her hair, remembering the sweat-soaked plea the girl had whispered so many years before.

"No, don't… Please, don't ask me. I don't want to live forever…"

She rocked the girl's still body back and forth until she heard the first falter of Brigid's heart. Deirdre's eyes cleared and she lifted a hand to smooth the hair back from Brigid's pale forehead. "Forgive me."

Wicklow
June 2010

Darkness. Fire. A twisting ache in her gut and a burning in her throat. Burning. Everything was burning.

"Brigid?"

She heard his voice calling from a distance. Was she dreaming? She'd thought she was in hell, but he wouldn't be there. No, he *couldn't* be there. He was good. Pure in a way that she'd never been. The smell of smoke filled her nose and the fire rippled along her skin, soothing and burning at the same time.

Pain.

It was the consuming thought in her mind.

Burning. Tingling. Snapping tiny bites along her flesh. Stripping bare every nerve with its vicious claws. Pain. Consuming, breath-stealing pain. But she was no longer breathing and suddenly, she knew.

Fire. She was immortal and she had been born into fire. She felt sharp fangs drop in her mouth, piercing her lips, and she tasted her own blood. It was sweet. Not metallic or bitter. Sweet.

Why? She wanted to scream. *Why, why, why?*

She was in Ioan's library in Wicklow, and Carwyn was moving toward her, calling, "It's me."

But it's not me, her heart screamed. *Stay back!*

She silently begged him to stay away. Fire vampires were volatile. They killed those who came close. She couldn't hurt him. She *couldn't.* She tried to breathe. To calm herself. It gave her no relief.

Just then, she heard him start to sing a lullaby and felt the tears roll down her face, sizzling and steaming as they touched her skin. He sang the silly, childish song she'd heard Ioan humming to her as a child. When was that? Had she ever been a child? Had she ever been innocent? She felt the anger well up and the fire started to snap along her body again. She curled into herself, willing him to stay away from the monster she had become.

"Brigid?"

No!

She could feel it snapping to the surface again. There was nothing to protect him from her rage. Nothing to shield him from the outpouring of pain and anger that she felt begin to consume her.

Please, God, she begged. *Let me be consumed. Don't let me hurt anyone else.*

He was at the threshold. She could *feel* him. She could feel his energy reaching out to her. Trying to surround her and comfort her, but she pushed it away.

"Brigid…"

Stay away! She lifted her eyes to meet his. The monster with the brilliant blue eyes stared back at her. Then he gasped, and she realized what he saw.

She was the monster now.

Brigid heard her feral scream erupt a moment before Carwyn's amnis rushed around her and the mountain crashed down.

He moved effortlessly through the silent earth, using his amnis to protect her from the fire, pushing away the rocks and rubble until he could sense her. He felt the hum of her amnis glowing like a banked fire in the darkness. Carwyn pushed through the soil until he was next to her, stretching his body out with the earth between them. Then he moved his hand, clearing a pocket around her face, but leaving the rest of her smothered in the cool soil. Her hollow eyes flickered open. He couldn't stop staring. The iris had been charred by her turning, and a deep grey border ringed the brown, creating a mesmerizing stare.

He said nothing. What was there to say?

Finally, she whispered, "It wasn't you. Was it Deirdre?"

"Yes."

She said nothing.

"Are you in pain?"

He could see the truth in her eyes, but she shook her head as much as she could. "The pressure feels good against my skin, in a strange way. Did I hurt anyone?"

Carwyn lifted a hand and brushed more soil from her face. He wished he had a wet cloth, or would that be too harsh on her newly turned skin? Her senses would be like a raw nerve now. He didn't remember his own turning, it had been too long, but he had sired eleven children, though none had been born to fire. He knew how to soothe a vampire of his own element, but what would comfort Brigid now?

"You didn't hurt anyone. Can you feel your amnis?"

"I understand why you call it a current now. I can feel it washing over me. It's like water. Only very, very hot. Like the hottest bath you could imagine."

"I know it hurts, but concentrate on pushing it over your body, if you can."

She took a breath and closed her eyes. "I ruined his library."

Carwyn forced a smile, cupping her cheek in his hand. It was scalding hot, but he didn't move it away. "Technically, I did. Don't worry, we'll build another one."

"Did I burn everything?"

"We'll build again."

"Ashes." He saw tears come to her eyes, but she refused to let them fall. "I saw the room. I left it in ashes."

"We can build again, Brigid. I promise. Even from ashes."

He heard her take a breath and could feel her amnis cover her cheek as his hand lay against it. They stared at each other, enveloped by the silent, eternal earth.

"Do you remember last year in the pub when you put your hand on my cheek because it was cold?"

Carwyn smiled. "I remember."

"It felt nice."

"It did."

"I don't like it when most people touch me, but I don't mind it when you do. Why do you think that is?"

He felt a burning in his throat and his eyes watered. "I don't know, but I'm glad."

"Me, too."

They were silent again, and Carwyn could feel her amnis growing stronger. Her shield was building even as he watched. So strong. She had always been so strong. So determined. "Were you trying to kill yourself, Brigid?"

She blinked. "I don't know, really. I just wanted to rest. I only wanted a little bit of peace. And now I'll never have any."

Carwyn swallowed back the harsh groan and said, "You must take care of yourself. Please, you must."

"I know." She sighed and the dust stirred in the air between them. "I was so tired. I only wanted to rest. Now I'm tired and hungry."

He bit back a growl when he saw the fangs fall in her mouth. He would feed her if she asked. He *wanted* her to ask, even though he knew it wasn't wise. He needed to get her blood soon, and a lot of it. Hopefully, Deirdre had made arrangements.

"We need to get you blood, and we need to dig out of this mountain."

"I'm hoping you can do the digging part, because I've no idea how."

He smiled. "I do. Why don't… Why don't you just let me take care of you for a bit?"

Brigid blinked her eyes again, watching him, as Carwyn felt the shifting in his heart.

He couldn't solve the ills of the world. He couldn't bring his son back to life, or heal his daughter's grief. And he knew he couldn't fix Brigid Connor, either. Not really. But he could help her. This young woman who had lived too much in her short life. He could help her take care of herself. Even if it was just for a while.

"Will you let me, Brigid?" *Please*.

Her eyebrows furrowed together. He could see the fear behind her eyes, the instinctive caution. Slowly, she nodded and Carwyn let out a breath. He cleared more room around her until they were huddled together in the ruins of the library. Then he stripped off his shirt and covered her. Brigid flinched when the cloth touched her sensitive skin, but he saw her force herself to relax.

Carwyn crouched down and lifted her in his arms, careful to make sure she was covered. Her skin was still burning hot as he sent out his energy to move the earth in front of them, slowly clearing a path out of the mountain. After a moment, he could hear movement as they broke through the rocks and roots, making their way to the surface. Deirdre called out, but he said nothing, conscious of Brigid's newly keen hearing.

"Just keep your eyes closed, love. You don't have to see or talk to anyone right now if you don't want to."

"Is everyone out there? I can smell them. Smell the humans." A low snarl ripped from her throat, but her voice was desperate. "Don't let me hurt anyone!"

"I won't." He clutched her tighter and felt the bite of her burning skin. "There's quite a few out there. They were trying to keep the other houses from burning."

"Oh, God!"

"Shhh," he whispered. "Remember, we'll build again. No one was hurt. Just wood and stone, Brigid."

"I'm a monster."

"No, you're not."

He took deep breaths, hoping she could mirror his movements. Her arms were wrapped around him and one hand lay over his heart. Carwyn gritted his teeth when he felt the blistering heat burn his skin, but said nothing. The outer crust of the mountain crumbled before him, and he pushed his way through, still holding tightly as he saw familiar faces.

"All humans," he roared, "get back now!"

His voice must have thundered in her ears because Brigid cringed and tried to escape his arms. He held her even more tightly and felt the bite of her fangs in his shoulder. He swallowed the groan. Deirdre's worried eyes met his, but he shook his head and she remained silent.

"She needs blood," he said roughly.

The humans fled and Carwyn searched for Anne's face. She had followed him from Galway and he was more grateful than ever for the caring and sensitive water vampire. Anne nodded in understanding and he saw her order Deirdre away as one of Ioan's children ushered them to a barn where Carwyn could hear cattle lowing. The other vampires on the farm looked on with wary eyes as the fire flickered along Brigid's neck.

"Everyone's looking at me, aren't they?" she whispered.

"Just hold on to me, Brigid." Her burning hands seared him again, but Carwyn held strong. "I've got you. Don't let go."

109

Building From Ashes

Book Two: Fire

You came near and stood at the foot of the mountain
while it blazed with fire to the very heavens,
With black clouds and deep darkness.

Deuteronomy 4:11

BUILDING FROM ASHES

CHAPTER TWELVE

Galway
August 2010

Brigid heard a crash down the hall as the ground shook when Carwyn and Deirdre started arguing again. Anne cocked an eyebrow and moved another chess piece, but didn't say a word.

Deirdre yelled, "Why don't you call Gio?"

"Gio is on the other side of the world. You expect him to leave Beatrice in China to come here and help her? Don't be ridiculous."

"Why does she need to leave at all?"

"Are you mad, Deirdre? She's a fire vampire. *Fire*. Not earth. I may be a thousand years old, but I can't teach her how to control fire, you idiot."

The earth gave another jolt, followed by another crash. Brigid only pursed her lips and looked up at Anne, moving her rook into position to take a black pawn. "Do you think it would matter if I told them what *I* want to do?" she asked.

Anne was the picture of calm as she said, "Probably not. Just let them fight. I think they enjoy it."

Brigid craned her neck to glance down the hall, but only saw the edge of Deirdre's wild red hair. "Fine with me."

"I hate that woman, Father. *Hate* her. Brigid is my child now, and I don't want her near—"

"That vampire is your sister-in-law, and you've been at each other's throats for over fifty years now. Get over it. She's family. More importantly, she's a fire vampire and she'll be able to teach Brigid things that you can't."

Brigid heard Deirdre growl and there was another crash.

She surveyed the board, carefully weighing her options, seeing every move and its consequence as her brain fired at lightning pace. "Is Cathy really that bad?"

Anne shook her head. "No. I've only met her a few times, but I liked her. If you ask me, she and Deirdre are too much alike. It's just that Cathy says whatever the hell is on her mind and Deirdre doesn't. That's why they don't get along."

"Sorry about your kitchen."

"I think they're only breaking dishes. Doubt they can help it. Earth vampires." Anne snorted. "It's fine. I didn't really like that set anyway. I'll make Carwyn buy me a new kitchen if it comes to it. He's got the money."

The two vampires continued to shout in the background as Brigid carefully proceeded with her offense. Anne had taught her to play chess when Brigid first came to stay with her in Galway five years before. Their friendship had remained one of the few constants in Brigid's life. She was glad to be with Anne, despite the circumstances.

Her first few nights in Wicklow had been a blur. Carwyn and Deirdre quickly dug shelter in the hills behind the ruined house, but Brigid knew she could not stay for long. The enticing smell of human was everywhere. Also, they had to keep buckets of water around to douse her anytime she got too heated. Mostly, she felt numb. Driving back to the misty shores of Anne's isolated home on the shore of Galway Bay had been a relief.

Within five moves, Brigid had put Anne in check. The water vampire smiled. "I can't believe how good you are now."

"I didn't believe Ioan, not really, but I *am* smarter. It's a bit startling. That'll come in handy when I can go back to work."

"See? And your hair will grow back." Anne's eyes twinkled. "Not a bad trade-off, really. And no wrinkles. You're determined to go back to Dublin?"

"If Murphy'll have me back after I leave work for over a year."

"A fire vampire on his security team? He'd be a fool to pass that up. And Patrick is anything but a fool."

Brigid took a deep breath and fingered the silk scarf that covered her head. She hoped her hair grew back by the time she returned to work. She could only imagine the jokes Jack would make. She looked like a cancer patient. Or a skinhead. Luckily, her eyebrows and her eyelashes had already started to grow. Anne said her hair would grow more slowly than it did when she had been human, but it would still grow. Her skin was pale and smooth; her body was quicker. She was strong, so strong that she often felt clumsy with it. But her eyes were what bothered her the most. How would she ever pass as human with them? She knew they looked awful, no matter what Carwyn said.

Carwyn, Anne, and Deirdre had spent a month teaching Brigid the basics of immortal life and trying to decide what to do with her for her first, most volatile, year. Brigid knew that returning to Dublin wasn't an option for some time. Even the scent of the humans a quarter mile from Anne's home made her growl with hunger. She needed to be somewhere deserted, and currently, Carwyn's sons' castle in the highlands of Scotland seemed the best option.

Brigid caught her new reflection in the mirror and quickly glanced away. "I can't get used to them."

"Your eyes? They're actually quite lovely. Very unusual."

Brigid muttered, "There's a lot unusual about me now. Fire. I had to become a fire vampire…"

Anne took a sip of wine. "There's always been something very special about you, Brigid. It's not a bad thing. A challenge, but you've overcome greater ones."

Brigid tasted the cup of blood that Deirdre had heated for her at nightfall. It was some kind of animal; she didn't ask what. It did not taste as good as the human blood Anne had provided the first few nights, but Anne, at over two hundred years old, didn't need to drink nearly as often as Brigid, so she didn't keep much extra around. Carwyn was going into the town every evening and getting blood from the local butcher for her. Brigid was trying to be grateful.

She curled her lip. "How do they drink this stuff?"

"Don't ask me. I think animal blood is vile. But most of Carwyn's clan follows his example. You know, he was likely a vegetarian in his human life. The church in Wales during the late medieval period…"

Carwyn.

Brigid glanced down the hall again. Who was he to her now?

Friend. Protector? Something else entirely more complicated?

Her feelings for him had always been so mixed. He'd danced on the edges of her world. A mythic figure to the child. A brief, unrequited crush to the teenager. He hadn't registered in a real way until he'd broken down the carefully built wall of secrecy she'd built in college. She'd been so angry with him then… but it wasn't all anger. And later?

He flirted with her, but then, he flirted with everyone. Brigid couldn't deny she'd enjoyed it. Then the Catholic in her felt guilty because he was a priest. But it wasn't as if Carwyn was like any other priest she'd ever met. How did he see her? How did she see him? She wasn't certain anymore. Nothing was certain. Her whole world, all her plans, all her routines, had been burned as surely as the old farmhouse in Wicklow.

"Brigid?" She looked up to see Anne giving her a guarded look.

"What?"

"You're heating up again. I can feel it. Try the breathing exercises."

Brigid nodded and began the slow, meditative breathing that Anne had practiced with her in the previous weeks. *In. Out. In. Out.* She closed her eyes.

"Hold on to me, Brigid."

Her heart sped as she remembered the careful way he lifted her from the ground and carried her out of the mountain. Gently. As if she was precious.

"I've got you. Don't let go."

But did he really want her to? Holding on to Carwyn at this point was liable to get him burned. Literally.

"There's one big thing you need to think about, Brigid. We made progress in treatment. A lot. You've come to terms with many things about your past, but you put off dealing with your anger, and it's never gone away." Anne spoke in a calm, soothing voice, but the words still pierced the hollow in Brigid's chest. "I knew it. You knew it. But I thought you'd have time to come to terms with it on your own. Then you lost Ioan. And now you've lost your mortal life."

In. Out. Slow, steady breaths. She felt a cool mist blow across her from Anne's raised fingers.

She asked, "What are you trying to say?"

"I'm saying that you can't put off dealing with your anger any longer. Putting it off could mean your death."

Brigid snorted. As if that meant anything to—

"Or the death of someone close to you," Anne said softly. "Someone you care about."

From the corner of her eye, Brigid could see Carwyn down the hall, leaning against one of Anne's kitchen counters as he and Deirdre talked. His red hair was mussed as if he'd been running his hands through it in frustration. His forehead was furrowed in thought and his arms—the arms that had held her so carefully—were crossed across his chest in a stubborn pose. His eyes rose and caught her glance; he let a crooked smile curve the corner of his mouth.

He wasn't going to leave her alone. She could feel it.

Brigid sighed. "Well, shit."

Two weeks later, Carwyn, Brigid, and Anne were bumping over deserted roads leading to the isolated castle owned by his two sons, Maxwell and Tavish Mackenzie.

"How far north do we have to go?"

Brigid was sitting in the passenger's seat with her hands folded carefully in her lap as they travelled over rocky roads. Carwyn asked, "Are you comfortable enough?"

"I'm fine. How much farther?"

She didn't look fine, he thought. She looked nervous, no doubt worried over what kind of hellish place she was going to spend the next year. Damn Deirdre. The stubborn Irishwoman had made her low opinion of Max's wife well-known. "Just a few hours."

The car fell silent again until Brigid spoke.

"What's the best thing about being a vampire?" she asked.

"Not having to breathe," Anne said. Carwyn looked over his shoulder. "What?" She shrugged. "I like to swim."

"Looking at the stars," he said quietly.

"Colors are much more vivid," Anne said.

"Music. Good music anyway."

Anne laughed. "No grey hair. Well, if you're not Tavish."

"Amnis. I'm not going to lie, it's fun messing with people sometimes."

"Amnis. It's amazing to be able to help humans the way I can."

He smiled. "Anne, have I told you that you're a truly lovely person lately?"

"No," she quipped. "I'm quite offended when I think about how long it's been."

"Independence," Carwyn said. "Because—let's face it—we all accumulate quite a bit of money over the years unless we're idiots. Hunting. And… no deterioration of my dashing good looks."

Anne laughed. Brigid just smiled.

"How much are we telling her, Carwyn?"

Brigid looked over her shoulder. "You're telling me all of it. I asked, didn't I?"

Anne just gave a wicked laugh. "Fine. Drinking from humans. Don't let the virtuous animal drinkers fool you. Once you've perfected control? It's *fantastic*."

He saw Brigid looking at him. "Don't ask me. My sire only drank from animals. That's how I was taught. The few sips of blood I've tasted over the years have been minimal, other than turning my children, but that's not the normal kind of drinking."

"But for sustenance, you've never…"

Carwyn kept his eyes firmly on the road. "No."

Anne said, "Carwyn is extra virtuous because drinking from humans also brings out our… other hungers, if you understand me."

Carwyn kept his eyes on the road as tension descended on them. Anne was right. Bloodlust and sexual lust were closely tied. For a mated vampire? Not a problem. For one who had accepted the celibacy his office demanded? Well…

"You know," Anne said, "sex is one of the—"

Brigid cleared her throat. "I get it, Anne. Thanks."

"I just mean that it's another thing that's better. Sex is fantastic. Particularly with another vampire."

Carwyn gritted his teeth, feeling his fangs fall as he stared ahead, never taking his eyes off the road. Anne just kept talking.

"You know, come to think of it, I think sex is the best part of being a vampire. You don't get tired or sweaty. And then, with the amnis, you have the added benefit of—"

Brigid's voice was hoarse when she interrupted. "Pretty sure I get it, Anne. Thanks."

Carwyn could smell the smoky sweetness of her scent as it filled the car, and he bit back a growl.

"Okay, moving on…" Brigid said. "What's the worst thing?"

Both Carwyn and Anne said together, "The sun."

Silence fell for a few minutes until Anne spoke. "The electronic thing has become very problematic, as well."

"Oh," Brigid groaned.

Carwyn said, "What?"

"I was just thinking about work. If I go back to work for Murphy after my year here, I'll have to hire a set of hands, like Declan. It might be too much bother."

He curled his lip thinking about Brigid going back to working for Patrick Murphy. "I think he'll be willing to put up with the bother."

"Boredom can be a problem when you live as long as we do." Anne paused. "Not boredom, exactly... aloofness. We tend to become quite separated from the world, if we let ourselves. Very set in our ways. I'm starting to feel it myself. Change, after so long, becomes quite difficult. But change is the only thing that keeps us truly alive, isn't it?"

Brigid answered softly, "I suppose so."

Her voice was so sad that Carwyn reached over and ran the back of his finger along her chin, flicking the corner of her mouth until she smiled.

Anne piped up from the back seat. "I'm going to zone out and read for a bit." Anne, Carwyn remembered, needed quiet. She always had earplugs with her.

He put his hands back on the wheel and there was silence for a few moments as Anne opened her book.

Finally, Brigid spoke. "So, being able to read without getting motion sick, is that one of the benefits?"

He smiled. "No. Afraid that's just Anne. I still get queasy. Especially in planes."

"Can you travel by plane? Can I?"

"There are a few very special planes that can take our sort. Gio has one, but I avoid it. Horrid thing."

He saw her shake her head out of the corner of his eye just a moment before a furry face poked between them and nudged his shoulder. "Settle, Madoc."

The wolfhound was only a puppy. Still, he calmed down and Carwyn saw Anne lift a hand to scratch his ears. A small snorting sound came from across the car. He glanced at Brigid's near-laugh. "What?"

"Why did you bring your dog?"

"Oh, he was missing me. Just a puppy and I left him all on his own for too long. Sister Maggie would have devised some medieval torture if I hadn't taken him off her hands. For me, not the dog."

Brigid looked back. "That is the largest puppy I have ever seen."

"He'll be almost as tall as you when he's full grown."

She shook her head. "Dogs."

"Not a cat person, are you?"

"Not an animal person."

"Shh." He frowned. "You'll hurt his feelings."

Madoc gave a mournful sigh from the backseat as they went over another bump in the road.

"Your friend, Gio. With the plane? He's a fire vampire, isn't he?"

"Yes."

"And he's around five hundred years old?"

Carwyn nodded. "I believe so, yes."

She was silent for a few moments. "Has he ever killed anyone?"

"Not by accident, if that's what you're asking." He caught her eye and winked at her. "Though, he had quite the reputation as a mercenary for a couple hundred years. Fire vamps tend to be the biggest bully on the block. Get a good handle on your element, and you won't find many foolish enough to challenge you, Brigid."

He could tell by the smile that curved her lips that she liked the idea of that. Ah, his combative Brigid. He knew once she got accustomed to the idea she'd like being a force to be reckoned with. She played with the end of her scarf where it lay against her neck. Carwyn tore his eyes away.

"Does Gio have all his hair?"

Carwyn said, "It's a bit of a sore point for him. His woman likes his hair longer, and he's always burning it off in places."

"Great."

He glanced at the grey scarf that covered her head. "Don't be too sad. Your hair will grow back, and at least you don't have an oddly shaped head." He reached over and palmed her scalp as she batted his hand away with a curled lip.

"Stop!"

Carwyn laughed. "You could have some strange lump on it, love. Now *that* would be embarrassing."

She was trying very hard not to smile. Stubborn girl. "Does your friend have a lump on his head?"

"No, but he has a mole shaped like the island of Cyprus behind his left ear." He caught her biting back the laugh. "I don't think he even knows about it. Don't have the heart to tell him. He's too vain."

"You're ridiculous."

"I am. Too much seriousness in the world as it is. It's my mission to bring levity."

"So that's your mission, heh? I've been wondering what the flowered shirts were for." In the blink of an eye, a dark look fell across her face. "I never wanted this."

Carwyn took a deep breath. He had sensed the heat in her, simmering below the surface. "Don't be too angry with Deirdre. She acted out of grief. If you're honest with yourself, you know Ioan would have done the same. She couldn't stand the idea of losing you."

"When things… when things were bad, I thought, 'At least it's not forever, Brigid. At least this life is short.'" He saw her blink back tears. "Growing up with Ioan and Deirdre, I knew better than anything that human life passed quickly. And I always thought, when the dreams were bad. When the dark parts were a little *too* dark... I thought, it's not forever. Life isn't forever."

"But now it is." His heart ached for her, and he resisted the urge to pull the car over just to hold her for a bit.

"I suppose it is." She reached over and patted his arm. "Don't worry. I'm not going to wander out into the sun."

His voice was hoarse. "Don't you dare."

"I am going to miss it, though. The sun."

"I can't blame you. I still miss it. Even after a thousand years."

"I always thought—" She broke off with a private smile.

"What?" He wished that she could still blush. She would have been.

"I always thought maybe that was why you liked those horrible Hawaiian shirts."

Carwyn looked at her. Then glanced back at the road. Then looked again. He burst into laughter.

"What?" Her eyes were wide. "Well, is it?"

She was brilliant. He could barely talk for gasping. "It probably is! I've never even thought about it before."

"They certainly don't do anything for your looks. You're far more handsome in non-florescent colors."

His grin only got wider. "You think I'm handsome?"

"What?" She scowled. "No, you're... horrid looking."

"You think I'm handsome." His heart pounded. "You said so."

"No. You have wild hair and—and your smile is..."

"What?"

"Too big."

He belly laughed. "Why do I love it when you insult me so?" He reached over and tugged at her ear, but she reached up, pinched his hand and shocked him. "Oh ho!" An evil glint came to his eye and he grabbed the squirt bottle that Anne had put on the dashboard, aiming it at her.

"You better not. Carwyn!" She tried to grab it while the car swerved. "That's just for emergencies!" Soon, Carwyn was roaring with laughter and Brigid was slapping his arm, trying to block the spray of water he aimed at her. Madoc was barking and jumping with excitement.

Anne must have pulled her earplugs out. "Really? Can't I leave the two of you to yourselves for a few minutes? Carwyn, don't run us off the road."

"He started it."

"She shocked me."

He saw Anne roll her eyes and return to her book. The dog settled down and Carwyn focused on driving. But, when he peeked at Brigid, a smile still lingered on her lips.

Northern Highlands, Scotland
September 2010

There was a light mist falling when they pulled up to the grey stone castle. It was L-shaped and tall, a relic of a far earlier time, and Brigid hoped that it was warmer inside than it looked from the outside. Though, she had to admit the pervasive mist felt cool and refreshing against her skin. Skin that constantly felt warm, as if she were running a permanent fever.

"Home, sweet home," Carwyn said. "Well, at least for the next year or so."

"I've never been to Scotland before."

"Not even on a school trip?"

"No."

Anne crawled out of the back seat a moment before Madoc burst out and shot across the grounds, yapping and howling his relief at finally being free of the cramped vehicle. "You'll like it here," Anne said. "Max and Cathy are wonderful fun."

"What about…"

"Tavish?" Carwyn smiled. "Tavish is… Tavish." He grabbed their bags from the trunk, holding all three suitcases in his massive hands and almost skipping up to the dark, wooden door. Anne folded Brigid's arm in hers.

"Carwyn loves it here. He and Max are very like-minded."

"Well…" Brigid smiled a little. "This should be interesting, then."

The Welshman was already banging on the door and yelling. "Open the door, you ungrateful children! Didn't you miss me?"

The door cracked open and a grey head peeked through. "Oh, it's you."

"Hello, son!" Carwyn laid a meaty hand on the shoulder of the vampire in front of him. He was tall and thin, but his years, however many they had been, had not treated him kindly. His shaggy grey hair fell into his face and his mouth was turned down in a permanent frown.

"I refuse to call you 'Father' when you look twenty years younger than me, Carwyn. But come in anyway."

"Always a joy to see you again, Tavish."

Tavish only grunted and stepped aside as Carwyn walked in the house.

"Highland hospitality," Anne whispered as they walked up to the door. "Hello, Tavish, lovely to see you. This is Brigid."

The vampire made more vague grunting sounds and waved them into a brightly lit living room just off the entryway before he picked up a book and disappeared down the hall.

Brigid looked around. It was everything she would have thought a Scottish castle would be, even down to the suit of armor standing in the corner of the room and the old shields hanging on the wall in a dignified line. A fire roared in a massive fireplace and her ears pricked up when she heard quick footsteps approaching.

This had to be Max. A handsome man with light brown hair and brilliant green eyes, he greeted them with a wide smile as he embraced Carwyn.

"Father! So happy you're here. You made good time. You just beat Cathy. She'll be here in a few."

"Coming from Edinburgh?"

"Of course." He turned and held a hand out to Brigid. "Maxwell Mackenzie at your service. You must be Brigid. I assume you met my rude brother."

"Brother?" Brigid looked over her shoulder, but Tavish was nowhere to be found. "You mean…" She frowned, then cocked her head. "You're brothers?"

They did look alike. If she thought about it, the two almost looked identical, only Tavish was an older, grumpier, version of the man in front of her.

"Yes. Twins, in fact. I just got the better end of things in the eternal youth department." He clapped his hands together and ushered them toward the fire, greeting Anne with a kiss on the cheek and taking everyone's coats. "Can I get you anything to drink? Beer? Wine? O-negative?" He winked at Brigid.

Anne asked for wine, and Carwyn asked for beer. Brigid wanted to curl into a ball and hide. She'd drunk several cups of blood when she woke in Glasgow that night, but she was hungry again. "Um… could I get some blood, please?"

"Of course! We have fresh animal or preserved human."

She looked to Anne, who shrugged and said, "They'll both fill you up the same."

Brigid cringed under Max's friendly, yet expectant, stare. "Human, please." It was strange to think about. It was even stranger to say. She felt like a freak. Like a parasite, like a— "On second thought, could I just have the animal? Is it… what is it?"

Max smiled. "We keep Highland cattle. There's as much cattle blood as you can drink around here."

Cattle. She nodded. Not all that different from steak, right? Maybe cattle blood was the best choice.

"Okay, let's do that."

She glanced over and saw Carwyn smiling at her. Anne just patted her hand and settled back into the couch as Max left to get their drinks. She tried to relax, but soon sat up when she heard a car pulling into the drive. A woman's raucous laughter rang out and Brigid heard a lower voice chime in after her. The smell of sweet human blood reached her nose and her fangs descended. In a split second, she had bolted for the door.

Carwyn grabbed her before she was halfway there.

"Ah, hold on now, love."

She snarled at him. "Let me go!"

"Not going to do that. You'll thank me later." A flame flared along her neck, but Carwyn took a soft throw that lay across a nearby couch and gently draped it over her back, smothering the flames. He made soothing sounds and pulled her into his chest as the footsteps approached and Brigid continued to snarl. Her throat was on fire.

"...come in for a drink after that drive."

"No!" Through the haze of bloodlust, she heard an American accent. "New vampire inside, Shane. Better keep away. In fact, just stay in the gamekeeper's lodge until you leave. Don't want to take any chances."

Carwyn's rumbling growl snapped Brigid out of her predatory stare, and Anne's cool mist enveloped her, hissing against her skin.

The human spoke again. "You got it, Cath. I'll see you later."

"Have a nice night."

A few moments later, a tall woman strode into the room, shaking off her overcoat and throwing it over the back of a chair. Her hair was cut in a curly bob, and black eyes danced in a pale face with a sprinkling of freckles. Her gaze swept the room, winking at Brigid who was still tangled in Carwyn's arms.

Completely nonplussed by the smoldering vampire, Cathy said, "If it isn't my favorite delusional father-in-law! How are you?"

Carwyn chuckled, and the familiar sound caused Brigid's fangs to retract. She took a deep breath. Then another. "If it isn't my favorite heathen." He cautiously set her on her feet. "How are you, Cathy?"

"Still an atheist. You?"

He took a step back from Brigid. "Still a priest. Imagine that."

"Damn, I keep hoping reason will find a way through your thick skull."

Carwyn's hand made small, soothing circles at the small of her back. "A thousand years, darling. I don't think you're going to change my mind now. This is Brigid."

Words failed her. How was she supposed to greet this whirlwind of a woman who had burst through the door, completely unafraid of the snarling, fang-baring new vampire being wrestled down in her living room? She had always thought Carwyn was larger than life, but Cathy Mackenzie filled up the room with her voice alone. Brigid felt tiny and strangely shy.

"Hello, Brigid! Welcome to the highlands. Nice to have another foreigner around."

She took a breath and held her hand out, trying hard not to wince at the snap of energy when their skin touched. The other fire vampire only grinned; Brigid could see the fangs hanging sharp in her mouth. "You're a live one, aren't you?"

Brigid cleared her throat. "I suppose so."

"Oh, the accent!" she said. "I do love that accent. Bet it's driving Deirdre absolutely bat-shit nuts that you're here, isn't it?"

Brigid lifted an eyebrow. She was willing to give this woman the benefit of the doubt, but she wouldn't stand for anyone insulting Deirdre, whatever her feelings for her sire might have been.

Cathy seemed to sense that a line had been crossed, so she backed away and went to greet Anne while Carwyn stood beside her and put an arm around her shoulders. Why did he do that?

And why the hell did she find it so soothing?

"Aye, my bonny lass has come back to me." Brigid heard Max lay on the Scottish brogue dramatically thick when he walked into the room. Cathy immediately abandoned Anne and ran to him. He set the tray of drinks down and caught her in his arms. They started kissing in front of the room.

Quite enthusiastically.

Anne cleared her throat and glanced away. "Newlyweds," she said, by way of explanation.

"Ah," Brigid mumbled. "How long have they been married?"

"Fifty years or so," Carwyn muttered, angling her back toward the fire. "Cathy works in Edinburgh, so they spend weeks apart at times."

"They, uh, seem to be making up for that."

She saw Tavish walk into the room and throw down his book on the end table in disgust. "Oh, for God's sakes. Get a room."

Max muttered between kisses. "Shut up, Tavish."

Tavish didn't say another word, but he picked up an apple from an arrangement in the entryway and tossed it at Cathy's head. Max caught it with one hand while Cathy stepped away from Max and snapped her fingers. Brigid jumped back when a fireball burst into her hand.

"Oh my God!"

Cathy hurled it at her brother-in-law, who quickly grabbed one of the shields hanging on the wall and deflected the whirling flames into the hearth where they were swallowed up in the crackling fire.

Brigid's mouth gaped open. What the hell had she stepped into?

Max winked at her and grinned. "Seventeenth-century armor. Not just for decoration in our home."

CHAPTER THIRTEEN

Castle Mackenzie, Scotland
October 2010

"Are they always like this?" Brigid leaned toward him and Carwyn tried to ignore the subtle, smoky scent she exuded. They had been in Scotland for three weeks and were listening to yet another shouting match between Cathy and Tavish refereed by a very unconcerned Max.

Carwyn cleared his throat. "The Mackenzie clan do not believe in holding their tongue. About anything."

"It's probably one of the reasons Cathy and Max spend so much time in Edinburgh," Anne said from her perch by the fire. She was knitting a sweater while Madoc lay at her feet. "Tavish is such a hermit."

She frowned at him. "Are you sure this is the best place for me to hide out and learn how *not* to kill people?"

Anne barked out a laugh. "Brigid, I couldn't think of a better place if I imagined it."

"What does that mean?"

Brigid looked up at Carwyn, but he only shrugged and tried to think about something other than how close her leg was to his as they sat on the couch. "Don't ask me."

Which didn't mean he didn't know exactly what Anne was talking about. If there was anyone who needed to say what was on her mind more, it was Brigid. As acerbic as her wit could be, when it came to personal things, she was as defensive as ever. And with her immortal powers and the protection of amnis, her mind was completely impenetrable, even to Anne.

"Brigid, why do you think Tavish and Cathy fight? Does it make you uncomfortable?" Anne asked.

"Oh no," Brigid said. Her eyes flicked toward Carwyn before she looked back at Anne. "We're not doing that here, Anne."

"Why not?"

Brigid's eyes flickered to his once more before she exchanged some sort of wordless conversation with the other woman. The water vampire finally shrugged and muttered, "Fine. It'll all come out at some point."

"Anne..." Brigid's voice was a low growl that made him bite his cheek.

Damn if every growl, every peek of fang, every glare from her inhuman eyes didn't put him on edge.

He'd tried, damn it. Carwyn had tried to push back the attraction he'd recognized so many months before, but once the trauma of Brigid's turning had passed, once they had established a more normal pace of life in the Highlands, it came roaring back, stronger than ever. She was immortal now. Every part of her called out to him. Her crackling energy. Her penetrating stare. Her sharp wit. The rugged heart of her, so strong despite all she had been through.

And layered beneath all of that, a vulnerability that she'd shown to precious few. So few that he counted himself lucky to have ever caught a glimpse. His feelings of pure, male attraction were quickly turning into something far more dangerous.

Brigid and Anne had slipped into Irish, which they often did when they were speaking of things the young vampire found uncomfortable.

"I think you're delaying dealing with things that—"

"I'm not talking about this right now."

"Why not? No one hides their feelings in this home, Brigid. It's one of the reasons I wanted to come here. The courtesy you were raised with has many fine qualities. I know you were always taught to be careful with your words and mind your tongue, but in this case, while we are here—"

"I'm not talking about it right now!"

Brigid stood up and stormed from the room. Madoc loped after her. A few moments later, Carwyn heard the front door slam and then the dog's howl as it set off across the grounds. Max and Cathy had sent away the human who traveled with them, so there were no mortals around for miles. She was safe and the pervasive mist that filled the hills would keep her from losing control of her fire.

"You need to stop needling her, Anne."

"You need to leave."

He started. "What?"

"You, Carwyn. Need. To. Leave."

He frowned. "Why?"

Anne let out an exasperated sigh. "Do you really not know?"

"I have no idea what you're talking about." He picked up a book and opened it.

Anne frowned and narrowed her eyes. "You're almost as interesting a case study as she is. Seemingly involved, and yet maintaining such a state of aloof separation. I suppose after a thousand years, the humor provides a kind of shield that—"

"Anne, I am not a patient. Stop it."

She broke into a grin. "Think. You know why you need to leave. Brigid's not here. It's just me. You can admit what you're feeling. I won't say a word."

Well, shit. He squirmed a little and took another drink of his beer. "I don't know what you're talking about."

"I'm talking about the way you look at her, Carwyn. I'm talking about her reaction to it, whether she realizes it or not."

His eyes darted up. "You think she realizes it?"

"Maybe not consciously, but Brigid avoids talking about things she thinks will upset you when you're around."

He held his breath for a moment before he let it out with a sigh. "The... feelings. They're not her problem. They're mine."

"What makes you think they're a problem at all? I'm not saying that."

"But you think I should leave her?" He set down the book he'd been pretending to read. "I told her I'd help her. I told her..." *to hold on to me.* He rubbed the red scar on his chest where her small hand had branded him.

Anne's face softened. "She's not a project, Carwyn."

He looked away and stared into the fire. "I know that, Anne. I'm not an idiot."

Anne offered him a sympathetic smile. "Brigid is a protector. That's how she deals with her past. And she senses that her distress causes you pain, so she's avoiding dealing with the things she needs to in order to gain control."

He let out a hoarse laugh. "You think... you think she's worried about *me*?"

"Yes."

"That's ridiculous."

"No, it's just who she is. It's her character, Carwyn, and it's not a bad thing. You're a comforter; she's a protector. But she doesn't need comfort right now. She needs to be able to be angry and learn how to deal with it, and for that, you need to leave."

His heart ached at the thought of leaving Brigid. Of being so far away, even if she was surrounded by friends and family. Carwyn had told her that he'd take care of her.

"I can't, Anne." His whisper was hoarse. "Do what you need to. I'll keep my distance, but don't ask me to leave."

Anne set her knitting aside and leaned forward. "I know you're not my patient, so consider this as a friend. Your world, the life and family you've spent a thousand years building, has suffered a tremendous loss. You are trying to help Brigid, but think for a moment. Do you want to stay for her? Or for yourself?"

He stared into the mirror over the dresser in his room, his right hand covering the delicate outline burned into his chest. Angry red bands wrapped around his shoulders where her arms had lain. The scars were still bright, though the skin was no longer blistered. How long would it take to heal?

Months? Years? His fingers traced the lines that lay over his heart.

A strange part of him treasured the evidence of her. After a thousand years of seeing the same reflection, Brigid's hand had marked him. Changed him. And in the back of his mind he knew that, even when the scars healed, he would never be the same.

A knock came, quickly followed by the door bursting open. Tavish stomped in with a pile of towels.

"Here."

"Thanks for knocking." Carwyn reached over and pulled on a garish shirt he hoped would make Brigid roll her eyes.

"You're welcome."

"What were you and Cathy fighting about earlier?"

"Couldn't you hear?"

"I was distracted."

Tavish only snorted and muttered something under his breath.

Carwyn cocked an eyebrow. "What was that?"

The surly vampire looked up with what could almost be considered a smile.

On a bulldog.

"I said I can't imagine what has been distracting you… Father."

"I've been contemplating the new breeding program you wrote me about for the cattle."

Tavish's eyes widened. "Really?"

"No, not really." He threw a wadded towel at him. "No one is as excited about cow genetics are you are."

An almost-wistful look crossed Tavish's lined face. "Ioan was."

Carwyn smiled. No, he wasn't. But his oldest son had been interested in any subject that any of his siblings was passionate about, from Highland Cattle to rainforest conservation to homeless children.

Carwyn nodded. "Did you get that article I sent a few months ago? He had it marked on his desk for you."

"I did." The gruff vampire cleared his throat. "Thanks. And Cathy and I were arguing about the girl."

"Who, Brigid?"

"No, the other new vampire you follow around."

"Shut it."

"Fine. I'm not one to pry. I'll only say that it's long overdue."

Carwyn frowned. "Nothing is going on. And even if it was, this is coming from you? The most confirmed bachelor I've ever met?"

Tavish rolled his eyes. "I don't like women. You do. You should have one. It would probably be a civilizing influence. And I actually… like the girl."

"You do?"

"I do. She's not frivolous."

Carwyn clapped Tavish on the shoulder. "Stop with the relentless flattery, son. I doubt she's interested in a decrepit vampire such as yourself."

Tavish crossed his arms. "Ha. She's smart and as long as she doesn't kill herself or anyone else, I don't mind having her around."

Carwyn was speechless. That was, perhaps, the nicest thing he'd ever heard his youngest child say about... anyone. Ever. Carwyn had saved Max from the battlefields of France during the First World War, not realizing that the young man had a twin. When he'd given in to Max's wishes to visit his ancestral home twenty years later, he'd had no idea that Tavish would storm after them into the night, calling his brother's name as if linked by some eternal and unbreakable bond.

Tavish must have seen the look on his face. "What are you getting maudlin about?"

"You and Max. Two children could never be more different, and yet you care so deeply for each other."

"I'd like him better if he hadn't waited twenty years to come home. He left me with all the damn work on this place and I knew he wasn't dead. Lazy arse. And I'd like him even more if he hadn't married the American harpy."

Carwyn gave him a rueful smile. "He's happy."

Tavish's face softened almost immediately. "Aye, he is. She makes him very happy. It'd be good to see another as happy, if you catch my meaning."

Castle Mackenzie, Scotland
November 2010

'We're going to our home in South America. She's devastated, Father. More than I've ever seen before. Since she's turned, she can't see any of her human family. She cannot see Benjamin. I'm asking for your help. I cannot watch her descend into despair like this. I cannot. She needs you, my friend. We both do.'

Carwyn clutched the letter that had finally reached him from China. He'd read it three times, but the contents never seemed to change.

Beatrice De Novo's father, whom they had searched the world for, was dead.

The book, the manuscript that Lorenzo had been looking for, was gone, taken back by the monster who had torn his family in two. Had Ioan known of the book, somehow? It contained a mysterious formula purported to be the Elixir of Life, but there were more questions than answers in its discovery. Had this been what Ioan had been tortured for? So many of the answers they sought had died with Ioan and now, Stephen De Novo. But... there was an elixir. An elixir for humans that a vampire wanted. It had to be connected somehow.

Beatrice, like Brigid, was a vampire. Her father, Stephen, had sired her only weeks before he had been murdered by the same scum who killed Ioan.

Carwyn's head fell in his hands. His friend had lost her father and her sire.

'She needs you, my friend. We both do.'

Giovanni Vecchio, the immortal Carwyn had called on so many times to protect his family or help a friend, asked him to come to comfort. To counsel. Carwyn sat on the edge of his bed and looked at the shaggy face of the wolfhound puppy who watched him. He took a deep breath and ran a rough hand though the scruff at the dog's chin.

"I have to go, Madoc."

The dog only offered a whine.

"I know. I won't make you go on the boat. Will you stay here? Keep an eye on things?" On her.

Brigid was stronger every day, and so was his fascination with the young vampire. Carwyn took a deep breath and a mental step back. He knew he needed distance. He had become infatuated with the girl, and he was coming to understand what Anne had been trying to say to him weeks ago. His reasons for staying were selfish.

He needed to leave.

His hand rubbed over the scar over his heart. Carwyn set the letter on the dressing table before he stood and opened the door. He paused on the stairs and caught the tail end of a conversation Brigid was having on the phone in the downstairs library.

"...I'd say no more than a year."

There was a pause as she let the other person talk.

"No, I'm doing quite well." Another pause. "Yes, Cathy Mackenzie from Edinburgh." A low laugh. "No, Murphy, she's not trying to get me to stay. I think one fire vampire per city is enough, don't you?"

Murphy. Carwyn smothered the low growl and continued walking.

"Don't tell me you've found someone to replace me already!" He could hear the smile in her voice. She was teasing the water vampire over the phone line. Friendly and familiar, with none of the awkwardness she often had in his presence.

"I'm grateful. No, I am. You don't have to do that, but I won't lie, I miss working. I hope... I just hope I can be the asset that you need."

She was grateful? His Brigid was grateful to the upstart Dubliner? Didn't she have any idea how valuable she was? Murphy should be thanking his lucky stars and all the saints that Brigid was willing to come back to the city that had so many unpleasant associations. With her skills, connections, and elemental ability, Brigid Connor could have had her pick of new beginnings. Terry and Gemma would love to snatch her for their organization in London. His allies in New York had long sought a more permanent connection with his clan. Not to mention all the people who owed him or Ioan favors. If Brigid had held a special status as a human, she had no idea how valuable and sought after she would be as a rare and well-connected fire vampire.

But Brigid was grateful to Murphy. It stuck in his throat.

"I need to go. It was great talking to you. And say hi to Angie and Tom. Declan, too." Another pause. "No, of course not Jack. Tell that arse he better invest in some fireproof pants."

Carwyn grinned. There she was. He saw the expected scowl when he walked into the library and she turned to look at him. Brigid lifted her hand in a small wave and turned back around.

"No... no, Murphy, I really need to go." She tapped her fingers on the table. "Okay. Okay. Bye."

He gave her a moment to collect herself. He could feel her hot energy spike as he came in the room, but he could also feel the waves of amnis that emanated from her begin to smooth and even out. Finally, she turned and leaned against the back of the sofa.

"You look serious," she said.

Carwyn closed the oak door and leaned against it. "I have to go."

She only blinked. "Where?"

"South America."

Brigid was frozen for only a moment before she spoke again. Her energy was heating up again, but not to an alarming level. "Is there anything wrong with Isabel and Gus?"

"No, it's my friends. Do you remember my friend, Giovanni? The fire vampire? His mate, Beatrice... they're on their way to South American now. She turned when she was in China and her sire—who was her human father, too—was killed shortly after."

He could see her eyes furrow in sympathy. "I'm so sorry. That's horrible."

"Lorenzo did it."

Her eyes flared and he saw smoke rising at her collar. He rushed over and put his hands on her shoulders, rubbing them and willing her to remain calm. "Calm, Brigid. Calm."

She took a deep breath and the smell of smoke dissipated. "Did they kill him?"

"No. He escaped with the book Stephen—B's father—had stolen from him. It was related to blood alchemy. Related to what Ioan was looking for, I think."

He could see a trace of tears in the corner of her eye before she blinked them away. "Well, you need to go, then. Go and help them find Lorenzo and this book. It's what Ioan would've wanted."

Carwyn couldn't seem to lift his hands from her shoulders. The edge of his thumb rested against the soft skin of her neck and he could hear the low thump of her heart as her blood churned. He felt as if he would be ripping himself in two to leave her.

"I said I would help you, Brigid."

She whispered, "I know."

He stepped even closer and leaned down. Her forehead was a whisper away from his lips. "I said... you could hold on to me."

A crooked smile lifted the corner of her mouth and she looked up. "I'm a big girl, Carwyn."

A reluctant smile came to his lips. "No, you're not. You're tiny."

"Careful, I'll shock ya." She lifted her hands and placed them over his as they rested on her shoulders.

He gave a rueful laugh. "You always do."

Carwyn couldn't look away. Neither, it seemed, could Brigid. Her voice was a whisper when she finally spoke. "I know it's not on the way, but can you look in on things in Dublin before you leave? Check on the investigation. I've talked to Murphy on the phone, but he'll tell you things he won't tell me, and—"

"Yes," he said. "I'll go by his office."

"There's still a local connection we haven't found. I know—I know they don't believe me. They think it ended when Lorenzo left Dublin, and I don't want them to lose the trace of any leads while I'm out here. I just know—"

"Brigid."

She took a deep breath and he could smell the smoky-sweet scent of her. "Yes?"

I'll miss you. More than I should. Do you feel this? Is it the same for you? Or am I some great hulking brute of a male who could never— should never...

His thumbs stroked along the skin at her collar. "I'll look into things in Dublin. Don't worry."

She took a breath and held it. "You should go. You can make Glasgow tonight if you leave now."

"I know." And yet, he couldn't seem to step away. She was so small and so strong. It was like tightly coiled steel held up her limbs. Resisting the urge to wrap his arms around her, he leaned down, pressing a kiss to the burning skin on her forehead. He closed his eyes and held his lips there, feeling the burn and the sharp bite of her fingernails as they dug into his hands.

She whispered. "You should go."

Finally, he drew away and lifted his hands from her. He took one step back. Then another. Then he turned and strode toward the door.

"Carwyn?"

He whirled around. "Yes?"

Brigid gave him a cautious smile. "Take care of yourself."

He forced a smile, and his heart gave a quiet thump. "I will."

CHAPTER FOURTEEN

Castle Mackenzie
January 2011

Nights in the Scottish highlands were cool and damp. They were also long. Brigid grinned as she turned and twisted her hands, letting the ball of fire roll down one arm and hover over the palm of her hand before she tossed it into the other and let her amnis move it up the other arm. Her energy pulsed and flowed along her skin, shielding and feeding her all at the same time.

Forget drugs, manipulating fire was the most intoxicating high she'd ever experienced.

"Good," Cathy said. "Now throw it. Far. Push it away from you and over the lake. You're going to have to channel a lot of energy from other parts of your body to get it that far, but I think you can do it."

"Okay." She closed her eyes and felt the tickling amnis flowing up from her legs. She was rooted to the earth and her energy flowed up. Up. Building and rising until she could feel it nudging her arms out from her body. Her fangs grew long as her blood pulsed. Then with one last push of her mind, she imagined the fireball flying out of her hands and over the lake.

And the minute she thought it, it happened. She held the ball, hovering over the water where its red glow illuminated the meadow surrounding them.

"Good! That's excellent, Brigid. You're a very fast learner."

Anne looked up from where she was sitting at the lake's edge. "It's so pretty. Your fire has the prettiest colors, Brigid. There's almost a greenish hue mixed in with all the red and gold. It's like an opal."

The water was freezing, but Anne didn't mind. The water vampire leaned back and pulled her skirt up farther, dipping her legs into the water and lying back in the tall grass as she looked up into the sky.

"Anne," Brigid called, "you look like a selkie. Are you sure you're not some magical creature?"

Just then, Anne lifted a delicate hand, and a spear of water shot up from the lake and swirled around the fire that Brigid had thrown. It split into sparkling tendrils and surrounded the glowing ball until Brigid narrowed her eyes and made the fire explode out. It shattered into sparks that she let drift and simmer into the cold, dark water as Anne and Cathy laughed.

"Show off!" Anne yelled, but she could tell her friend was pleased with her. Everyone was pleased. They were impressed. For the first time in her life, Brigid felt confident and strong. Carwyn had been right. There were more than a few benefits to this whole immortal package.

As soon as she thought it, a wave of exhaustion took over and she swayed a little.

Cathy chuckled. "Whoa there, I think we better get you back to your room."

"No," she murmured, even though she could feel the heaviness begin to descend. "It's still dark."

"It is, but you know how long the nights are in winter. Your body doesn't care. You're young; it still wants you to get in those twelve hours."

"Come on." Anne rose from the lake's edge and grabbed one of Brigid's arms. Cathy grabbed her other one and they helped her up to her room. Brigid was careful to make sure her door was securely bolted before she went to lie down in the feather bed that smelled like lavender and lemon.

Sleep.

As her eyes flickered closed, she smiled. The best thing about being a vampire? It wasn't not needing to breathe or night vision. It was sleep. Vampire sleep, quite simply, kicked ass. No dreams. No nightmares. Nothing interrupted the sweet oblivion of rest. So far, it was her favorite thing about immortality. With a soft sigh, she let the blissful exhaustion take her.

Her eyes flickered open hours later. She glanced at the clock on the wall, then at her body, which still lay in the same position as the night before. For a few minutes, she enjoyed the utter silence of the castle and thought about the previous months. Peaceful. It was the most peace she'd ever felt, despite the loud arguments that filled the hall. Castle Mackenzie was a happy and cheerful place, full of laughter and love. Max was the prankster. Tavish the straight man. And Cathy was the live wire that everyone reacted to.

Her rooms were in their own wing. Part of that was probably because everyone liked their privacy, though she'd certainly had to become accustomed to hearing Cathy and Max going at it on a regular basis. No vampire hearing was going to miss that; Cathy was loud. But Brigid's rooms, for the most part, were isolated. Tavish had some small burrow in the basement where he huddled, and Anne had taken one of the lavish guest rooms, leaving Brigid in the south tower by herself.

She knew that, partly, it was a safety measure. On the off chance that she exploded, she didn't want to take anyone with her. Though, from what Deirdre had said, she'd exploded when she first woke up and hadn't left a mark on herself. They were still trying to figure that one out.

She ran a hand over the short crop of hair that covered her skull. Cathy told her she looked like a pixie. Anne said she looked like Audrey Hepburn. Brigid thought she was a little closer to a Sinead O'Connor look-alike with funky eyes. She got out of bed and dressed in the leggings and T-shirt she wore for practice. She'd learned her lesson about wearing loose clothing the first night and had the smudged burns to prove it.

Just then, she heard a scratching at the door. Sighing, she rose to open it and Madoc pushed in.

"Why? We go through this every night, dog."

The large puppy ignored her; then he walked over to the heather-green sweater that was draped over the chair in the corner and pulled it. It fell on the floor where Madoc promptly turned in a circle and laid on top of it. Brigid rushed over and pulled at the sweater as the dog whined.

"Don't! You beast, you'll get fur all over it. That's not yours."

It wasn't hers, either. Carwyn had left it in the library, and she'd found it after he'd left. She was just keeping it for him. She pulled up and the dog released the sweater with a whine.

"No. You can't have it. I've told you before." She held it in both hands and sat on the edge of the bed, fingering a frayed edge along the collar. She wondered if Anne could teach her how to fix it. It wasn't as if she didn't have time to learn a new hobby. Plus, knitting needles were sharp and could double as a handy weapon, should the need arise. The wolfhound came over and put his chin in her lap, looking up with mournful black eyes. Reluctantly, she lifted a hand and put it on his head, rubbing the coarse grey fur between her fingers. "I know," she whispered. "I miss him, too."

"Brigid!" She heard Cathy's call from across the castle.

She set Carwyn's sweater on her bed and gave Madoc one last pat before she stood.

"Time to eat, drink, and…" She looked down at the dog, who really was becoming alarmingly big. "Drink some more."

The wolfhound huffed and walked to the door.

"Well, I don't see you offering, dog."

Madoc barked and sat back on his haunches as she locked her door and pocketed the old key. Then the small woman and the giant dog set off down the hall.

"I was just joking, you know. The way you smell, I can't imagine your blood tastes very good."

"Again!"

She built the fire up along her arms, then snuffed it out, and the flames appeared to sink into her skin. Every time she did it, there was a sharp tingling sensation that reminded her of needles. She looked up into the full moon and took a deep breath, calming the race of her heart.

"Again."

"Shit," she muttered. It wasn't painful in the way that she remembered pain as a human, but it was still uncomfortable, and she'd been repeating the exercise for over an hour while Anne and Cathy chatted near the lake's edge. She built the fire again. Then snuffed it out. Again. Cathy claimed that learning to put out the flames was just as important, if not more, than learning how to control them.

"Once more."

Brigid locked her jaw and felt her fangs slide down, but she did it again.

"Okay, one more time."

"Are you fecking kidding me?" she finally exploded. "I've been doing this for over an hour!"

Cathy rose and rushed to her. "Are you questioning me?" The spicy smoke of the other fire vampire tingled in her nose, but she did not back down.

"Yes, I'm questioning you. I'm questioning the idiocy of going over and over the same drill for an hour when I've obviously mastered it."

Anne said quietly, "Calm down, both of you."

Cathy leaned down, growling in Brigid's face. "You've mastered it when I say you've mastered it, little girl. Do it again."

"No."

Cathy's hand shot out and gripped her neck, lifting her feet off the ground as Brigid tugged at her hands.

"I can't—"

"Do it." Cathy growled with bared fangs. "Again."

Brigid tried to ignore the instinctual panic, knowing she didn't need to breathe, but for a brief second, she was a small girl again, hiding in a closet with stifling hot air. She tried to build up the fire along her arms, but it swirled and sparked completely out of control. Cathy dropped her and she tumbled to the ground.

"You're weak and immature. Do it again."

Brigid felt the flames erupt from her hands just as Anne sent a cool mist over her. It sizzled against smooth skin. She'd burned off all the soft hair on her arms. Again. She lifted a hand to check her head and Cathy saw her.

"Don't worry about your fucking hair!"

She shot to her feet. "Don't tell me what to do!"

Cathy roared in her face. "You're an idiot, Brigid. Don't you realize? It's not going to be when you're in some controlled place that you have to worry. It's going to be when you're angry or afraid. That's when all of this is going to have to be like second nature. *That's* when you're going to have to control yourself."

Her heart was pounding. Her breath came hot and fast. "I always control myself."

"You didn't just now, did you?"

Brigid's fangs were long in her mouth. She felt the blood drip over her lower lip where they pierced the skin. "You were deliberately provoking me."

"I know!"

She and Cathy began to circle each other like two animals spoiling for a fight. The amnis washed over her. Hot. Angry. She could feel the air shimmer around her.

"Brigid." Anne's soft voice drifted to her, piercing the red haze that fell over her eyes. "Brigid, what are you really angry about?"

She blinked. "What?"

"Why are you angry with Cathy? She's your teacher. She's only trying to help."

"She's treating me like a child."

Cathy scoffed. "You *are* a child."

"I am not!" She tasted more blood in her mouth, and her throat burned as she glared at Cathy. "Children are weak. I'm not weak!"

"Brigid," Anne's voice came again, even as her eyes were locked on Cathy's. Circling. Growing closer. Closer... "Why do you say children are weak? They're not weak. They're children."

"They snivel and cry and need too much attention."

"But they're children, Brigid."

Brigid and Cathy circled each other in the meadow, both staring at each other as Anne continued to ask her maddening questions. Sparks lit between them. Brigid balanced on the knife-edge of control and chaos. Part of her, she realized with a sick twist in her stomach, was enjoying it.

She growled through bared fangs. "I *never* cried."

"Of course you cried when you were a babe, Brigid. It's natural. There's nothing weak about that."

"No." The flames licked down her arms. Over her fingertips, dying to reach out.

"Everyone cries. It's a perfectly healthy response to stress or grief." Brigid listened to Anne, but her eyes were locked with Cathy's. The other fire vampire sauntered slowly around her, eyeing her like a plaything. "When was the last time you cried, Brigid? Did you cry when Ioan died?"

"No."

Cathy sneered. "Typical self-centered human."

The fire leapt out from her arms. "Shut up! You don't know anything."

"I know you're a frigid bitch who doesn't give a shit about anyone but herself. I know that."

Brigid snarled and flung herself at Cathy, but the older vampire only batted her back with one hand.

"I'll kill you!" she screamed and jumped up.

"Brigid, you loved Ioan. Why didn't you cry?" Anne's voice was still soft, but closer.

She shook her head, looking back and forth between Cathy's sneering face and Anne's soft, concerned eyes. "I… I can't cry."

"Why not?"

"I can't, Anne!"

"Why?"

The fire reached out, circling around her. "You know why!"

"Tell me."

"Because she would hear me!" The flames shot toward a clump of nearby gorse, which exploded in the still night air. Cathy grew still, watching as Brigid turned her focus on Anne. A terrible burning started in her chest.

Her counselor's voice was almost a whisper. "Who would hear you?"

"Mum would hear me. I'd get in trouble. He told me."

"Brigid—"

She paced back and forth as the grass singed under her bare feet. "Why don't you understand? It's too ugly. I know what you're trying to do, dammit! But if I let one thing out, it will all come out and there'll be no end to it!" Anne and Cathy backed away slowly as Brigid came to a halt, burning alive in the desolate meadow. "It'll swallow me up! I'd never be myself again. There's too…"

"Too what?"

A sob she didn't recognize tore from her throat. "Too much!"

Anne's eyes bled tears. "Too much what?"

"Everything!"

"Let yourself feel it, Brigid."

"No! That's what everyone says, but what does that do for you? You only lose control of the *one thing* that's yours. And then, you have nothing. They've taken everything from you, and there's nothing left. Nothing will be safe."

Cathy spoke up. "Brigid, you have people who love you. Who want to help—"

She spun on her. "That's a lie."

Anne looked confused. "Brigid, you know we want to—"

"No one will take care of you but yourself. That's the only person you can depend on."

Cathy snorted and Brigid's ire spiked. "Well, that's horse shit."

Brigid's eyes narrowed. "No, it's not."

"Who told you that? Your mother? Your step-father?"

"Shut up, you bitch."

BUILDING FROM ASHES

"Because I sure as hell know that Deirdre and Ioan loved you. Especially Ioan. Your Aunt Sinead. Carwyn. So who are you going to believe?"

"Shut up!"

Cathy shook her head. "You're an idiot."

Brigid started toward her. "I am not, you miserable cow!"

Cathy didn't back down. She pointed a finger in Brigid's furious face. "You're the one believing the lie, instead of the people who love you."

"I do not!"

"Yes, you do," Cathy said. "You just said so. And you're full of shit. You can't cry? You're crying right now. Can't you feel it?"

Brigid blinked and brought a hand up to her face, starting when her fingertips sizzled on the bloody tears. "I'm... I'm not—"

"I guess *you* don't even believe the shit you're spewing."

Brigid's shock dropped away, and a murderous rage took over. She felt the fire building along her skin. It surged from the small of her back, and she felt the cool air as her clothing fell away. The flames covered her. Swirling over her like a living shield.

Cathy still looked unafraid. "It's a good thing Ioan never knew what a liar you are."

Brigid let loose a scream as the rage burst out. It exploded away from her, shooting in every direction in one terrifying flood of energy. She held it for a brief moment before she felt her amnis shrink back, curling around her like a warm shroud. Brigid fell to her knees, weeping gut-wrenching sobs that tore her throat. The earth around her was burned black, the grass curled into ash, but she was untouched. She lay frozen in the middle of the scorched earth as a blanket of water fell over her. Anne's hands sizzled against her back as she pulled Brigid up and embraced her.

"I have you, Brigid. You're fine. I have you now."

"Anne—" Brigid choked. "I didn't... I didn't lie to Ioan."

"I know, darling." She soaked the front of Anne's shirt with her tears. The water was already steaming off her skin, and she felt a shivering kind of weakness envelop her. She was exposed. Raw.

She tried to pull away from Anne's embrace. "I... I can't—"

"Don't." Her friend's arms tightened around her. "You deserve to be heard. And held. This is not weakness." Anne bent over and whispered in her ear. "Let me hear it. Even the ugly things."

"There are so many ugly things."

"Then let them out so you can be rid of them. You don't need to carry them around for eternity."

"I didn't want Ioan and Deirdre to know."

"Know what?"

"The ugliness. The anger." She sniffed. "He was better than me. All that he and Deirdre did for me? They didn't deserve that."

Anne pulled back and framed Brigid's face with her hands. "They aren't better. Or worse. Just different. We all have our demons, Brigid. Let me help you with yours. That way, you don't keep hurting yourself."

"Or other people," Cathy croaked from across the meadow. She crawled toward them with a grin on her face and a curl still smoking over her forehead. "And all emotional revelations aside… that, Brigid Connor, was very fucking interesting."

CHAPTER FIFTEEN

Valle de Cochamó, Chile
February 2011

"Squeal in terror, tiny human."

"Forget it, old man. You're going down."

"You are wildly optimistic for a loser."

"Keep trash talking. It'll just make it sweeter when I—what was that?" Ben's mouth dropped open as he stared at Carwyn's coin count shoot up.

"Ha!"

"What was that? Where did those coins come from?"

"Catch up now, slowpoke." Carwyn quickly punched in the cheat code, and his car shot forward.

"You're cheating at Mario Kart! I thought you were supposed to be a priest!"

"Doesn't mean I'm a good one."

The young man was indignant. "Cheater!" Ben furiously pressed buttons to steer around the cars that had bunched up in front of him, but Carwyn only grinned as the checkered flag waved and electronic confetti sprinkled down across the screen. He stood, raising his arms in a victorious pose.

"And I am, again, the undefeated champion of—oof!" Ben tackled him from behind, but Carwyn only laughed and let him knock him to the floor.

"You're such a cheater! Why do I even play with you?"

"Because I'm the only one here who doesn't fry the equipment?"

Ben punched his arm and rolled off the giant vampire. Carwyn was still laughing and gasping for breath.

"Well, I'm not playing with you again unless it's Resident Evil."

"Oh," Carwyn pouted. "You always win at that one."

"Damn right, I do. I kick your ass at killing zombies."

Isabel's voice drifted in from the front porch. "Language, Benjamin."

Ben Vecchio rolled his eyes at her voice, but Carwyn tapped him on the back of the head, shaking his head and giving the boy a look. Isabel may have been the strictest of his children—and the most devout—but Carwyn wouldn't put up with any disrespect from Giovanni's nephew, who was staying with Isabel and Gus while Giovanni took care of Beatrice during her first, most volatile year as a vampire.

The Cochamó Valley had changed little in the previous hundred years. Carwyn's daughter and her husband still brought most things in by horse or boat. There were no roads and only a few tourists during the busy season, which they happened to be in the middle of. The balmy southern air of the valley brought travelers from the Northern Hemisphere to enjoy the rock-climbing, hiking, and horseback trails that still ran through the mountain valley. It was a pocket of wild in a rapidly changing world, and the perfect refuge for a close-knit clan of earth vampires. Giovanni Vecchio and his new wife, Beatrice De Novo, had become adopted members of their clan.

"Ben!" Isabel's husband, Gustavo, called from outside. "Time to practice."

The boy's head fell back and he groaned. "Not wrestling again."

Carwyn shoved him up. "Go. Practice. Or you'll never hear the end of it from your aunt."

The quick sadness flashed in the boy's eyes. Ben hadn't seen Beatrice in months, and Carwyn knew any reunion was still months away as his friend learned to control her bloodlust.

"Okay." As always, Ben immediately complied when Beatrice was brought up. He dragged himself off the floor and stomped outside for his *jiu jitsu* lesson from Gustavo.

Beatrice was a new vampire and far too unpredictable and hungry to be safe around humans, even humans she loved. So Ben spoke to her on the radio phone a few times a week and saw his uncle at Isabel and Gus's house for lessons. But Carwyn could tell that the boy was still lonely in the strange place. Luckily, he knew the time would fly. For mortals, it always did.

"He's been better since you've come." Isabel slipped in the house and sat on the couch, watching as Carwyn put away the game controllers and turned off the television. He took off the leather gloves that enabled him to use the video game equipment and tucked them in with the controllers. "He's a good boy, but he misses Gio and B terribly. He acts out. I'm glad you're here."

He nodded. "I'm glad I came, too." Mostly. His thoughts still turned to Scotland far more than they probably should. "Ben is a good boy."

"He is. He's had a hard life, but he's very resilient."

Carwyn grimaced. "Pain tolerance seems to be a requirement in our family recently."

"We've been fortunate. Our clan lived a charmed existence until recently."

He grunted. "It was not without effort."

"I know your sacrifices. And Ioan's, too."

Carwyn turned and looked at his daughter. Like Tavish, Isabel looked older than him, but unlike Tavish, had always treated him with far more respect. She had been born in Spain and lived a full human life before her change. She had been a wife. A mother. A grandmother, even. In some ways, Carwyn thought Isabel understood him more than his other children because of that.

"You're different," she said quietly as he sat next to her on the worn couch.

"How?"

"You are… unsettled."

He studied her face, frozen in time in her mid-forties. "How did you stand it? When your children died? I lost two as babes. The others lived full lives I wasn't even part of. With Ioan… it is different, isn't it?"

Isabel's sons had been taken by plague as adults, along with their wives and children. He found her in the aftermath, bleeding and terrified. Afraid of the fires of hell for giving in to her despair and trying to end her own life. Carwyn had changed her from pity, a rash decision that was unlike him, but one that he had thanked God for many times over. Isabel had lived a happy and peaceful life in the five hundred years since. Her husband, Gustavo, was another welcome addition to his clan.

Isabel smiled. "Ioan lived a wonderful life. A life of joy and companionship and love. But to lose a child, no matter how long you have loved them, is to lose part of your own heart." She shook her head. "Humans take so much for granted now. I considered myself lucky to see my two sons live to have their own children."

"But then you lost them, too."

"I did." Isabel gave him a sad smile and leaned against his shoulder. "It is not a unique loss, Father. You will move on from this. Ioan would have expected it. It is Deirdre I am more concerned about."

Carwyn took a deep breath. "She sired Brigid out of her grief. It was not the young woman's choice."

"Does she have peace about it?"

"Deirdre or Brigid?"

Isabel shrugged. "Both, I suppose."

He cocked his head. "They will find their peace. They have time."

"Time…" Isabel reached up to squeeze his hand. "We all have time. Beatrice will have time to recover from her father's loss and find joy again in her union with Gio. Deirdre will have time to mourn Ioan and maybe, one day, she will find love again. Brigid will have time to find her place in this world she did not choose." Isabel paused. "What will you do with your time, Carwyn?"

"What I have always done, I suppose." His daughter was silent. Carwyn looked at her. She had an odd, thoughtful look on her face. "What?"

"Why?"

"Why what?"

"Why do you resist change?"

He blinked. "I—I don't."

"You do." She leaned away from him and crossed her arms. "As rebellious as you can be, you resist change... maybe more than any other immortal I have known. You know what respect I have for you, for the Church, for an eternal calling, but..."

"But what?"

"I wonder..." She frowned. "Who is watching over your flock, Father?"

"I am. Though there is a young priest from Cardiff who the bishop sent up to fill in while I'm dealing with family issues. Sister Maggie says he's doing very well. He's very popular with the young people in the village."

Isabel nodded. "And who is watching over our clan?"

His voice was hoarse. "I am. As well as I can."

Isabel squeezed his hand again. "You do very well, Father. We're all well, even if we mourn. We are safe. Secure. You have blessed us with your wisdom for hundreds of years."

Carwyn leaned over and pressed a kiss to his daughter's forehead. "Thank you, Isa."

"And who is watching over *you*, Father?"

He drew back. "What?"

She patted his chest, covered in a purple and green floral shirt that night. Isabel tugged at the collar and smiled. "Your heart has been pulled in so many directions for so long. You have to run away from all of us from time to time just to stay sane. And I don't blame you. You have lived a life dedicated to others for hundreds of years. Dedicated to the church. Your family. Your friends."

"What are you trying to say?"

She frowned a little. "Ioan's death changes things. He was as much your brother as your son. Other than Gio, he was your best friend. Definitely your oldest one."

"He did too much. There were too many things I left him to deal with on his own that I should have—"

"What?" Isabel broke in. "We're not children. We call you Father, but we are all quite capable of taking care of our own affairs. We love you, Carwyn, but we don't *need* you. Not like we did when we were young. Most of us have our own mates and our own clans now. We're safe. Secure —"

"Not secure enough."

"There is no such thing as secure enough. There are always dangers in the world, but you..."

He shifted in his seat and crossed his arms, frowning at her. "What?"

Isabel struggled, but eventually, her face broke into a grin. "You need to get a life!"

His mouth dropped open. "I don't know what you're talking about."

"Yes, you do."

"I have a very full life. Too full at times."

"Yes, but it is full of other's needs." Isabel grabbed his collar and pulled it together at his throat. "You use your collar—the Roman one, not the flowered one—as an excuse. A shield, in some ways. You've been alive for a thousand years, Father. Even I would say that you've paid your dues to the church."

"It is my calling."

"But it is no longer your joy. Not as it was. Does God want that?"

He growled and pulled away. "Vows are not always about enjoyment, Isabel."

"I know they're not. I'm married, aren't I?"

Carwyn rolled his eyes and stood up, pacing the length of the small den. "So you know—"

"I know that you will always be a servant of God. You will always be the one to comfort and care for whoever is in need. But you have devoted a thousand years to serving others."

"A leader *should* be a servant."

"But should he always serve alone?"

Carwyn shook his head and tried to brush the memory of smoke-tinged eyes from his mind. "I don't know what you think you see, but—"

"I see *you*." Isabel stood and walked to him. "I see the way you look at Gio and Beatrice."

He frowned. "What are you talking about? Beatrice is my friend. I have no—"

"Not her. *Them*. Your best friend has finally found his partner in eternity. His true mate. Like Ioan did. Like I did. And I see how you look at them, Carwyn."

He stood stock-still, his heart pounding in his chest. "I do not envy you."

"Not envy." She shook her head. "Not envy. *Desire*. It is not a sin to want someone to walk through eternity by your side."

Carwyn said, "It is if you're a priest."

Isabel raised an eyebrow. "Do you really believe that?"

Carwyn looked away from her piercing gaze. He had never felt guilty as a mortal for loving his wife and his calling in the church at the same time. His own father, an abbot, had taught him that the love between a man and wife should be the purest reflection of God's love for the church. A joy and testament to the people they guided.

In his heart of hearts, he knew what Isabel saw.

"I'm... lonely," he finally said. "I can accept that."

Isabel smiled and a pink sheen of tears came to her eyes. "You shouldn't have to. Not if there is someone God has brought into your life."

He cut his eyes at her. "You and your siblings talk too much."

She smiled innocently. "I don't know what you're talking about."

"And you're a horrible liar." He walked over and pressed her cheeks between his hands, looking down at her lovely face. "I love you all *so much*. You have given me so much joy and companionship. I love my family."

Isabel patted his chest where the red outline of Brigid's hand still marked him. "And we love you. But it's not the same."

He finally smiled and shook his head. "No. It's not the same." He pulled his daughter into a tight hug.

"It's a good thing that breathing is no longer a requirement, Carwyn."

He laughed and set her down, feeling lighter than he had in months. Perhaps years. He put his hands on his hips and looked around the room, suddenly feeling restless.

Isabel watched him with a smile. "You look ready for something, I'm just not sure what."

He grinned. "Neither am I."

"Ready for a change?"

"I think so." A knot of discomfort settled in his stomach. "I hope so."

"Ioan would like this."

"He would, wouldn't he?" Carwyn nodded.

He moved to the window, watching Gus and Ben grapple along the edge of the meadow. The boy was growing fast and strong. Adapting quickly to his new reality. A wry smile twisted his lips. If a thirteen-year-old runaway could adapt, then a thousand-year-old vampire should be able to, as well.

Isabel asked, "Will you leave the church?"

"I don't know." He looked over his shoulder. "Do you think I need to?"

She paused. "There's no need to make any decisions right now. But I'm glad you're thinking about it. Even the most devoted servant can have a change in calling."

"True." He pursed his lips. "Perhaps I should just give it some thought."

She smiled and patted his shoulder. "You have time."

And so did someone else. Carwyn rubbed the scar over his heart and glanced out the window into the black night. "We have time."

He was perusing the one book of Ioan's that Gustavo had borrowed about vampire biology years before. Gus's interest had been in muscular development, but it did have some of Ioan's theories about blood, as well.

'Because of the elemental nature of our energy and our need for blood as sustenance, it stands to reason that there is a connection between the four elements and our blood. In comparing phases of matter, we see that

the ties between classical elemental theory and modern science begin to find some common ground...'

He heard Giovanni approaching. The fire vampire had been ensconced in his remote cabin with his wife for almost a week. Carwyn had been seeing to Ben's lessons.

Sort of.

Giovanni said, "Good evening."

He glanced up. "Hello there, Sparky. How's the wife?"

"Doing well. She's swimming right now. And I think she and Gus are practicing some grappling later."

Carwyn smirked at the carefully restrained growl in his friend's throat. Would he ever get over seeing Beatrice as someone to be protected? The young woman's strength was quickly becoming formidable as an immortal. Then he thought about his own instinctive reaction to Brigid Connor working security for Murphy and decided not to say anything.

Giovanni unwound the scarf from around his neck and hung it on the peg by the door. A thought tickled the back of his mind. Something Brigid had said.

"Why do you wear scarves? It's not as if you get cold."

"I like the feel of them," he said with a shrug. "That's all."

He frowned. Brigid had liked the pressure of the earth against her skin. "Is that because of the fire?"

Giovanni sat across from him, pulling a letter from his pocket. "Possibly. I think it's different for all vampires. But for fire vampires, there is a kind of... prickling sensation under our skin most of the time. Not uncomfortable or painful. It just... is." He shrugged. "Clothing irritates it. So it's most comfortable to be clothed from head to foot or not at all."

Carwyn's breath caught when the idea of 'not at all' and Brigid Connor collided.

"Oh, God."

"What?"

He cleared his throat and willed away the mental images. "Nothing. What's the letter?"

"It's from Tywyll in London." Giovanni set his elbows on the kitchen table and looked at him. "I'm going to have to leave. I've already called the plane to Santiago. Can you stay?"

"Of course." He ignored the pang of disappointment. He had hoped to get back to Scotland in the next couple of weeks. "What's in London?"

"The irritating bastard has journals that Stephen left with him for Beatrice. I have a feeling they have to do with the elixir, so we need to get them and he won't send them. He's asking me to come fetch them myself."

"That *is* irritating, but I'm guessing they're important."

"I won't know for sure until I see them, but I hope they might shed more light on the elixir Stephen was so concerned about. And since I'm going to be there, I thought I'd try to meet with Jean in France and Terry and Gemma, as well. Should I go by to see Deirdre?"

Carwyn shook his head. "I don't think you need to. She's quite busy right now. There was some damage to the house in Wicklow. They're having to rebuild."

"Oh?"

He debated telling Giovanni about Brigid, but what was there to say?

I'm irritatingly fascinated with a woman for the first time in hundreds of years. She's young, intriguing, and I'm suddenly feeling older than dirt. She's also Roman Catholic, so she probably won't touch me with a ten-foot pole.

He cleared his throat. "Nothing to concern yourself with. How long do you think you'll be gone?"

"I'm aiming for no more than two weeks, but we'll see. Who knows how long it will take me to track down Tywyll once I'm there."

"He does operate on his own timetable." The enigmatic water vampire always had. He was an information trader, or that was as much as anyone seemed to know about him. Tywyll went where his whispering sources led him, up and down the River Thames as he had for thousands of years. His wells of information were vast and mysterious. Who knew what he might know?

Giovanni was still talking. "And I think we'll probably end up going to Rome soon. Stephen mentioned a contact there, and I have a few ideas about who that might have been."

"Oh?" He cringed internally. Carwyn hated Rome, but if Giovanni and Beatrice went looking for clues into Ioan's murderer, he'd go.

"I want those journals before I draw too many conclusions, but this elixir…" Giovanni crossed his arms and shook his head. "When I first heard of it, I had so many hopes that it might be a cure for our thirst, but the more I find out, the more dangerous it seems."

Carwyn frowned and a thought began to tickle the back of his mind. "So… this elixir. It was supposed to give humans vampire-like health and healing?"

"Yes."

"And then if a vampire drank from one of them, it was supposed to cure bloodlust so we wouldn't need to drink again?" He had to admit, the thought of being free from bloodlust was more than appealing.

"That's what the book Stephen found said. It was written by Geber, a medieval Persian alchemist. He was working with four vampires, one of each element, and his manuscript said that he had stabilized vampire blood so that human beings could ingest it and reap the benefits."

Carwyn rubbed a hand along the stubble that dotted his chin. "A cure for bloodlust?"

"Apparently."

"Given by altering human blood."

"That's what it sounds like. What are you thinking?"

Pieces of a conversation months before drifted to his mind.

"She asked me if there were any drugs that could be intoxicating to immortals."

"Ridiculous question. ...alcohol and drugs do nothing to us... nothing. Trust me, I've tried."

Carwyn frowned. "I'm thinking that this elixir sounds an awful lot like a kind of drug for immortals."

"I suppose..." Giovanni shrugged. "In a way, I suppose it is."

Both immortals fell into silence until Giovanni said, "I should get back to my wife."

A sharp longing rose in Carwyn as he remembered his conversation with Isabel. What would it feel like to find that person? The one who completed you. The one who embodied home and belonging. It was hard to imagine. He had been alone for so, so long.

"Give her my best. Tell her I'll be up later tonight, if she'd like some company. And she should call Ben when she gets a chance."

The dark-haired vampire chuckled. "Yes, Father."

CHAPTER SIXTEEN

Scotland
March 2011

Brigid was lying in bed, her eyes closed, trying to picture the last image of the sun that she could conjure. When was the last time she'd looked at her shadow? At the light reflecting off the river? She had woken for the night and opened the shutters to a beautiful full moon, but her thoughts had immediately turned to its more vivid cousin.

"Brigid?"

A quiet knock came at the door. It was Max. She exchanged a glance with Madoc, whose ears had perked when he heard the sound. "Yes?"

"You've a guest downstairs."

She frowned. "A guest?"

"Someone Cathy brought from town."

Brigid rose and slipped on her shoes, tucking the journal she'd been writing in under her mattress. She walked to the door and opened it; the dog poked his head through. Max was looking sheepish.

"Who is it?" A warm rush filled her chest. Could it be Carwyn? She dismissed the thought almost as soon as it arose. Max would never announce Carwyn. He was as welcome here the same as any of his family's homes.

"It's Patrick Murphy." Madoc gave a soft huff and pushed through the door, headed to the stairs.

Brigid was still trying to gather her thoughts. She'd spoken to her employer the week before. Surely he would have mentioned coming to Scotland. Wouldn't he?

She narrowed her eyes. "Are you sure it's him?"

Max said, "I have met the man before, Brigid. Yes, it's Murphy. Cathy said he had to make some last minute trip to Edinburgh. She ran into him. He asked to come up to the house." There was an awkward pause. "Are you refusing to see him?"

She looked up from contemplating the floorboards. "What? No! I was just surprised. Why would he want to see me? I'm…" *Thirsty. Confused. Edgy. Without my live-in psychologist.* "Hungry."

Max smothered a grin and nodded. "Of course. I'll warm some blood for you and bring it. He's in the front parlor."

"There's a front parlor?" Brigid looked down at the black leggings and large green sweater she was wearing. Then she imagined Murphy in his tailored suits and perfectly knotted tie. She looked up at Max. "I'd better change."

Just ten minutes later, she pushed open the huge door to the front parlor. At least, she was guessing it was the front parlor door. She'd changed into a fitted button-down shirt and pressed slacks she hadn't worn since she'd left Dublin. The clothing felt itchy and constraining against her sensitive skin. She heard Max and Murphy's voices from inside the room. "Hello?"

Sure enough. It was Murphy. And he looked just as he always did. If he dressed casually, she had never seen it. Of course, she had only ever seen him at the office. She heard stories of the bare-knuckles boxing matches that were held at his club in the early morning hours. Brigid certainly couldn't imagine him wearing a suit while he beat the stuffing out of someone in the ring. The Dubliner turned and flashed a roguish grin. Her heart immediately gave an involuntary thump.

"Brigid," he said and walked toward her. "You're looking extraordinarily well. The short hair suits you."

"Um… thanks."

"And I'm so pleased to finally see you again."

Murphy's eyes were warm and familiar in a way that was more comforting than she had expected. It *was* nice to see him again. It reminded her of home and work. Suddenly, she smiled. "I didn't—well, why didn't you say you were coming when we spoke last week?" She grasped the hand he held out. His fingers enclosed hers. Cool. Refreshing, in a similar way to Anne. She wondered whether it was just a product of his water element. As he held her hand, a soft pulse, like a friendly hug, caressed her arm.

"I hope you forgive the intrusion. It was a last minute impulse when I had to make the trip to Scotland. Deirdre was in town last month and mentioned how well you were doing. When I ran into Cathy yesterday, I asked her if I could stop by."

Why was he here? She thought they had covered most of the duties she would be performing once she came back to work in the new year. January would put her in Dublin eighteen months after she had been sired. A respectable and safe projection from what Cathy and Max had said. And Anne, who'd had to leave for the summer, would be back in the fall and could resume their counseling sessions to further prepare her to return to normal—well, *almost* normal—life.

"I'm sorry. Was there something you forgot to ask on the telephone? You didn't have to come all the way out here." She quickly added, "Not that it's not nice to see you, of course."

The dimple that occasionally peeked from his left cheek came out. "It's just a social call, Brigid. You're missed back home."

By whom? She smiled. "That's nice to know."

"I understand you just woke for the evening. May I join you?" Murphy held a hand out, motioning to the low couches surrounding a table laid with the vampire version of afternoon tea. Small sandwiches. Bits of fruit and cheese. Mild foods that wouldn't taste too strong to her sensitive tongue. Tea, of course. And then a steaming carafe of what Brigid guessed was fresh cow blood.

Appetizing.

"Thanks, yes. Help yourself." She looked at Max, who was hovering in the corner and trying to be inconspicuous. "Max? Will you join us?"

He shook his head. "I'll leave you to chat about work if you're comfortable, Brigid. I haven't given Cathy a proper hello since she's been back."

Lovely man. She smiled at his thoughtfulness. "Go to the back wing of the castle," she teased him. "We don't want to have to shout over her."

Max threw his head back in laughter before he sped from the room.

Brigid just cocked an eyebrow at an amused Murphy. "Notice he didn't correct me."

"My dear Brigid—" Murphy smirked. "I can't imagine what you're referring to."

She snorted as she sat at the table. "Right. This family isn't the shy type."

"Now that is something I do know." He sat across from her. "Are you enjoying your time here?"

"I am. Cathy's been a wonderful teacher. As much as we… see things differently at times, I'm learning so much from her."

"Well, I'll admit that I was surprised when the news came." Murphy poured her a cup of tea before he served one to himself. Brigid was already draining her first mug of blood. "Both that you'd turned and that you were sired to fire." He studied her carefully masked face. No one outside the family knew that she hadn't chosen to turn. As far as she was concerned, it could stay that way. It was family business.

"It was a surprise. But fire usually is."

"I understand no one was hurt."

"That's correct. And I've become quite adept at handling my element. Cathy said my other training is going very well. I'm becoming very good at manipulating amnis for questioning. My physical reaction times are very good. My reflexes have adapted." She gave him a rueful smile. "As much as I may have hated the PT that Tom forced on me, it appears to have been an excellent preparation for immortality."

"So you said over the phone." He took a sip of the tea. The delicate china might have made a less masculine man look dainty. Patrick Murphy did not have that problem. He was the picture of elegance with an edge of danger. "I'm sure Tom will be happy to hear it. But it doesn't surprise me that you can wield fire effectively. In fact, if I could have predicted any person becoming a fire vampire, it would have been you."

She almost choked on the mouthful of blood. "What, me? Why?" Was that a compliment? Insult?

"You have one of the most passionate personalities I've encountered in… well, hundreds of years. And yet, you keep such a tightly controlled exterior, Brigid. It's really rather extraordinary. I don't doubt you'll wield your element effectively through sheer force of will, if nothing else."

Brigid blinked and set down her mug. She swallowed, then picked up the tea he had poured her, drinking it black. "Um… thank you?"

Murphy laughed and the dimple made another appearance. "You're welcome. It *is* a compliment. I admired you as a human," his eyes darted over her face. "And I'm eager to know you in your immortal life as well. I'm very excited to have you in my organization. As is Tom. The whole team is ready to have you back home as soon as you're able."

"How is everyone?"

"Doing well." He quickly steered the conversation away from Brigid and onto the other members of the security team, which was a relief.

As much gut-wrenching emotional work as she'd done in the previous three months, she was happy to have the focus off her. The intense counseling sessions with Anne were as exhausting as the elemental lessons with Cathy. But while Brigid was quickly gaining confidence with her new physical strength, she was still wrung dry by her talks about her past. The immortal psychologist had needed to return to her home for the summer months, but had encouraged Brigid to keep a journal while she was gone.

Murphy served her a small sandwich she'd been eyeing and helped himself to another cup of tea.

"Thank you," she said.

"You're very welcome. I'm trying to remember if we've ever shared a meal."

"You interrupted Jack and me while he was feeding from a dealer once, but I'm not sure that counts."

His rich laugh filled the room. "No, it doesn't. Ah, Jack…" He shook his head. "A troublemaker to the bone. But a loyal one. He's been making noises about dreading your arrival, but I'm fairly sure he's counting the days. No one else gives him as much grief as you did."

"I'll have to call Angie and see if I can give her some tips."

"Do. He gets more annoying without someone to keep him in check. He thinks he's making headway with the local connection, though." Their eyes met for a moment and held. "He met with me just after we spoke last week."

"That's good! It seemed like we kept running into dead ends before I left." She leaned forward, her food forgotten. "What is it? What did he find?"

"He was looking around the warehouse where they'd been holding Ioan…" Brigid thanked the heavens that her color could no longer give her away. That was the place where she'd overdosed. The place Deirdre had fed her immortal blood, changing her irrevocably into what she had become. Would Jack have caught the scent? Did he know how it had happened?

She shook her head and focused on what Murphy was saying. It didn't matter. For some reason, she doubted that Jack would say anything if he did know.

"…So it appears that someone is using the warehouse again. I know you heard about it at a party Lorenzo held while he was in town last. Declan said you'd called it a club of some sort. An after-hours place like mine on the riverfront?"

She searched her memories of the party where she had met the two vampires belonging to Carwyn's old enemy who had killed Ioan in revenge. "Josh—the American one—he said that they just 'hung out' there. That it was kind of a club, but a private one. I had the feeling it would be where they would bring human girls to feed. Have sex. That kind of thing. But he also said that Emily had been there, too. She's human, of course, but she was like me. Knew everything. She was dating one of your sort—" Brigid broke off as Murphy smiled. "Well, *my* sort now, I suppose. He was a friend of theirs, it sounded like." She took another sip of tea, wondering how badly she'd stuck her foot in it. "Anyway, the American said Emily had been there. He invited me, too. I had no intention of going."

"So, your friend—the human dating an immortal—had been there. Did you ever ask her about it?"

Brigid shook her head. "I lost touch with Emily after Ioan died, to be honest. All I was thinking of after the disappearance was finding him. Then after he died… well, I didn't do much besides work. Emily tried to contact me a few times, but I wasn't receptive."

"Completely understandable." His eyes were kind and concerned. She looked away and took another bite of a pâté that Max had made. He was a surprisingly good cook. Most vampires weren't. "Brigid, who was the vampire Emily was dating?"

She sipped her tea before she answered. "His name was Axel." An image of the smiling blond vampire came to her. His model-handsome face and lazy blue eyes. "To be honest, Murphy, I don't think you should worry about Axel. He isn't…" Was it a vampire faux pas to insult the intelligence of another immortal? Why didn't anyone go over this stuff with her?

Oh yes. They spent most of their time trying to keep her from combusting.

Murphy asked, "He isn't what?"

Well, honesty had always worked before...

"He's dumb," Brigid said. "For the life of me, I don't understand why anyone would have turned him. He's slow as a box of rocks. He's very handsome, so I supposed someone could have just turned him to keep him around. Do vampires do that? Have you ever done anything like that? Changed someone just because they were pretty?"

His eyebrow arched, and she had the distinct impression that she'd insulted him. "Certainly not. Accidents do happen, but it's very irresponsible to turn someone for superficial reasons. To tie yourself to someone for eternity who you will always have a responsibility toward? It must be someone you have confidence in. A child should always be someone with an independent nature, in my opinion. You have to be able to care for yourself."

She nodded, thinking back to an argument she'd had with Cathy and Anne the week before when she'd refused their offer to help with something. At least Murphy seemed to understand why it was so important to do things yourself.

"Of course, the longer I live, the more I am convinced that we also need to know when to ask for help. It's part of maturity, I think, knowing your own limitations."

Well, damn.

She turned the subject back to Axel. "So, you can look into him, or have Jack do it, but I don't think there's anything there. He's not malicious, or smart enough, to be the ringleader. But I could be wrong." She hoped not. Emily—if they were still seeing each other—would be crushed.

"I'll pass the information along. Thank you. Is there anything else you remember?"

She tried to think, chewed on her lip as she ran over and over the memories of that night. Why, oh why, had she not seen the two vampires for what they were? "No, there's nothing else I remember. If there's anything..."

"You'll call." He smiled, flashing his dimple again. Murphy really did have the most disarming smile. It set Brigid at ease and set her heart pounding all at the same time. "I appreciate it. Most of us take some personal time after we turn to be cared for by our sires, and here you are, working as always."

"I like to work. I'd have gone back to Dublin right after if it had been safe."

"Why does that not surprise me?" He laughed. "If anything else comes up while you're here, I'll let you know. I don't want you to feel uninformed."

"Thanks."

He took another sip of tea and glanced at the clock over the old wooden mantle. "I should be going. I have to get back to the city before dawn, which is coming earlier and earlier this time of year."

"It is, yes."

They both finished their tea and stood. Murphy, like Carwyn, towered over her, but he had a leaner build and moved with a quick elegance. He walked to the door with her. "Thank you for the tea, Brigid. It was lovely to see you."

"Thank Max." She shrugged. "I'm not exactly the best hostess."

"But you're excellent company." He leaned down, ever so slightly. Brigid could smell the clean scent that rose from his neck. "Now that our schedules are more in sync, I'll see you at the office when you come back. I'm looking forward to it."

Good Lord, was Murphy… flirting with her? Oh no. She'd always been spectacularly bad at flirting, and she doubted turning into a vampire had helped.

"Um… thanks. I am, too."

She turned her face up so she could see his reaction when he looked into her inhuman gaze.

His voice was rough. "Your eyes did change."

"A bit freaky, I know."

"No." He shook his head. "They're beautiful."

What was this reaction? The tightness in her chest. The rush of blood in her veins. "Murphy… I don't know—"

"I need to go," he said abruptly and stepped back. "I'm sorry. Can we continue this conversation when you get back to Ireland?" His tone may have been formal, but his eyes burned hot as they stared into hers. That damn dimple almost taunted her. "We don't have as much time here as I'd like."

"Of course, Murphy. Good—"

She sucked in a breath when he leaned down and brushed a kiss across her cheek. He murmured, "Please, Brigid. Call me Patrick."

"Tavish, how does one go about… dating when they're a vampire?"

The gruff old man looked at her in annoyance as he pried a stone from his prize cow's hoof. "You're asking *me*? About courting?"

They were standing outside in the misty night air. Brigid had been forced into helping Tavish since his favorite herding dog had a broken leg from getting kicked by one of the bulls. A few spring calves already dotted the hills. Brigid took a deep breath. The calves smelled far better than the grown cattle, but Tavish gave her dirty looks every time she mentioned taking a sip from one of his babies.

"What's courting? I'm talking about dating. Seeing people socially who you're interested in on more than a friendly level."

Tavish just gaped at her. "Are you daft, girl? What makes you think I know anything about dating? Or that I even care, for that matter?"

"Well…" That was a good point. Why *was* she asking Tavish? Oh yes. "I'd ask Anne, but she's gone. I can't ask Max because he'd immediately call Deirdre to gossip about it. And Cathy—"

"No explanation needed there. She'd probably tell you to leap on the first lad you come across and just keep trying till one tickles in the right spot. Heathen."

She blinked. "Well, I wasn't going to put it that way, but—"

"She's a different temperament than you, Brigid. Temperament's important." He stood and looked over the hills, dotted with the shaggy, russet herd. He squinted into the night. "You know, I probably do have some advice."

"Really?" Brigid didn't actually expect him to give her any insight. Frankly, she'd been avoiding thinking about both Patrick Murphy and… other people that she shouldn't be thinking about, but the subject kept circling her brain. "So, what's your advice, Bovine Casanova?"

"You may joke, but look out there." Tavish nodded to the herd. "That's not purebred Highland Cattle there. That's a healthy hybrid lot. There's no mistaking the strength of this herd. I've built a very strong bloodline over the years."

"So, what you're saying is you can give me advice on *dating* because you're good at breeding cattle." Brigid squeezed her eyes shut. This was ridiculous. Where were the sheep? She'd round them up and bring them in, then go to her room and hide under her covers in embarrassment.

"It's all the same basic idea."

She started to walk away. "It is not. Never mind."

Tavish grabbed her shoulder. "It is, Brigid."

"Fine. Enlighten me."

The vampire frowned. "It's all about finding the right match. Find the right partner. The one who fills in the weaknesses in yourself and you do the same for them. This bull is hardy, but stupid. That cow is delicate, but keener. Together, their calves will be strong and keen. Same idea. I don't know about foolish things like dating—ridiculous modern concept—but cows. Vampires. Both need to find the one that makes them better. The match that fits best."

Brigid's mouth had fallen open right about the time he'd motioned to her while mentioning the cow. Still… "Tavish, that's surprisingly insightful."

"Told you. It's all about crossbreeding for hybrid—"

"Stop while you're ahead, old man." He tossed the pebble he'd pulled from the cow's hoof at her head. "Ow!"

"Who are you thinking about dating, anyway? The be-flowered one?"

Her eyes popped open. "Wh—what?"

"My sire. The vampire who asks about you when he calls to speak to Max. Which is far more often than normal, I might add."

She couldn't blush, could she? Still, she could feel her cheeks warm at the thought. Carwyn wasn't—*couldn't* be—interested in her that way.

Could he? She ignored the thump of her heart, wishing Tavish couldn't hear it. If he did, he ignored her. "Carwyn's a priest. Don't be ridiculous."

"You're such a Catholic."

"And you're such a Presbyterian. What does it matter?"

"He was married before."

"And hasn't been married since."

He shook his head. "Well, maybe he just hasn't found his match yet."

"In a thousand years?"

Tavish shrugged and slapped the side of the cow he'd been standing near. The giant animal lumbered off. "Some bulls are very, very stupid. You have to put the female right in front of them and just hope they figure it out."

"Please, let's not continue this comparison any longer. Please."

"And by 'bull,' I mean—"

"I get it, Tavish!"

He nodded and pulled on her arm. "Good. Now, enough of this girlish chitchat. Let's get the sheep in. You're getting better with the commands. Almost as good as Rufus."

Almost as good as the dog? With Tavish, that was as effusive as it got.

The next night, she was staring at the ceiling. She'd found a poster in the back of one of the spare room closets. A sunrise over the ocean. It was tucked behind a pile of coats and blankets, as if the sunny reminder had been retired with the out-of-season clothes. She'd stolen some tape from the kitchen and somehow attached it to the ceiling, the bored wolfhound cocking his head as he watched her.

Well, it wasn't as good as the real thing, but maybe it would make her feel a bit better about the endless night. Wasn't there some depression you could get from not enough sun? How did vampires combat that? She'd have to remember to ask Anne. She sure as hell didn't need any more depression.

"Brigid!" Tavish's shout came from the hall a moment before he pounded on the door. "You've a package. Eat something, then come help me with the sheep."

She opened the door, but he'd already left. A small package lay on the floor in front of her room. Deirdre? Anne? She picked it up and looked at the return address.

Chile, S.A.

She spun and slammed the door shut, immediately forgetting about both the blood she hungered for and the wandering sheep. Madoc whined in excitement and sniffed the package, as if he could smell the traces of his master in the brown paper she tore from the small box. Inside was a simple white envelope and red box with Spanish writing she couldn't decipher. She opened the envelope, and tears welled at the corner of her eyes as she read:

'Just in case you miss the sun.'

She swallowed the lump in her throat and opened the box. Nestled under tissue paper was a mass of bright colors. Red, blue, green, yellow, purple. She pulled the silk scarf from the box and held it against her cheek.

It was soft and silly. Flamboyant. She could see him picking it out with a mischievous grin on his face or a laugh.

Brigid would never wear something so frivolous. She wore dark colors. Sensible fabrics. If he had been in the room, she probably would have rolled her eyes as he teased her.

But Carwyn was nowhere in sight, so she wound the scarf around her neck and lifted the ends to cover her eyes. Then Brigid lay back on the bed, opened her eyes, and looked into the brilliant blooming night.

Chapter Seventeen

The Atlantic Ocean
May 2011

Carwyn stretched out as much as he could on the small bed as he crossed the Atlantic, wondering why, exactly, his children had decided to live in such inconvenient places. As much as he traveled, he still hated it every time. Unless he could tunnel under the earth as God intended earth vampires to do, travel was something he only ever put up with.

Air vampires could fly once they had grown old enough; one hundred years or so was common. Water vampires, obviously, were comfortable crossing even vast oceans with their elemental strength. Fire vampires could bully their way into any passage they preferred, as long as it didn't involve too much electricity.

But earth vampires, being the most domestic of the four elements, tended to stay near their homes in remote places. When they had to travel, large sun-shielded vessels like the freighter were their best option. This one belonged to his son-in-law in London, Gemma's husband, a water vampire who did large amounts of trade between Europe and the Americas. Terrance Ramsay—eager to take advantage of his wife's connections—happily loaned Carwyn any room he asked for. Terry's generosity allowed Carwyn the opportunity to travel wherever he needed, though he would never enjoy being on the water.

It was the most vulnerable position for any earth vampire. Surrounded by vast amounts of water, Carwyn was still strong, but his amnis was dampened. Still, it was the only option, and he needed to get back to Britain. For… lots of reasons.

"It is not a sin to want someone to walk through eternity by your side."
"It is if you're a priest!"
"Do you really believe that?"

His conversation with Isabel had haunted his thoughts for months. He tried to distract himself in the notes he had taken from Beatrice. She had made notes about the effect of Geber's elixir of life, the ancient formula that sounded more and more like the drug Ioan may have been thinking of. The more he learned of it, the more his suspicions grew.

'Human subjects who had taken the elixir—most on the verge of death —showed improvement within hours of taking it. Their color and appetite returned within days. In the single vampire trial, the immortal subject who drank from an elixired human showed evidence of increased strength, a surge of elemental ability, and no evidence of further hunger for human or animal blood. In the year of observation, the only negative side effect seemed to be a slight increase in necessary sleep.'

Increased strength. Stronger amnis. No bloodlust.
Was it possible?
It seemed more like the performance-enhancing drugs that professional athletes used than the oblivion-producing drugs that humans favored. And while oblivion was actually something that many immortals craved after hundreds or thousands of years, his kind lived in a dangerous world. A world fueled by webs of alliances and power. A world where the strongest and richest really did survive the longest. This elixir—if it did what it promised—would be very, very attractive to those seeking power and control.

Carwyn had always steered clear of politics. He took care of his own; that was all he wanted. And though he had always been a man of God, he was the head of his clan, as well. His singular desire in increasing his strength and guarding his reputation was to protect those who belonged to him.

Carwyn closed his eyes and thought. A vampire drug. It had been exactly what Ioan had feared, a drug added to human blood that could affect vampires. But this drug wouldn't weaken the immortals who drank it. In fact, it would seem like a miracle. Health for the human. Strength for the vampire. What was the downside?

There was *always* a downside.

Cardiff, Wales
May 2011

"Hugh?"
Carwyn poked his head through the old priest's door. The old man was sitting curled over his writing desk, his simple black pants and neatly pressed shirt showing signs of both wear and age.

"Hugh," Carwyn called again and stepped forward. The old man finally looked toward the door, and his eyes lit up.

"Father Carwyn!" he called, reaching up to switch on the hearing aid that had, apparently, been turned off. "I have to say that the benefits of hearing loss far outweigh the negatives when one is trying to finish writing letters. Why, just a quick switch of the batteries and I am plunged into a most pleasant silence, the likes of which not even Father Simon can disturb with his chattering."

Father Hugh stood and ambled over to the hulking immortal. He wrapped spindly arms around Carwyn's shoulders as they embraced.

Carwyn said, "It's good to see you, my friend."

"I think it may be one of the last times," the priest said with cheer. "I feel my homecoming may be soon."

The vampire smiled. "Now, Hugh. I think that's a bit hard to—"

"No, no." Hugh waved a dismissive hand. "Don't spoil my excitement. I'm quite ready to exchange the earthly body for the celestial one, thank you. My walks around the garden are getting shorter and shorter, and I can hardly taste food anymore. It's about time." Father Hugh patted Carwyn's shoulder and led them toward the low chairs that surrounded the fire in the sitting room.

"And you'd force me to bid good-bye to another friend when I've just said good-bye to Ioan?"

Carwyn was mostly joking. He'd known his old friend was failing for a few years. The signs and scents of impending death were evident. It would be a matter of months until Father Hugh went to his eternal home.

The priest looked up and smiled wistfully. "Surely God knew that I would be arriving shortly. Why else would he call my old friend Ioan to keep me company in eternity?"

The familiar bitter ache curled in his belly. Another age, another friend lost. Carwyn's voice was hoarse. "Well, our Father must have needed a few bad jokes about Irishmen."

Father Hugh's eyes twinkled. "Carwyn, *everyone* needs a few bad jokes about Irishmen."

Carwyn laughed as the old man settled into the chair and pointed the vampire toward the sherry. "Help yourself. If you could pour me just a small glass, I'd be glad."

"Of course." He walked over and poured a small amount of the wine into two glasses and brought them over.

"How is your family? I received a lovely letter from Deirdre when I wrote her after Ioan's loss. She seems to be doing as well as she can."

"She is. And she has a new member of her clan who has… kept her busy."

"A new child?" Father Hugh's eyes furrowed. "Someone in need of healing?"

Carwyn had never elaborated on the specifics of siring vampires with the old priest. His thoughts turned to Brigid for the thousandth time. *'Someone in need of healing…'*

"Yes." He nodded. "It was a… a friend in need of healing. She seems to be doing very well in immortality, so we are grateful for that."

"Why the unexpected visit? I hope Sister Maggie is satisfied with Father Samuel. He's sent me regular updates and seems very happy in the village." Father Hugh's eyes twinkled. "A very enthusiastic boy. The young ones are often like that."

"And often lose it in time, Hugh. You are a rare one."

"I have been given the gift of joy. Something I think we've always shared, though…"

Carwyn looked up in concern, noting the old man's downcast expression. "What is it, Hugh? Are you all right?"

"It's not me." Hugh smiled. "What is troubling *you*, old friend?"

Carwyn leaned back and sighed. "You've always been a sharp one."

"Found out what you were, didn't I?"

"That, you did."

"What is it? I don't have eternity like some people."

He laughed and took a sip of wine. "I'm thinking of leaving. The priesthood, I mean."

Hugh's mouth dropped open. "Leaving the church?"

"Not the *church*." He shook his head. "The priesthood."

"Why?" Hugh scooted toward him. "Do not mistake me. I am not wholly surprised by this. After all, a thousand years of service is incomprehensible to me. You have blessed so many. But I always thought you had resigned yourself to your solitude."

Carwyn tapped his chin. "It was solitude, wasn't it? I don't think I ever saw it that way until recently."

"Our parishioners are a kind of family. Your immortal clan is another. I know you speak of many friends. But…" Hugh offered a gentle smile. "We see life. As priests, we are observers, but often stand alone with our God and our calling. For a mortal man, it is a joyful sacrifice. But to face eternity without a mate, as you have, is something altogether different. I know that it was something Ioan and I spoke of."

"I'm well aware of his views of my celibacy. I didn't know that you'd spoken about them."

"Well not in detail!" Hugh laughed. "What sort of men do you think we are?"

"Do you really want me to answer that?" Carwyn shook his head and said, "I don't think I saw it that way until recently."

"What? As solitude?"

"Yes."

Hugh shrugged. "Well, you have always been busy. Tending your own flock. Seeing to your family. But that kind of company is not the same as the beauty of marriage that God consecrated for mankind."

"True."

Hugh's eyes danced. "Is there someone who may have caused you to think differently?"

Carwyn had the urge to squirm like a schoolboy. Awkward, considering he'd known the old man across from him when *he* was a schoolboy. "I don't need to go to confession, Hugh. Not yet, anyway. But there may be… someone."

"She would be a fortunate woman to find a mate as devoted as you, Carwyn."

Tears almost came to his eyes. He felt unexpectedly absolved by the approval of his old friend. "I believe I would be the lucky one. And I need to speak to Rome if I'm serious about things."

"Arturo?"

Carwyn nodded, thinking about the cardinal based in Rome who oversaw the more… unusual members of the priesthood. "He won't like it."

"Does it matter?"

He grinned. "Not really."

"What are they going to do? You serve a higher power than Rome."

Carwyn lifted his glass to Hugh. "Spoken like a true Welshman."

"Exactly. Now, as for your church, I think I shall ask Samuel to consider you 'on sabbatical' until further notice. I'll send him a letter shortly letting him know that the care of the church is his until further notice."

Carwyn thought about the small village he had called home for so many hundreds of years. The quiet strength and faithfulness of its people. "He's good?" he asked in a rough voice. "This Samuel. He's cares about the village?"

"He does. And his energy, enthusiasm, *and* ability to go out in sunlight may be just what the town needs."

"Ha! I think you may be right." Carwyn sat back, and an unexpected peace stole over him. "Thank you, Hugh."

"You're welcome. But don't think in a million years I'm going to be the one to write to Sister Maggie. I don't like you that much."

"Coward."

Dublin, Ireland
May 2011

The very proper secretary smiled at him and lifted a hand to her earpiece. Then she looked up at Carwyn, who waited in the small sitting area of Murphy's Dublin office. He had not been waiting long.

"Murphy will see you now." She rose and showed him to the door.

Carwyn stood and followed her. "Are you Angie?"

Her eyes smiled. "I am."

"Brigid speaks very highly of you."

"Oh!" Angie's face glowed. "Have you seen her? I wasn't sure. Is she doing well? Those boys don't tell me anything."

'Those boys' were—Carwyn suspected—at least a hundred years older than the human secretary, judging from the level of energy he'd detected when they'd met him in the hall. His visit to Murphy's office had not been expected and the vampire's security had reacted predictably.

"She's doing very well, last I saw her. And I'll see her again soon. Shall I pass along a greeting?"

"Yes, please do. I understand she's planning to come back to work in January. God knows I'm grateful." She waved a hand around the office and opened Murphy's door. "Pains in the arse, every last one of them."

Murphy met them at the door and leaned down to brush a kiss along Angie's cheek. "You know you love us, Ange."

"You're the worst one."

Murphy's eyes danced looking at her. He allowed his amusement to drift over to Carwyn. "The adoring respect my staff offers me is its own reward for my labor." He stuck his hand out and Carwyn shook it as he was ushered into the room. "Carwyn, it's good to see you. I understand you've been traveling."

"I have." He sat across from the water vampire in the luxurious modern office building. Shutters had been drawn back and the black span of the river, lit by the twinkling lights of the new Docklands developments, spread out behind the vampire's desk. Murphy's empire. Ships. Real estate. Business and trade. He suspected the old gambler reveled in playing the humans of Dublin as he had his marks in mortal life.

"So, what brings you to Dublin?"

"Just wanted to check in on the investigation." Tension immediately descended on the office. Neither vampire had forgotten that it was immortals in Murphy's city, unmonitored and hostile, who had taken and killed Carwyn's son. And Brigid seemed to think that Murphy and his people were overlooking a local connection. Carwyn hated to be suspicious, but a thousand years had honed his instincts. And his instincts told him that Brigid was seeing something no one else did. Speaking of Brigid... "Brigid also asked me to keep her updated when we spoke last."

Brigid's name and smug satisfaction chased the tension from Murphy's face. "No need for that. I saw her last week. I've kept her informed about our progress."

Carwyn smothered the growl that threatened his throat. "Oh?"

"I was in Edinburgh for some business and ran into Cathy. I called on Brigid the next night. She's looking phenomenal. I'm looking forward to having her back."

Don't kill the water vampire, Carwyn. You don't want to run Dublin. Besides, technically, Murphy is an ally.

"I don't find that surprising in the least. She's a very attractive asset. Did you see her work with fire at all?"

"Sadly, no."

Carwyn smiled. "Unfortunate. She's breathtaking when she's training. All that tightly coiled control released. Careful you don't get too close, though." Carwyn rubbed his chest. "She stings." *And I crush.*

Murphy's eyes narrowed. "How can I help you, Father?"

"I want to know if you've made any headway with the local connection. Brigid seemed very certain there was a vampire other than Lorenzo involved in Ioan's death."

"I know her theories, though I'm not sure what she's basing them on. Our own investigation is ongoing."

"The party she went to that Lorenzo hosted. She went with a friend of hers, didn't she?"

"Yes, not her normal scene, but her friend was—*is*—seeing a vampire socially."

His instincts triggered. "Who?"

Murphy shook his head. "Something of a local. He's Scandinavian. Not very old. And not very smart. Hardly someone Lorenzo would depend on. We've looked into him, but we don't think he's worth pursuing."

"What's his name?"

The water vampire narrowed his eyes. "We've looked into him. Not a likely suspect."

Carwyn shifted in his seat. He'd only ask one more time before things became... interesting. "His *name*, Murphy."

The two vampires measured each other. Murphy had people. People surrounding him who were loyal. He was strong and ambitious. But his few hundred years were nothing compared to Carwyn's strength. Or his vast network of family connections. If Carwyn wanted to rule Ireland, it wouldn't be much of a fight. He could take Murphy out with one battle and a few well-timed telephone calls. He may not even need the battle.

And Patrick Murphy knew it.

"His name is Axel Anderson," he finally said. "False, I'm sure, but that's what he goes by. No idea who his sire is. He's lived in Dublin for around twenty years. Does a little shipping. Has traded in some recreational drugs like Ecstasy and marijuana, but I put a stop to that after I found out he was the one supplying Brigid in college. She doesn't know that, by the way. I'd like your discretion. The vampire is dating one of the few friends she has in town, and I'd hate to see her lose that."

That information was going to piss Brigid off royally when he told her, which he had every intention of doing. "We'll see," he said as he rose. The other vampire stepped out from behind the desk. Carwyn said, "I want to be kept informed. Send messages by way of Deirdre if I'm out of town. Things are a bit unpredictable for me right now, but I'll be around more."

Murphy did not look pleased. "The Father has left his flock? I thought you liked your quiet mountains, Carwyn."

He shrugged, and a slight smile lifted the corner of his mouth. "I like all sorts of things. And I protect what's important to me." He stepped a bit closer. "Don't make the mistake of forgetting that."

Murphy's face was blank. "I don't forget much."

"Good." Carwyn thought for a moment, weighing the intrinsic value of information against the possible threat against innocent mortals and immortals under Murphy's aegis and territory. The innocents won. "There's another drug you should be aware of. Something that may have just resurfaced. I'm still gathering information, but it's targeted at immortals."

Murphy said, "A drug for vampires? Careful, Father, things like that are what urban legends are made of."

He snorted. "Like I said, I'm still getting information. I'm working with Giovanni Vecchio and his wife on the research. I'm sure you know their reputations."

The mention of the famed fire vampire and scholar halted the amusement on Murphy's face. "Of course."

"I'll keep you updated, particularly since it seems to be related to Ioan's death. In the meantime, if you see any immortals who are acting out of character... seem to have increased strength or aren't feeding as much, let me know."

Murphy gave a slow nod. "You can be sure of it."

Carwyn walked toward the door and turned. "So Brigid still wants to work for you?"

"January. She'll be coming back in the new year."

He cocked an eyebrow at Murphy. "You're a lucky..." *boy*. "... employer, Murphy. To have her on your team."

"I know it."

Carwyn smirked before he strode out the door. "Just don't forget it."

Chapter Eighteen

Scotland
June 2011

Brigid held her hand up, a single flame hovering over one finger, as she sang in the misty night. Madoc watched with disapproving brown eyes.

"Happy death day to me, happy death day to me, happy death day, dear Brigid… happy death day to me." She stared at the single flame for another minute before blowing it out and turning to the wolfhound. "Don't look at me like that. It's an odd kind of thing to celebrate." She stood and brushed the grass from her leggings. Brigid had been at a bit of a loss for what to do to mark the one-year anniversary of her new life. A life, she had to admit, she grew to like more and more as her control grew. Cathy and Max were in Edinburgh. Anne was still out of the country. Tavish was the only one who acknowledged the date at all.

"Hasn't it been about a year now?"
"Yes."
"Killed anyone? Max isn't here; you can tell me."
"Nope. Though that annoying man that lurks around the pub in town has been tempting."
"Can't blame you for that. Still, more trouble than it's worth. Probably."

And that had been the extent of Tavish's words of wisdom.

Brigid strolled through the grounds with Madoc following her. In the months that Carwyn had left the beast in her care, the dog had wormed its way into her heart, following her around the property when she walked or ran, chasing after the deer with her when she could hunt, and curling at the foot of her bed as she slept. She knew that her room was secure. Knew that even if anyone managed to break in, the dog wouldn't be able to wake her. Still, for the first time in her life, Brigid had rested easy with another living creature in close proximity. Madoc's gentle presence had been soothing instead of nerve-wracking. Brigid was grateful for the company and proud of her trust in the gentle beast.

She walked along the edge of the lake, stripping off her sweater to play with the gold fire that had become her companion. Like the dog, its presence had become soothing. Fire was her armor. Her protector. She felt its residence under her skin like a familiar, if volatile, friend. Brigid let the amnis run down the back of her neck, over her shoulders and arms, until it bloomed in her hands. She pushed it away from herself, letting the twin globes of fire hang over the water and reflect in the dark ripples of the lake. Madoc grew excited as she played, yipping and dancing in circles like the overgrown puppy he was.

She focused on the flames as the dog's excited barks grew. Soon, he was circling a rise in the hill, jumping and dancing in the moonlight.

"Madoc?" What was he on about? He never reacted like this when Tavish was approaching. "What is it, you mad beast?"

The fire drifted away, and Brigid's heart began to pick up a slow beat as she saw the ground shift under Madoc's feet. What the—

The ground burst open with a shout as Madoc pounced. Brigid ran over, her arms lit, ready to burn whatever had attacked her dog. She immediately halted when she heard the familiar laugh and the loud voice.

"I heard you barking from twenty feet below, you mad hound! Haven't you ever heard of the element of surprise? I'll not be taking you on any missions of stealth, you can be sure of that."

His dark red hair was flaked with dirt, and his skin was black with mud, but when Carwyn turned to her, there was no mistaking his vivid blue eyes. She broke into a smile just as he rose to his feet. She started toward him, but he only held up a finger.

"One moment," he said with a grin. Then he stripped off his shirt, tossed it onto grass and dove into the water with glee. Madoc barked along the edge of the lake, waiting for his master to emerge.

He was back.

Her heart was racing now. Did he remember it had been a year? Did he come back for her?

She banished the thought from her mind. Of course he didn't come back for *her*. Not like that. He was watching out for her. Like… a priest. Or a friend. Which he was. A priest. A friendly priest.

Then he rose from the lake, the water scattering from his arms as he pushed back his unruly wet hair. Rivulets ran over the dark freckles on his shoulders and down his torso. Thick muscles flexed as the cool moon reflected off the solid planes of his chest. Dark red hair ran in a line down his flat stomach and into dripping wet trousers that covered his hips and muscular legs. Brigid was struck again by his size. Carwyn was enormous. Tall as a small tree and solid as the earth he controlled. He should have been intimidating. But he wasn't.

He was back.

Damn it.

Priest! Her mind yelled. But Father Jacob didn't look anything like that. Had Carwyn always had so many muscles? There seemed to be more than the last time she had seen him. Did that happen with vampires? Had he been... working out? He strode toward her with a smile.

"Surprised to see me? Despite this mutt's warning?"

"Um..." Wasn't there some rule that priests had to be thin and academic?

"Brigid?"

Or fat and jolly? Safe and approachable?

Carwyn was standing in front of her. "Are you all right?"

"I'm... fine!" she squeaked.

"Are you sure? Sorry I gave you a start."

She squeezed her eyes shut. Father Carwyn ap Bryn was approachable, all right, but not for any reasons the pope would approve of. She could feel the heat rising along her neck. Her heart thumped in her chest and her skin prickled as her eyes landed on a thick cord of muscle at the side of Carwyn's neck. Her fangs fell down in sudden, passionate awareness as she imagined sinking her teeth into his neck, sucking on the sweet, hot blood that would run—

Oh, she was going to hell.

Just then, her eyes landed on the red outline of a palm on Carwyn's chest and she froze. Her fangs retracted. Her heart stilled.

A small hand had branded him, searing away the scattered hair that covered his chest, raising an angry red welt. It had healed smooth, but the mark was still there.

"I did that," she whispered, staring at the scars that marred his skin.

His voice dropped. "Brigid—"

"I *did* that." She spread her hand and placed it over the burn. "I burned you. I *hurt* you."

"It's nothing," he said in a hoarse voice. He pressed his hand over hers and held it there. She could feel the calm thump of his heart and her eyes rose to his. "It's nothing, Brigid. A wound that has already healed. Please, don't—"

"I'm sorry."

"I'm not."

Their eyes locked and Brigid knew he was telling the truth, but she still wondered, had every touch hurt him? Her eyes raced over his skin, and a gasp tore from her throat. A red band from her arm. Fingerprints on his neck where she'd clutched him as he carried her. She felt strong fingers grasp her chin as Carwyn forced her to meet his eyes.

"Don't you dare! I won't have you blame yourself. You allowed me to help you when you wouldn't let others." His voice caught. "It was an honor. That's all these scars mean to me. No blame, Brigid. I won't allow it."

She blinked back the tears that threatened her eyes. "You're not my boss."

A smile crinkled the corners of his eyes. "Doesn't matter. Now give me a hug and welcome me back, you brat. You've spoiled my jovial entrance with your Irish guilt."

A reluctant smile worked its way over her face, then Brigid lifted her arms and wrapped them around his huge shoulders and she held. To his goodness. His kindness. The unexpected comfort of his touch. She could feel the laugh rumbling in his chest when he picked her up and swung her around.

"A year immortal and no slips, am I right? That ironclad discipline won't allow it." He held her around the waist, her feet dangling in the air, but she wasn't afraid to fall. She knew he would hold her. Madoc danced around them, yipping and bouncing in excitement.

"No slips. No kills anyway. I can't stand the all-beef diet you, Tavish, and Max adhere to, so I have been going into town to drink. Cathy's been teaching me how to do it safely."

"It's not for everyone, love. You make your own choices." He still held her against his chest, and Brigid began to grow more and more heated. Her fingertips sizzled against the wet skin of his neck as the water dripped from his hair.

'*Love*.' He called her 'love.' He did that with lots of people, didn't he? It was just a friendly endearment.

She asked, "Are you going to set me down anytime soon?"

"I haven't decided yet. You're very tiny. Have you always been this tiny, or has immortality caused you to shrink?"

"You're ridiculous."

"I know. Don't pretend you don't like it." Carwyn finally set her at her feet and stepped back. Her eyes were drawn to his chest again as she examined the scars in the dark.

She had marked him. *She* had. Her fangs fell again, and a strange, instinctive reaction welled up inside her. It wasn't guilt.

Mine.

Madoc's shove against her legs sent her stumbling back, breaking the spell the burns seemed to have on her. Carwyn grabbed her arm with a laugh and tugged the dog by the scruff of the neck affectionately.

"How have you put up with this beast? I'm pleasantly surprised to find him still groomed and fed, by the way. I thought for sure you'd have run him off to live with the sheep by now."

"I'm not cruel, Carwyn. I wouldn't put him at Tavish's mercy."

She watched him lean over and pick up his shirt. And wasn't the back view just as nice as the front?

Oh yes, she was definitely going to hell.

Immortality suddenly seemed like a particularly fine idea if it meant she didn't have to face eternal damnation for being attracted to a priest.

Carwyn slung the shirt over his damp shoulder and whistled for Madoc to follow them up to the castle. He slowed his long strides to match hers as they walked and the dog danced around them.

"I thought you didn't like animals," he said.

She cleared her throat. "Well, sometimes you get attached to the ridiculous ones."

Tavish greeted them at the door with his typical grunt, then disappeared to the basement. Carwyn gave an affectionate smile as he watched his youngest 'child' wander away. "Where are Cathy and Max?" he asked.

"Edinburgh. Cathy's boss had some interview she needed to be there for. Max tagged along."

"You prepared for that kind of thing?" Carwyn eyed her warily. "The kind of security work that Cathy does—that you'll be expected to do—it's different than what you did as a human."

She nodded and led him to the kitchen. "I know. I'm prepared for that. I've been practicing questioning people with amnis in the village with Cathy. Using my power in more offensive, as well as defensive, ways. It's fascinating, really."

Carwyn looked amused. "Questioning people, eh? How's that going?"

She cocked an eyebrow as she opened the refrigerator door. "It might be a good thing you're here, Father. These people need to confess to someone more proper than me."

That seemed particularly amusing to him for some reason. He sat down and watched as she prepared a sandwich.

"Are you hungry?" she asked.

"Yes."

She turned to see his eyes dart away from her and over to the radio, which was playing some news program. "Roast beef all right?"

"Fine, thanks. Finally feeling at home here?"

"Hard not to with the Mackenzie clan. After the first month or so, they expect you to fend for yourself. I can make a mean mutton stew now, too."

"Aren't you the domestic one?"

"Ha!" She shook her head. "Actually, I learned how to set a formal table at age eight. I could probably still throw a dinner party in my sleep after seeing my mother host so many. I just don't like company all that much." He was so silent she turned to look at him. "What?"

"I've never heard you talk about her."

"My mother?"

"Yes."

Brigid shrugged and turned back to slice the bread that Max had baked and frozen the week before. "I've been told that it's not healthy to pretend the first ten years of my life didn't exist."

Another pause. "Where's Anne?"

"Galway." Brigid smiled at him over her shoulder. "I'm not her only basket case, you know."

"Don't talk about yourself that way."

"I'm joking. Aren't you the one who never takes things seriously?"

His voice was sharp. "Is that what you think?"

Brigid smirked. "I'm not—"

"I take things seriously when they need to be."

Her eyebrows raised as she examined him. The look in his eyes was unfamiliar. Raw. Vulnerable, in a way. "I know you do, Carwyn."

He blinked and looked away, then rose to come stand beside her. "Can I help?"

"Why do men always offer to help when the job is almost finished?"

He grinned and grabbed two plates. "We're smart that way. Why ruin the rare pleasure of watching a woman see to your needs?"

Now why did that make her skin heat? He was talking about food. Wasn't he? Brigid shoved back the other images that sprang to her mind.

Wasn't he?

She was definitely going to hell.

Carwyn leaned over her shoulder and took a deep breath.

"Smells fantastic, Brigid. Thank you." She was frozen when he grabbed the two sandwiches and put them on the plates. Brigid turned around and watched him carry everything to the small table in the corner of the kitchen. He set them down and asked, "What would you like to drink, love? I'll get it."

Her eyes flicked to his neck a moment before she turned back to the counter to put away the plate of beef.

"Whiskey," she said in a strangled voice. "Please."

He didn't respond, except to dart to the living room and fetch her a glass. Then he sat down with a beer and dug into his sandwich with gusto.

"When did you come back from South America?"

"A few weeks ago. Went to Cardiff first, then Dublin."

Her ears perked up. "Dublin?"

Carwyn nodded. "Saw Murphy while I was there. Angie says hello, by the way. Sounds like you're greatly missed."

A soft smile stole over her face when he mentioned Angie. She had to confess she had been worried what the older woman's reaction would be to her new immortality. She should have known. "Angie's a good friend."

"And I asked Murphy about your friend Emily's boyfriend."

"Axel? What did Murphy say?"

"He doesn't appear to be taking it as seriously as you do. Seems to put more faith in his boys."

"Declan and Jack."

"Aye." He frowned and took a drink from the bottle of beer he'd pulled from the fridge. "Why are you so certain that Lorenzo had a local connection? Murphy seems quite sure that this Axel was not involved."

"He might not have been, but I'm surprised Jack hasn't looked into it more. He was with me. We worked the streets together on the dealer thing. We both thought Lorenzo had to be the one funneling the new drugs into Dublin, because they died off quickly once he was gone. It was only weeks and the dealers were scrambling to get more. With him gone, the supplies had dried up. Lorenzo had to be the connection."

"Then why would a local be necessary?"

"The drops they were making. The meeting points and the dealer network? According to your American friends, Lorenzo had been underground for years, not in Dublin. And it was too smooth to be someone new. There was no violence when the purer drugs first started showing up. No change in employees. The same people were getting the drugs out; they just had stronger stuff."

"So you think Lorenzo made a local contact that he started supplying and that's who helped him abduct Ioan. Maybe it was the Irish boy he'd turned?"

She shook her head. "No one knew him in the scene. I asked around. If he'd been the one, someone would have told me or Jack, especially after he was dead. No, it was someone else, and I think they're still there."

"Still selling drugs?"

"Why would they stop? They still have to make money. They still have to supply their dealers. They just have to be more desperate now since their supplies have dried up."

Carwyn paused for a moment, staring at her as if deliberating something. Finally, he said, "Axel is the one who was selling Emily the drugs she gave you, Brigid."

She blinked. "What? Axel?"

"Are you surprised?"

She thought. Was she? "A little. But I suppose it makes sense that she'd get them from him. I always figured he was shady in some way, but the drugs surprise me a little. He must have been dealing on a smaller level from someone—"

"Why are you so sure he's not the connection?"

"I just…" She sipped her drink. "He's not smart enough, Carwyn. I mean, you don't have to be smart to use drugs, or even to deal. But to organize a network like what was in Dublin when I first got there? There were so few arrests by the human police. It was so carefully structured to keep the lower level—even the upper level—dealers in the dark. Someone smart was fixing it. Someone far smarter than Axel, anyway."

He nodded and leaned back. "Fair enough. You'll keep looking when you get back. If there are more people who were involved in Ioan's death, I want to know who. And if Murphy is not following through, I know you will."

"Count on it."

"I'll be following up with Gio and B, so I may have to leave again. According to them, we have far bigger things to worry about from Lorenzo. He's acquired a book, a very dangerous one if the stories are true. One that might contain the formula to an elixir that makes vampires stronger and quells bloodlust."

Brigid's heart beat faster. "What? An elixir? Like a drug? A vampire drug?"

He paused and took a sip of his beer. "Ioan was right. You were right. Apparently, it is possible. It's an elixir for humans, but vampires who drink from them are affected as well. We still don't know exactly how."

Thoughts tumbled through her head. A drug that affected vampires. It had been a mad kind of 'what if' she had spoken aloud. Then Ioan had taken off with the idea...

"Is that why he was killed? Is that why Ioan was murdered? Because he found this?"

Carwyn shook his head. "I don't know. There's no way of knowing. It might have been something he discovered after you'd asked him about it, but it might have been some of his earlier research, too. He was well known for his studies into vampire biology. An authority in our world. Or it might have been retaliation at me and had nothing to do with this drug. It might have been a coincidence."

"And it might not have been."

"Brigid, I won't have you feeling guilty for this. The only ones responsible for Ioan's death are the vampires who killed him and those who funded them."

Her eyes hardened and rose to meet his. "I know that. It just means that my list of people to kill got a bit longer."

When Brigid finally made her way up to her bedroom, she was almost stumbling into walls. Carwyn had offered to help her to her room, but Brigid made excuses, knowing that once he was there, the urge to pull him in with her might be too much to resist. She wanted to curl up against him and purr.

She was definitely going to hell.

Madoc trailed after her. He had gone back and forth between the two vampires in the hall like a conflicted child, until Carwyn had shooed the dog in her direction. He nosed open the door to Brigid's room a moment before she stumbled in. Brigid carefully latched the door, then collapsed in bed. Just before she fell asleep, she pulled the silk scarf from beneath her pillow. She tucked it under her cheek and closed her eyes, but the last image she had was not the colorful blooms of the exotic silk. It was the warmth of a pair of vivid blue eyes the color of the summer sky.

CHAPTER NINETEEN

Scotland
June 2011

"What happened to the pinball machine?" Carwyn scowled at the rectangular box that used to light up. He checked the plug, but it still wouldn't turn on.

"Brigid got to it," Tavish said as he lounged in the den in the basement. "Fire vampires. Burn out everything."

"Hey." The fire vampire in question walked past Tavish and knocked the back of his head before she grabbed a book from the pile on the coffee table. "Not my fault it had faulty wiring. And Carwyn, consider it payback for you cheating at cards last night."

Max and Cathy had returned home the night before, happy to see Carwyn. The family had played poker late into the night, Cathy finally throwing up her hands at Max and Carwyn's obvious tricks.

Tavish grunted. "Cathy says she won't play cards with you anymore, Father."

Carwyn only shrugged. "She says that every year."

"Why do you cheat so badly?" Brigid asked.

"He likes cheating. Makes him and Max feel clever."

Brigid rolled her eyes, and Carwyn grinned. "I know that, old man. I just meant, why does he cheat so *badly*? You'd think, after a thousand years, he'd have learned better tricks."

"Oh..." Carwyn chuckled. "I have plenty of good tricks." *You just haven't seen them yet.*

He had been at Castle Mackenzie for two weeks and had found particular enjoyment flustering the usually very controlled Brigid. He could only hope that he was flustering her as much as she was getting to him. She seemed nervous around him. Joking like normal one moment, silent and squirming the next. And he had yet to hear the girl give him a single real laugh, which irked him to no end.

But she looked... mouthwatering. When he'd emerged from the earth, he saw her rushing toward him, fire blazing, eyes lit with protective fury at whatever appeared to be attacking the dog. Then she'd halted in her tracks and given him a rare smile. She had never looked more beautiful. Carwyn's heart actually pounded.

The dark cap of velvet brown hair covered her head, highlighting her pixie features and eerily beautiful eyes. Her body was strong and compact in the tight black T-shirt and leggings she wore as she walked along the lake. He thought she'd been practicing her element, because the smell of smoke still hung in the air. He'd thrown himself into the freezing cold water of the lake before his reaction gave him away.

It was useless fighting his attraction to Brigid Connor. And foolish. If God had placed the right woman in his path after a thousand years, then he wasn't going to argue with providence. Besides, he was having fun ruffling the young woman's very orderly feathers. Brigid was still cautious around him, and Carwyn had to know whether she felt any real attraction for him before he pressed further. He couldn't afford to lose the precious friendship they already shared if she wasn't interested in more.

Carwyn heard Max and Cathy chase each other down the stairs, laughing. They turned the corner and Cathy rushed to Brigid's side.

"Have you shown him yet?"

Brigid looked up in surprise. "Shown who what?"

"The high and mighty father, of course. Have you shown him what you can do?"

"Oh." Carwyn cocked his head. This had the potential to be very interesting. "Shown me what?"

Brigid squirmed, and he resisted the simultaneous urge to comfort and needle her just to provoke a reaction. Sometimes, he really was an overgrown child. He could admit it.

"It's fantastic!" Cathy turned to Carwyn with a grin. "She's a total freak show. And I mean that in the best way possible."

"Hideous American harpy," Tavish muttered. "She's not a trained seal."

"Shut up, you old bag. Brigid does great tricks. And very handy ones, I might add. And I'm curious whether his ancient-ness has ever seen anything like it."

Now Carwyn was just intrigued. "Seen anything like what?"

Cathy grinned and poked at Brigid's arm. "Come on."

"Cathy," Brigid said. "I really don't—"

"Come on, get your lazy ass up to the lake and show him your trick!"

The smoke had already started on Brigid's collar as she curled her lip. "I'm not lazy. Leave me alone. I don't want to—"

"Damn it," Tavish shouted. "She's smoking already. If you burn my den again—"

"It wouldn't be a problem if Brigid would just move her ass!"

The shouting grew as Carwyn looked on. Max, he noticed, had stepped back from the two vampires surrounding Brigid, and Carwyn's senses were starting to go haywire at the smoke drifting through the room. Oak and hawthorne. Brigid and Cathy's elemental natures were quickly making themselves known.

What was Cathy doing? Carwyn could see the heat waves shimmer around Brigid, as if the fire could burst forth at any moment. As the three shouted over each other, the energy in the room only mounted. He stepped forward, hoping to calm them just before Brigid finally burst.

"Will all of you just shut the feck up!" she screamed a moment before a quick burst of fire shot out in all directions. Instead of burning her where she stood, it pulsed away from Brigid, tearing off her clothes in a furious wave that knocked Tavish and Cathy to the ground and left Brigid angry and panting in the middle of the burned circle.

And naked. Rather gloriously and beautifully naked.

"Oh…" His imagination hadn't done her justice.

Carwyn's eyes lingered only a moment before the cloud from the fire extinguisher filled the room from the corner Max had hidden in. Shock gave way to confusion as everyone began talking at once.

Brigid shouted, "I hate it when you two do that!"

"You had to do it in my den, didn't you? You're paying for a new couch if she's ruined this one, too."

"I tried to get her outside; she's just so damn uncooperative."

"I hate all of you! Now will someone hand me a blanket?"

He heard Cathy say, "That was phenomenal, Brigid! You're exhibiting more control even when you let the fire loose. So well done."

"I still hate you."

Max calmly walked over and threw a blanket over Brigid's shoulders, shooting a stream from the extinguisher at a pile of newspapers that were still lit. Luckily—or probably by design—Cathy had drawn Brigid to the most empty space in the room, so not much was burned beyond a small end table, Tavish's eyebrows, and the rug that Brigid had been standing on.

And her clothes. Carwyn was still thinking about the clothes.

He finally shouted over the tumult of voices, "Will someone tell me what the hell that was?"

"For most fire vampires," Cathy said, "the flames are both our greatest weapon and our greatest threat. We control them, to an extent, but the fire can sometimes have a mind of its own. And since fire is one of the few ways vampires can be killed, it can be deadly to the one who wields it. It's why so many of us die when we're first sired. There's no way to predict a vampire turning to fire, so it often causes our death and the death of anyone close to us when we first manifest."

Carwyn nodded as the five sat at the large dining table. Brigid was sitting next to him, sipping a whiskey, still glaring at her teacher. "I know all this, Cathy. One of my best friends in the world is a fire vampire. But that didn't look like anything I've ever seen Gio do before. Or you, for that matter."

Cathy sat back and smiled. "I wondered. I haven't either, but you're a lot older than me."

"I'll ask again—what was that?"

"Brigid's fire *always* moves away from her. She controls it well, but everyone has slips, which are the most dangerous times. Especially when you're young. But when Brigid loses control, it shoots out in a radius around her body. It never seems to turn on her."

Carwyn reached out and put a hand over Brigid's where it lay on the table. "So, it isn't a danger to her?"

Max shook his head. "No. Every time she's lost control, it rolls away from her, almost like an electromagnetic pulse. I think that may even be part of it. She's knocked out numerous pieces of electronic equipment from far away when she lights up."

Brigid muttered, "Well, if you three would stop provoking me in the house—"

"Whatever the cause," Cathy continued, "whether it's her natural defensiveness, her self-control, instinctive shields—whatever it is—it's unique, as far as I know. And good news for her, in the long run, though she still needs practice to learn more control."

Brigid lay her head down on the table, seemingly exhausted. Her eyes were weary when they met his. "One thing," she whispered. "Is it too much to hope that one thing would be like everyone else?"

He leaned down and stroked her hair. "Do you remember the library in Wicklow, love? When you first woke up?"

She shook her head and Carwyn continued, ignoring the curious faces around him as he spoke softly to the tired girl. "It was just as they say. All the furniture had been pushed back against the walls, as if an explosion had gone off. I didn't think about it until now, but I remember. And there you were, right in the middle of the flames, curled up with not a mark on you. No hair, but no burns either."

Brigid reached out a hand and placed it over his heart. "There were burns."

He shook his head. "Not important, remember?"

She closed her eyes and he could almost feel her drooping. "I'm so tired, Carwyn."

He didn't spare a glance for Max, Cathy, or Tavish. He didn't stop to ask. He just stood, scooped Brigid up where she sat, and left the room. He carried her down the hall and toward the tower where he knew she rested, Madoc following them.

Her small voice tore at his heart. "Sometimes I'm tired of being strong."

"So don't be," he said hoarsely. "Just for a little while. We'll do something fun and silly tomorrow night when you wake. Maybe I'll even get you to laugh."

"I know you consider it a personal challenge at this point, but I wouldn't hold your breath."

"I'm a vampire. Don't really need to breathe, do I?"

"So you're just going to wait forever?"

If I have to.

He followed Madoc, who sat waiting by one door. Carwyn pushed it open and looked around the room. Simple. Spartan. A few pictures on the dresser were all the decoration she allowed. One of Brigid and her Aunt Sinead. One of her as a child, sitting next to Ioan in the library. The only art was a poster of a sunset over Loch Torridon, the sky painted vivid red, purple, and gold. It was taped over her bed where she would see it when she woke. He smiled as he laid her down and stroked a hand over her cheek. One hand came up to touch his chest and his heart gave a quick thump under her fingers.

"Going to hell for sure," she murmured.

"What are you talking about?" But before she closed her eyes, he caught it. The look she would never have allowed if she weren't so exhausted: pure, feminine hunger. *Want.* For him. Carwyn almost threw his head back and howled in triumph.

"Nothing. I'm talking about nothing. Let's do something fun tomorrow night, like you said. Even if I don't laugh, you will."

He knelt down and whispered a kiss over her cheek, fighting back the urge to crawl in next to her. "I bet you're gorgeous when you laugh." Brigid opened her mouth to speak, but her eyes fluttered closed again, and she let out a soft sigh before she slipped into sleep.

"Why… why is he tapping out? He could easily get out of that! Oh, it's so obvious that was a set up."

Tavish rolled his eyes. "Of course it was a set up. It's *all* set up. It's professional wrestling."

"Shut up, Tavish," Max said.

Cathy shook her head. "Look at his manager. He's up to something."

Carwyn grunted. "You know he broke up with his girlfriend last month. I wonder if that's thrown him off."

"His girlfriend?" Max asked. "You mean the one who does tag team with the redhead?"

"Yep, that's the one."

"They were dating for months. No wonder he's off his game."

"So ridiculous," muttered Tavish. "You know it's all—"

"*Shut up, Tavish!*"

Cathy, Max, and Carwyn were staring in fascination at the spectacle on the screen. Tavish was reading an agricultural journal and rolling his eyes at his family. Carwyn had woken in the early afternoon and immediately decided to answer Brigid's long-standing suspicion about professional wrestling. It was just the sort of ridiculous escape the girl needed.

The next match was cued up by the excited announcers with the American accents that Cathy imitated to everyone's amusement. The three were watching the main event with such attention that Carwyn barely registered the soft footfalls that entered the room. They paused at the door. Came closer. Then a giggle came from the back of the room. He turned his head.

It was Brigid.

"You…" She snickered. "You really…" Her face fell and she burst into peals of laughter as her eyes darted between the television and the four vampires who sat in front of it.

Carwyn shot to his feet, the fight on the screen forgotten. She was laughing—*really* laughing—and he'd been right; she was glorious.

"You *do* watch it!" She gasped, clutching her stomach. "That's the most… I can't believe you're actually watching it!" She burst into another round of laughter while she wiped bloody tears from her eyes with the edge of her shirt. "I mean, I didn't really believe them when they told me. Why on earth would anyone…" She gasped again and her eyes met his. "A thousand years old? And you— why? It's *so* ridiculous!"

"And fake!" Tavish called out, but he ignored him. Carwyn ignored everyone in the room except for the beautiful woman who laughed in front of him. Brigid's face was lit with a fire within. Joy. She was overflowing with it. Pure, carefree…

"Oh, God," he breathed out. "I love you."

The crowd on the screen erupted in applause, but the laughter died on her face, overtaken by sheer panic. Brigid's mouth dropped open, her eyes widened, her breath caught and held a second before she bolted from the silent room. The front door slammed a moment later.

Carwyn turned to see the shocked faces that were ignoring the final round on the screen.

"I said that out loud, didn't I?"

Max nodded.

Tavish said, "That was far more amusing than professional wrestling."

Cathy only shook her head. "Bit rusty on the wooing skills, aren't we, Father?"

Max finally rose to his feet. "You idiot!" he hissed. "Go after her before she's halfway to Glasgow."

His heart was pounding when he sped from the room.

Smooth, Carwyn. 'A bit rusty' was an understatement.

He slipped off his shoes when he reached the door and stretched out with his senses. He felt a trail of her energy speeding away from the house and toward the dark trees where the deer often took shelter. He grinned and followed her.

"Brigid!"

He tracked her past the tree line. Along a narrow stream. She was fast; he'd give her that. But then, perhaps the shock of his confession had terrified her even more than a raging predator. For a moment, he slowed. Had he truly frightened her? Then he remembered the soft, trusting look in her eye the night before. The hunger. The glorious, long-awaited joy he'd only ever imagined lighting her face. He had to see it again. He *loved* her.

It was so glaringly obvious, he laughed. His possessive behavior around the little shit Murphy. The overwhelming desire for her, when so few women in a thousand years had even tempted him. The ache in his chest when he thought of her strength and determination.

He loved her.

Carwyn found her pacing in a clearing, as if readying for battle. Her head was down, her shoulders stiff, and her hands clenched.

"Brigid?"

She looked at him like a frightened animal caught in a trap.

"Brigid, I'm sorry. That wasn't the way—"

"Is that what you meant?" she shouted. "Something ridiculous? Something to make me laugh?"

He stopped dead in his tracks. "No!"

"Because that ridiculous joke—"

"Was not a joke!" he roared.

She stopped pacing and glared at him. "Of course it was. You can't love me."

He stepped toward her. "Says who?"

Brigid held up a trembling finger. "The pope, for one. And... the church. And I'm fairly sure Father Jacob would have something to say... along with the pope." Her hand fell, but the glare had turned back to panic as he approached her cautiously.

Carwyn tried to smother his smile. "So, I'm not allowed to love you... because it would anger the pope?"

The panic was growing as he drew closer. "Yes! You're a priest."

He lowered his voice to a soothing murmur. "I cheat at poker. And Mario Kart."

"Still a priest."

He came closer, but she backed away. *Slowly. Carefully.* "I watch professional wrestling and use bad language."

She whispered, "Still a priest."

"Let's not even mention the Hawaiian shirts during mass," he whispered.

Brigid swallowed and took a ragged breath. "Carw—"

"I want you," he said roughly as her back met a tree. He pressed closer. "More than I have ever wanted any woman in a thousand years."

Her chest heaved, and she lifted tortured eyes to his. "I can't!"

Carwyn smiled and shook his head. "Silly Brigid. It's not anything you can or can't do. It's me. I love you. You can argue with me, but it doesn't change anything."

He could hear her heart pounding. Smell the rush of her panicked blood.

She whispered, "It changes everything."

"No." He braced his arms on the tree behind her and gave into the desire that had eaten at him for months. He leaned down, letting his lips brush over her forehead. *Soft.* Stroke her temple. *Hot.* Relaxing her inch by inch with his touch. "I love you. That's all."

"You can't love me, Carwyn. You can't. This is… some infatuation."

A low chuckle rumbled from his chest. "Infatuation. Yes." Testing lips nipped at her cheek. The taste of her lingered on his lips, and he licked them. He felt her temperature rise and her amnis tentatively reach toward his. He held back a shudder. "Desire."

Her shoulders relaxed, and her hips shifted slightly toward his.

He put his hand on her cheek. "But it's more than that. And you know it."

Another nip at her chin when she sighed. Her hands came up to rest lightly on his shoulders, and he could feel the pulse of her amnis through his clothes.

"Love, Brigid." He trailed one finger from her collar up her neck, tilting her chin up until their eyes met. She was trembling beneath his touch. "I love you."

"Why?" she whispered.

"Because you're… you."

"Ridiculous man," she murmured a moment before her hands grasped his neck and brought his mouth down to meet hers.

Glorious.

Their mouths met in a bruising, hungry kiss that reached down and filled the aching hollow in the center of his chest. His heart pounded as he drew her closer, fumbling like a schoolboy for a moment before instinct took over. The few dalliances that had tempted him had been nothing like this. Brigid *consumed* him.

He braced his hand against the trunk of the oak as he felt the earth's energy rush up his body to steady him. From his bare feet, up his spine, and down the thick arms that held her.

He had crushed boulders with these arms. Killed immortals older and more powerful than himself. Ripped the earth with his hands and rendered mountains at will. But Carwyn held something precious now, so he coaxed the earth beneath him with a whisper. The ground beneath her rose up, pushing their bodies together as his other hand gripped the small of her back. She pulled away for a minute, her mouth flushed red, but he growled softly and pulled her back.

"Oh," she breathed out. "The earth really *does* move."

He kissed her again, and a low purr left her throat the same time she dug her fingers into the thick muscle at his shoulders. Carwyn felt the burning tips push against his skin and he reveled in the sensation as he pressed her closer.

Mark me.

Brand me.

Claim me.

Brigid's hand tugged at his hair, tilting his neck back before she ran scorching lips down his neck till he felt the sharp point of her fangs slide across his skin. His own fangs grew long in his mouth.

Yes. Yes. Yes!

"I love you," he groaned.

A soft moan answered him. "Oh..." she said. "This is wrong."

He pulled her mouth back to his. "No, it's not."

"Going to hell," she mumbled between kisses.

"They can't have you. You're mine." He nipped at her lower lip, drawing a tiny bead of blood that he licked away and swallowed greedily. "Sweet," he gasped. He sank to his knees in front of her, the taste of her blood rushing to his head like a drug.

More, more, more!

Carwyn wrapped his arms around her hips and pressed his face to her soft breast. "So sweet, Brigid."

Her hands skimmed over his shoulders as he closed his eyes and pressed her closer.

"I love you," he whispered again. "How did I not see it before?"

Her heart was pounding. He could hear it. Her temperature was rising. The aching grew in his chest. His groin. The need for her was roaring through him. Take. Drink. Possess. Carwyn wanted every inch of her. Her body and her heart.

A primal knowledge reared its head. *Mate.* Here was his mate. She was his, and he... he was utterly and completely hers. Their energy crashed together as her hands dug into his neck, and he couldn't stop the slight wince when her skin met his.

She drew her hands back bracing them against the tree, and the bark blackened beneath her palms. Brigid stared at him in horror, and he tried to hold onto her.

"I did it again."

He shook his head. "No, Brigid. Don't. I'm fi—"

"I did it again!" she cried, the tears flooding her eyes. She dashed them away, and her hot fingers sizzled against her own skin. Carwyn tried to grab her hands, but she twisted out of his embrace and sped through the trees.

"Brigid!"

She didn't turn back. Carwyn turned and slumped against the trunk of the scalded oak tree, confused, aching, and alone.

CHAPTER TWENTY

Scotland
July 2011

Brigid tossed the small throwing knife into the air, watching it flip in the low light as she lay in bed and the fire she had started crackled in the grate. Madoc snored by the door as she catalogued her accomplishments for the previous month:

Finally rounded up the sheep faster than the dog. Check.

Learned how to bake bread with Max. Check.

Burned off Tavish's eyebrows. Double check.

Lusted after a priest. Triple check?

Kissed a priest in the most mind-numbingly intense encounter she'd ever had with a man.

Burned a priest while engaged in previously mentioned mind-numbing kissing.

Ran away from priest after kissing and burning.

She should really stop counting checks.

Brigid sighed. Going to hell wasn't even a question anymore.

She squeezed her eyes shut and prayed.

Dear God, I'm not sure if the kissing and the lusting and the burning is a mortal sin. Even worse, I can't really bring myself to feel repentant about the kissing and the lusting bits, so it probably doesn't matter anyway.

I can't, God, because Carwyn saying that he loves me was the most illogical, ridiculous, gorgeous thing that's ever happened in my entire life. And I'm a ragged mess. And I don't deserve a bit of it. I don't really know what to do about it at all, except avoid him like I've been doing for the past week. But...

If any of this is part of some strange plan for me or him or maybe even some future idea of us... please don't let me mess it up.

Or send me to hell if I blow myself up.

Amen.

Brigid sighed and opened her eyes.

He loved her? Stupid man. Stupid, gorgeous, wonderful man. She wanted to cry just thinking about it. The crazy wrestling program. Brigid had never laughed so hard. The memory alone wanted to make her giggle. Then his face and the soft look in his eyes.

"I love you."

And she ran away. Because Carwyn loving her was completely illogical. It had to have been a joke. A prank like the ones he was always pulling. But then, then he ran after her.

He ran after her!

And then he said it again. And again.

And then...

Brigid remembered the shiver of his lips as they stroked along her forehead. Testing. Tasting. Soft and hesitant. His hands had been almost reverent when they touched her the first time. Even a little awkward.

Then... not. Nope. Not awkward at all. Apparently, there were some things one really didn't forget even after a thousand years. Brigid groaned in frustration and threw the knife into the opposite wall, where it stuck.

She was going to hell. And she wasn't walking, she was running, because she felt her fangs descend at the thought of Carwyn's mouth. The earthy spice of his scent when she ran her fangs along his neck. What would his blood taste like? She bit her lip. Carwyn had touched her before. Embraced her even. But the twisting, curling flood of his energy as it poured from his lips and ignited her senses had brought the fire to her skin.

"I want you. More than I have ever wanted any woman in a thousand years."

She pressed her palms to her eyes and tried not to cry in frustration. Nothing about her was worth waiting a thousand years for! She was prickly and defensive. Damaged and carrying more scars inside than the ones she'd branded Carwyn with. She wasn't even all that pretty. Her nose was pinched and her lips were too thin. Her elbows were bony and her eyes—which she had once thought were her best feature—were completely inhuman. Whisky brown that looked like they had charred along the edges. They were a perfect metaphor for everything she had become.

Strange. Unnatural. Frightening.

"You can argue with me, but it doesn't change anything."

Brigid shook her head and pulled the flowered scarf he had given her from beneath her pillow. She draped the bright silk over her eyes and looked up into the brilliant color before she closed them. The memories assaulted her. His lips pressing against hers. Soft, then harder. The power of his amnis when it touched her own in passion. Carefully banked desire held back on a razor-thin leash. His massive hands holding her so gently. The earth itself pushing her into his arms.

"Ridiculous man," she whispered. "Don't you know? It does change everything." Unrequited desire was one thing. But this?

There was a knock at the door.

"Brigid?" It was Cathy. "Tavish and Max took him to town for the night, so you can come out of hiding."

Brigid opened the door with narrowed eyes. "I'm not hiding."

"Of course you are. Let's go down to the lake."

Cathy turned and walked down the hall. Brigid peeked out, but she couldn't hear anyone around the house. There was a television playing in the study and a faint human heartbeat. It was probably Cathy's driver and assistant who was back living on the grounds when they weren't in Edinburgh. Brigid wouldn't feed from him, but her fangs descended automatically at the smell.

"Cathy," she called. "I'm going to grab some dinner before we start practice."

"No, you're not!" She heard a faint reply. "Hunger is part of what we're doing tonight, so don't eat."

"Heinous cow…" Brigid muttered, stomping out the front door before she sped down to the lake, the dog racing after her. Cathy was already waiting, and Max was with her.

Brigid halted. "I thought you said they were gone!"

Max smiled. "I sent them a bit ahead. I'll follow in just a minute, but we needed to give a demonstration first."

"What?" Brigid asked. Max was a great friend, but he never helped with her lessons. He was an earth vampire.

An earth vampire who reached over, grabbed his wife, and started kissing her very enthusiastically. Right in front of Brigid.

"Well then…" She cleared her throat and said, "Do I really need to be here for this?"

Cathy finally broke away from Max's mouth and grinned. "Yes, you do. And more importantly, Max had to be here for this."

Max gave Cathy one last kiss, then strode over with a smile. He held up his hands and said, "You don't have to say anything. I just want you to look." He stood in front of Brigid and turned his neck to the side. Brigid wanted to look away in embarrassment, but her curiosity overwhelmed the awkwardness when Max loosened his collar and spread it for her eyes. "Just look, Brigid."

There was a slight reddening where Cathy's fingers had been holding him, but no burns. As passionate as she knew their relationship was, Max bore no visible scars from his lover. Brigid didn't say anything, just turned her face away and nodded. Max walked back to Cathy gave her a quick kiss before he sped over the hills and out of sight.

Cathy said, "Being a fire vampire is tough. We have to have mountains of self-control. We're always seen as a threat, and we're targeted because of it."

"I know."

"Some of us—" She stepped closer. "—spend our whole lives alone."

Cathy didn't talk about her past. Brigid knew she was far older than Max, but didn't know by how much.

"Hundreds of years… an eternity." Then she smiled. "But sometimes, we find the right person."

The longing almost overwhelmed her. "I'm happy for you, Cathy. For you and Max, both."

"Being a fire vampire doesn't mean that you're going to hurt anyone you get close to. Don't use it as an excuse to run away."

Brigid stiffened and turned away. "I appreciate the useful information. Please thank Max as well. Now, I'm going to go to the kitchen and get some—"

"You hurt him more by running than you did by burning him."

Brigid spun around and hissed, "That's none of your business."

"Yes, it is."

"No, it's not." She turned back toward the castle, but Cathy intercepted her and tugged on her arm. Brigid immediately sent out a quick burst of energy, which caused Cathy to stumble back.

"Will you stop?" she yelled. "You bet it's my business! Carwyn is part of my family. He's my husband's sire, and he's also a friend."

She just kept walking.

"What are you afraid of?" Cathy yelled.

Brigid spun around. "Everything! Don't you understand that?"

Cathy frowned. "But I just showed you—"

"I'm a mess, Cathy!" Brigid walked toward her slowly with her arms spread out. "A horrible, destructive, damaged mess. Before I was a vampire, I had to take drugs just to let a man touch me. My anxiety may be gone, but now…" Brigid stopped and drew in a ragged breath, determined not to cry. "I hurt everything I touch. Not just physically.

"It doesn't have to be that way!"

"I'm a mess," she continued. "And he's a priest. I shouldn't even allow myself to think about him that way because he's so… so good. And I'm not. I don't know what he thinks he sees in me, but—"

"Shut up!" Cathy glared. "Just shut up. Don't insult yourself and him by finishing that sentence." The taller woman paused, then looked out over the lake until she turned back to Brigid. "I understand that you have problems, Brigid. Both of you. And I may not believe the same things that Carwyn does regarding God and the church, but I respect that he does. And it's something he's dedicated a thousand years to. Think about *that* before you dismiss his feelings, because it's not a step he would have taken lightly."

Brigid swallowed the lump in her throat. "I know."

Cathy's eyes softened. "Don't lose something precious because the timing doesn't seem right. I almost did and it would have killed me. You have time, Brigid. Time to mess up and make up. Time to figure things out. Together." Suddenly, Cathy laughed. "Remember, when it comes to relationships, he's probably just as clueless as you are!"

"That's both comforting and offensive at the same time," she muttered.

"Take your time, but don't throw it away, Brigid. You'll regret it forever."

Time. Brigid took a deep breath and relaxed. She kept forgetting how much time she had. An eternity of it now, if she wanted.

"Thank you."

"You're welcome."

"And thank Max, too."

"Oh, he doesn't mind. He likes showing off his scars, too."

Brigid's eyes widened. "I thought you said—"

"You don't *have* to hurt your lover." Cathy gave a wicked grin. "Doesn't mean they might not want you to."

Brigid shook her head. "Speaking of things I didn't need to know."

Cathy laughed. "Also, a warning. Never underestimate the possessive streak we all carry. Fire vampires tend to be worse than others. I'm not saying it's a bad thing. It's just a reality, so don't forget it."

Brigid thought about her reaction to seeing the scars she's put on Carwyn's body. Horror. Guilt. Sorrow. Then... desire. Possession.

Mine.

Her thoughts must have shown on her face because Cathy burst into laughter. "I knew it," she said. "You can argue as much as you want, but you're so done for. Totally nuts about him."

"Shut up, Cathy."

When the other vampire finally stopped laughing, she said, "And don't forget, showers are your friends. And baths. When you really want to let loose, that's probably your best option. Especially when you're young."

"I get the idea."

"Once you get in the throes—"

"Please." Brigid winced. "Please stop now."

"I've heard Carwyn is very fond of the beach. Just thought I'd mention that."

Brigid just groaned and covered her face.

"Hey, the guy hasn't been laid in a thousand years. It's about time."

"I'm going to go curl up in my room and die now."

"Whatever, Guilt-Girl. This is why you should be an atheist."

Brigid just shook her head and kept walking.

"Hey, Brigid?" Cathy called behind her. "Tell me, did the earth move? Because, you know, it can! Having sex outside takes on a whole new dimension when you're with an earth vampire. Just another thing I wanted to mention."

"Shut up, Cathy!"

Carwyn stared into his beer. "Who knew that the most effective way of keeping modern women away was to tell them you were in love with them?"

He let the sounds of the pub wash over him, ignoring the football game in the background, ignoring the chattering of his two sons, and ignoring the persistent ache in his chest that pulled his thoughts back toward the castle and Brigid.

Brigid, who had avoided him for almost seven days.

Carwyn knew that, superficially, he was a handsome man. He'd always drawn female attention, whether he wanted it or not. And he loved women. He loved the layers of them. Loved the tangles and hidden corners of their minds and hearts. He'd loved the many female friends he'd had over the centuries. And he'd certainly never complained about the sight of a beautiful girl. Women were the crown of God's creation. Ignoring their beauty was akin to sacrilege. And more than one had taken a fancy to him over the centuries; some he indulged more than others. Harmless flirtation had been a game to him. Though many had tried to take it further, he'd pushed them away with a gentle nudge.

Who knew that a declaration of love was the surest deterrent?

"Oh, Brigid," he groaned quietly. A thousand years old and he felt clueless as a boy. The woman might be the death of him. He ached for her. Dreamed about her.

"You're pathetic," Tavish said.

He sighed. "I know."

"Why are you down here at the pub?"

"Because you and Max insisted I give her some space."

Tavish shrugged. "Well, we were wrong. Go get your woman, Father."

Carwyn frowned. "Why are you suddenly so eager to see me leave?"

"Because you're sighing into your beer and ruining the match. You're pathetic. Go convince her she's not going to hell for kissing you, then live happily ever after or something. But stop sighing into your beer."

Max slid next to him and set down another pint. "And stop being pathetic."

"Wonderful children, both of you. Such support and love. And why does Brigid think she's going to hell for kissing me?"

Tavish rolled his eyes, clearly disgusted. "Very, very dumb bull."

Max laughed at his brother, then turned to Carwyn and lowered his voice in the quiet corner of the pub where they were sitting. "Carwyn, are you forgetting who she is? You're not dealing with an immortal of age and perspective. She's young. And yes, Brigid knows when you were human priests often married and had families. Yes, she knows that you are a thousand-year-old earth vampire who doesn't often abide by the orthodoxies of your faith. I'd even say she loves you, too. But she's also an Irish Catholic who has seen you wearing a collar. Of course she has reservations."

Carwyn sat, blinking in surprise. "You think she loves me, too?"

Tavish snarled. "Pathetic! Go away. Maybe you should take up writing sonnets in your spare time."

Max shook his head, smiling. "Tavish was right about one thing. This is going to be more entertaining than wrestling."

An hour before dawn, Carwyn was still mulling over what Max had said as he wandered back to the castle. He cut through the woods where he had kissed Brigid.

Oh, that kiss.

Too much and not enough. Kissing Brigid had been like pressing his lips to bottled fire. Her passion was a revelation. As he passed by the clearing, he caught her scent and approached quietly, resisting the urge to pounce.

She was standing in front of the tree where he'd cornered her. She had her hand pressed against the black outline she'd left in the trunk of the oak and wore a concentrated frown. He stood behind some thick brush and watched her for a minute.

"I know you're there, Carwyn."

He smiled and stepped into the clearing. "Of course you do."

"Besides, the rather powerful feel of your amnis, you're not very stealthy when you move above ground."

Carwyn leaned against a tree, careful to keep his distance. He ached for her, but he wanted to talk to her more. "I'll keep that in mind. How are you?"

She finally looked at him and the corner of her mouth turned up. "Complicated."

"Good. I hate being bored."

A sad uncertainty came into her eyes. "Carwyn, I just don't know what you expect from—"

"Do you really think you're going to hell because I kissed you? Is it the collar? Is that why you ran away?"

The sadness turned stricken, and her mouth gaped open in shock. Then Brigid turned heel and ran.

His head fell back against the tree and he groaned. "You've really got to stop doing that, love."

Carwyn took off after her, his long strides eating up the distance between them. He tackled her just before she reached the castle; then he picked her up, kicked open the door, and carried her toward the basement living room.

"You bastard, put me down!" She beat on his back as they walked down the stairs, but he didn't release her. If she really wanted to be let down, all she'd have to do was—

"Bloody hell!" he yelped when she pulled up the back of his shirt and lay two burning hands on the small of his back. He dropped her immediately, but luckily, they were already in the den. "That hurts, Brigid!"

"I told you to put me down, you big brute! Next time, listen to me."

"Is it so wrong that I want to talk to you and not worry about you running away?"

She opened her mouth to speak, but no words came out. Carwyn just stood, staring at her, blocking the door, and waiting.

Finally, she blurted out, "I had a crush on you when I was sixteen!"

He smothered a smile. "You did?" Well that was... completely adorable. He tried to remember what she had looked like when she was sixteen.

"It was *ridiculous*. I'd built you up in my mind like some kind of knight who had rescued me from the dragon. And—and you were so handsome, and I just... I had a massive crush on you. But then, you came to visit Ioan once, and you had just come from some meeting in Dublin with the bishop, and you had on your collar and your jacket and you just looked so... so *holy*."

Carwyn stood, actually rendered speechless. Which was an accomplishment, he had to admit. Brigid was still rambling.

"And I felt so guilty. So, *so* guilty. I went and confessed to Father Jacob. I told him... well, not everything, of course, but he knew you were a priest. And that I had lustful thoughts toward you and that—"

"You had lustful thoughts?" That was promising.

She glared at him. "I did a lot of penance! I actually added to what he gave me because it didn't really seem like enough. So, to answer your question, *yes*. I know it's not entirely logical, but a very deep 'raised by my aunt' part of me feels like I am absolutely going to hell for kissing you and enjoying it so damn much that it's almost all I can think of. And I want to do it again. A lot. And..."

She trailed off, a dazed look in her eye. Then she fell to the floor in a dead heap. Carwyn's heart gave a leap as he sped over to catch her. "Brigid?"

He looked at the clock. Sunrise. Damn. That had to be the most inconvenient interrupted conversation that he'd ever been a part of. Still, he smiled as he looked into her peaceful face. Then he grinned.

"You enjoyed it? A lot? I'll be hearing more about that very soon." He lifted her up and took her to the couch. "I want to kiss you again, but it seems a bit wrong when you're asleep. I can be patient." He settled down on the couch and tucked her into his side, making sure her head was tilted so that he could look at her. "And yes, I know this is somewhat creepy, but

I'll fall asleep soon, too. So you don't have to worry about me staring at you all day."

Brigid didn't say a word. She was sleeping the sleep of the newly immortal. At times it was hard to remember that she was so young. But she was. He ran soft fingers through her cap of dark hair. She was young in some ways, but perhaps even older than he was in others. She had suffered. She had fought. His Brigid had conquered demons and beaten back fire. She was remarkable.

"It's no wonder that I love you so much, Brigid Connor. Now, I just have to convince you that all of this is God's plan." He kissed her forehead and leaned back, closing his eyes. "We're meant, love. You'll see."

Brigid woke slowly. There was a luscious scent in her nose and the comforting smell of a warm fire. She could hear Madoc's snores in the background. Her pillow was warm and firm beneath her cheek. It rose in a comforting breath as she opened her eyes.

Not a pillow.

She froze when she came to and her face was nestled in the crook of Carwyn's shoulder. His arm was draped around her shoulders and his fingers trailed lightly along her wrist. He took deep steady breaths as her eyes closed again.

Brigid was resting with him. And she didn't feel uncomfortable; it felt… right. It was Carwyn. And she knew without a doubt that he would sooner tear off his own arm than see any harm come to her while she slept. He must have known she was awake because his breathing changed slightly and a low heartbeat sounded beneath her ear as it lay on his chest.

"Carwyn?" she whispered.

He spoke in a soft voice when he answered. "Yes, love?"

She kept her eyes closed, trying to hold on to the peace of the moment. "Did I sleep here all day?"

"Mmmhmm."

"Sorry I fell asleep."

"Don't worry about it. It's natural. Your body needed the rest."

They fell silent again, and the only sound was the soft tick of the clock on the wall. What had they been talking about when she fell asleep? Oh, God. Her pathetic schoolgirl crush… When she remembered, she tried to pull away, but his arm tightened around her, holding her in place.

"I've been thinking," he said in a soft voice.

"About my embarrassing confession?"

"No. Well, yes, but I don't consider it embarrassing. I'm quite flattered, really."

"Of course you are. And I'm going to die of embarrassment now."

"No embarrassment." He leaned over and kissed the top of her head. She felt the current of it spread over her skin. Past her shoulders. Straight down to her…

"I am definitely going to hell."

She felt, rather than heard, the low chuckle. "Now who's being silly?" Carwyn paused, but didn't stop stroking the inside of her wrist. It was hypnotic. She wanted to curl into his lap and stay forever. "I don't want to talk about my collar, or your problems. I'm not denying them. I'm just not interested in all the marks against us tonight." His fingers left her wrist to tilt up her chin so their eyes met.

"What do you want from me, Carwyn?"

"Many things." A lazy smile spread over his face. "But tonight, I want to hold you, and kiss you, and tell you that I love you as often as I like. And you're not going to run away—"

"But—"

"Or argue." He pressed a finger to her lips before he traced around them with care. Brigid's skin was on fire. "Shhh," he soothed her. "I'm not asking you to say anything. Or do anything. Just… let me love you for a bit like I want. Please, Brigid?"

His blue eyes burned into hers, her heart gave a quick lurch, and she fell. Utterly and completely.

But she couldn't say the words. Couldn't say them when he thought it might be in thanks or out of obligation. So she knit their fingers together and lifted her face to kiss his lips.

Oh, it was *sweet*. Achingly slow and gentle. One hand pressed against his chest and she felt the sure, steady heart give a solitary thump. Slowly, as if he was trying not to startle her, Carwyn pulled her onto his lap so they were face-to-face. One hand rested lightly at her waist, and the other made a slow, soothing circuit up and down her back, occasionally stopping to play along her neck and the fine, dark hair that covered the nape.

She melted into his arms as he made love to her mouth, interspersing light kisses with teasing bites.

"I love you," he whispered. "I've waited so long for you, Brigid."

It made her ache. *Why me?*

As if he could hear her thoughts, he whispered again, "I love your strong heart. I love your mind and your passion. When you fall in love with me, you're going to love me madly. Completely. Because that's who you are."

I do! She almost cried as he kissed her.

"I should also point out that I'm extremely fond of your mouth at the moment."

She smiled against his lips. How could he do it? How could he make her heart bleed and laugh at the same time? How could she ever be his equal?

"Carwyn, I…"

He pulled back slightly. "What?"

I love you, and I'm so hopelessly incapable of being who you need me to be. "I… don't know what to say."

He smiled at her. That teasing smile that made her insides melt. "Then don't say anything." He kissed her again. "I love you. That's all. I love you."

There was nothing to say. Nothing. So Brigid gave herself fully over to his kiss. To the comfort and strength of his arms. And she loved him.

They spent hours in the den. Kissing. Laughing quietly. And she lost count of how many times Carwyn told her he loved her. That she was beautiful. That she was a treasure. It was as if he were making up for a thousand years of loneliness and filling her to the brim with tenderness all at the same time. She was heady with it, and grateful that he made no other move than to tuck her more firmly into his side or nestle her head against his chest.

"Carwyn?" she whispered to him hours later.

"Yes, love?"

"Can I ask you to do something for me?"

"Of course."

"When Anne gets back next month... When she comes back, I need you to leave again."

His arms tightened around her and his voice was hoarse when he said, "Why?"

She steeled her resolve and picked her head up. "You know why."

His brows furrowed together and he placed a hand on her cheek. "I want to help you."

"But you know there are some things I have to do myself. You know this."

She could see the resignation on his face, but his eyes still argued with her.

Brigid said, "I need to make myself better. For me. For you. For my future. I need to work on myself, so I'm not such a mess. So I can be good for you." She saw him begin to argue, so she put a quick hand to his lips. "And for me. I have this new life stretched in front of me and a pit of human problems I need to sort out. I need to not worry that I'm going to hurt you in the process. So, what I'm asking for..." She leaned forward and placed soft lips over his heart. "Is time. If you love me, please give me time. We have it. An eternity of it, if you want. I'm only asking for a few months."

He tilted her chin up so their eyes met. "Months?"

"I'll be back in Dublin in January. Give me till then?"

"If you give me this month. Till Anne gets back in August, give me this month with you?"

She smiled. "If you're willing to risk the fire."

A fierce light flared in his eyes, and he grasped her around the waist, pulling her hard against his body as his mouth descended on hers. A keen edge came to his lips as they pressed against her own and a soft whimper escaped her throat as her temperature soared. Carwyn pulled back, panting, and placed his forehead against her own.

He whispered, "Love is as strong as fire."

Building From Ashes

Book Three: The Seal

Place me like a seal over your heart,
like a seal on your arm;
for love is as strong as death,
its jealousy unyeilding as the grave.
It burns like a blazing fire,
like a mighty flame.

Song of Solomon 8:6

Building From Ashes

CHAPTER TWENTY-ONE

Dublin
March 2012

The news from Murphy was world-changing.

"We don't know its name, but it is a drug targeted at immortals. We're still learning more, but this could change everything if it does what it seems. I'm on the phone with every contact I have, but keep your ears tuned. I want to know what you're hearing on the street. In the clubs. Everywhere that vampires gather." Murphy's voice was grim as he addressed the group. Tom, Declan, Jack, and Brigid were gathered in his office, having been called into a surprise visit as soon as they'd all arrived at the office that evening. None of the humans—not even Angie—were present.

Tom's voice was quiet and calm. "What does it do, Murphy? What are the effects?"

"It seems to quell bloodlust."

Brigid could see Declan sit up straight. "What, completely?" he asked.

"According to reports."

Jack's eyes narrowed. "What else?"

Declan said, "What else does there need to be?"

"There's something else," Brigid murmured. "There's always something else." A drug that would kill bloodlust and allow her to live more normally? As much as she liked the taste of human blood, a cure was ferociously attractive. Even as she'd gained control, it was a constant battle. A gust of wind passing by a human's warm neck and she was right back to the mindless hunger of a newborn; even if she reined it in, it was there. Always. Calling her. Making her blood boil and her fangs drop. The idea of not feeling that hunger again was more seductive than the blissful oblivion heroin once provided.

Murphy said, "We're not sure what else it does. It's something that's given to humans. Puts them in amazing health, from all reports. A kind of miracle cure. Heals wounds. Cures disease. And once a human takes it, the vampire feeds from them."

Tom said, "And then?"

"Reports are saying that the vampire has no hunger but the human kind. Normal food and liquid intake. There's an increase in elemental power. Surge of strength—"

"Forget battling it," Declan said. "How can we import it?"

Tom's voice was a warning. "Declan…"

"Come on!" The usually pragmatic immortal's voice hummed with excitement. "Murphy, this is an *opportunity*. This isn't like the self-destructive shit that humans take. This doesn't sound like a drug at all. It sounds like the answer to a bloody problem."

"Literally," Jack said.

"The problem"—Murphy held up a hand—"is that the source of this drug is a ninth century manuscript that Lorenzo stole. We all know Lorenzo. We're not talking about a humanitarian, gentlemen. If he wants it, there's another side to the story."

The four men began arguing, but Brigid sat back in her chair and let her mind drift.

So, this was the book that Carwyn had told her about. The book his friends, Giovanni Vecchio and Beatrice De Novo, had lost. Carwyn's old enemy, Lorenzo, had stolen it. Killed innocents for it. And it contained the formula for the drug that Ioan had wondered about. A drug that could affect immortals. Change them. But how? Brigid had to agree with Murphy; there was another side to this story.

Murphy was still talking. "I'm talking about pragmatism, boys. I'm talking about looking out for the greater good and not letting our enthusiasm run away with us. The bastard killed the most respected vampire in Ireland to get information about this drug. And the reports I'm getting—"

"What are these reports you keep talking about?" Brigid broke in quietly, and the whole room turned to her with guarded eyes. "Where are you getting them? What's the source of the information, Murphy? Can we trust it?"

A quick glance between Murphy and Tom roused her suspicions. "I received a call from Deirdre earlier this afternoon."

"Deirdre?" Her sire. Why was Deirdre calling Murphy instead of her?

They'd come to an uneasy truce, her immortal mother and herself. Yes, Deirdre had sired Brigid without her consent, but with Anne's help and the gift of time and distance, Brigid had found peace about her new life. She hadn't wanted to die and was grateful that Deirdre had saved her. She had things to look forward to now. She had friends. A future. She had—

"Carwyn has been in Wicklow looking through the remains of Ioan's library with Deirdre. Apparently, there are missing papers regarding blood research, but he has no idea what is gone."

Carwyn? Brigid's brain locked up.

"Carwyn ap Bryn?" Declan asked with evident respect. "The priest? I thought he'd gone back to Wales. He's here?"

Carwyn was in Ireland? But...

Murphy's eyes darted toward hers. "Yes, he's been here for a number of months now. In Wicklow with his family."

And not with her. Brigid quashed the rush of heat that tried to overtake her. The fire simmered just under her skin, prickling and dancing as she inwardly fumed.

He was in Wicklow?

Three months she'd been in Dublin. The first month, she settled, knowing that he had been spending the Christmas holidays in South America with family and friends. He'd told her before he left in August that he'd be gone. That he'd be back. How could he not? After their month together, the perfect month they'd spent talking and laughing. Kissing like sweethearts and holding hands. He'd never pushed her. He said that he could be patient. That she was worth the wait. There was still so much to work out. But they had time, he said. And she agreed.

But she'd missed him when he didn't show up the first month. Then the second month came and there was no word. Then the third. And Brigid didn't know what to think.

She slid back into work as if she had never been gone, the only difference being hours and the set of hands that Murphy had hired for her. The 'hands' were named Sara and belonged to a very nice human girl whose parents, like Emily's, had worked for Murphy since she was born. She was a quick, no-nonsense twenty-four-year-old Trinity graduate who did her work efficiently and seemed completely unimpressed with Jack's flirtations.

Brigid had liked her almost immediately.

Seven months had passed with no sign of him, and a crack had formed in the delicate trust they'd built. Brigid blinked and tried to focus on what Murphy was saying.

"Until we know more about this drug, about its effects and the long-term ramifications, I want all of you to be very, very careful. We know he intends to produce it, but we don't know where. We don't know if it's even detectable in humans, so be very careful whom you drink from. And if you see any of the usual humans who like being bitten seem to have a surge in health or activity, beware. Our first priority is still finding local connections Lorenzo might have used when he was distributing heroin here. Logic says that he'll use the same connections with this new drug as the old, so keep up with your investigations. Now that Brigid is back"— He grinned and winked at her—"those who kick up a fuss have more incentive to cooperate."

"Just call me Miss Incentive," Brigid muttered and snapped her fingers, immediately tossing the two glowing balls of red fire in her hands.

"Jesus, Connor, don't scare the lads." Tom chuckled as Jack inched away from her and Declan's eyes darted away.

Oh yes, they were all scared of her now. Tom and Murphy not as much as the rest. Part of her reveled in it, loving the power. The other part missed the easy acceptance she'd become accustomed to in Scotland. Normal immortal society had a very different attitude toward fire vampires than the Mackenzie clan. She was feared. Always set just a bit apart. Even with Deirdre, she could see the hint of caution every time they spoke.

She missed Cathy. Missed Anne, who was back in Galway. Missed Max and his easy manner. She even missed Tavish's gruff bossiness. He'd never feared her, even when she singed his eyebrows off for the fourth time.

And, oh, she missed Carwyn.

She ignored the ache in her chest as Murphy finished the meeting. She was tucking her notes into her messenger bag when she heard her boss's voice.

"Brigid? A word before you leave?"

"Sure thing."

Unlike Carwyn, Murphy had been making his interest in her more than clear. He sent her flowers when she'd moved into her new house in Ringsend. Had arranged movers for her things, which had laid untouched in her apartment in his building the entire year and a half she'd been away. He'd never let anyone into her space. He'd asked her for a drink. Then dinner. He'd asked her to concerts and clubs. He was polite, but friendly. He seemed to take nothing for granted.

So far, she'd been able to resist. But Patrick Murphy was like a modern day James Bond, with more class and a meaner right hook. If Brigid started to get hungry, he was there to escort her to the kitchen or the donor rooms where some humans in Murphy's employ offered their blood in exchange for a bump in salary.

If she was looking for a file on Angie's desk, he was there a moment before her, offering it with a smile.

Handkerchief? He had one tucked in his front pocket.

Cup of tea? He knew exactly how much milk she liked.

Brigid had the feeling if she asked for a breath mint, he'd have a tin of them in his perfectly pressed suit. She was glaring at his suit pocket in suspicion as he approached.

"Brigid?"

She blinked and looked up. Oh yes, he'd wanted a word. And probably not about breath mints.

"Yes?"

He hesitated, and it was such an unusual expression on him that Brigid stood up. "What's up, Murphy?"

He grinned, disarming her with his smile and that damn dimple. "Will you ever call me Patrick?"

"Not at work."

He cocked an eyebrow. "So, how about after work?" He stepped a bit closer. "I have theater tickets for tomorrow evening. I'd love to take you."

She kept turning him down. Politely. He was more than attractive, but she'd considered herself... well, if not committed, then at least... unavailable? But Carwyn had been in Wicklow three months. Three months, and he hadn't even called her.

Brigid stuttered. "I—I don't know, Murphy."

Sensing an opening, he stepped closer. "It's a wonderful play, and I have the extra ticket. The seat would just be empty if you didn't join me."

She scoffed, thinking of the scores of willing women who made themselves available to the immortal ruler of Dublin at any time of his choosing. "I don't think you'd have trouble finding someone to fill the seat."

He stepped even closer, and she could feel the heat rise on her body. He smelled amazing. Cool and crisp like the ocean. "I don't want just anyone to fill the seat, Brigid. I want you." She forced herself to raise her eyes, despite the rush of blood that started in her veins and the instinct to escape. "I've been trying to make that clear."

"I don't think—"

"Surely you can see what a match we'd make, Brigid. With our power and connections combined, we'd be unstoppable. And I've always—*always*—found you very attractive."

Her heart was pounding now. "Murphy—"

"Patrick." He cut her off and leaned down slowly. Brigid gulped nervously. He was going to kiss her. She should stop it. It wasn't right. She closed her eyes and Carwyn's face floated in her mind. There had to be an explanation. He wouldn't have just—

"Stop," she whispered, putting a hand to Murphy's chest. The suit was crisp under her fingers, and he halted immediately. His eyes ducked down to meet hers. "I can't."

"Why, Brigid? Is it the priest?" Murphy whispered. "Is there something between you? I thought when he came to see me last year, but... He's been back in the country for months, and he hasn't been to town. I'd know if he had. So what's stopping you?"

"I—I don't know. It's not that I don't find you attractive, Patrick. You know I do, but—"

"But what?"

"Carwyn—" She broke off when she heard the crack of Murphy's office door as it slammed open. "Is here." Brigid groaned. "Of *all* the moments to show up..."

Carwyn rushed into the room. In the blink of an eye, the enraged immortal had Murphy lifted in a chokehold and pushed against the far wall. Murphy was powerful, but nothing compared to Carwyn. At over a thousand years, the Welsh vampire had the strength of a mountain. A mountain that was currently furious. His amnis whipped over his body. She could feel it pulse in the air. Angie's voice rose out in the hallway and she heard the rush of feet as Murphy's men ran toward their leader. Her mind raced. This could end very badly.

Brigid yelled, "Carwyn, stop!"

He snarled and did not release the vampire. Murphy's feet dangled in the air, but he hung still, staring into Carwyn's face with a kind of detached calm. Brigid pulled at his shoulder, but she might as well have pushed against a cliff, for all the good it did.

Brigid whirled to the door, where Tom, Declan, and Jack were poised and ready to strike.

She brought flames to her hands and her eyes burned. "Stop! Everyone, just stop right now!"

Finally, Carwyn growled, "Your heart. I heard your heart racing. Who scared you? What did he do?"

She took a deep breath. "I wasn't scared, Carwyn."

"But—"

"It wasn't fear that made my heart race."

Carwyn's eyes flickered toward hers for a minute, confused. Slowly, he set Murphy on his feet, not releasing his neck. Nevertheless, Murphy glanced over at Tom and nodded toward the door; Brigid heard the three vampires slowly back away.

"Father, if you could release my neck, I'd be most appreciative," Murphy spoke evenly, and Brigid could tell he was carefully restraining his ire. Murphy was being smart, but she could tell he was furious. He glared at Carwyn, but the earth immortal didn't spare him a glance. He only had eyes for Brigid.

She stood silently, meeting his glare without fear. Finally, Carwyn released Murphy and walked toward her.

"Not fear?" he growled around his fangs. He looked brutal. Feral and wild in a way she had never seen before. Her temperature spiked, but she tried to keep her voice steady and her eyes on him.

"Murphy was not threatening me."

His eyes narrowed. "Not fear?"

His head ducked down to her neck, inhaling a deep breath, testing her scent. Whatever was there made him growl even lower and she caught a glimpse of his fangs. Long, thick. Shining in his mouth like blades. Carwyn's head whipped around to Murphy's and he snarled at him in Welsh. She didn't catch it; she'd never understood the language, despite the lessons Ioan had tried to give her.

Carwyn ducked down as if to kiss her, but pulled away with a blistering anger in his eyes. Murphy stepped toward them and Carwyn's hand shot out, grabbed Murphy by the throat again and threw him across the room before he stormed away.

Brigid was still holding her breath when Murphy walked toward her, dusting plaster from his shoulders where he'd slammed into a wall. The look in his eyes was amused. "So, nothing going on there, I take it."

She gulped. "Murphy—"

"Do me a small favor and go after him, Brigid. I'd prefer not to do further repairs to my city if at all possible."

"Sorry about that," she muttered before she sped from the room.

Well, that certainly wasn't how she'd imagined their reunion.

Carwyn had growled at the Dubliner like an animal.

'My woman.'

Brigid hadn't understood him, but Murphy sure as hell spoke Welsh.

Rage simmered under the surface as he walked along the river, breathing deeply. He tucked his scarf more securely around his neck as his breath fogged in the cool night. It was midnight. He had gone to Murphy's office directly after his meeting with the bishop, which was his first stop in town. There were few humans in sight as he crossed the bridge and headed back to his resting place. It was on the edge of one of the seedier parts of town, an old warehouse that Ioan had used at times for clinics. But it had comfortable, secure quarters hidden in it, as well. He'd planned on being in town for some time to see Brigid.

He'd missed her. He'd ached for her.

"It wasn't fear that made my heart race."

Not fear. Murphy. The little shit had taken his opportunity. Carwyn kept forgetting how young she was. Three months seemed like nothing to him, but it probably seemed an eternity to her. He should have called. He should have come sooner.

But three *fecking* months?

Was their connection really that inconsequential to her?

He heard footsteps running after him.

"Carwyn!"

It was Brigid, and he was still angry. In fact, the more he thought about it, the angrier he became. Fecking Murphy. Not fear. Murphy had been about to kiss his Brigid, and her heart was racing in *excitement*. The fact that the Dubliner still lived was gift enough. He didn't need to hear her excuses.

"Carwyn, stop, damn you!"

He kept walking, turning the corner into the alley behind the warehouse.

"Who's running now, you big brute?"

Fine.

Carwyn's eyes narrowed as he spun around. Brigid almost crashed into his chest. His hands caught her, steadying her shoulders as she swayed. She was such a tiny thing. Tiny and furious.

And beautiful. It rushed over him then, the longing for her that had driven him in Wicklow. Driven him to find the answers that would keep her safe. Keep them all safe. But he had lost her in the process.

"Three months?" he said roughly, grabbing at the back of her neck so she was forced to look into his eyes. He pushed them up against a wall, blocking her in and cushioning her head so it didn't touch the grimy stone. "Three months and I lose you? Three months was too long to wait?"

"Carwyn, you need to listen—"

He cut her off with a furious kiss, groaning into her mouth when she pulled him closer. He'd been so careful with her in Scotland, patient to the point of pain, but he didn't hold back now. It might be the last time he kissed her.

Carwyn dove into the kiss with abandon. Her mouth parted and her burning tongue met his own. She clutched him closer, digging into his back as he shoved a knee between her legs, pulling her into his aching body. She was burning up. Anger? Desire? He didn't care.

Her hands reached up to tug at his hair and he lifted her against the wall. He reached down to the curve of her hips, back, around to the soft swell of her bottom. His hands cupped, pressing the aching length of his arousal against her heat.

"Oh, God!" she cried out as he continued the assault with his lips. Tongue. His fangs ached in his jaw and he let the length of them run along the satin skin of her neck. A low rumble built in his chest as his amnis reached out to her, twining around her limbs, begging him to sink his fangs into her body and claim her.

Mine.

Not Murphy's. His.

My mate. Mine.

Forget Murphy. He'd waited a thousand years for her and no one would love her as well as he would. Brigid was his.

He finally tore his mouth away and looked at her. She was panting. Her eyes were clouded with lust and her skin was steaming in the misty night air.

"Did you sleep with him?"

Her eyes cleared and blinked at him in confusion. Then righteous anger. "What?"

Oh… He'd misread that one, hadn't he?

He ducked away as Brigid swung at him.

"You ass! You think I slept with Murphy?" She shoved him back, her anger instantly killing his arousal, as he set her back on the ground.

Well, almost instantly.

She took a step forward and he backed away. "I didn't even kiss him, you idiot! I was waiting for *you*! Where the hell have you been?"

"I've been in Wicklow. There's been a bit going on, if you hadn't heard."

"I know that. You couldn't even call?"

"You're the one who sent me away in the first place! You wanted time; I was giving you time."

"I've been back for three months."

"Three months?" He ran his hands through his hair in frustration. "Three months is nothing, Brigid."

"It is to me," she hissed. "Some of us aren't a thousand years old."

He rolled his eyes. "Well, *that* much is obvious."

"Are you implying that I'm being immature?" Her eyes narrowed. Carwyn had a feeling he needed to tread carefully.

"No... maybe a little? If you think about things from my perspective, you're really quite young."

Wrong thing to say. Why the hell were women so complicated? Brigid just looked more furious.

"Oh"—she stepped closer and Carwyn shrank back from the tiny bundle of mad—"so I'm just supposed to wait by the telephone until you decide to ring me? When was that going to be? A hundred years or so? And I'm supposed to put my life on hold while you're off saving the world? How long were you in Wicklow? You couldn't even tell me; I had to find out from my boss!"

Carwyn glued his lips together. He was fairly certain there were no right answers to those questions. Diversion tactics were necessary. He gathered his courage and lifted his hands to frame her face, stroking her cheeks with his thumbs. She stopped in her tracks, looking confused.

"I've been in Wicklow for three months sorting through Ioan's papers, and every minute, I wished I was with you," he said softly. "That I could hold you and kiss you and hear your voice. I missed you, love. So much. But I knew you needed to settle in and get back to work. I didn't want to interfere with that. And I've been focused on finding Ioan's research because I think it's important. I think there's something very bad coming, and I'm hoping something he discovered might help stop it. I have to keep you safe. I couldn't bear it if you were in danger." He leaned down and whispered a kiss across her lips. "I couldn't bear it. I have to keep you safe, Brigid. Forgive me?"

She melted under his words, and Carwyn pulled her into his chest, wrapping his arms around her as she lifted her mouth for a kiss. Oh, she was a prickly one, his Brigid, but softhearted for him, and he wasn't above using it. He knew she was in love with him. She just hadn't let herself admit it yet.

Sweet woman. *His* sweet woman.

"Mmm," he hummed into her mouth and lifted her again. She wrapped her legs around his waist as he leaned against the wall. "Oh, love..."

"Carwyn..." Her voice was a soft plea. "I missed you so much." Her hands clung to him and her fingers twisted in the coarse hair that hung at the nape of his neck. She tugged at his scarf, searching for his skin.

"I missed you, too."

Hot. She was so hot the night fog was steaming off her. He wanted to make love to her in the ocean, with the waves crashing and churning around them. He wanted to love her in the wild with the earth feeding his energy as he sank his fangs deep into her throat and thrust into her body. He wanted her forever. An eternal night lit by the glow of her fire.

"Brigid," he breathed out as he thrilled at the feel of her lips on his neck, her fangs scraping his skin. "I want you… forever. Marry me, Brigid."

She froze, her arms still wrapped around him, her hand buried in his collar. Slowly, she pulled away, tugging at his scarf as she slid down his body, still hard from his desire. She pulled and stepped. Pulled until the wool slipped over his shoulder, exposing the pure white band underneath his jacket. He swallowed once as she stepped away and leaned against the dirty wall, squeezing her eyes shut as her head fell.

How could she have forgotten? He made it too easy to forget. What was she thinking? He was a priest. A priest who loved her. Who *she* loved. She knew that. Here was a man she could spend eternity loving.

Marry me, Brigid.

Her heart screamed yes, and her mind said no.

"You can't ask me that," she whispered.

"I had a meeting with the bishop," he said. "That's the only reason I wore—"

"It doesn't matter, does it?" Her voice was so small she barely heard it herself. "Whether you wear it or not, it's there. I'm pretending that you're free when you're not."

"You know when I was human—"

"But you're not human, Carwyn!" She shook her head and felt tears in the corner of her eyes. "It's not a thousand years ago. You're devoted to something that will never accept us being together, whatever you might wish. And being with you goes against everything that I was raised to believe. Our time in Scotland. Even being together here… we're pretending at things that can't happen."

"Pretending?" His eyes narrowed. "You think I'm pretending?"

"Not about your feelings. I'm not doubting those. But as long as you wear a collar, this is not going to work. However much you might want it too."

"Brigid, you have to—"

"Loving you is a sin," she whispered. She wanted to bite back the words as soon as they left her mouth.

"A sin?" A hard mask fell over his face. A dull anger came to his eyes as he stepped toward her and took the scarf from her hands. He dropped it on the ground and lifted her chin. "Loving me is a sin?"

She shook her head, trying to backtrack. "That's not what I meant."

"Do you know what I did the night I took my vows to the church, Brigid?"

She tried pulling away, but he had boxed her in. "No. And I didn't mean—"

"I took my vows in front of my family, with my father blessing me and my mother watching proudly. And that night, I went home with my wife. With my Efa. And we prayed together. We smiled and laughed, and I kissed every inch of her body and made love to her for hours. I lay awake the whole night with my arms wrapped around her thanking *God* for blessing me with such a woman. And such a calling in my heart."

Bloody tears slipped down her cheeks, and she looked away. Carwyn brushed them from her face and leaned down to place a single, chaste kiss on her lips. "I'm sorry."

"Love is *not* a sin, Brigid. There is no shame in what I feel for you. When you understand that, please let me know."

He released her and backed away, walking farther down the alley as she stood watching him in the night. He turned after half a block and said, "I may be going to Rome soon. My friends need my help and… there are things to see to. Will you think of me?"

Would she think of anything else?

"You know I will." Brigid took a deep breath before she asked, "Do you still love me?"

A slow smiled crooked the corner of his mouth. "Course I do. I meant what I said, Brigid. Nothing is more important to me than keeping you safe. I'll do whatever I have to do."

"You meant what you said?" She swallowed the lump in her throat.

'*Marry me.*'

She wanted to rush to him. To kiss him and hold him. To drag him back to her house and make love to him all night. But she knew it wouldn't happen. And it shouldn't. Not like that. Not for him.

Carwyn's smile grew into a grin. "You know I meant every word."

She couldn't stop the smile that lifted the corner of her mouth. "I'll be here. I'll keep looking, too. Keep me updated?"

"As much as I'm able." She started toward the opposite end of the alley, but turned when she heard his voice. "Brigid?"

"Yes?"

"Remind Murphy that I take care of what's mine." Then he winked and disappeared around a corner as Brigid frowned.

"Takes care of what's '*his*?'" she muttered. "What, *me*? He's talking about me? Ugh! That egotistical, bullheaded, infuriating…"

She was completely in love with him.

CHAPTER TWENTY-TWO

Wales
April 2012

Carwyn sat at his kitchen table, listening to the chattering of Father Samuel as he filled him in on the activities of the parish. The young priest had taken over the small cottage behind the church in town and was rapidly making changes in the village. There were church festivals planned and computer courses for adults taught by Father Samuel himself. Some of the women in the parish were using the church buildings to start childcare for the working mothers and an after-school program for the older children. The village was entering the modern age.

And the young priest was exactly the right man for the job.

Carwyn smiled and sipped the tea the young Englishman poured. Enthusiasm filled the air, and Sister Maggie was glowing. After another hour of visiting, the priest and the sister made their way back to the old house in the mountains. The moon was full over them and the ground was muddy from a spring shower that had fallen that afternoon.

"You should take a house in town," Carwyn said. "You'll be more use there than up at the house."

She frowned. "Who'd watch over the place, then?"

Carwyn shrugged. "I'll shut it up for a while. Probably best that I disappear for a bit so that the village forgets me, if you get my meaning."

Sister Maggie halted and put a hand on his shoulder. "They still ask about you, Father." She smiled. "The people still care."

"I'm glad." He put an arm over the stout woman's shoulders and tugged her down the path. "But this is good. This is what needs to happen, I think. The village was dying, Maggie. I'd taken care of it as well as I could, but in this age, it needed... something more. Someone human. Someone who could take a bigger part in the whole community, not just shepherd the church."

"Are you going away, then? Permanently?" Her eyes wore a worried frown.

"Well... mostly." He paused. "I think there's a new calling for me, Sister. There are things in my life that I've put off. People who need me."

They both fell silent for a few moments. Finally, she said, "You're leaving the church, aren't you?"

"I think I am."

"Is it a crisis of faith, Father? Do you need counsel? I often feel that there is so little wisdom I could share with you, but I can offer a willing ear."

"Ah, Maggie." He squeezed her shoulder. "What a fine friend you are. It's not a crisis of faith. Just a change in calling. Since Ioan's death, I've been unsettled."

"How?" They approached the old stone house and a thin trail of smoke snaked out of the chimney. It was still chilly at night, so Carwyn was happy he'd left the fire burning for the sister. As vigorous as Maggie was, she was getting older, too. She often seemed to ache in the mornings, though she never complained.

"I think I realized that, by trying to be all things, I was truly being none. I was pulled in too many directions. And..." He pulled the door open for her. "I'm... lonely."

A glint came into her eyes. "You've met a woman, haven't you?"

He cleared his throat. "I—why do you say that?"

Sister Maggie snickered. "Because you didn't deny it immediately."

"Oh, fishing for information, are we? There is... someone. I think."

The sister smiled and unpinned the cloak she wore around her old grey dress. "I'm amazed you've lasted this long. You've far more self-control than most men, particularly with all the attention the fairer sex has given you over the years."

Carwyn unwrapped his jacket, loosening the tight collar he'd worn for Father Samuel's benefit while they met. He could at least pretend to be proper... until he abandoned it completely.

"For your information, Sister, I had determined to leave the ministry—mostly—before the woman happened."

"And what happened?" She grabbed two beers and opened them, handing him one as they sat across from each other at the scarred kitchen table. The same table where they'd counseled each other, harassed each other, and joked for over thirty years. Carwyn smiled as he raised his beer. "Cheers."

He would miss her. He would miss them all.

"It's time," he said quietly. "One thousand, forty-four years ago, I was turned into an immortal in these mountains. It wasn't a day's walk from here, Maggie. I'd been traveling from our community to another in the North. My mother and father were watching the children. My wife had died the previous spring and I was in a deep melancholy, so my father sent me on an errand. A simple errand." His eyes drifted toward the fire, lost in his thoughts. "It should have been simple. But the storm hit very suddenly. The snow covered the path and I tripped in a hole."

He shrugged. "A simple thing now. A broken leg. Go to the physician and have it set. But then, I was alone on my journey. I'd wanted it that way. I passed out from the pain after some time and when I woke, I'd lost my sense of direction. But I could see smoke in the distance, so I went toward it." He ran a hand roughly through his shaggy hair. "Maelona was there. And I was dying. I wanted to live. No matter what."

Sister Maggie was watching him carefully. "You still want to live, Carwyn. Perhaps more than any person I have ever met. You love life. You love your family. And now you love another, don't you?"

His voice was hoarse. "With my whole heart."

"Of course you would. You love everything that way, don't you?" She smiled, drained her beer, and patted his hand. "So, what's her name?"

"Brigid." Just the name made him ache with longing.

"A good name. A saint and a goddess. Straddling two worlds. A powerful name." Maggie nodded in approval. "Brigid was a leader. A protector. She held the fire of knowledge in her hands. And she is an immortal?"

"Yes, a young one."

"Well, she'd have to be. Who else would put up with you? She must not know any better. And does she love you, too?"

"Yes." He grinned. "Won't admit it, though."

Sister Maggie snorted. "Arrogant man. Typical. Have you made your intentions known to her? Does she know what you want?"

He frowned. "She's bothered by the collar."

"Well, that just makes her a good Catholic. Nothing wrong with that. You've told her that you're leaving the priesthood, of course." Maggie stood and took the empty bottles as she began to tidy the kitchen. "It might still be a bit awkward for her, but if she's accustomed herself to drinking blood to survive, loving an ex-priest won't be that much more difficult."

Carwyn squirmed in his seat. "I… I didn't tell her I was leaving the Church."

A pan clattered in the sink as Maggie whirled around. "Why not?"

"I wanted… well, I wanted her to accept me as I am. Collar or not. She knows I was married before."

Maggie's mouth gaped. "Men are idiots no matter how old they are!"

"And I asked her to marry me."

Maggie walked to the icebox, took out two more beers, opened them, and sat across from him. "I think you'd better start at the beginning, Father."

Gemma frowned, a tiny line marring the delicate pale skin between her groomed brows. "So… you took her to Max's, then left her there for a year. Returned. Declared your love for her within weeks… left again, then showed up three months after she'd asked you to. Upon meeting her again, you physically assaulted her employer—Terry's going to enjoy that story, by the way—stormed out of the room, then asked her to marry you. Do I have the facts correct?"

Carwyn thought. It sounded so much worse when his daughter said it. "Yes."

"I'd laugh, except I feel rather sorry for Brigid."

"I'm starting to feel sorry for her as well. Think I should drop the whole thing?"

"Not unless you want me to kill you myself."

They were walking through the dark streets of London while Carwyn and Gemma updated each other on family news. Since Ioan's death, Gemma was the oldest of his children, and as she was also one of the ruling vampires of London, it was important to keep her informed.

Gemma fluttered a hand. "I have no doubt that she would have shoved you off if she wasn't interested, so I can only assume that she returns your affections. As well as liking the young woman, she's extraordinarily bright, a fire vampire who'll be less volatile than Cathy, and has direct loyalty to our clan through Deirdre and soon, you. She's an excellent choice, Father. Will you be basing yourself in Dublin? I'd try to move you both to London, but I have a feeling Murphy is going to need the help, and he's an ally."

He tucked the mention of Murphy away with a mental note to ask her later. Trust Gemma to put the most pragmatic spin on the situation. "I love her, as well," he said. "There is that."

Her face softened into a smile, and she tucked her arm into his. "I can tell. You look very happy and very frustrated at the same time. Obviously a man in love."

"I have a rather uncertain future at the moment. I need to go to Rome, help Gio and B figure out this mess with his father's books, speak to a cardinal, and try to convince Brigid to marry me." He frowned. "I need a clone, actually, so I can be in two places at once."

"Or a minion. I'm very fond of my minions for that reason."

He had to smile. Gemma may have put on a hard front, but it wasn't one of her numerous employees walking through the seedy neighborhood late at night scoping out buildings for another shelter.

Carwyn said, "I love you, Gem. You're a grand friend and a wonderful daughter."

"I'm your best daughter, and you know it. But I promise not to tell the others you said so. I am surprised about Brigid, though. She's far too sensible for you. I remember seeing her when she was first working for Murphy. So bright. I was hoping she'd choose immortality like a good girl. She was too valuable to waste on one lifetime. How ever did you persuade her to fall in love with you?"

"I'm not entirely sure I have yet, to be quite honest."

"Well good. A woman deserves to be courted. It's your job to convince her."

"Courted?" It was an old-fashioned concept, but he liked it. He'd consider it his own personal campaign to prove to Brigid why she should marry him.

"Of course, courted. You're rather rusty at this, aren't you?"

"My last marriage was arranged. Courting never happened. But I'll keep it in mind, my wise daughter. Now, tell me what you meant by Murphy needing the help. I may not like him personally, but I have a vested interest in that city remaining stable."

She shook her head and a keen edge came to her eyes. "He's keeping it quiet, but there've been problems. Some of the same problems we're dealing with here. More vampires than usual showing up in town, then moving out quickly without notice. A surge in minor criminal activity—drugs and such." She looked around and lowered her voice even more, despite their location. They were the only people he could see on the street. "All this is from our own sources in Dublin, but they're reliable. There have been challenges."

"Challenges?" If Murphy's leadership had been challenged, that meant Brigid might be walking into a minefield working for him.

"It started out rather casually in his club. Just some boys from out of town who made trouble, then left." The buildings seemed to loom over them as Gemma continued speaking. "Did you know Murphy was a Traveler as a human? He doesn't speak of it much, but he's kept a close relationship with the gypsies, and one of the groups near Dublin—one he has family ties to—was attacked. Their caravans burned. They never discovered who did it, and it made him lose face with them. He's been slowly consolidating his allies. Visiting the MacGregors in Edinburgh, meeting with Terry more. He's being very smart about it, but I'm glad he has Brigid there. Having a fire vampire from Ioan and Deirdre's clan among his people is sure to smooth some channels and instill fear at the same time."

"I'm beginning to like that man less and less. And I don't like Brigid working for him."

"She can take care of herself. She's Deirdre's daughter, and Cathy trained her. Murphy will put her to good use."

Carwyn looked around, his senses alerting him to something nearing. There was an energy signature that was weak, but growing. They might have just been approaching a building with numerous humans occupying it, or the energy could be coming from a few immortals. With the hum of electricity that surrounded him in cities, it was hard to tell. Gemma was still talking.

"Terry would do the same. And that's part of the reason he didn't use his connection to Deirdre to try to woo the girl to London. We want Murphy stable there. In fact, all our allies need—"

"Gemma, there's someone here." He was sure of it now. Four immortals approaching. One from the air. Three on the ground.

She halted immediately, the proper young woman disappeared and the killer opened her eyes with a feral smile. "Excellent. It's been months since I've had that kind of fun."

His eyes skimmed the deserted street. No water nearby. The ground was covered in concrete. Unless there was a fire immortal approaching, the only one with an elemental advantage was the wind immortal. Gemma stood still, small and delicate in the glow of the streetlamp.

Carwyn chuckled under his breath. Looks could be so deceiving.

In a blink, she turned her head to the side and was gone, leaping onto a narrow balcony like a cat, then waited crouched as Carwyn leaned against the corner of a building and watched.

The wind vampire came first. Foolishly low, he didn't even realize that he was dead until Gemma sprang on his back, knocking him to the ground. With a quick twist and a wet rip, his blood was spilling over the dirty street as she tossed his head to the side.

"Stranger, I hope?" Carwyn asked in whisper.

"A troublemaker. I recognized his scent. That's why he's dead first. Stupid man."

She recognized his scent? Carwyn frowned. What was going on in London?

Before he could ask, the dead vampire's friends caught up with him. They sped around the corner, obviously expecting their friend to have corralled their prey, only to slip on the wide pool of blood spilled next to his body.

Gemma hissed and Carwyn spared no time, barreling into two of them with his arms held out. He grasped both by the neck and knocked their heads together, more for his own amusement than anything else.

"Stop playing, Father!"

He grinned and shook the two dazed vampires, who he was fairly certain, belonged to water. "Why? I need the exercise."

Gemma snorted as she batted away the remaining vampire who charged her. "No, you don't."

"Are we keeping any alive?" One managed to kick Carwyn's knee while he held them both by the neck. Cheeky.

"Maybe just one to question. Which should we choose?"

Gemma's attacker ran toward her again, but she grabbed him around the neck and head-butted him before she tucked him under her arm and waited.

"Why don't we see which one is smartest?"

She shot him a smile. "Excellent idea!"

Carwyn tossed the two kicking vampires into a pile in the center of the street, not far from the growing pool of the wind vampire's blood. Gemma tossed hers as well. Then, they both waited while the three rose to their feet.

Two knelt into a crouch, baring their fangs as Carwyn and Gemma watched. The third vampire rose behind his friends, scanned Gemma first, then Carwyn... then proceeded to turn tail and run as quickly as he could down the dark street.

"Smart one," Carwyn and Gemma said together.

"Catch the runner," he said. "I'll take care of these two."

Gemma shot off without a word and Carwyn was left with the idiots. His fangs fell in delight. "Hello, boys."

They grunted, snarling in what someone probably told them was a menacing way. Not very smart, these two. The most dangerous vampires he'd ever encountered usually looked the most harmless. Like Gemma.

Carwyn smirked. "Compensating much?"

The snarls turned into sneers, and one leapt. With one hand, Carwyn caught him and threw him into a wall, where he crumpled to the ground. The other pulled out a gun.

"Really?" Carwyn groaned. "Well, that's just unimaginative." In a blink, he'd rushed the vampire. He grabbed the gun and twisted it out of the other man's hand. "Particularly when these"—with one strong hand, he slowly squeezed—"don't do much to me." The semiautomatic bent as if it was made of tinfoil. With three quick squeezes, the gun was balled up in Carwyn's hands and the vampire's teeth retracted in his mouth.

Carwyn winced. "Embarrassing when that happens, isn't it?" The vampire lifted his eyes to his in terror, just as the other leapt onto him from behind and sunk a knife into his shoulder. Carwyn reached over, plucked the immortal off his back, twisted his head off, and dropped the body on the street. Then his smile fell, he grabbed the knife out of his back and sliced at the staring vampire's neck as his blood spurted out.

In two quick slashes, it was all over.

Three bodies lay at his feet. The blood, he knew, would burn away at dawn, but he didn't want to chance some poor fool stumbling over the remains. Gemma would have taken the survivor off to Terry's already.

Carwyn stared at the ground and scowled. "Typical children. I always have to clean up the messes."

He decided it was amusing to watch Terry fuss over Gemma. The vampire paced the room, yelling at Gemma at the top of his lungs with some of the most inventive swearing Carwyn had heard in some time.

"—bloody, mule-headed woman, Gem! When I tell you to take guards, fucking take guards. These bastards owe me their fucking loyalty for a reason and if I tell them to hold your fucking handbag and paint your toenails, they'll bloody do it!" He spun at the guard who was standing silently by the door. "If any of you ever paint her toenails, I'll fucking kill you."

"Yes, boss," he murmured before Terry started pacing again, running a frustrated hand over his close-cropped buzz cut.

Gemma's fiancé, who was considerably younger than his daughter, was a handsome man in a rough, lantern-jawed way. A bruiser in his human years, the water vampire still carried the look of the streets about him, but had one of the keenest strategic minds Carwyn had ever met. He also had more than enough confidence in Gemma, which meant that this fussing meant Terry was genuinely worried.

That worried Carwyn.

"All of you bastards get the fuck out," Terry said. "And Roger?"

Terry's lieutenant stepped forward. "Yes, boss?"

"Get that slimy French bastard ready for me to question and send another team to the docks. Carwyn, you're sure they were water?"

"Fairly safe bet."

"I'm still here, you know." Gemma rolled her eyes. "Feel free to ask me, as well. I know I'm not a big strapping man, but I might just stumble through it."

Terry glared at her and pointed at the door. All his men left in a blur. Then Terry rushed to Gemma, pulled her up, and landed a furious kiss on her mouth. Carwyn smiled when he saw Gemma's knees buckle, ever so slightly. Then Terry's angry kiss turned into something far more tender, and he cradled his mate's head in his hands and whispered into her ear.

"You scared me, luv. I don't appreciate being scared. See to that, will you? Take the guards."

Gemma spoke quietly. "I was never in any danger, Terry. Especially with Father there."

Terry turned to him and gave him a piercing stare. He pulled Gemma onto his knee while he sat across from Carwyn on the couch.

"Ever since that Italian friend of yours was here last year, there've been problems. I'm not withdrawing my support. Giovanni Vecchio is a good ally to have, but this business with finding some old books is not just about bloody books."

Carwyn said, "That seems to be the consensus, yes."

"Something's stirring, Father. Something much bigger than a personal quest about an old library. I've talked to Murphy. Been in contact with Jean Desmarais on the French coast. Been speaking with Leanor in Spain, too. Things are happening. All my allies—those with serious power—are being felt out. Like someone's out there is taking jabs to see who squeals the quickest. Nothing big, just little things. Annoyances, if they weren't all happening at the same time."

"You think it's coordinated?"

"Yes, I do. And whoever is behind it is testing for weaknesses."

Carwyn paused and thought. "To what end?"

Gemma shrugged. "We're not sure yet, but if there is some sort of power shift like what happened in the eighteenth century, we need to be prepared. And maybe more interesting is who is *not* being tested. Germany is quiet. As are most of the Scandinavian countries. Russia? Well, it's always hard to know, but no reports so far. North Africa is surprisingly steady. Northern France and the Low Countries are peaceful, though with their tendency toward neutrality, that's hardly surprising."

A suspicion tickled the back of his mind. There had been one very notable exception. "And Rome? What about Rome?"

Terry growled and his fangs descended. "Silent as a bloody tomb."

London
April 27, 2012

Dear Brigid,

I love you.

Just thought I'd mention that. I'm going to Rome tomorrow. Well, actually, I'm going to Le Havre, where I will catch a ride on a freighter to Genoa, and then I will go to Rome. I hope the food is tolerable. I'm going to help Gio and Beatrice. I've told you about them, haven't I? Gio's one of my oldest friends. The fire vampire. Nice chap. Rather stuffy in a very Italian, academic way. His wife's a dear friend and far more fun. They've stumbled across something. And I think it's something bad. The book I was talking about before. I think it may all be a thing together, Brigid. Ioan's death. The book. The drugs.

I hate being away from you. It's harder than I expected.

Take care of yourself. This is bigger than us. Bigger than my friends. There's a pattern to the threats. Watch out for small things. Things that seem minor, because they might not be. I don't know how much you should tell Murphy, but if there's danger, go to Deirdre. If Ireland's not safe, go to Max and Tavish. I know you're capable, but this is different than an open challenge. Dublin may not know how to handle it. Be smart. If it comes down to it, trust family and yourself. No one else.

And be careful, Brigid. You're holding my heart.
Carwyn

P.S. Don't go out with Murphy.

Chapter Twenty-Three

Dublin
May 2012

Brigid sipped her tea and read the letter from Carwyn.

And be careful, Brigid. You're holding my heart.

Among the grating routine of her nights, the sentiment of his words melted her.

P.S. Don't go out with Murphy.

She narrowed her eyes. "Oh, for heaven's sake, the idiotic—"
"Not talking about me, are you?" She glanced up at her boss, who was standing next to her in the café in the lobby of the building. A smile flirted around his mouth and she caught him trying to glance at the note in her hands. She quickly tucked it away.
"Not you. What's the story tonight?"
"Declan and Jack are out at that club you tipped them off about. Tom's in the office with Sara. Taking a quick break?"
"Just for a few. Did they see my note about the girl?"
"I believe so."
"She was a bartender at Riot until January, then she disappeared. She'd given me quite a bit of information before I... went to Scotland, so I was checking up on her. Went by her apartment, her friends' places. Some of them mentioned The Abby, so I thought it might be a new place."
"It sounds like a place Jack mentioned last month." He shrugged. "We'll look into it. I'll need you in a meeting later."
"Business stuff?" She curled her lip as Murphy chuckled.
"Aren't you glad you came to work for me? Yes, just a meeting with a chap from Lisbon. Trade deal."
She sighed. Since she'd come back, she spent more time standing in the corner of Murphy's office looking menacing than she did investigating the

trickle of information they were getting about this drug from the continent. Jack had assured Murphy he was more than capable of heading the investigation. Declan continued to coordinate his army of human hands to control and monitor the shipping operations. Tom coordinated security for the Docklands building and other businesses. Angie still ruled the office with a smile, and Brigid had become Murphy's constant shadow during most night hours.

Trade meeting? She was there.

Tour of the city with the cagey German? Brigid was happy to assist.

Interrogation of a vampire suspected of smuggling goods from the North without informing Murphy… well, that part was a bit fun.

"The meeting is at three a.m., so please be there around two thirty or so. Angie will brief you."

Brigid offered him a polite smile. "Sure thing. See you then."

Murphy strolled off after flashing a smile at her waitress, who almost poured the tea on Brigid's lap instead of in her cup. She sighed and caught the small stream before it hit her pants as the waitress apologized profusely.

Ah, Murphy.

She was just finishing her tea and reading Carwyn's letter for the third time when she sensed someone approaching. A deliciously sweet smell hit her nose and the chair across from her scraped back. A familiar figure slid into it.

Brigid blinked, gaping. "Emily?"

Her old friend smiled cautiously. "Hello, Brig."

It had been almost two years since she'd seen her. The last night had been the one when she'd pounded on Emily's door, demanding she give her the heroin that had caused Brigid to overdose. Brigid knew Emily had a supplier, even though she'd only ever used drugs to party. She hadn't known that the supplier had been Emily's vampire boyfriend, Axel.

Emily spoke quietly. "Nothing to say?"

"I'm… surprised to see you." She was. As far as she knew, Emily had stopped working for Murphy shortly after and no one seemed to know where she had disappeared to. "You're looking well, Em. How've you been?"

"Locked up," she said with a small smile. "Well, in a treatment program, anyway. My parents finally caught up with me. I… well, I'm better now. Thanks to them."

Brigid looked around the room in a panic. She had no idea how to react to her old friend.

Emily looked just as uncomfortable. "I know this is a bit awkward."

She snorted. "A bit, yeah."

"I…" Tears came to Emily's eyes. "I never wanted to—"

"I never blamed you, you know?" Brigid may not have known how to feel about seeing the girl—woman—again, but she didn't want Emily carrying any guilt for things that she was responsible for herself. "I wasn't in a right state, Em. I probably would have bloodied you up if you hadn't have given me anything that night. You should know that. I don't blame you for my own stupidity."

Emily nodded and Brigid could see the relief in her eyes. "I appreciate that. But I was still responsible. And I wanted to apologize. I've been trying to work up the nerve for months now, ever since I heard you were back in town. And it's something I need to do for my own recovery. Making amends, you know?"

"Oh really?"

Emily gave a rueful grin and the playful girl that Brigid had bonded with at Parliament House peeked out. "You know how organized I am. Got to check all the boxes off or I'll go insane."

"Might not be the best joke when you've been locked up for a bit, eh?"

Emily let out a laugh, and Brigid joined her. Finally, Emily wiped the tears from her eyes. "Jeez, it's good to see you again. And you look amazing. The immortal thing really works for you."

For some reason, the approval of her old friend warmed her. "Does it?"

The human smiled. "You already had that intense, badass thing going for you. Now you just have the fangs to back it up."

Brigid grinned and let her fangs run down. Emily couldn't help but stare at them. "Pretty cool, right?"

"Very cool. And the blood thing? Should I be wearing a metal scarf?"

"No." Brigid laughed. "Though, I'll confess that you smell pretty amazing. It's funny the things you notice. Hope I'm not scaring you, but if you've always smelled like that, it's no wonder Axel couldn't keep his fangs off you."

She blushed, which only made the smell stronger. Brigid shook herself. Her friend smelled like some exotic sweet fruit. Her skin glowed and she looked ripe for the picking. Apparently, sobriety agreed with Emily.

"You look great, too," Brigid said. "I think you look younger now than when we were in school. Really good. Healthy. I'm happy for you."

Emily smiled and looked away in embarrassment. "I wasn't for a while, but I'm feeling much better now. Who knew clean living was the best beauty treatment, eh?"

"Are you and Axel still...?" She'd been making quiet inquiries about Emily's old boyfriend, but no one in Dublin would admit to seeing him.

"No," she said quickly. "That wasn't the healthiest relationship, was it? I, uh... I loved him. Madly. And he didn't want to break up, but when I went into treatment... He didn't understand."

"The treatment program?"

"I think it was the addiction. He didn't understand why I just didn't stop and move on with my life."

"Ah." Brigid sipped her tea, which suddenly seemed bland, despite the sugar she'd added to it. "It's a mindset, isn't it? Getting off the drugs. It's far more than the physical symptoms. You have to leave behind the things that hold you back."

Emily paused, twisting her fingers together and looking around the room. "I don't think vampires—" she said softly "—unless they had an addiction when they were human, really understand that."

Brigid raised an eyebrow. "I don't know. We're all addicted to blood, aren't we?"

"I guess so." Emily shrugged. "I bet you conquered it quick, didn't you?"

"What?"

"The blood thing. You'd already had practice getting off drugs. Blood was probably a cinch."

Brigid smirked. "I've never thought about it that way. You might be right; I'm very strict about that part of my life. Now it's easier, of course."

Emily's face lit up. "That's great!"

"Though I'll confess, the way you smell is testing my control, Em." Brigid pretended to plug her nose and Emily smiled and leaned away.

"Sorry."

"Find a different perfume, will you?" Brigid was mostly joking, but Emily did smell mouthwatering. Rather inconvenient if she wanted to remain friends with the woman.

Emily started to stand. "I know you're working, so I won't keep you. I'd like to keep in touch, if that's something you'd like, too. I'd understand if you didn't. I'm staying with my parents." Emily handed her a small card with a phone number and address. "Call if you like. I'm just getting back into things here. Found a nice job working for a friend of my mum's. Still accounting, but no vampires this time." She trailed off, looking a bit lost and more than a little nervous.

Brigid thought back to their time in university, and it wasn't the drugs or partying she remembered. She remembered a nervous girl from the country and a warm and welcoming hand of friendship. She remembered Emily's patience during the worst of Brigid's social anxiety and her encouragement when Brigid was frustrated with her old, human limitations. She smiled at the young woman and held out a hand for the card.

"I'd like that, Emily. I wouldn't want to lose you."

Rome, Italy
May 26, 2012

When is your birthday? I should know these things since I'm in love with you. I don't know when mine was. I was born in the winter. And my mother complained that I came out of the womb causing trouble. I don't believe her. I blame my older sisters. I always did.

Did you want children? It pains me that it might have been something you didn't have the chance for in your human life. But don't worry, we can always adopt, if you'd like. Whether we add any human children to my crazy brood is entirely up to you. I'm rather fond of children. Haven't had one around in quite some time, though. It would probably be entertaining.

But I'm getting ahead of myself, aren't I? I'm good at that.

Gemma told me that women like being courted, so please read the following reasons that you should marry me. (I only included five. I didn't want to overwhelm you.) And yes, I realize this isn't a traditional courtship. It'll work anyway; I'm irresistible.

"Arrogant ass," she whispered, trying to ignore the smile flirting around her lips.

The top five reasons that you should marry me:

1. My Hawaiian shirt collection. It's extensive. There have actually been overtures from some museums to add it to their exhibits. I know you pretend to think that they're ugly, but I see right through you, my sweet Brigid. You're in love. (With my shirts... and me.)

2. I'm extremely rich, particularly for a priest. I never did all that well with the vow of poverty thing. See, when you've been alive a thousand years, it's just idiotic not to invest. So, I'm very comfortable financially. Not that I think this is a concern to you, but it would be irresponsible not to mention it.

3. My good looks are obvious, so I won't expound on them.

"This is possibly the worst 'courtship' in history," she muttered. "I don't really think it's supposed to work this way, Carwyn."

4. A thousand years. That's a lot to make up for. My enthusiasm for certain activities will be rather boundless, and I can promise neither of us will go unsatisfied. Please, use your imagination to fill in the rest. (Then tell me about it later.) By the way, your mouth is glorious. I'm thinking about kissing you right now. And Gio is watching me. Awkward. Best leave the room.

She bit back a laugh and kept reading.

5. And I'm back. The last thing I'll mention is just this: I love you. I've lived as an immortal for a thousand years and I've never met a woman who warmed my heart, my body, and my soul the way you have. I admired the woman you were as a human, and I'm even more excited to see who you become in this new life. I think you're extraordinary.

Love to you, Carwyn

Trust him to leave her a bit weepy right before she was supposed to go out on patrol with Declan.

P.S. The collar is optional, you know.

Brigid stood up suddenly, shouting, "What the hell does that mean?" Declan and Tom turned to her, both looking as if she'd just slapped a nun. "Sorry... just something unexpected."

"Everything all right back in Wicklow?" Tom asked.

She nodded with a tight smile, folding the letter in half. "Yes. Fine." She folded it again. "Just fine. Just..." She folded the letter again. It was around the size of a business card. She tucked it in her pocket and walked from the room. "It's all just... *fine*. Let me grab a quick bite and I'll be ready to go."

An hour later, Brigid and Declan were leaning against the back wall of The Abbey, a club in town that catered to vampires and their human guests. Murphy was out of the office that night, so Brigid had eagerly volunteered to join Declan as he monitored Dublin's newest hotspot.

It was a new club, one that Murphy hadn't approved before it was built, but once the owners made their very generous tribute to the leader of Dublin, allowances were made and the club remained in business. They had a man stationed there every night who reported in. Jack had argued that shutting it down would just force the club underground, and Brigid had to agree.

But she still didn't trust the owners. They were two Norwegian humans who had letters of introduction from the immortal leader in Oslo. Murphy was being cautious, but politically smart by allowing the club to remain open as a favor to the other vampire, who had powerful connections in shipping that he wanted to exploit. The political considerations grated on Brigid, who was sure the club was funneling drugs. She just wasn't sure through whom.

"Where the hell is Jack?" she muttered, kicking a loose pebble in the street.

"He probably found a sweet-smelling girl and is taking a nip."

"He was supposed to meet us half an hour ago."

Declan shrugged. "It's Jack."

"Does that vampire understand the concept of 'on time?'"

"What do you think?"

Just then, the alley door opened and a body was tossed out into the road. Brigid smirked. Stupid, drunk human...

"Jack?" she gasped when she recognized the mussed hair and torn shirt. She rushed over. Declan was just behind her. "Jack, what the hell?"

Declan flipped him over. "He's... passed out? It's nowhere near dawn, how can he be—"

"Feel him." Brigid put both hands on his face. One on his neck. "Feel his amnis. It's all..."

"Scrambled," Declan mumbled. "It's like it's coming in short bursts. What the hell is this?"

It was unlike anything Brigid had ever felt before. Jack's amnis was still there, still a current running under his skin, but it jumped and died under her hands, as if an electrical surge had knocked out the power and his computer was restarting.

"Have you ever felt anything like this?" she whispered.

"Never," Declan said. "Jack?" He patted his friend's cheek. "Jack, wake up."

"I've never seen one of us passed out before."

"It must have something to do with his amnis. We need to call Murphy."

"As soon as he's awake." Brigid was trying not to panic. "I don't even know what to tell him."

The starts and stops were evening out and she could see Jack's eyes fluttering open. His pupils were dilated and he was... wet. Soaking wet, she'd just noticed. As if someone had thrown him in the bath with his clothes still on. Worry gave way to irritation. What the hell had the vampire gotten himself into now?

"Jack!" Brigid slapped him. Just to wake him up. Mostly.

He groaned. "Feck, Brigid, stop hitting me. I promised to stop making passes at your friend."

She glanced at Declan. "Doesn't seem to have scrambled his brain any more than it was already."

"Jack." Declan pulled at one of his eyelids, checking his pupils as Jack tried to bat him away. "What happened?"

"Well, there was this girl..."

"How did I know it was going to start out that way?" Brigid muttered.

"Shut up, Brigid. I'm not afraid of your fire-y, fang-y ways. I hate that you have such a great ass, though. Makes it hard to keep focus sometimes."

She snarled and Declan pulled Jack up by his shoulder. "Jack," he said. "Watch your mouth and tell us what happened."

"This girl took me to one of the private rooms for a quick snack and..." He glanced at Brigid. "...well, a quick snack. She was gorgeous. And she smelled so good, I practically came just from sniffing her—"

"Just the facts, please," Brigid said.

Jack scowled at her, but continued. "We were just getting down to business when I... What happened?" He squinted. "I don't fecking remember, Dec. I think..." Jack reached over his shoulder. "Something pinched me."

Declan frowned. "Pinched you?"

Jack was rubbing his shoulder, then his hand drifted over the base of his neck, slid down. "Not a pinch. More like—"

"A bite?" Brigid hissed as she looked over his shoulder to the twin holes in the back of Jack's shirt, right between his shoulder blades. She quickly split Jack's shirt so she could see his skin.

"Jesus, Brigid, if you wanted my clothes off, all you had to do was ask."

"Declan, look at this." There were two punctures in Jack's skin, not unlike small tears. They weren't bites, didn't seem to go very deep, and they were already healing. The area around the punctures was singed, as if Jack had been hit by two very small beams of sunlight. "What the hell is this?"

"I think I know." Declan's voice was grim. "I've seen it on humans before, just not vampires."

"What is it?" Jack was reaching to feel the wounds. "It actually hurts. That's... odd."

Declan was furious. "Why the hell haven't we thought of this before?"

She was still confused. "What are you talking about?"

"I think... it's from a Taser."

Her heart dropped. "Oh hell."

Of all the weapons that could be used against them, Brigid had been warned about swords most of all. It may have sounded medieval, but cutting off a vampire's head or burning it were really the only two ways they could be killed. Guns, knives, none of them were truly dangerous unless the spinal column was severed at the neck. They were immune and self-healing, even able to regenerate limbs over long periods of time. The sun or fire could burn them, and burns took a long time to heal—as evidenced by the scars on Carwyn's chest—but even those did mend eventually.

Amnis, everyone repeated. It was the key. Amnis was what regenerated them. Kept them strong. Let them connect to their element and manipulate their energy. It was the electrical current that ran under their skin, the unseen armor that every immortal depended on.

So why had she never considered a Taser?

"I don't know why we never considered it before," Murphy said quietly. They were sitting in the office. He'd sent Angie home, so it was just Tom, Declan, Brigid, and a still-recovering Jack. He was shaky and drinking a bag of donated blood cold. "It makes so much sense. Bloody technology will kill us all in the end."

"Hits us right where we're most vulnerable," Tom said. "Amnis controls everything. It may seem like magic sometimes, but it's all just energy, isn't it? Same as electricity. If you shock us—"

"It'd be like a power surge in a computer," Declan interrupted. "We'll restart, but be all scrambled. We're used to being the ones frying electronics, not being fried. If a human—"

"Or a vampire," Brigid interjected. "A vamp could customize one. We've all become used to making accommodations for other electronics. Plastic coatings and cases. If a vampire wore gloves, they could probably use a Taser."

"You're right," Murphy said. "And if you used one of the ones that shoots out the wires, you could shock a victim without getting close enough to have it affect you, too."

Brigid said, "Damn it, this is the perfect weapon." She frowned. "But why was he soaking wet?"

All five were silent for some time. Finally Jack said, "What if it's a result of the shock?"

Everyone turned to him.

"Think about it. What if it makes your amnis… *surge* right before it shorts you out? If that happened, your element would react. We've all had that experience before. Our amnis gets excited by something and we have an elemental reaction. All the water in the air might have been drawn to me like a magnet, which would drench me and make the electrocution from the Taser worse, too."

Brigid gasped, thinking about what her own reaction might be. "Oh, this is not good."

"Any word from The Abbey?" Murphy asked Tom.

"I sent men over to question the guests and employees, even had them use amnis, but no one claims to know anything. A few people saw the girl Jack disappeared with, but she was already gone and no one recognized her. Not a regular."

"The owners?" Declan said.

Murphy answered. "I've already called them in for a meeting tomorrow night. They claim to know nothing, of course. Apologized for a lack of security, but then asked why my men hadn't made their club safer, considering all the tribute they were paying me."

"What?" Brigid said. She felt her fangs descend. "They should have their own—"

"We'll make it clear tomorrow, Brigid. Calm down." Murphy stood up and patted Jack on the shoulder. "Time to head home for the day. Everyone take precautions and avoid being alone, if possible. This is… new."

Brigid fell silent. New drugs. New weapons. New enemies.

Things in Dublin had just become very, very interesting.

CHAPTER TWENTY-FOUR

Vatican City
May 2012

Carwyn tugged on his collar as he walked down yet another lavish hallway. The timid priest in front of him glanced over his shoulder with a smile.

"Just down this corridor, Father."

He grunted and tried not think unkindly of the young man who represented so much of what annoyed him about Rome. Soft. The city was soft. He wondered if the young priest had ever picked up a dying child who was lying in a gutter. Or cared for a human who smelled of disease. Had he ever prayed with a family who had just lost a loved one? He tried not to be judgmental, but it was difficult in a city known for its layers of complicated historical bureaucracy that separated its residents from the world. The Vatican was even isolated from the very city that surrounded it.

He hated Rome. "When did they change the offices?"

"I believe it was ten years ago."

Ten years? Had it really been that long since he'd had to visit Arturo? The irritating Spaniard was probably grey-headed by now. To most, the office he was visiting was a small one that oversaw some of the more private finances of the papal household. The current *Camerlengo* was an old friend of Carwyn's; they corresponded regularly. Officially, this was a friendly visit, and the stop by the Cardinal's administration offices was merely a formality so his assistant could meet with him on some minor matter.

Unofficially, the priest Carwyn was meeting oversaw all "supernatural" members of the church.

Carwyn had no idea how many immortals there were in the world. He'd never really bothered trying to guess. He had even less of an idea how many identified as Catholic, but he imagined it was a fairly large percentage. After all, vampires liked to know what to expect, and few institutions were more predictable than the Roman Catholic Church. But he had no idea what the numbers were. Really, who cared?

Arturo Leon did.

The young priest gave a polite knock, ushered him through the door, then disappeared. Carwyn walked into the office of the assistant-vice-something or other in the office of the *Camerlengo* of the Holy Roman Church. The trim Spaniard rose to greet him behind an immaculate marble-topped desk. He held out a soft, manicured hand, which Carwyn took and considered crushing, just to be contrary. Arturo raised an amused eyebrow at him before he motioned to the seat across from him.

"Thank you for visiting with me before your meeting with the *Camerlengo*. I appreciate your time, Father."

"And I appreciate dropping the pretenses, Arturo. We both know my meeting here is really with you. I'll stop by for drinks with Raoul, but you're the one I really need to speak to."

The Spaniard had a confident manner and a trustworthy bearing. Salt-and-pepper hair was cut neatly around a pleasant, though not particularly attractive, face. His eyes were hooded in a lazy expression that belied the brilliant mind behind them. No one really spent that much time keeping notes on papal household expenditures. Arturo dealt in far more valuable currency than gold. The priest dealt in information, and no one was better at obtaining it, in Carwyn's experience.

"Oh?" Arturo said with forced innocence. "Whatever could I help you with, Carwyn? My previous requests for your help obtaining information —"

"I'm not one of your spies, Arturo."

"Simple requests for information do not constitute spying."

"Nothing is simple in my world."

"It's the same world I live in, Father. I just don't have fangs." Carwyn glared at Arturo until the formal mask dropped. "Fine," the Vatican official said. "You're leaving the church. Am I supposed to be surprised now?"

Carwyn forced his face to remain blank. "I am." The Spanish priest remained silent until Carwyn spoke again. "How did you—?"

"The signs have been there for years, Welshman." Arturo just sounded bored. "You had become peripherally involved with too many other things. Which is understandable, but not conducive to active church ministry. Further, I believe that certain conflicts of interest have arisen between your duties as head of a large immortal clan and your vows to the church." The priest's eyes flickered with interest. "Your... actions in France regarding the death of two young men—"

"The two vampires who murdered my child?" Carwyn bit out. "Those two?"

Arturo gave Carwyn a lazy shrug. "Do you think I was condemning your actions? I know nothing for certain, only rumors." Arturo leaned forward with a predatory stare. "After all, I highly doubt a priest of your age and faith would have given a boy absolution, then stood by while he was executed. Not when you could have stopped it." The lazy black eyes glittered with interest. "After all, you know the Church's position on capital punishment."

A position untenable in the immortal world. "Of course I do."

"I am merely mentioning this because it is not without precedent that an immortal priest of your age and position has conflicting interests. Interests that might keep him from being completely loyal to the Church. Leaving at this point may be the wisest course. For you."

Carwyn examined the man across from him. Arturo was angling for something. Normally, a priest abandoning his vows was a matter met with counsel. Prayers were offered and received. Carwyn had expected to face weeks of careful and concerned faces who would try to dissuade him from leaving his calling.

So why did he get the distinct impression that he shouldn't let the door hit him on the way out?

Still…

Carwyn smoothed a hand over the formal clothes he'd put on for the meeting. "After a thousand years of service to the Church, I find that my responsibilities to my family and clan have begun to take away from my duties to my parish. It is for that reason that I desire release from my vows to the church."

"And is that your only reason? The responsibilities to your family?"

"Why do you ask?"

Arturo reached into his desk, removed a thin file, and opened it, spreading his hands over the contents. "Tell me about Brigid Connor."

Carwyn was silent. He should have known that others would find out about his interest. He hadn't exactly been subtle about it. Still, it was none of Arturo's business, as far as he was concerned. "She's a new member of my clan. Recently turned."

"She's a confirmed member of the church."

"And still practices, as far as I am aware. She was raised in the church and sees no conflict between her immortal state and her faith."

"She's a fire vampire. Very valuable, isn't she? And under your aegis?"

He felt a twitch in his eye. "She is under my daughter's aegis. She and Brigid were friends in her human life."

Arturo paged through the file. "Vampire 'families' can be quite complicated, can't they?"

"I suppose so."

"Based on so much more than biology. It's fascinating, really."

Now Carwyn was just getting annoyed. "Get to the point, Arturo."

"Your feelings for Brigid Connor have nothing to do with your desire to leave the church?"

Carwyn could feel the anger building. "Who told you about her?" Murphy had close ties to the bishop in Dublin. Was this his doing?

Arturo leaned back in his chair, examining him as if he were some interesting specimen under a microscope. "I have my sources, Carwyn ap Bryn. Are you refusing to answer the question I asked you?"

"I want to know what business it is of yours."

"She's a member of the church. That makes it my business."

"You take such an interest in every Catholic? How noble."

"What is your relationship with her?"

"So you can use it against me? Or her?" He shook his head. "She's none of your concern. See to your spies, Arturo. Leave Brigid Connor alone. She's not a pawn for you to use."

A single hand slammed down on the marble desk and the Spaniard leaned forward. "I want to know because she is a child of God, who has—according to all reports—led a very difficult life. I'm asking, Carwyn, because as powerful as she is, she's also vulnerable."

Carwyn blinked. "You mean... you're actually concerned about her? Not the political implications of this or her possible use to your network?"

Arturo glared. "I'm not a complete monster. Her sire is your own child and holds no authority over you. Therefore, there is no one in the immortal world who can interfere should you try to take advantage of her."

Carwyn bared his fangs. "You think I would try to—"

"What are your intentions toward the young woman, Carwyn?" Arturo's nostrils flared. It was more reaction from the human than Carwyn had seen all night. "Her sire cannot ask, but I can. Your interest has been noted by more than me. *What do you intend?*"

"I intend to marry her, you infuriating dolt!"

Arturo's shoulders relaxed and he sat back in his chair. "Why didn't you just say so?"

His fangs were still long, so he muttered around them. "It's none of your business."

"Technically, it is." He closed the file and slipped it into his desk drawer. "I knew there was more than just family obligations. Calm down. Do you think you're the first priest to leave the church for love?" Arturo rolled his eyes and took out other papers, shuffling them around the desk in an efficient manner. "Frankly, I'm amazed you've stuck around this long."

"This church is my home." He spoke softly, finally calming from his previous rage. "It has been my calling and purpose for longer than you can imagine. It's not a decision I came to without prayer and deliberation."

"I believe you." Arturo had relaxed into his seat. "The other reason I ask is, while the request for laicization is somewhat routine, a release from your vow of celibacy—which I'm assuming a married man would want—needs to be approved by the Holy Father. That, my friend, is why it is my business."

"Not trying to convince me to stay?"

"Could I?" He looked amused. "I'm not going to fight you on this Carwyn." A kind light finally shone through the human's dark eyes. "You have been a faithful—if not entirely obedient—servant of the Church for over a thousand years. I would be happy if you stayed, but I'm not going to sabotage myself by hindering you." Just like that, the kindness disappeared and the calculation returned. "Let me get these papers approved. Then, we'll meet again. The last thing I want is to sever our relationship. I think both of us could benefit from... mutual cooperation in these complicated times."

Rome
June 2012

"Thank you, Emil."

"Giovanni is not in any danger until Livia has felt out the city. She's insecure right now, has poured millions of Euros into something she's pinning her hopes on."

"Oh?" Was it this elixir that everyone kept mentioning? The vampire empress of Rome certainly had the means, but what was her motivation? Purely financial?

"Taking your friend prisoner was not a smart move, Carwyn. We both know it. It leaves her looking rash and unstable. Not to mention that Giovanni's wife has built quite a reputation."

"She's earned it." He saw Beatrice enter the library, still hollow-eyed from the shock of Giovanni's arrest.

They had stumbled into a viper's nest in Rome. What was supposed to be an information gathering trip had turned into open confrontation. Lorenzo had appeared. Giovanni had been arrested. And it was all over a book.

But not really. He was positive the elixir the book contained the formula for was the reason for the escalating violence in Ireland. He had a feeling that this was a far bigger problem than even Giovanni or Beatrice realized. And if they thought that finding it and destroying the secret formula was going to work, they were delusional. Carwyn was well acquainted with secrets. He'd held them for a thousand years. Big secrets and little ones, he heard them all. And secrets had a tendency to wiggle their way out of the shadows until they were the center of attention.

"I'll talk to you later, Emil."

"I'll call when I have more information."

Carwyn walked over to Beatrice, sat down next to her, and put an arm around her shoulders. "Do you remember that night on the beach years ago? Right after you had moved to L.A.?"

"Yeah." Her voice was hoarse.

"We were watching fireworks, and you cringed every time the waves crashed."

"I remember."

"And now you could control the ocean itself." He felt her tense up and pulled her closer. "That problem seemed huge then. But now, as an immortal, water is your ally."

She sighed and put her head on his shoulder. "What are you trying to say?"

What *was* he trying to say? He looked at Beatrice's dark hair and couldn't help but think of Brigid. The two women looked nothing alike, but they were still two of the strongest young vampires he'd ever met. And both had overcome so many challenges.

Carwyn said, "The things that seem insurmountable in the moment have a way of working themselves out."

"Like false imprisonment?"

He snorted. "Yes. And crazed Roman she-devils."

"Missing manuscripts."

"Thousand-year-old commitments that you struggle to let go."

She jolted up. "What?"

"Nothing. Tell me more about this elixir."

Beatrice narrowed her eyes at him, but launched into an explanation of the alchemic formula developed in the Middle East in the ninth century. It had been developed by the alchemist, Geber, who was trying to find a way for humans to ingest vampire blood. The formula was supposed to allow humans to heal the same way vampires could. It was intended for healing. To prolong life. But it had other, perhaps unintended, effects, as well.

He turned when he heard a stumbling in the hall. Lucien Thrax walked into the library, almost turning over a Chinese vase that stood near the door.

"Careful now, Doctor. You know how our friend gets about his pretties."

That provoked a small, amused sound from Beatrice, and Lucien smiled as he walked toward them. Lucien had been one of his son's dearest friends. A kindred spirit who had roamed the world, searching for better ways to heal humanity. But the vampire had also drunk from an old lover who had taken an early form of Lorenzo's elixir and was experiencing strange symptoms.

"How is everyone this evening? Any news about Giovanni?"

"Emil is still poking around. He'll be a good ally for you to cultivate, B."

"I'll keep it in mind. Lucien, how are you feeling tonight?"

Carwyn motioned to the chairs in front of the fireplace. Something about Ioan's old friend was off. He had to sleep far more than what was normal for an earth vampire of his age. Lucien lowered his lanky body onto a chair and pushed back his shaggy brown hair.

"I am still unwell," he said. "Which is very strange when I have been living for as many years as I have."

"Any word from your sire?" Carwyn asked. Lucien's sire, Saba, was the oldest vampire Carwyn had ever heard of. An ancient woman from the Ethiopian highlands, she was also a renowned healer. All earth vampires could probably trace their roots to Saba. Perhaps all vampires could. If anyone could understand the mysterious "Elixir of Life," it would probably be her.

"No word so far. I had to send a messenger, of course. And there's no telling where she is."

Beatrice asked, "Do you think she's heard of the manuscript?"

"If she has, she's never mentioned it."

Carwyn ears perked up. He heard Beatrice's nephew, Benjamin, calling from downstairs that she was needed.

"Better go." She kissed his cheek before walking to Lucian and patting him on the shoulder and darting out of the room. "He's a bit lost without Gio."

So was she, but Carwyn didn't mention it. He wondered whether Brigid would ever worry about him the same way that Beatrice worried about Giovanni.

"They're still looking for a book," he heard Lucien muse.

"What?" Carwyn turned his attention back to the other vampire. "Of course they are. That's what we need to find, isn't it?"

He was waving a hand. "Forget the manuscript. This is far bigger than one book now. Far, far bigger. They've made copies. I know Livia. She's made copies of copies if she thinks it's valuable. Which means that it's also been stolen by someone by now. If information is valuable, then it will be stolen. It's practically part of natural law."

"So this drug—"

"Finally!" Lucien threw up his hands. "Someone calls it what it is."

"A drug?"

"It *is* a drug! Not the elixir of life. For some reason, that was annoying me. Give things their proper names. Elixir implies that it's a cure of some kind. And it's not. Well…" He frowned and shook his head. "It's a kind of cure, in a way…"

Carwyn frowned as Lucien drifted off. It was odd. His manner. His way of speaking. Something about Lucien spoke of confusion, which was unheard of. Immortal minds were sharp. More than even the brightest humans, the increased electricity that their bodies generated spurred faster processing, better memories, and far better reflexes. All that Lucien seemed to be lacking.

"Pomegranates," Lucien whispered as he stared into the cold fireplace. "Did I tell you she smelled of pomegranates? Like fruit ripe in the sun,

Carwyn. Do you remember that smell? And the smell of sunshine? Even with the sickness, she still smelled so sweet. Tasted... She tasted like the sweetest honey."

Was Lucien talking about his lover? The one he had drunk from? "What are you talking about?"

"Silly me," he whispered. "It felt so good at first."

Alarm was beginning to grow in Carwyn's chest. "Are you talking about this drug? How it made you feel? I thought you felt unwell."

"Now I do. But at first..." Lucien's eyes glowed. "Drinking her blood made me feel like a god."

Vatican City
June 2012

Arturo was running late. But then, this was a last-minute meeting that Carwyn had called, so he couldn't really blame the human. He wasn't dressed in his clerical uniform this time. He wore black jeans and a black T-shirt with sturdy boots. He hadn't shaved in months, and the slow-growing stubble cast a dark shadow on his face. He knew he looked like one of Terry's ruffians, but the grim colors reflected the mood he was in.

He'd be leaving Rome soon. Beatrice had come up with a plan that was going to plunge him into more danger than he'd ever faced in his long life. He and Giovanni would have to find two vampires who were supposed to have died hundreds of years before. The fiercest kings of the ancient world. It was so far from his quiet mountain home it was laughable. The plan was madness—sheer, utter madness.

But it was the only way to learn the absolute truth about the origins of this drug.

If he survived, he was grabbing hold of Brigid Connor and never letting go.

The Spaniard bustled into the room shortly after Carwyn sat down. He placed several files on his desk, shuffling them around as Carwyn watched.

"Now," Arturo said, "as I expected, this has all been routine. There will be a few things to sign, but permission of the Holy Father has already been granted. Privately, I can say that you have his sincere blessing and thanks for your long service to the church. Some of the Cardinals are unhappy, but as you haven't officially existed since the tenth century, they can't say much, can they?"

"Wait!" His heart had begun pounding as soon as Arturo opened his mouth.

'...routine... permission granted...'

It was an odd feeling. Carwyn felt lost and found all at once. "So, it's official? I'm not a priest anymore?"

For better or worse, the Catholic Church had been his home for over a thousand years. It had given him purpose. Had offered an unchanging bedrock in a constantly changing world. Though release was what he wanted, a corner of his heart still grieved.

Arturo straightened his shoulders and lifted his chin proudly. "You will always be a priest in your heart. It is part of your soul. 'You are a priest forever, like Melchizedek of old.' The church is only releasing you from your vows. The only responsibility you have is to hear the penitence of the dying. That will always be your blessing and your burden."

He took a deep breath. A priest forever... but released from his obligations to the church. Free to live as he chose. Free to devote himself to his family and friends. Free to love the woman who had become so precious to him.

Free.

"Thank you, Arturo."

"Thank *you*. Now, what is this meeting really about? We were not scheduled to meet until next week. I was surprised when you called."

"I will be leaving Rome shortly, and there are matters happening among my kind that I wish to speak to you about."

"Is it this so-called 'Elixir of Life?'"

Carwyn cocked his head and smiled. "One of these days, I'll figure out where you get your information, human."

Arturo shrugged and crossed his arms over his chest. An enigmatic smile flickered on his lips. "Where do you think I get it? I'm sure you can make a decent guess."

Carwyn narrowed his eyes and thought. How many immortal priests or nuns were scattered around the globe, intimately involved with their communities? Hundreds? Thousands? How many more vampires like him who retained strong ties to the church? How many did Arturo speak to on a regular basis?

He mused, "No wonder you made this easy for me. You want me to stay in contact. You want to use me for information."

"Of course I do." Arturo leaned forward. "We have great resources. Chief among them is our people. And misconception. How many of the more unsavory characters in the immortal world believe the nonsense about being demons and rejected by God? How many more dismiss the Church as no longer having any influence in matters of state? My office is quiet and efficient. We have a mission to promote God's kingdom. To keep the Church and its flock—mortal *and* immortal—safe. I will use any and all resources at my disposal to do that. I think you understand my mission. I think you approve of it. So why don't you tell me why you were wearing such a thunderous expression when I first walked into the room? Why don't you tell me the real story behind this 'elixir' and why I'm beginning to hear mention of it from various corners of the globe?"

"Which corners?"

Arturo took a deep breath. "Russia. Eastern Europe. A rumor in India. Whispers in the Eastern church."

"Lorenzo has been producing it in Bulgaria."

The Spaniard raised an eyebrow. "Do you truly think that is the extent of this madness? One plant?"

His breath caught. "Of course. There's more, isn't there? There has to be."

"What I know about Lorenzo tells me that he is all about profit," said Arturo. "Livia is about power. But profit trumps power, and Livia is *not* Lorenzo's only backer. We don't know who, but we're quite sure of that. The elixir is being produced elsewhere."

"Can it be contained?"

"I don't think so. Perhaps if we understood it more, but we don't. Two things have been my priorities: finding out what is does and how it can be detected. For humans and vampires both. We know the formula is given to humans who then give blood to vampires, but what are the effects? We're getting mixed reports, and nothing like this has been seen as far as I know."

How much could he tell the human? Carwyn weighed his options and decided that Arturo was a worthy ally.

"Currently, my people don't know much more than you do. We know that it does appear to heal humans who take it, but there are side effects for vampires."

"What side effects?"

Carwyn crossed his arms and laid out what he knew. "The first side effects are an immediate cure for bloodlust—"

"Not a bad thing."

"—and increased strength. I suspect elemental power, too."

Arturo grimaced. "That is somewhat frightening, considering all the power you already have. All humanitarian arguments aside, why would this be a concern to vampires? Those are all positives for you." The priest narrowed his eyes. "You said the *first* side effects—"

"The negative effects come later. Increased sleep. Mental confusion. Lost time."

"Lost time?"

"Fugue states that seem to strike out of nowhere."

Arturo's eyes gleamed. "Now that could be very, very dangerous for those who cannot survive sunlight."

"Indeed. We're attempting to learn more. You might contact Lucien Thrax while he's still in Rome. He has taken it and is suffering the consequences."

The Spaniard sat up and straightened his shoulders. "The physician? I will do that. For now, I will alert my people that this elixir—"

"It's a drug, Arturo. Call it what it is."

He nodded. "Fine. This *drug* is harmful, and they should avoid it. The problem, of course, is how? If a human has already taken this drug, they are a walking poison for your kind. A danger to the those who would drink from them, or kill them because of the threat. There has to be some way of detecting it. We just don't know what it is."

Carwyn sighed and closed his eyes. "Then I suppose I have my new mission."

"I suppose you do."

~~~

Plovdiv, Bulgaria
July 2012

Dear Brigid,

We've learned more about the elixir, but it doesn't sound good. Keep on your guard; this had the potential to be very dangerous. I know that you prefer feeding from human donors, but please consider drinking animal blood until I can find out more. We must learn how to detect this drug in humans. Otherwise, any of us could drink it without being aware, and the side effects are beginning to sound more and more severe the more we learn.

Giovanni and I are leaving Rome to try to find more answers. I may not be able to write for some time. I'll contact you as soon as I get back to Dublin. I don't want to say too much in a letter. (Also, Bulgaria is beautiful. We should consider coming here for our honeymoon.)

I miss you. I think of you every day. Pray for our safety.

Love, Carwyn

P.S. Would you consider going to Wicklow and fetching Madoc? I'm fairly sure the dog is miserable without me there. Sinead may have mentioned it once or twenty times to Deirdre.

P.P.S. I just realized my dog is going to share your bed before I do. Lucky mongrel.

Chapter Twenty-Five

Dublin
October 2012

Brigid opened the door. Deirdre stood with her hand raised to knock, seemingly startled to be caught in the act.

"Hello," Brigid said.

"Hello."

There was an awkward pause. "Am I supposed to call you 'Mother' now?"

Deirdre snorted and pushed into the house. "Don't be ridiculous. I'm hardly the most maternal person, and you've never wanted a mum."

"You're back from Rome."

"I am."

Deirdre had been called away months before to help Carwyn and his friends in Rome. She'd been back for weeks, but had stopped in London and Wicklow before coming to Dublin.

A smile lifted the corner of Deirdre's mouth as she angled past Brigid and slipped down the hallway. "Thanks for inviting me in."

"So, you got the letter from Murphy?" She turned to watch Deirdre standing in her small living room, examining it. For some reason, the perusal of her sire made her nervous. It was the first time Deirdre had been to her home. "The letter, did you get it?"

"I did. That's why I came back from Italy." Then she muttered under her breath, "That, and an annoying Scot."

Brigid frowned. "Is there any—?"

"No news." Deirdre turned and looked with haunted eyes. "Nothing since Istanbul."

Brigid nodded. For months, she'd received letters from Carwyn. Silly letters with stories to make her laugh. Serious letters filled with warnings and information about the drug they were investigating. Long, loving letters filled with sweet words that made her sigh. And every letter just made her fall further in love with him.

Brigid bit her lip nervously. "My last letter was from Istanbul, too."

Deirdre cocked her head and smiled. "He'll be fine. He's with Gio, and no one's more dangerous when his friends or family are threatened."

"So I've heard." Still didn't make her feel much better. She'd rather be the one starting fires.

Deirdre roamed about the room, examining her books and the art on the walls. "Father's very close-mouthed about your relationship. I have to confess to being very curious."

"We're…" *In love. Involved.* Dating was too silly a word and it wasn't as if they'd gone out for drinks and a show. What did Carwyn call it again?

Brigid cleared her throat. "He says he's 'courting' me. I don't really know what that means, but I'm fairly certain the church would frown on it."

Deirdre looked like she was about to burst out laughing. "Is that so? Well, good luck to him. I very much doubt the church is going to have much say in the matter, so the next time you see him, tell him—as your sire—I'm demanding at least two dozen sheep for you and a stout draft horse."

Brigid narrowed her eyes. "I'm not sure whether I should be flattered by that or not."

"Considering he won't be getting any fine, strong sons from your fertile loins, he'll probably consider it a bargain."

She rolled her eyes and fought the urge to burst out laughing. "You did come from medieval times, didn't you?"

"Not me, but he did." Deirdre walked past, patting her shoulder as she continued exploring the house. "Literally. Medieval."

"Don't remind me."

"So was Ioan. Luckily, the Welsh of that age were unusually progressive. They make excellent husbands, if you can find them." She smiled sadly as she touched a picture of Ioan and Brigid that was tucked onto the shelf of one bookcase. "He was such a fine husband."

"I miss him every day. Well… night." Brigid blinked back the tears that came to her eyes. "You know, growing up I always thought…"

"What?"

Her voice was almost a whisper. "If I could find anyone to love me like Ioan loved you, I'd be the luckiest girl in the world."

Within seconds, Brigid was squeezed in a tight embrace. "He does. Carwyn does love you like that. And if you return it, then you're both the lucky ones."

And in another instant, she was gone, standing in front of the refrigerator with the door hanging open.

"What do you have to drink?"

Brigid heated the pig's blood she'd bought from the butcher. Since the word had spread through Murphy's offices—by way of Carwyn's letters to her—most of the staff had begun to drink animal blood. No one liked it, and after several months, Brigid had noticed that she felt weaker and was sleeping more. Less strength, far less tasty, but safer until they could learn how to avoid the elixir. She heated the cold bag in the simmering water before she snipped the corner and poured it into a mug for Deirdre.

"Cheers." She clinked her cup with the other vampire's as she sat down.

"Is everyone drinking animal now?"

"Mostly those on staff. Murphy's being cautious about not causing a panic until we know more. I think Jack still takes a nip from the girls every now and then, though."

Deirdre shook her head and took a sip. "Playing with fire."

"No." She grinned. "That's me."

Deirdre laughed as Brigid tossed a small flame toward a candle in the center of the table.

"Really though…" Deirdre fell serious. "It's not a joke. This drug is incredibly damaging. One of Ioan's oldest friends has drunk elixired blood. He's far older than Carwyn, and his sire is one of the ancients of our kind. Still, one drink from a human who had taken it has weakened him dangerously."

"There has to be some way to detect it. No one would create something like this without putting in some kind of—of marker, or sign, or something. And humans must have some noticeable symptoms. Maybe not at first, but—"

"I agree." Deirdre nodded. "Any vampire who produced it would put in some safeguard or marker. Our kind is too cautious not to."

"Do we have any idea when we'll know more from Rome?"

Deirdre shook her head. "I'm sure, as soon as Beatrice—Giovanni's wife—knows, she'll spread the word. She's young like you, and not as secretive as the older ones."

"And Carwyn?" Her voice lifted in hope. "Any idea when he'll be…" She almost said 'home,' then realized that his home was actually in Wales, which didn't suit her at all.

Her sire's eyes twinkled. "He'll come back as soon as he can. Your guess is probably better than mine. I'm fairly certain Dublin will be his first stop."

A smile fought its way to Brigid's mouth. "Well, he's missed." She took a drink and made a horrified face. "And I'll be extremely grateful to figure out some way to eat properly again, as well."

Deirdre threw her head back and laughed. "It's not that bad!"

"Yes, it is. How do you stand it?"

She winked. "Well, I've been known to take a nip now and then from a human. Don't tell Father."

"Oh really?" She smiled, feeling like she and Deirdre were sharing girlhood secrets. "He knows I don't drink animal blood as a rule. Doesn't seem to bother him."

"He's not judgmental." Deirdre paused. "Plus, after all this time, he's probably curious what your blood will taste like when he drinks from you."

Brigid almost snorted the pig's blood through her nose. "W—what?"

A wicked grin crossed her sire's face. "Well now, it looks like Cathy and Anne didn't get to have *all* the fun with the new girl. Brigid, my dear, it's time for an entirely *different* kind of 'special talk.'"

She couldn't decide what was making her skin heat. Embarrassment or curiosity. Probably both.

After a few more hours having her ears scorched by far more than she ever wanted to know about vampire sex and mating habits, Brigid was back at The Abbey, the club where Jack had been attacked. It remained open, more as a place to gather information than anything else. Over the previous three months, it had become the vampire 'place to be seen and drink' so it had attracted a large immortal clientele, as well as humans who liked to be bitten. A win for everyone. Especially the club owners, who were turning an even larger portion of their earnings over to Murphy.

She sat, bored, watching the stupid and the desperate. Many of the humans wore the hollow eyes of those looking for oblivion, so much like the aching girl she had been, it made Brigid want to weep. When she thought about her life seven years before, she wanted to wring her own neck.

What did she think she was running from? As painful as reliving and working through her abuse had been—still was—she had come to a place of peace that the human Brigid never could have imagined.

Her thoughts were interrupted by Jack, who had come back to the table looking flushed and evil.

Brigid frowned. "I don't particularly like you, Jack, but I'd miss you if you lost your mind. Cut it out, will you?"

He only shrugged. "It's not like I haven't lived past my allotted time anyway, Connor. If the good Lord decides to take me for enjoying the neck of a plump young thing… well, it's been a good run."

"Idiot."

"Prude."

"Lot you know."

"Brigid, your man is a priest. If that isn't a recipe for sexual frustration, I don't know what is."

She fell silent, thinking about Deirdre's visit. And Istanbul. And dangerous places she couldn't roam.

"Hey." Jack tugged on her arm. "I'm just teasing you, Brigid. And don't get that sad, weepy look. Your man's one of the most powerful vamps I've ever met. And he's a tricky one. He'll be fine."

"Tricky?" She frowned, as Jack leaned back with a lazy smile and spread his arms across the back of the booth. "Why do you say that?" Brigid thought Carwyn was one of the most straightforward people she'd ever met.

"Think about it. He's terribly clever. Comes across as a very jovial chap, the Father does. Crazy Hawaiian shirts and loud laugh. The life of the party and everyone's favorite friend." A keen glint came to Jack's eye. "But push him past that joking manner and he's rather unpredictable. A thousand years old, after all. In our young corner of the world, that's something. I've seen him fight." Brigid looked at him and he gave a slow nod. "Once. And I learned a valuable lesson."

"Oh? What's that?"

He smiled slowly. "Always let your enemies underestimate you."

"He won?" A smile flicked over her face. "Of course he won."

Jack chuckled. "Never seen a dozen Frenchmen so surprised."

Just then, a long sweep of hair caught her attention. A broad shoulder peeked from the shadows in the corner of the club.

"Jack." Brigid nudged him. "I think that's someone we know."

The other vampire threw back the pint he'd ordered. It was warm, but immortals tended not to like cold beer anyway. "Oh aye," Jack murmured. "Hello, pretty boy. We've been looking for you."

It was, undoubtedly, Axel. Emily's ex-boyfriend and former drug dealer had disappeared for months. Brigid didn't even know if he'd stayed in Dublin. Emily claimed to have nothing to do with him since rehab, and Jack had been frustrated, since he thought Axel had something to do with whoever was shipping drugs into Dublin. While the heroin problem seemed to be tapering off, the whispers about the new "vampire drug" were growing louder.

Brigid still had her doubts whether he had the brains to mastermind an operation, which had gone undetected under Murphy's nose, but his disappearance, and now reappearance, was certainly speaking in favor of Axel being more than just a pretty face and a long set of fangs.

"You want to grab him?" she asked Jack.

"Yes. I don't think he's noticed me. Grab the human he just sent to the bar and meet me in the alley. I have a few questions for our dear Dane."

"He's Norwegian." She slid out from the booth eagerly. Finally, the night had become more interesting.

She waded through the sea of dancers, using the crowd to hide her approach from the girl who stood twitching at the bar. *User.* The girl looked like she needed a fix. Her balance was uneven and Brigid could see the beginning of ribs showing though the skintight black dress she wore. Her light brown hair hung limp at her shoulders. Brigid sidled up to her, glancing over her shoulder to see Jack approaching Axel from the far side of the club.

No scenes. Just a friendly chat with Axel's current—

She looked over, stunned. "Emily?"

It couldn't be.

It had been four months since they'd met for a drink. After their meeting in May, they'd talked on the phone a few times. Brigid had gone to Emily's house to meet her family, all of whom seemed understandably wary of the vampire. The two friends had kept in contact, but only over the phone the last few months, she suddenly realized. Otherwise, Brigid would have noticed Emily's rapid deterioration.

"Brigid… hello. I'm just—"

"Em, what's wrong with you?"

The thin smile Emily had been trying to muster fell. "Nice to see you too. Been a while. How's life? How's immortal health? Must be nice."

Brigid shook her head and glanced rapidly between where Axel had been standing and back to Emily. Jack must have already taken the other vampire out to the alley. "I'm just… I'm not going to lie, Emily. You look sick. How…?" Brigid's voice dropped and she stepped closer, closing her nostrils to the sickly sweet scent of Emily's illness. "Are you using again? It's okay. Everyone slips. I'll get you help. We don't even have to tell your parents if you don't want to. I have some money and I can—"

Emily tore her thin arm away from Brigid's warm hand. "You think I'm on drugs again?"

"You're skin and bones! I mean… what the hell? The last time I saw you, you'd lost some weight, but you said you'd found a new diet and you felt wonderful. Now, you look like a—a skeleton. I'm worried about you!"

"Well, don't be." She handed her cash over to the bartender and took her drinks. She turned, but Axel was nowhere to be found.

"What are you doing with Axel? Are you two back together?"

Emily's eyes flickered over the crowd, and Brigid had the distinct impression that she'd already been forgotten. "We're just friends," the woman murmured, clutching the two martini glasses between bony fingers. "We just hang out. It's not like he's dealing drugs anymore."

"He better not be." She was drifting away, and Brigid was torn between wanting to shove the girl in a cab and send her to her parent's house— possibly along with some chicken soup if she could find it—and trying to find Jack and Axel. She didn't buy for one moment that Emily wasn't using again. And if Axel was the one to blame…

Brigid blinked. In the split second that she'd glanced toward the alley, Emily was gone. She searched the club with her eyes, but the thin woman wasn't in the shadows or the mess of surging dancers in the middle of the floor.

"Shit!" Where could she have gone so fast? Brigid bolted down a narrow hallway and out the alley door. She stepped into the dark street and looked around. There were two figures near the dumpster. She could hear voices, but nothing distinct. Brigid scowled. They must have been vampires. Only other immortals could drop their voice to a low whisper that was only intelligible to others with preternatural hearing. She walked toward them.

"Oy!" She reached for the pistol at the small of her back.

They were cloaked in thick darkness, but her eyes caught the profile of the shorter one as he began to turn.

Her breath caught. "What—?"

The pinch caught her at the base of the neck a moment before she sensed the vampire behind her. It was like being blasted by fire from the inside out, and the crackling energy that lived under her skin froze for a split second before time seemed to stop.

The dust motes hung still in the glowing streetlights. She tasted the acid on her tongue. Silence blanketed the cold alley.

A familiar voice screamed '*No!*' as her heart took off in a panicked gallop. The air around her seemed to contract a second before the fire exploded out and everything went black.

When Brigid woke, it was approaching dawn. She was naked and alone in the alley, and a black ring scorched the earth around her. Her fangs fell down at the scent of human blood; then she gagged as the smell of burning flesh touched her nose. She turned, and there was a pile of black flakes scattered out behind her and the twisted body of a human a few feet away.

She crawled toward the human remains. The mostly intact shoes marked it as a male. Probably young from the style. She guessed he'd been wearing a jacket, but the blast had ripped it back, melting his keys and wallet into the scorched ribcage, just below his heart.

Brigid crawled away, disgusted, trying to remember what had happened. Trying not to retch.

The club.

Music. Pounding. A dance floor. She'd been looking for someone.

Emily.

Had she followed Emily out to the alley and lost her temper? Brigid didn't remember. She didn't remember *anything*. She hadn't lost control like that since… not since she had first turned in the library in Wicklow.

Her stomach twisted as she stared at the charred bones. Had she meant to kill the human? Was she defending herself? Who was it?

She looked around at the alley. She needed to find answers. She needed to get to shelter. And—she rubbed hands over her bare arms—she really needed some clothes, as well.

Brigid could feel the rips on her knees closing as she lurched to her feet. She was starving. Clearly, whatever fire had overtaken her had drained her body *and* her amnis. She needed food. She stumbled toward the back door of the club, hoping she could find clothes inside.

As she walked past the human's body, a gold glint caught her eye in the streetlight.

She bent down. Melted into the side of the body, under what was left of the man's back, was a warped glass bottle. The lid was gold and it was made of frosted red glass, like an expensive perfume or lotion. But Brigid was fairly sure that the human wasn't carrying perfume in his jacket.

Because when she picked it up and brushed the black scorch marks away from the bottle, only one word was etched onto the dirty red glass.

ELIXIR.

CHAPTER TWENTY-SIX

Dear Brigid,

It's silly the things we do, sometimes. Like writing letters no one will ever read.

I'm in a cave in the Caucasus Mountains. It's midday and Giovanni is sleeping. I might die tomorrow night, and the only thing I can think of is that I wish I'd had time to make love to you once. Just once. To know you that way. To love you. I don't want to die. I'm greedy, aren't I? A thousand years isn't enough.

I wish that I'd had the feel of your skin against mine. To wake next to you at nightfall.

I love you, Brigid.

So, I'll pray the prayer of a greedy man and ask for another thousand years. Maybe that will be enough.

Part of me wishes I could turn back. Go to you. Hide away and steal those years, but then I wouldn't be good enough for you. You've never run from a fight in your life. Not even when it was against yourself. Have I told you how I admire you? I do.

You'll never read this letter. And I'll have faith that God would not have brought us together without a purpose. The hardships in your life have only prepared you for this fight. And I have to believe I will be at your side.

Whatever happens in these mountains, this evil will not end here. It will not end in Rome. Perhaps it will not end. And I must seek the truth to make us safe. That is the only thing keeping me from you, love.

I pray for your safety.

Take care of yourself, Brigid. Until I can.

Carwyn

CHAPTER TWENTY-SEVEN

Dublin
December 2012

Brigid listened as Deirdre sat in Murphy's office, briefing them about the events in Rome.

"Livia is finished," she said. "The power in Rome lays in Emil Conti's hands now."

"He's an ally," Murphy muttered. "Not a strong one, but we'll cultivate it. And the elixir?"

"The plant in Bulgaria has been shut down. The elixir that has already been produced there has been destroyed. Father assured me of this."

Declan leaned forward. "That's all fine, but what of the bottle that Brigid found on the body here in Dublin? Whoever attacked her may have been killed, but they're not working alone. We've had more and more reports of immortals with odd behavior. Vampires leaving town unexpectedly. Humans in our community disappearing. Something is going on. This elixir is here and we still have no idea how to detect humans that have taken it."

Brigid asked, "This Lucien Thrax, the physician. He's taken it?"

Deirdre said. "Lorenzo gave him the elixir in Eastern Europe over a year ago. When I left Rome, he was failing, though Carwyn writes that his sire came for him and they think—*think*—that a sire's blood will heal an affected vampire."

"But it was Lorenzo who gave it to him. Not Livia?"

Deirdre nodded.

Murphy asked, "What are you thinking, Brigid?"

"Who's to say that Lorenzo didn't have his own supply? I doubt he trusted anyone but himself. If he gave some to Lucien, perhaps he gave some to others, too."

Silence blanketed the room.

It was Tom who finally spoke. "It would fit with what we know. He was the one trafficking heroin in Dublin—probably to fund this elixir production. When Ioan was killed and he disappeared, the purer heroin dried up. Almost completely. We have a year or two of quiet before we start hearing rumors about this vampire drug. Deirdre, does that sound about right?"

"It does," she said softly. "Fits the timeline."

"He probably just quit with the human drugs and focused on the vampire one. I'm sure it'll make him more money."

Declan said, "And now someone is picking up right where he left off. Probably the local that Brigid was always on about."

Jack shook his head. "Even if people believe the rumors out of Rome about the effects, many won't believe it. Besides, it's still attractive. It quells bloodlust, increases elemental strength—"

"Causes you to lose your mind," Brigid said. "Slowly, but surely kills you."

Murphy said, "So does heroin, but humans become addicted to it nonetheless. And for immortals who already believe they're superior to humanity, this drug will be even more attractive. No one will believe it's harmful until they see the effects themselves. We all believe what we want until we're forced to face reality."

Deirdre said, "Carwyn says that it's foolish to think that we can stop it at this point. Maybe it was hidden for hundreds of years, but the secret's out now. And there will always be vampires and humans willing to exploit the ignorance of others. But they won't do it without some kind of safety net. Not for something this dangerous."

Brigid nodded. "There has to be some way to detect it in humans."

"Agreed," Tom said. "There's some way of detecting a human that's been tainted. Otherwise, the ones profiting from it are poisoning their own food supply. The smartest dealers never use themselves. Human. Vampire. Same thing."

Murphy asked, "Did Carwyn tell you anything else?"

Deirdre said, "No. I believe he's been having meetings with someone in Vatican City, but he's been quite vague. But he's in Italy until after the New Year, so he has to have a reason. Otherwise..." Deirdre glanced at Brigid. "I doubt he'd stay away from Dublin for this long."

Brigid studiously ignored the pointed glances that bounced around the room. He hadn't written to her. Hadn't called. And he was getting information from the Vatican, which probably had big, important sources around the globe. No doubt, an ally that Carwyn would not want to lose. Especially now. After all, this problem was far bigger than sentiment. A heavy weight settled over her heart and any hope she had of Carwyn leaving the priesthood fled. Just as quickly, she brushed her own feelings aside. They were facing a new, incredibly dangerous threat, and she was acting like a lovesick schoolgirl.

Idiot.

As Deirdre finished up with the briefing, Brigid took quick notes that she just as quickly committed to memory.

The drug, Elixir, had been produced as a partnership between Livia, the former leader of Rome, and Lorenzo, the vampire who had killed Ioan.

Ioan's research before his death had been confirmed by Lucien Thrax, an ancient physician who had become infected with the elixir himself. It *was* possible to create a drug that would affect vampires. While the initial effects of the drug were positive, like all drugs, it would eventually kill the user. The ancient vampires that Carwyn and Giovanni Vecchio found had confirmed that the elixir would, over time, destroy an immortal's amnis and ability to function by killing the mind. The results took time to manifest, but were inevitable. Only the ingestion of untainted blood from a vampire's sire could heal the amnis and return an immortal to health.

Despite the deaths of both Livia and Lorenzo, the drug was still being produced. They had found more than one bottle floating around Dublin. One, on the body of the human Brigid had killed after being shocked. Jack also said he'd killed two vampires who were giving it to girls at clubs. Even he had stopped drinking from any human after he'd discovered that.

"Brigid?" She blinked and looked up to see Murphy staring at her. "What's up?"

"You with us? I was asking if you'd found your friend."

"Emily? No, not yet. Her parents haven't seen her. The more I find out, the more I think that she must have taken Elixir. Axel probably gave it to her. We know he had ties to Lorenzo, so he's probably the local connection that we've been looking for. You were right."

She saw Jack frown in the corner of the room. "Why would Pretty Boy give it to Emily?" he asked. "He drank from her. Do you think he didn't know what it did?"

Brigid shrugged. "Is it that far of a stretch to think Lorenzo wouldn't have confided in him? If he was the one coordinating the heroin trafficking a few years ago, it's possible that Lorenzo just shipped him the drug and told him to sell it. Lorenzo wouldn't have cared what happened to Axel or anyone else. It was profit to him. And if the cut for the local dealers was big enough, I doubt anyone would question it."

Tom asked, "Any more memories of the night you were attacked? It could give us a clue if there's anyone else he's working with."

She shook her head. "Nothing. The last thing I remember was talking to Emily, then waking up in the alley. I didn't have a scratch on me, so I don't think I was attacked, but I don't remember anything."

Jack nodded. "That fits with my experience with the Taser, too. Just a big blank. Fairly happy I'm not a fire vamp, though." Jack's eyes gleamed. "That's a neat trick, Brigid. How'd you stay alive?"

Something about the way everyone was looking at her gave Brigid pause. She met Deirdre's eyes and her sire gave her head an almost infinitesimal shake.

"No idea, Jack," she said. "Just luck, I suppose." Brigid realized that, if anyone knew how a Taser blast affected immortals, they would easily think it was a way to kill her. After all, fire was one of the few ways an immortal could be killed. If she was a normal fire vampire and her element turned on her, she would be dead.

Jack's mouth lifted at the corner. "Very good luck, indeed."

The meeting quickly wrapped up, and Deirdre walked Brigid home where one of her humans was waiting to take her back to Wicklow.

"I want you to watch your back, Brigid," she said quietly. "There was something in that room that I couldn't quite put my finger on. I know that all those men are your friends, but they're not family, so be careful."

Her heart rebelled at the thought of any of her team members using knowledge of her weaknesses against her, but she knew Deirdre was right.

"I'll be careful," she said.

"Let's keep the extent of your power under wraps for the moment. No need for everyone to know that your main weakness as a fire vampire isn't truly a weakness."

Brigid gave a rueful smile. "Who knew my natural prickliness would manifest in such a useful way?"

Deirdre barked out a laugh. "I'm going back to Wicklow tonight. I may go to Anne's for a bit. Pick her brain about a few things."

"Tell her I said hello."

"I will. And give Father my greetings when he gets back to town."

"Deirdre—"

"Which I have no doubt he'll be doing as soon as possible," her sire said with a grin. "And tell him I'll expect the livestock within a month's time or I'm withdrawing my offer."

They had stopped at Brigid's front door and Deirdre's car was puffing out exhaust into the damp, winter air as it idled at the curb.

Brigid shook her head. "I don't think Carwyn's going to risk his sources through the church right now to... whatever it is he thinks he's doing. Whatever we are—or were—it's not more important than stopping this drug from spreading."

Deirdre frowned for a moment before catching Brigid in a quick, one-armed hug that she'd become accustomed to from her sire. "Nothing's more important than love," she said.

"That's not true. You're the leader of a huge clan. You know that there are more important considerations than—"

"Ioan told me that, Brigid," Deirdre said. For a moment, she caught the pink glow in Deirdre's eyes. "Ioan told me that long ago. Before I was immortal, he told me that love was the bond that tied his family together. And together they could face any challenge the world throws at them. Love is the foundation of strength." She cocked her eyebrow and smiled a little. "Wonder where he learned that?"

Then the tall redhead slipped into the dark sedan and it pulled away.

BUILDING FROM ASHES

January 2013

Brigid scanned the list of names in front of her.

Dillon McCaffrey-114 years
Cristina Leon-65 years
Otto Smith-320 years

The list went on from there. Over twenty names. Some newly turned and others older. All who had been reported missing from Dublin or the surrounding areas. Vampires had the habit of moving from place to place —particularly the older ones—so some of these would be false alarms. Friends or clan members who would turn up in six months or six years on the other side of the globe. Others would have gone into hiding alone or with friends if their health seemed to be in peril.

And some might turn up as ashes, like newly turned Joseph Van Elsen, whose sire had discovered his remains in the garden at twilight when she came to check on her child. The sire had been worried about Joseph's unusual behavior the previous months, but had never suspected that a drug could have caused it. Brigid only knew about the loss because Joseph's sire was one of Murphy's former lovers and had come to him for answers.

Panic was growing, which meant vampires and the humans who were under their aegis were growing *more* silent and secretive, not less. Which made looking for missing vampires even more difficult.

And Brigid had given up hope of ever finding the humans.

The human list was longer. Much longer. And she had given up on every name except for one.

Emily Neely.

Brigid took a sip of the warm pig's blood in her travel mug and made a face as the phone rang. She glanced around, but there was no one in the office except her, so she ignored the gloves she usually slipped on to answer the phone and punched the speaker button with her pencil.

"This is Connor."

There was a pause.

"Um... hello?" A timid voice filled the empty office.

"Yes?"

"Is this Emily's friend, Brigid?"

She blinked and leaned closer to the phone, resisting the impulse to pick it up. "Yes. Is this... is this Mrs. Neely?"

"Yes, it is. I remember you called a few weeks ago. You'd left your card and asked me to call if there was any news."

Brigid's heart began to race. "Have you found her? Is she all right?"

There was a low sniff and a thread of steel filled the voice. "No. I mean —yes, we've found her. She's... in the hospital, but she's not all right. I know we're under Murphy's aegis, so we should call the main office, but you said that you worked for him, and she asked me to call you so—"

"It's fine. Tell me where she is. I'll come right now." It was after three in the morning, but this was more important than the sorting and filing she'd been doing while Declan and Jack were out on patrol. Mrs. Neely gave her the address of the hospital in suburban Dublin and Brigid called for a car.

Half an hour later, she was pulling up to the emergency entrance and asking the driver to wait. Brigid walked in, her touch persuading the nurse in the Emergency department to escort her to the private room where Emily lay. She walked into the room and paused, shocked by the scene. Brigid's mother and father sat on one side of the bed, staring with hollow eyes at the shell of their daughter in the bed.

Emily was covered with a white sheet, the formerly vibrant girl thin and sallow beneath the florescent lights. Her arms looked like twigs. Her hair was limp and uneven around her face. She appeared to be sleeping and monitors around her beeped and jumped as Brigid approached. She tried not to get too close, having no idea how she would affect the equipment that was monitoring her old friend or keeping her alive, she wasn't sure which.

"Don't worry." She heard a croak from the sheets. "If you short any of it out, it'll just make the nurses panic. Nothing's really keeping me alive," Emily said with a thin voice. Her eyes had still not opened. "Mum, Dad, can you let me and Brigid talk for a bit?"

Brigid could tell that Mr. and Mrs. Neely didn't want to leave, but they measured Brigid in her work clothes, which that night consisted of black combat pants, a black T-shirt, and a leather jacket, and decided not to challenge the grim-looking vampire their daughter wanted to speak with.

Emily's mother whispered, "We'll be right down the hall, dear." Then she left the bedside and shot Brigid a hateful look.

She blames a vampire for this.

She was probably right.

Emily finally opened her eyes and lifted a hand. "Hey."

"Hey, Em."

"You can come closer. Like I said, nothing's keeping me alive at this point anyway."

"What happened? This isn't drugs."

Emily curled a finger to bring her closer and whispered, "If I speak this low can you hear me? Don't want Mum and Dad to hear."

Brigid nodded and leaned closer. The machines beeped and went blank for a moment before she drew back. Emily grasped her hand in a surprisingly powerful grip.

"Don't. Don't worry about that. This is more important. You need to listen to me, Brig."

"What is it?" Her nose twitched and an ancient instinct alerted her. Emily was dying. The sickly sweet smell of disease emanated from her friend, and Brigid tried not to curl her lip. Her stomach twisted in the same way she remembered it had as a human when she smelled spoiled meat.

"I know I'm dying. I don't want you to make me a vampire, but that's not why I wanted to talk to you."

Brigid was grateful that Emily wasn't going to ask. As much as it twisted her heart to see her friend in pain, she'd been warned by both Deirdre and Cathy about humans who were too sick. They often didn't survive turning and, if they did, were weak and unstable in immortality. Besides, Brigid had a suspicion that drinking Emily's blood could be lethal for both of them.

"What happened to you?"

A heartbreaking smile crossed Emily's lips. "He said it would make me beautiful forever. I was so vain. Stupid, stupid girl."

"You're not stupid."

"I was." She sighed and her eyes slipped close again. "I wouldn't turn. He wanted me to, but I didn't want to give up the sun. He told me… it was the elixir of life. I would live forever and be young and beautiful, just like him. And at first, I thought he was right."

"Who, Em? Was it Axel?"

Emily nodded.

"When?"

"About a year ago, right after I quit using."

She brushed a bloody tear from her eye as she watched her friend dying before her eyes. "Just a year?"

"I'd been having a hard time. You know how it feels. I felt years older. I looked awful. I thought for sure that Axel was going to break things off. Then, he got a shipment of Elixir from Europe. I think… maybe Germany? Said it was for humans. More like a supplement than a drug. I took it, and I felt…" She sighed as her eyes drifted closed. "Amazing. My skin glowed. I had so much energy. No more cravings… I didn't feel high, just healthy. For the first time in so long, I felt vital. I didn't need much sleep. Had an amazing sex drive. It was like I was me, but better."

"What happened? When did you start to notice a change?"

"Right around the time we broke up. When I first saw you, Axel and I had just split up. I lied. We hadn't been separated for months like I said. I knew Murphy's people were looking for him, but I didn't want to betray him. He had always been so sweet with me, but he'd been getting… different. Hostile. Not like himself and it seemed like he blamed me for it. I didn't know why."

Brigid whispered, "He was probably starting to suffer the effects from the Elixir. It wasn't your fault."

"He drank from me so much. He said my blood tasted sweeter. That I smelled like ripe fruit." She sniffed. "But I was poisoning him, and I didn't even know it."

Brigid's senses alerted. "Like ripe fruit?" She remembered when she had met Emily in the spring. What did she smell like? It *had* been fruit. Something distinctive. It wasn't just sweet. Sharp smelling. What was it? "Did he say anything else?"

She shook her head. "He was evasive. I should have known then that it wasn't a good idea, but he seemed so enthusiastic about it. He couldn't keep his hands off me after I took it. It was almost as if he was high after he drank my blood. And he would say the oddest things. Probably talking about whoever he got it from. 'He's brilliant. We'll make a fortune.' Stuff like that."

"Did he mention any names?"

She shook her head weakly. "No, nothing. Wait... there was one he mentioned when he was speaking to someone in another language on the phone once. He usually didn't make calls in front of me, but I think he thought I was sleeping. He was speaking German, I think. But the name... 'Jacques,' maybe?" Emily began to sniff. "I wish I knew for sure. I'm sorry."

"Shhh," Brigid soothed her, wishing there was something she could do. But no cure had been found for tainted humans. They didn't even know where to start looking. "You're doing fine, Emily. You've been an amazing help."

"I was a crap friend, Brig."

"No, you weren't." Brigid could feel the tears come to her eyes. "You were my only friend."

"I wish I'd never taken you out partying. That was so awful of me."

"No." Brigid's voice was hoarse. "You know, everything happens for a reason. I didn't see it at the time, but looking back... there's nothing in my life that I'd change. As horrible as some of it has been, it's all worked together to make me who I am. And... I like that person. I finally do. I'm strong. I've learned a lot. I have things to offer now. I don't want to give that up."

Emily blinked slowly and a dreamy smile crossed her lips. "Are you in love, Brigid? You should be. You deserve love. You deserve the happiest happy ending in the world."

She sat down and leaned her elbow on the edge of the bed. For a moment, they were two girls in college, confiding their secrets again.

"Can I tell you a secret?"

"I'm dying, so I won't have much time to gossip. I think you're safe."

Brigid said, "I'm in love with a priest."

Emily blinked, opened her mouth, then closed it again. Finally, she said, "You really don't do anything the easy way, do you?"

She let her head fall forward and muffled a quiet laugh. "No, I guess not."

"Does he love you back?"

She nodded. "He says he's *courting* me. Wants to marry me. When he was a human, priests could marry, so he doesn't see a problem with it."

"But you do." It wasn't a question.

Brigid hesitated. "I do—I did. I don't know anymore. Those rules get drilled in young. But the longer he's gone..." She blinked back tears again and lifted her eyes to meet Emily's. "I think, Em, that as long as he comes back safe from wherever he is, I'll take him any way I can get him. Collar or not."

Emily shrugged. "If it doesn't bother him, then don't let it bother you. He's a vampire, of course."

"Yes."

"Well then, both of you will just have to live forever so you avoid eternal damnation. Convenient when you think about it."

Brigid continued to watch Emily as her breathing became labored. The monitors stalled for a moment, probably from Brigid's energy, then they smoothed out again and Emily took a deep breath.

"Part of me," she gasped. "Part of me wants to ask if you'd kill me, Brigid. I don't know how long I'll last like this. They don't know what's wrong with me, just that I'm wasting away. None of the food they give me, not even the feeding tube, seems to do anything. So, I'm going to die. And it's going to be painful, probably. And part of me wants to avoid that." Emily's eyes rose to Brigid's, which were filled with bloody tears she wiped on her shirt sleeve. "But then part of me knows that I'd lose the last bit of time with my parents. That it would kill you to do it, even though you probably would if I asked."

I would, Brigid thought. If Emily truly wanted, she would do it. She wouldn't drink from her, but there were other ways that wouldn't hurt. She could use her amnis to calm her friend so she drifted away and felt no pain. She swallowed hard as Emily continued speaking.

"You would do it because you never shrank from doing the hard thing. But I won't ask. It's like you said earlier, everything happens for a reason. Life. Death. Suffering and joy. There is a frightening beauty in all this that I don't want to lose, even if there's pain, too."

"Are you sure, Em?"

"I am." She closed her eyes and Brigid could feel her begin to drift into sleep. "I'll be here for as long as I am. And when I die, have a damn fruity drink in my honor. You'll hate it, but it'll make you smile. Even if you don't want to."

"I love you, Emily."

Emily smiled, though her eyes did not open. "Thanks, Brig. That's better than I deserve. You should go now. It's getting close to sunrise, isn't it? Take care of yourself."

Brigid sniffed and rose to her feet, brushing back Emily's hair from her forehead as she heard Mr. and Mrs. Neely approaching in the hall.

"I always do," she whispered. "Good-bye."

Brigid stumbled into her house just as she started feeling the pull of day. As soon as she did, her sleepy senses went on alert.

There was someone in her house! Old energy. And… panting?

She blinked once as Madoc bounded down the hall and pushed into her legs. She swayed and tilted. What was Madoc doing there? Deirdre had taken the dog back to Wicklow when she returned from Rome. Unless…

"You mutt." She heard him call. "Don't knock her over; it's almost dawn. She's probably exhausted."

Carwyn was back.

A brilliant smile lit up her face when she saw him approaching. Her vision was swimming, but he was still the most wonderful sight in the world.

"Brigid?"

She was grinning like an idiot and still couldn't speak. There were too many things to say and she was going to pass out on her face. How completely romantic and elegant of her. Luckily, Carwyn caught her in his arms and she took a deep breath of his scent. Dark earth and wind and a woody kind of spice. Home. She let out a breath and wound her arms around his neck as he lifted her up.

"We've rendered the woman speechless, Madoc." He walked to her darkened bedroom, but not before securing the locks on the door behind her. "Well done. Enjoy the moment."

"You're here," she finally whispered. "You're safe. I missed you so much."

Brigid felt him press a kiss to her forehead. "And the moment passes. Forgive me for breaking in, love. I couldn't wait to see you. Thought you'd be home earlier."

"I was at the hospital. Emily… my friend is sick."

His voice was soft as he tucked her into bed. "I'm so sorry, love."

She pulled on his hand. "Stay with me."

Carwyn winked. "If you insist."

"I insist."

He slipped in behind her and wrapped her in his warm arms. She felt his breath as he buried his face in her hair and sighed in relief. It was right. She didn't care about anything else anymore. The world, the church, their families. They could think what they wanted. Carwyn was exactly where he was supposed to be, and she was never letting him go.

Brigid whispered, "Two dozen sheep and a... draft horse, Carwyn."

"What?" She heard him laugh at her.

"Sheep. Horse. Ask... Deirdre."

"What are you talking about?"

"Us. Silly. Marry you. You forgot already."

"Brigid?" His voice sounded so far away.

She sighed and let the dark envelop her. "Love you..."

Chapter Twenty-Eight

Dublin, Ireland
January 2013

He was frozen, staring at the top of her dark head as she sank into sleep.

"Brigid?"

Carwyn blinked and shook her shoulder. What was she talking about?

"Sheep. Horse…"

He poked her side. "What did you say?"

"Marry you. You forgot already… Love you…"

His heart raced, but she was utterly and completely still.

"Brigid Connor, you can't say things like that and then fall asleep!"

He rolled her over and stared at her. "Did you just agree to marry me?"

No response.

"I think you did. Did you?"

She was sleeping the sleep of a baby vampire.

"Aargh!" He rolled over on his back and stared at the ceiling.

"Love you…"

He rolled back toward her and narrowed his eyes. "Are you really sleeping or are you teasing me?" He poked her side. "Brigid?"

She lay completely still. She wasn't even breathing. He poked her once more. Again. He might have lifted her eyelid, just to be sure.

"Brigid Connor!" he yelled. She didn't even flinch. He glanced at the clock. Seven in the morning. She wouldn't wake for another twelve hours.

"Twelve hours…" he muttered. "Twelve *hours*?"

Carwyn ran a frustrated hand through his hair and rolled her on her side so he could face her. Madoc stood on the other side of the bed with his head propped on her hip. Carwyn glared at him. "Back off. You've already shared her bed."

He gathered her into his arms, kissing her forehead and singing her name in a coaxing voice. "Brigid, wake up. I brought you something very silly from Florence. Wake up, love. Please…"

Carwyn peppered her face with kisses. He begged. He bargained. And Brigid was just as asleep after twenty minutes of his most concentrated efforts. He rolled out of bed and resisted punching the wall.

"I travel hundreds of miles—*in a boat!*—and you tell me you love me… I think. And maybe agree to marry me. I think? And then you fall asleep." He groaned. "Oh, wake up, Brigid."

He sighed and collapsed on the bed next to her. "You're not waking up are you?"

He knew, logically, that she wasn't going to wake. It had taken him decades to wake during the day. Even now, it still took effort during parts of the afternoon. A vampire as young as Brigid wouldn't wake for at least twelve hours. He would have to be patient.

"Love you…"

"Oh, Brigid." He settled next to her and cuddled her sleeping body into his chest. "I'm yours. Completely." He kissed her forehead. "Utterly yours. Even if you're sleeping."

Madoc gave a mournful sigh on the other side of the room and Carwyn glanced at him.

"Agreed, my friend, this didn't fit my plan, either."

Wait, she'd said something about Deirdre…

Deirdre would still be awake, and no doubt she'd be happy to hear that he was back in the country. She hadn't been in Wicklow when he'd visited to pick up the dog. He'd traveled up from Waterford after catching a boat in Genoa. Days on a freighter. Days waiting to claim his woman. Only to have her stumble in the door and fall asleep almost immediately. At some point, he was sure to see the humor in the situation.

Eventually.

Restless, he eventually got up and prowled around her small house. The windows had all been equipped with automatic shutters, so he could snoop at his leisure. He poked through her bookcases, randomly offering commentary to the sleeping woman and the dog, who trailed after him, looking on accusingly.

"What?" he scowled at the wolfhound. "If she didn't want me to snoop, she would have stayed awake."

The dog huffed.

"Fine, she has no control over that. I'm just being nosey. Aw, love, look at that." He smiled when he saw a picture of himself and Ioan taken ten years before on a trip to Wales. "Where did you find that? Wicklow, no doubt. Maggie probably sent a copy to Deirdre."

There were a few more mementos from her childhood. A picture of Brigid in a dance costume. One of her and a friend at university. "Look at your hair, Brigid… It was so long. You were so darling."

Carwyn puttered and poked around the house, grabbing a pint of blood from the refrigerator before he decided to call Deirdre and catch up on the most recent news. After a conversation that made him worry and laugh in equal measure, he lay back down next to Brigid, rife with plans for the coming night. Finally, he closed his eyes and prayed that the hours would fly.

He heard her stir before she woke. He rolled over and watched her eyes flutter open, smiling when he saw the grey-brown gaze meet his own. He'd been patient all day.

Patience had run its course.

He scooted down and placed a soft kiss on her lips. They barely moved against his own.

"Brigid?" he whispered. "Can you hear me?"

Just barely, she gave a nod, a smile ghosting over her lips. Which he kissed again before he scooted down and kissed her neck. Her skin was delicious.

"You're really here," she murmured.

"I am. Now, darling, I know you're still sleepy, but I should inform you that two dozen sheep and a draft horse are being delivered to the farm in Wicklow as we speak." He glanced over his shoulder at the clock as he felt her tense beneath him. "Actually, I believe they've already arrived."

She frowned. "Carwyn…"

"And since the bride price has been met, and I am back in the country, we can now be married. Don't worry, I've already spoken to Deirdre and your aunt. Obviously, they're disappointed not to be able to attend the wedding, but since we'll be married immediately…" He trailed off, teasing her collarbone with his lips and anticipating the howling protest that he'd face as soon as she roused to full consciousness. "They gave their blessing anyway."

Her voice was a little louder and her hands reached up to his head. "But Carwyn—"

"Ah ha!" He looked up at her with a grin, pausing in his exploration to watch her. "Speechless. You're obviously as excited as I am."

"Hello to you, too!" Her fingers tightened in his hair, pulling at the roots as she narrowed her eyes. "You've got this all figured out, haven't you? Been plotting all day?"

"Maybe a little."

"And on the trip here?"

"There was a boat. Lots of time to think on a boat."

An evil gleam lit her eye. This was going to be fun. "So, you mean to say we can be married right away?"

"Oh yes." His face was the picture of innocence. "No need to postpone the imminent joy."

She cocked her head to the side thoughtfully. "I think you're on to something."

"Currently, I'm on you." He wiggled his eyebrows. "And quite happy about it."

"Careful. You'll have to confess."

His mouth dipped down to skim over her shoulder. "No need. I plan to honor the marriage bed." A low rumbling sound grew in his chest. "Very, *very* thoroughly."

She pulled on his ear to bring his eyes back to hers. "Excellent idea. It's hardly orthodox, but I can't imagine you've forgotten the ceremony." She snickered. "Even if you are somewhat distracted at the moment."

He was fully expecting her to punch him at any moment for his presumptions. He grinned anyway. "Exactly!"

"Well then, Father Carwyn." She scooted down to meet his mouth, kneading her hands into his shoulders and distracting him as she mumbled, "Proceed."

"What? Right now?"

"Oh yes. The collar, let's face it, is kind of kinky." She pulled away, purring. "Oooh, do you have it with you?"

"Um…" He frowned. She wasn't reacting at all as he'd expected. "Brigid, what—"

"It's okay if you don't. You can always put it on later."

He frowned. What was she playing at? "Brigid—"

She pulled back and her eyes met his with feverish excitement. "Do you think you could find me a nun's habit?"

Carwyn reared back as if she'd burst into flames. "Now, wait just a moment! Some things really are…" Then he trailed off when her mouth spread into a grin. "You're such a brat, Brigid. Don't tease me about nuns. They're frightening, holy creatures."

She burst into laughter. "Well, good to know there are no latent fantasies going on there."

Carwyn tackled her, rolling them over so that she was lying on top of him. He looked up at her. "Say it again," he said softly.

She frowned. "Do you think you could find me a nun's habit?"

Carwyn reached down and pinched her ass. It was, he had to admit, a very nice ass, so he soothed it with a greedy hand. "Not that! What you said…" He brought her face down to his and placed a lingering kiss on her mouth. "Before you fell asleep."

She let out a deep satisfied sigh. "Two dozen sheep, a stout draft horse, and I'm yours, you ridiculous man. I love you."

He'd known it, but hearing her say it was different. "Again."

"I love you."

He sighed in contentment. "Once more."

"You're insatiable. I love you." She kissed his chin. "I love you." Bit his earlobe as he groaned. "Mad, foolish man. I'm in love with you, Carwyn ap Bryn."

Carwyn dove in deep, seduced by her burning lips as they moved against his own. He was already aroused almost painfully when she arched her hips against his. "Brigid, we should probably—"

"Were you serious about the sheep?"

He snorted. "What? No. I don't have random livestock handy, I'm afraid."

"Too bad. I do want to get married, and tonight is as good a time as any."

Carwyn said, "Very funny."

"Do you think I'm joking?" He blinked as she began to tug at the T-shirt covering his torso. "I want to marry you, Carwyn. Why wait?"

She laid burning lips over the scars on his chest. It was getting harder and harder to think straight. "Brigid... wait."

"Why?" She pulled away, suddenly blinking back tears. "I thought I was going to *lose* you," she whispered. "Those months I didn't get any news, I thought I would lose you, and you would be gone, and I'd never get the chance to tell you." She kissed his lips, a tinge of desperation flavoring them. "I'd never get the chance to show you that I love you. I knew a year ago, and I didn't tell you then. I don't even remember why."

"Brigid..." He reached up a hand to stroke along her cheek, soothing her. There were still tears in her eyes.

"And the collar? I don't care about it anymore. I'll marry you, Carwyn. We'll figure it out. I walked in my house this morning and you were *here*. And it was right. And I want to see you there every night and every day. If that means that we have to be married privately, we'll do it. If that means we have to move somewhere—"

"Brigid." He put a hand over her lips and smiled. "I would never hide you. And also... I—I'm not exactly a priest anymore."

She halted. Blinked. "Wha—what?"

"I'm not a priest. I've left the priesthood. The pope even gave me his blessing."

She was frowning. "But... when did you..."

"I knew before I went to Rome that I was leaving the church."

Suddenly, confusion turned to something else. "You knew in March?"

"Um..." Did he not mention that to her? Right. He'd forgotten about that. Well, this would be interesting.

"In *March*?"

That probably wasn't the best way to tell her. Still... she was rather stunning when she was angry. He could feel the heat coming off her skin.

"March! I put up with *months* of guilt and mental anguish over violating the tenets of my childhood faith—"

"Well—"

"And you already *knew?*"

Yep. Madder by the minute. How did one distract a righteously angry woman?

"You *knew* you were leaving and—"

Carwyn grabbed her and kissed her, fully expecting her to injure him in some way. Really, though, it would be worth it. He was aching for her. He dove into her mouth, hoping that would keep her from berating him more. She tried to speak, but finally gave a groan and surrendered to it. Mouth. Hands. Her legs tangled up in his as he rolled over and pressed her into the bed.

Finally, he pulled away, panting. The anger in her eyes was gone, replaced by an edgy hunger that mirrored his own. Oh, he wanted her. A thousand years of desire began to curl in his belly. "I should have told you that I was considering it months ago, but I was being stupid and stubborn, and I wanted you to choose me as I was. I should have told you, Brigid."

She rolled him onto his back, straddling him, and the heat built on her skin wherever he touched. Her neck. The small of her back. He sat up and slid shaking hands along the soft hair at the nape of her neck as she said, "I should have told you I loved you. Loving you was never a sin. I was scared of so much more than that. It was just an excuse."

"I think I knew that," he said. His heart pounded as his fingers dug into the soft flesh of her thighs. "But I'm still glad you said it. Brigid, I'm... impulsive."

"I know."

"Stubborn."

"We won't be bored."

He couldn't stop the laugh. "I'm crazy in love with you."

A gorgeous smile spread over her face. "I know that, too."

"You deserve—"

"You." She pressed her lips to his in a lingering kiss. "I deserve you. For all eternity, I deserve you."

He smiled. "You really want to marry me?"

Her eyes met his with wicked light. "Oh yes."

"Right now?"

"Now."

"I... suppose I can agree to that." Carwyn rolled her under his body, pushing her hands over her head as she arched back into the bed and he began to lick and nibble along her skin. He didn't care about witnesses. Brigid would be his before God, and that was all he desired.

She was his. He was hers. That was all, and it was everything.

"Marry us, Carwyn," she whispered into the dark room. "There's no reason to wait."

He chuckled and let his fingers push her T-shirt up, revealing a belly button pierced with a thin gold ring. Carwyn licked his lips and bent his head, tugging on the decadent gold and closing his mouth over the flesh to suck as her shivering energy leapt in excitement. "Well, I don't know." His tongue played with the ring as she moaned. "You haven't spent much time courting me, Brigid."

"Call me a modern girl, but I'm not paying more than a dozen sheep for you."

He laughed against her skin, then halted and cocked his head, looking at her carefully. Despite the mischievous look in her eye, there was a resolute confidence, as well.

"You're sure of this." It wasn't a question.

"I am. Getting cold feet now?"

He pulled away and looked at her. She was laid out before him like a gift. She *was* a gift. A heart created to love him. A mind to match his own. A body made to be worshiped. And a soul burned, but never destroyed. The fires that had touched her life had only refined her, molding her into the woman she had become. Strong. Loving. Courageous in ways that he could only imagine.

His mate.

Carwyn sat up straight and slowly pulled his shirt over his head, baring his scarred chest to her. Brigid's eyes raked over his bare torso, and a possessive gleam lit in them. Carwyn pulled her up to her knees and placed her palm over the faint scar that still marked his skin. He swallowed the lump in his throat before he spoke hoarsely. "Brigid Connor, will you take me as your husband before God? For the rest of our days on this earth, will you love me and remain faithful to me?"

Her eyes filled with tears when she heard the words. She leaned forward, touching her forehead to his as she said, "Before God, you are my husband. You and no other."

Had his heart ever beat like this before? His amnis reached out to hers. Heat against heat that wove them together as surely as their vows. He touched the face of the extraordinary creature who had claimed him, and returned, "Before God, you are my wife. You and no other."

Their lips met in a single kiss before he drew away. "Is it enough?" he whispered.

"Is it enough for you?"

He nodded. "More than enough."

She gave him a crooked grin. "Just make sure you follow through on the horse."

Carwyn burst into laughter, and Brigid threw her arms around him, tackling him to the bed, which creaked at the motion.

"Brigid," he said as she tore at the buttons on his jeans. "I believe—oh, that's good—I am going to buy you a new bed for a wedding present."

"What—oh!" He nipped at her collar, reached up, and tore the shirt she'd been wearing down the middle with his hands. He tossed it to the side as he stared at her smooth, bare skin. "What's wrong with this bed?" she asked.

He quickly rid her of the scrap of lace she called an undergarment before his mouth latched onto her small breast. She gasped, and his eyes closed in rapture. Her skin was silk under his tongue. He lifted his mouth for a moment and smiled. "Sadly, my wife, this bed is not long for this world. And you taste like heaven."

"We'll give it a—yes, more—proper burial, then." She hooked his pants with her toes and shoved them over his hips.

"Such a talented—*oh*, right there—woman you are." Her body was a revelation. So many sweet curves and corners to explore. It would take years to learn her.

"I'll return the compliment. And that's… impressive."

"I'm not going to say 'I told you so.' Just let me know if there are any pieces of furniture you're fond of." He braced his foot on the end of the bed and heard it give a solid 'crack' under the pressure as his body surged toward hers and he ripped the last of her clothing away.

She pulled him over her. "Wicked…" She let her fangs trail along the edge of his jaw. "Wicked man. Destroying the furniture like that."

He stilled, everything coming into focus in that instant. Brigid under him. Bodies pressed together and amnis entwined. Her scent and heat were a drug to his senses, but he stilled. "No, Brigid. Not wicked," he whispered. "Pure. I was made to love you like this."

"Carwyn—"

He stopped her mouth with his, murmuring sweet words as her body cradled him. "'You have ravished my heart, my bride, with one look of your eyes…'"

"I'm… I'm hot," she whispered. "I don't want to hurt you."

"Shh," he dipped down to her burning lips. "You would never."

The fire that churned beneath her skin was building, almost startling in its intensity. Carwyn could see the air around her shimmer, and suddenly, he knew how to calm her. It was all so clear. He reached out and his amnis wrapped around her as he gently coaxed the heat away, drawing it into his own body as her flesh welcomed his and she cried out. He slid within her, staring into her eyes as they widened in surprise and joy.

Body. Heart. Soul. Together.

Brigid smiled and touched his cheek. "And the two will become one."

Carwyn rocked in her, leaning down to taste her lips. He whispered, "'Behold, you are fair, my love… your lips are like a strand of scarlet, and your mouth…'" He pressed another kiss to her lips as she gasped his name. "'Your mouth is *lovely*.'"

His right arm slid under her shoulders as he braced himself and felt the bed crack again. Brigid's eyes were glazed over as he made love to her, her body a shivering mass of coiled heat, waiting to release. He held her on the edge, slowly and thoroughly acquainting himself with the feel of his body and hers together. He clenched onto every ounce of control he owned so he could savor their union.

It had been so very long.

"What are you doing to me?" Her voice was a high keen and she clutched his neck, holding him so tightly he knew he would have brands in the morning. The thought only made him smile in sensual greed. Let her mark him. He eyed the curve of her neck, a thousand years of self-restraint falling away. He bared his fangs, bent down to her skin, and let them scratch slowly up from her collarbone.

Brigid arched into him, wrapping her legs around his hips. "*Yes.*"

He sucked and pulled, willing her vein to swell for his bite. Then, with one final slow thrust, he held her at the peak and bit.

Her body shuddered and pulled at his as her blood slid down his throat and she sobbed in release. Rich. Thick with the essence of her. Sweeter than any wine. More satisfying than any food. He was heady with it. Carwyn took deep draws before he pulled away, baring his own neck to her so she could strike.

She rolled them over and he felt one of the legs on the bed give out, the resulting jolt sending a wave of pleasure up his back, making his spine arch just as Brigid bent down and slid sharp fangs into his neck. The combined pleasure of her body and bite rocketed through Carwyn and he could no longer hold back. He roared in release and threw his arms out, gripping the bedposts until they snapped like twigs beneath his fingers as the earth beneath him gave a slow roll.

Hours later, Brigid lay limp, her cheeks flush with Carwyn's blood and her own pleasure as he wrapped his arms around her. He held her as his heart slowed its galloping pace. Finally, she let out a soft sigh and relaxed completely. Her body draped over his broad chest as he trailed fingers up and down the delicate ridges of her spine.

"I love you, wife," he whispered.

"I love you, husband." She nuzzled her face into his neck, tasting his earlobe with her tongue until he groaned and rolled her over. Her eyes widened when she saw the clear intent.

"Again?"

He cocked an eyebrow. "A thousand years is a lot to make up for." He glanced around the room. The bed was already splintered and the table by the bed was knocked over. The lamp lay flickering on the floor and a bookcase lay on its side. He deliberated as his hands and mouth began moving again. "There may be some foundation damage... On second thought, why don't I just buy you a new house?"

"You think that's going to be necessary?"

"*Very.*"

CHAPTER TWENTY-NINE

Dublin
January 2013

Brigid stood in the doorway of her small kitchen, surveying the damage. Pots that had hung over the counter were scattered on the ground. Cupboard doors hung open. The bowl of fruit—one of the few human foods that Brigid still enjoyed—was tossed over and the apples rolled over the wood floor, which had obviously buckled in places. She walked over and lit the stove, curious whether it would work. A blue flame popped up and she put on a pot of water to heat two bags of blood.

She was glad that the damage appeared to be localized. No doubt further… activities would have woken the neighbors, but for the moment her enthusiastic new husband appeared to be distracted.

Husband.

She had a husband. Brigid stifled a laugh and tried to wrap her mind around the ridiculous, thrill-inducing thought.

She reached over to the refrigerator just as she felt the rush of energy snake behind her. A long arm curled around her waist and her neck tilted to the side when she felt him nuzzle in for a quick bite. Brigid smiled and enjoyed the shiver of pleasure that tickled down her spine as Carwyn's fangs slid into the soft, tender flesh.

"You really have quite the appetite, don't you?" she laughed.

"Mmhmm." He only took a few drops, choosing instead to let his mouth linger as he pierced his tongue and sealed the tiny wounds. "You're delicious."

"Well, thank you. You're not bad, either."

She felt a low, satisfied rumble in his chest as the water heated.

Carwyn asked, "Why don't you just heat the blood with your hands?"

"Plastic. Melting. Horrid smell. I learned my lesson early on that one. I haven't figured out quite how to heat them up slowly yet."

"Hmmm." He seemed to enjoy just feeling her skin. Large hands slipped under the T-shirt she'd put on. His cheek lay against the nape of her neck.

Brigid smiled. "You're quite cuddly for an ancient monster of terrible strength, you know."

"Quake with fear, my love." He nibbled on her earlobe. "I'll be attacking something very soon."

She shook her head. "No more quakes for a bit, please. It's a miracle the house is still standing."

"No, it's not. I went outside and made sure to shore up the foundation and feel around under the house after you got out of bed. No obvious structural damage."

"You mean…" She bit her lip. "You rearranged the earth to make sure the house didn't fall over?"

He spun her around and his smile was more than a little conceited. "Well, since I was the one causing the earth to move earlier, it only seemed fair."

"You're never going to get tired of that joke, are you?"

"No. Want to go outside?" He ducked down and sucked at what she was already thinking of as his favorite spot on her neck. "I have ideas."

"Well, your ideas should wait until we've had something to eat." She slapped a hand over his mouth as his eyes lit with mischief. "Something other than *that*! We do have to get sustenance from more than each other, Carwyn."

"Not as much, though," he mumbled through her fingers, nipping at them until she shook her head and turned back to the stove. He righted the chairs in the kitchen and sat down. "We won't have to drink as much now that we're exchanging blood."

Her heart began to beat faster when she thought of the first moment she had felt it. Carwyn above her. Surrounding her. The cracks in her heart filling with his love. The acceptance. The rightness as his body cleaved her and his fangs pierced her skin. Her blood entered his body as he entered her. Their amnis weaving together until…

"We're one," she whispered. "I never understood what that meant until now."

She could see the red rim his eyes. Oh, her sweet man. He had such a huge, strong heart. So full of joy and faith. What had she done to deserve the gift of his love?

Grace. In that moment, Brigid Connor understood grace.

"Thank you for being my wife." He winked at her with shining eyes. "We're going to have so much fun."

She smiled, trying to hold in the laugh, but it didn't work. She was giggling like a schoolgirl. "We…" She shook her head. "We didn't really think this through, did we?"

"What do you mean?"

She laughed again. "We jumped into it! I mean, you show up one night and by the next—"

"Be honest, how long have you had feelings for me, woman?"

That brought her up short. "What? How long?" She tried to think. "Are we counting the embarrassing teenage infatuation?"

He grinned. "Can we?"

She rolled her eyes, which only made him laugh again. "No. Okay, not counting that…" She sighed. "Probably since you called me on the drugs in college."

His eyebrows raised. "Really?"

"Yes. I was relieved you found out." She shook her head. "I tried to be mad—I *was* mad! But I was relieved, too. And then… then I thought, 'If I can make it through this, it will impress him.' I don't even think I realized what that meant at the time. But then years went by, and the next time I saw you—"

"At Christmas," he said. "You'd just started working for Murphy."

"And you asked about my hair." She smiled. "And I fell in love with you a little for remembering that it used to be purple."

"How could I forget? You look fantastic in purple. Almost as good as you do in nothing at all."

Brigid said, "And you? When did you have feelings for me?"

"I think around Christmas, as well. But I was relatively clueless. It wasn't until that second night at the Ha'Penny when I realized I was attracted to you."

"I knew you seemed odd that night!" She chuckled. "But surely that wasn't anything new. You've been around for a thousand years, and you're a man."

"Oh, but it *was* new. Because it wasn't a fleeting thing. It was you. And you were… you." He rose and stood behind her again, hugging her to his chest. "So, you see, it's been something like seven years, Brigid. This is the longest courtship in history."

She snorted. "We weren't courting that whole time. We were… friends. Good friends. And then, we were more."

He laughed in her ear. Leaning down, he whispered, "Silly Brigid. Love *is* friendship. Just with less clothes, which makes it far more brilliant."

Carwyn took her out to the garden after they'd fed, the cool earth cradling them and heightening their pleasure as they made love under the stars. Brigid decided she was glad she'd purchased a house with a very high hedge. Finally, they rested, and Carwyn brought a blanket from the living room to shield them as they both lay on the soft grass.

"Tell me about your friend," he urged softly.

She'd told him that Emily had taken the elixir. He was concerned, but she could also see the curiosity in his eyes. Brigid felt his arm wrap around her more securely. "Axel—her boyfriend—gave it to her. I think he was the one who was working with Lorenzo on the heroin before."

"I remember that. But you said he didn't have the smarts for it."

"I must have been wrong. Because once Ioan was killed, when Lorenzo's heroin operation was halted, things settled down. Then, there were the rumors. And right about the time you left for Rome, Elixir started showing up. I think he used the same distribution network. The same clubs and dealers. He gave it to her over a year ago. And I saw him at the same club where she was. He has to be the connection."

"It sounds like it was around the same time that Lucien drank from Rada."

"Who?"

He cleared his throat. "Ioan's friend. The doctor? He had a research assistant—an old lover—who had cancer. She was dying, and Lorenzo showed up in Eastern Europe with a miracle. After she'd been healed, Lucien drank from her. He was elated at first. Thought he had healed Rada and conquered bloodlust all at the same time. Then he started losing time. His mind became hazy.

"It affected his amnis. Damaged it."

"Yes. Most of us—older vampires especially—rebel against the thought. We've all become accustomed to thinking of our amnis as this impenetrable shield. Nothing can harm it. It's what protects our minds. Lets us control the elements. That's why we have to feed from humans or animals. It's the energy in their blood. It's more than just the physical substance; it's mortal energy we feed on, Brigid."

"Almost like it recharges our batteries," she mused. "That makes sense. And the elixir breaks it. Disrupts the flow of the current, like our wiring becomes twisted."

He paused. "That's a very good way of putting it. Maybe it's easier for younger vampires who grew up around technology to understand. Was Emily sick when Axel gave her the drug?"

She shook her head. "No, but she'd just come off drugs. Her health had taken a hit from years of use, and then she went through withdrawal. She said…" Brigid felt her voice grow thick with emotion. "Axel told her that it would make her healthy and beautiful again. Even though she wasn't ill, she took it."

"Vanity?"

"Maybe a little. She loved him and she thought the elixir would let her stay with him forever."

"Poor thing," he murmured.

"Her health was already damaged, but now she can't seem to digest anything. She's starving to death, but her body rejects all nutrition."

He paused, and Brigid glanced over her shoulder. "It's exactly the same as what happens to vampires. Those who are affected can't feed their amnis with blood. And the human body can't retain the nutrients that it needs, either. The elixir starves both the human body and the vampire mind."

"And you haven't found a way to detect it."

She could tell he was frustrated. "Not yet. We haven't had many humans that we *know* are infected. We can't run tests on it. It's too dangerous. And those humans we do know about are very ill. I tried to get Lucien to share more information about Rada, but it was hard to talk to him after a while. He just kept going on about her scent and how good she smelled."

A memory pricked her mind. "How good she smelled?"

"Yes, he said she smelled... sweet. Sweeter than she had in the past."

"Like fruit..." Brigid whispered, and her heart began to race. "She smelled like ripe fruit, didn't she?"

Carwyn's eyes narrowed. "Yes. Like... what was it?" He blinked and he sat up next to her. "Pomegranates. He said she smelled like *pomegranates*. Did Emily—"

"That's it! I remember thinking when I met her last spring that she smelled delicious, but I'd never seen her as a vampire before. I thought it was just her natural scent. But she smelled like fruit. Something distinctive, but I couldn't quite place it. It was pomegranates, Carwyn. Why..." Her forehead furrowed in confusion. "Why would she smell like pomegranates?"

Carwyn rose and pulled her up by the arm, tugging her into the house. They pulled on clothes as he ran his fingers through his hair, thinking. "The elixir was made by plant alchemy developed in the Middle East during the ninth century. I'll bet you that one of the main ingredients is pomegranate."

"What's so special about pomegranates?"

"I have no idea." He stopped in the living room, scanning her bookcases. "Do you have any books about gardening? Botanical... mythology?"

She blinked at him. "Do I look like a gardener?"

"Aargh! Why don't I have Gio or Beatrice here? They're both walking encyclopedias about things like this."

"Can you call them?"

He cocked his head. "I can try. What time is it?"

"Four in the morning."

"They'll be awake. Phone?"

She pointed toward the kitchen where her phone lived. She followed Carwyn and sat at the table as he paced and tried to connect. She could hear the ringing on the other line before a woman picked up.

"Hello?"

He punched the button for the speakerphone. "B! How are you, darling girl? I need your help with something."

"Carwyn... where are you?" The voice was American. This had to be Giovanni's wife, Beatrice. Brigid felt strangely nervous. She'd met much of Carwyn's family, but these were his friends.

"I'm in Dublin, and you're on speaker phone."

"Who else is there? Is it Deirdre? Hi, Deirdre!"

"No…" Carwyn rubbed the back of his neck. "It's… um, it's Brigid."

The woman's excited yelp traveled across the Atlantic, and Brigid's eyes widened.

"Brigid! You're with Brigid? Gio!"

She could hear the sound of something being thrown across the room. It sounded like fluttering. A book? A low voice with an Italian accent came over the line.

"Why are you throwing paperbacks, Tesoro?"

"It's Carwyn! He's on the phone… with Brigid."

"The mysterious Brigid? Father, you have some explaining to do. She's been going on and on about this for months now."

She hid her face in her hands. What had he told them about her? She could hear her husband snickering across the room and she picked up an apple and tossed it at his head. He ducked and burst into laughter.

"What did you say about me?" she hissed.

Beatrice's voiced jumped out. *"He didn't say anything about you! I tried and tried—once, he let your name slip, but—"*

"Brigid, by any chance, was Carwyn writing you letters last fall? Because he was being very secretive about—"

"Hush! Both of you." Carwyn chuckled and dodged another apple that almost tagged him in the ear. "Gio, does your wife throw things at you? Because mine throws fruit with amazing accuracy, and I just want to know if this is typical behavior."

Stunned silence filled the room, and Brigid felt the almost irresistible urge to hide under the table.

"Um… she tends to throw books at me. Mass market paperbacks, mostly. And I avoid her when she's reading Tolstoy."

"Good to know."

Another long silence filled the room, until Brigid heard sniffing. She looked around in alarm. "Who's crying?"

He closed his eyes and bit his lip to keep from laughing. "It's B," he whispered. "Don't worry. She's a bit of a weeper."

"Oh, no." These were some of Carwyn's closest friends, and they were probably going to hate her for—

"You got married? I'm so happy for you! I can't wait to meet her. When are you coming to America? We have to meet her! Why isn't she talking? Is she still there?" A quick pause… *"I can't believe you didn't even tell us, Carwyn!"*

He leaned toward the phone. "Turnabout is fair play, Mrs. Vecchio. Besides, we *just* got married. And it's not actually the reason we were calling. We need your brains, please."

Someone cleared their throat on the other line. *"So… what? You were just going to skip over this little bit of news until the next time we—"*

"Beatrice..." The low murmur came from Giovanni. *"Later,"* he whispered. *"Carwyn, Brigid, what can we help you with?"*

Brigid took a deep breath, pleased to be talking about murderous plots and conspiracies again. "What can you tell us about pomegranates?"

"Pomegranates?"

"Yes, we think the elixir may be produced using pomegranates, and we might be able to detect it in humans using the scent."

There was a long pause; then Beatrice's somber voice filled the room. *"They're still making it, aren't they?"*

Carwyn said, "Yes."

Brigid heard two sighs.

"After everything we did..."

Giovanni said quietly, *"We tried to tell the truth about it. Why didn't they listen?"*

"Greed," Brigid said. "A willingness to exploit the weakness of others. They'll justify it to themselves any way they can."

"It's a poison."

"It's a drug. And when I was human, I took drugs even though I knew they could kill me. Never underestimate the power of delusion."

"We're not going to stop it," Carwyn said. "Our best bet is to learn how to detect it and hopefully find a cure."

"And you think pomegranates might have something to do with it?"

"With detection, at least. We know of two elixired humans who both smelled distinctly of pomegranates."

There was a pause, then the sound of movement on the other line. Giovanni spoke. *"I believe that one of the ingredients in the elixir was pomegranate. Beatrice and Dez have the manuscript, and Dez has been trying to find someone here who might be able to research it further. Unfortunately, there aren't many experienced alchemists in Southern California."*

"Brigid," Beatrice said. *"There's a lot of mythology and symbolism related to pomegranates, so I'll just give you the highlights. They're Persian. Very ancient. Some think the fruit Adam and Eve ate in the Garden of Eden was actually a pomegranate."*

"Not an apple?" Carwyn chuckled and bit into one of the fruits she'd tossed at him.

"No. In Greek mythology, they're associated with death. Persephone was tricked into eating pomegranate by Hades and doomed to live in the Underworld. There are lots of stories, but there are health benefits, too."

"Oh?"

"Pomegranates have been used in medieval remedies and folk medicine throughout Asia and the Mediterranean for hundreds—maybe thousands—of years."

"And now they're being used to weaken vampires and kill humans," Brigid whispered. "Like Emily."

Another silence filled the room, and Carwyn walked to her, lifting her up and cradling her in his arms.

"I'm so sorry, love."

She blinked back tears and nodded. "Beatrice, Gio, thank you so much for the help. Carwyn's right. You two really are walking encyclopedias."

Brigid heard Giovanni's low laugh. *"You're more than welcome. It sounds like you two are busy, but keep in touch. And whenever you're able, please, come visit. We'd love to meet you, Brigid. And we'll even put up with Carwyn if we must."*

Brigid snorted. "Thanks. It was nice to speak to you both."

"It's nice to finally know who Carwyn's mystery woman is," Beatrice shouted.

Carwyn sat at the table and she perched in his lap. "I'm never going to hear the end of this, am I?"

"Give me a couple hundred years, and I'll think about letting you off the hook. Bye, Father!"

"Um…" Didn't they know? She had assumed that Carwyn would tell them. "Carwyn, did you…"

There was a scuffle of voices on the other end.

"You know he's not a—"

"I forgot! I've called him that the entire time I've known—"

"It might bother his wife to hear him called 'Father.' If I can get out of the habit—"

"Don't use the professor voice on me, Gio."

Carwyn interrupted the quietly escalating argument. "Good-bye, both of you. We'll talk to you soon." Then he clicked off the phone without another word.

"So…" he said, leaning back in his chair.

"They seem nice."

He grinned. "They're going to love you."

"You really didn't tell anyone about me?" She didn't know how to feel about that.

"Oh," he said. "I let your name slip once and B grabbed onto it. But… I didn't know where we stood then, and I didn't… I didn't know."

Her heart hurt at his rare show of vulnerability, and she leaned on his shoulder. "I'm sorry we separated without you knowing how I felt."

Carwyn hugged her tightly. "I know now."

She twisted their fingers together as she glanced out the window. The sky was starting to lighten. They'd spent the whole night either making love or talking about a deadly elixir. Brigid had a sneaking suspicion that she'd just had a glimpse of her foreseeable future. "There's no telling where all this is leading. And it's going to be impossible to stop it."

"I know."

She sighed. "And if my time with Murphy has taught me anything, it's that immortals aren't the most cooperative bunch. Your friends excepted, of course."

"No, you're right. We're stubborn, secretive, territorial—"

"Violent. Cunning."

"We move in a world that runs a lot like the human world did in the Middle Ages. Everyone is their own small kingdom, and there's no central government or authority. This problem is going to be impossible to contain."

"True."

"Still…" He paused. "I suppose with my contacts and connections…"

She nodded. "Which are extensive."

"And your innate ass-kicking abilities and penchant for pyrotechnics…"

"You say the sweetest things…"

They both trailed off, lost in their own thoughts. Finally, Carwyn laughed ruefully. "I told you we wouldn't be bored."

Brigid groaned. "This is a nightmare."

"It's very serious, but we do know a few things now." He held up fingers as he counted off. "We know that humans who take it smell like pomegranates, which is a distinctive smell. We know that vampires who take it have increased strength and amnis—"

"At least at first."

"And we also believe—not sure on this one—that the blood of your sire or your direct line can heal an immortal from the effects of amnis."

"So earth vampires…"

"Are actually some of the most protected, considering we tend to have large clans and close ties. You're protected as long as Deirdre is, and even my blood could help you."

"Since you're Deirdre's sire."

He frowned. "Is it too strange?"

She shrugged. "You're a former priest who likes beer, professional wrestling, and ugly Hawaiian shirts. You gave up the priesthood after a thousand years and paid two dozen sheep and a draft horse so you could marry a slightly crazy fire vampire who'll probably burn you every night."

"Only if I'm *very* well-behaved," he said with grin.

She rolled her eyes and elbowed him as he roared in laughter. "Carwyn, the fact that you sired Deirdre is hardly the strangest thing about our relationship."

He tugged on her ear. "Have I told you how much I love you?"

"You have." She snuggled into his side and stared at the growing light. She was already starting to feel sluggish. "You know what?" she murmured as her body began to tire.

"What?" He stroked her hair absently.

"I didn't even call into work tonight." She snorted. "I'm surprised Murphy isn't banging on the door wondering where I am."

Carwyn grunted. "If he has any questions, he can ask me. Besides, as soon as we're able, we're going to take a proper honeymoon."

"Oh?"

"Yes. We may have had an unconventional wedding—"

"You could definitely say that."

"But the honeymoon is non-negotiable. Beaches in moonlight." He nibbled on her neck. "And making love in the waves."

She smiled. "That will keep me cool. And hot. At the same time."

"Ideas. I have many, many ideas…" He paused and she could feel his tension ratchet up. "Someone is coming toward the house."

She froze, her senses reaching out cautiously for a moment before she relaxed. "It's fine," she said as she rose and walked toward the door. "Just one of the boys from work."

"Not Murphy?"

"No, not Murphy."

She was still smiling as she opened the door. She laughed for a moment, not even the sight of Jack dampening her happy mood. "Jack," she said. "You're never going to believe what I did earlier tonight."

"Oh?" Jack smirked, and Brigid's eyes widened when she saw a vampire step out from the bushes at the street. His amnis must have been weak, but then, Axel had been drinking from Emily for over a year. "Do tell, Brigid. I'm ever so eager to catch up on news.

She blinked and a scene flashed before her eyes.

A dark alley. Two vampires, one blond, one sandy-haired. Red frosted glass passing from hand to hand. A wicked laugh and a bright flash.

"It was you… Of course," she murmured as Axel stepped closer. "There were always too many dead ends."

Her head was swimming with exhaustion and shock when she heard a shout and a crash as windows shattered in her house. A loud buzzing sound came from behind her, and the ground beneath her feet rocked as she fell to her knees. Arms caught her as she fell and someone threw her over a shoulder.

No, no! Her stomach roiled. She fought to stay awake, but the last sight she caught was the roof of her house falling in as her eyelids fell shut.

CHAPTER THIRTY

Dublin
January 2013

Carwyn could hear before he could see.

"…realize what's happening to you, Axel."

"Jack said I shouldn't talk to you."

It was Brigid's voice, but it echoed. Where were they? He kept his eyes closed, trying to remember.

"Someone is coming toward the house."

"It's fine… Just one of the boys from work."

"Not Murphy?"

"No, not Murphy."

"Jack, you're never going to believe what I did earlier tonight."

Shattering glass and a sharp pinch on his neck. He'd been so occupied trying to sense who was approaching from the front that he'd forgotten to check the back. He'd been entirely focused on Brigid. A bright flash of light followed by blackness. What had hit him? Had he actually been… unconscious?

"Axel, we were friends. I know you didn't mean to hurt Emily, but she's dying now. And you're ill. You must know that something is wrong. You must know that he's lied to you."

She continued speaking calmly. She didn't sound hurt, so he kept his eyes closed and tried to sense around him, slowly filling with dread when he realized where they were.

Under water.

Of course they were. Jack and Axel were both water vampires. Brigid and Carwyn were definitely not. A ship? A freighter, perhaps. Surrounded in a chamber that echoed like metal. They were probably in a cargo hold of some kind. His amnis creeped out, looking for some trace of his element to connect with, but he could feel nothing. They were far from land. The only energy he felt was Brigid's warm fire across the chamber and the rippling, unsteady energy of their captor.

Why wasn't she attacking him? If she could get away, he could tear a hole in the belly of the ship and escape.

Carwyn finally opened his eyes, still keeping them lowered to avoid notice. He caught movement from the corner. In the corner Brigid was tied up with what looked like wire, her arms, legs, and neck secured by a thin gauge metal cutting into her skin. A line of blood trickled down her throat every time she spoke and a long electric cattle prod was pointed at the base of her neck. He stifled the growl that rumbled in his chest and concentrated on his own surroundings.

"Jack says he knows how to cure me. He says that the condition is only temporary. He watches out for me."

"Think, Axel, have you ever seen him drink from a human who had taken the elixir? Did he ever use it on himself? Think about human drugs. Did the dealers—the smart ones—ever use? No, because they knew not to use the shit they sold, Axel. Why do you think Jack's never taken it? *Think.*"

From what Brigid had told him, Axel thinking *before* the elixir was hit or miss. After was going to be practically impossible. Still, he would let her reason with him while he tried to get his bearings.

How the hell had they taken him? Nothing had ever knocked him out before, but Carwyn had a feeling the electric gadget that was pointed at his mate had something to do with it. Normally, any electronics would short out in close proximity to them. But a contraption made to electrocute? Well, that might be an entirely different thing. It didn't matter. Whatever the reasons, it was keeping Brigid from fighting back, which meant she was afraid, which made him furious.

He could feel his anger mounting and Brigid started to talk faster. "Axel, I don't want you to get hurt. *Think.* That vampire you have locked in the corner is going to get out, no matter what kind of cage Jack has put him in, and he is far more powerful than either of us. After all, *the metal's not very thick* and there appears to be a *distinct gap* in the frame that connects it to the freighter hull. If he happened to pull it open, we would both be at his mercy, even though *he'd need to be very careful* to not rip open the hull of this leaking old bucket whose rivets appear weak from age and probable past structural damage."

Axel sounded even more confused than before. "What are you talking about, Brigid?"

Of course, she could sense him now. Carwyn kept his eyes closed and stifled a smile.

"And if he gets out or you poke me with that cattle prod, then I would feel threatened, which would make me burst into flames in a small space, killing all of us. I don't think *any of us* wants that to happen, do we?"

A warning for them both. Carwyn's previous optimism dampened, but didn't flee.

They were trapped in an old freighter, which was leaking and unstable. Their hosts, being water vampires, would be quite comfortable and far more powerful surrounded by their element. Brigid would be at her weakest in water. Carwyn would also, despite his age. Add that to Brigid's natural volatility and they were in an interesting situation.

He tried not to smile. This was more fun than he'd had since almost being burned alive in the Caucasus Mountains the previous year! But Brigid might worry.

Axel said, "Jack will be back soon. Don't light up, okay? By the way, it's really good to see you, Brigid. You're looking very well. Is the big earth vampire your boyfriend? That's good. Have you seen Emily? How is she? She stopped returning my phone calls, and I don't like it."

Poor sod was so lost. Had he always been this dumb?

"She's not well, Axel." Brigid spoke in a softer voice while Carwyn thought. "If you help us out of here, then I'll take you to see her. I know she'd love to see you."

Thank God they had exchanged blood. For a young immortal like Brigid, that would be more helpful in keeping her grounded and in tune with him than anything else. Though blood exchange wouldn't give her the ability to sense his emotions or thoughts, it did mean that their amnis was in tune, which would give them a greater awareness of each other while fighting.

She knew he was awake. It was evident in the tone of her voice. "I know you said he'll be back soon, along with *the four guards with weapons* that I saw, but surely you can help me out. I know you're not a bad person. You didn't want to hurt Emily."

CHAPTER THIRTY-ONE

Surely, he had to be getting the message. She'd been dropping enough obvious hints about who they were up against that anyone less stupid than Axel would certainly have muzzled her. Brigid could sense when Carwyn woke, but he stayed still and she didn't know how rattled he still was from the shock of the cattle prod they had used to take him down. The punch of his massive elemental energy when that had shocked him must have been enough to rock her neighborhood.

Brigid had woken at what must have been nightfall, arms and hands tied with wire that cut into her skin. One wrist felt like it had been cut to the bone. Her immortal body kept trying to repair itself, healing around the wire, but then she would twist again and her flesh would tear. It was painful and she was losing more blood than was comfortable. She should have been stronger, but then normally, she would drink a few bags of blood when she woke.

Tonight's view hadn't been the comfortable refuge of her bedroom, curled up with her new husband and enjoying his attentions. This night had been cold metal, twisted wire, and the view of a vampire she had hoped to never see again. Even if he was an idiot, she would never forgive Axel for poisoning Emily like he had.

"Of course I didn't want to hurt Emily, but I can't help you," he whined. "Jack says he has the antidote to make me better. He says if I cooperate that he'll make Emily better, too. See?" His voice sounded like a child's seeking approval. "I only want the best for her. She'll get better as soon as Jack gets rid of the people standing in his way. Then he can take charge of Dublin and get all the supplies of the elixir he needs. That's what he says. He just says that we have to take more. That as long as we keep taking it—"

"It's not going to help you. And Emily will be dead by then. Who did he say would send him more elixir?" Maybe, if nothing else, Axel knew who was making it. Jack may have been the elusive Dublin connection, but she doubted he was manufacturing the drug. That had to have been someplace else. It had all become so clear once she made the connection. Jack had been her guide to the city and its nightlife for years. She knew he was ambitious, but had no idea that he ever would have betrayed Murphy the way he had. He held little regard for humans other than as a source to sate his hungers. And if there was one person who would have been able to steer her in the wrong direction, make promising leads turn into dead ends, it was Jack.

Which also meant that he had taken part in Ioan's death.

Every comforting embrace he offered, every understanding shoulder now sickened her. She thirsted for his blood and her fangs grew long in her mouth.

If she could just get Axel to untie her…

Carwyn peeked from the corner of his eye again before he raised his head. Axel was staring at Brigid, completely ignoring him. He looked up to take in their surroundings, which were exactly as Brigid had described. An old, leaking ship and a cage that looked like it was used to transport animals.

The idiots. How weak did they think he was? Even if he was underwater, he was still a thousand years old. The only thing that truly worried him was Brigid bursting into flames. Though the air was damp, there was no doubt a shock would be quite explosive. He didn't think she could hurt herself, but burning *him* to a crisp was definitely a possibility.

He narrowed his eyes at Axel, wondering how difficult it would be to leap on the immortal. Would he be fast enough? Could he kill Axel before the idiot could shock his wife?

"Just take the cattle prod from my neck," she said. "If it does the same thing as a Taser, the first time it touches me, I'll burst into flames and kill you, no matter how dripping this place is. Jack told you that, didn't he?"

Axel cocked his head. "No."

Carwyn rolled his eyes. *Could it be the evil drug dealer didn't have your best interests at heart, you utter and complete moron?*

"Why don't you just grab those wire snippers and cut me out? We'll figure this out between us. But it hurts." Her voice turned uncharacteristically weak. "I can't think like this."

"I'm so sorry, Brigid." Axel started to move toward a low workbench in a corner just as Carwyn heard steps approaching.

Damn.

He dropped his head to his chest as Jack opened the door, followed by four guards he watched from the corner of his eye. Two wore swords, one wore a semi-automatic, and one wore an odd kind of plastic gun at his waist. They certainly had all the bases covered. Carwyn felt an unexpected wave of nostalgia for the days when bare hands or a sword would kill just about anything that moved, mortal or immortal.

Oh well. Times were changing in all sorts of ways. Suddenly, he recognized the device.

A *Taser*. So that was the pinch he'd felt that blacked him out. Ingenious little bastards.

"Axel, why are you speaking to her?" Jack said, walking over and slapping Axel in the face. "I told you not to do that."

"Sorry, Jack." Axel wiped a trickle of blood from his lip and stepped back. Then Jack walked over and slapped Brigid. Carwyn heard it echo around the chamber and could no longer stifle his anger. A low growl came from his throat. Jack spun around, grinning.

"Our surprise guest! What a treat it was to find you. My associate was *very* pleased. Glad I had a few boys with stun guns going through the back so Brigid wouldn't bolt. Odd of you to sleep for as long as you did. It must have done a number on you. Only felt it once, myself. We were experimenting with the effects and, since I was the strongest, I volunteered so we could see what it did to someone with power. I thought the effects on you might be impressive."

"You were the strongest?" Carwyn forced himself to remain sitting against the hull of the ship. He stretched his arms over his head and knit his hands together. "That must have been a sad company. So who are you working with? You have the look of a puppet, not the master."

He could tell Jack's pride had been wounded, but he only sneered and walked closer. "You know, I recall your son Ioan saying something like that to Lorenzo years ago as the Italian was torturing him. 'Who are you working with? What are you after? Why must you keep slicing off pieces of me as I scream?' Well, he might not have said that last part." Jack glanced over his shoulder in amusement as Brigid snarled. "But it was implied."

Carwyn ignored the rage and tried to think through it. "So, you've been working with Lorenzo from the beginning? You were the one running drugs in Dublin. Then you just switched over to the elixir. But Lorenzo is dead, so who's giving it to you now?"

Jack only laughed and crouched down so they were face-to-face, metal bars separating them. "You think you're going to get away, too. Just like he did. You won't."

"I will, actually. I'm much stronger than you."

"Oh, I know." Jack ran a hand along the rusted bars of the cage leisurely. What was he up to? He was strangely unconcerned about the idea of Carwyn killing him. "I learned something very valuable from you, Father. Always make your enemies underestimate you. Who would think a ridiculous priest in a Hawaiian shirt was the most dangerous vampire in the room?"

"Who indeed?"

Jack glanced over at Brigid. "But then again, you won't want to chance your favorite little vampire losing control, would you?"

"No."

BUILDING FROM ASHES

"No…" Jack hung his hands in his pockets lazily. Carwyn crouched in a corner of the cage.

"What do you want? Jack, is it? You took us for a reason."

Jack shrugged. "It was getting harder and harder to deter Brigid. And I was never quite sure if she would remember seeing me in that alley. One of my boys shocked her and got himself killed, but I could never be sure. And the whole thing just made her more curious in the end. Irritating little girl. You were just a bonus. Had no idea you'd be at her house that night. Good luck for me."

Carwyn heard Brigid snarl from the far wall, and he smirked. "You're not very smart, are you?"

"I certainly make it seem that way, don't I?" A wicked grin took over his face. "Rascal Jack behind the drug trafficking? Not even Murphy caught it. But then, he was always so small-minded."

"Yes, I've thought the same thing." Carwyn paused. "Wait, no, I haven't, you idiot." He rocked forward, studying Jack. "Right now you're a dead man. A walking dead man. Even if I don't kill you, Murphy will. But if you run now, you might live. So go. Just leave us here and run—or swim—as fast as you can. I'll catch up with you eventually, but you might get a few more weeks of life. Take them."

Jack ignored him. "Your son was right, by the way. Lorenzo was a puppet, which was why I pursued my own connections after he left Ireland. I always knew he would fail. He was too emotional. But the people I work with now?" Jack smiled. "They're businessmen. Nothing more. Nothing less. Makes them nice and predictable. Not unlike you, Father."

"Oh?"

"Yes. You see, I know that you can break out of that cage easily, but you'll try to lull me into giving you information before you do. Predictable. Just so you know, you're not going to be able to stop this elixir. It's out there. On the wind, so to speak. In so many grubby hands and dirty alleys that you'd have to burn down the world to contain it. So don't try to be a hero." Jack rolled his eyes. "You'll ignore me, of course. So predictable."

"So glad you've figured me out."

Jack was starting to irritate Carwyn, and he didn't seem to be willing to give up any information. Which made him less and less valuable as the minutes ticked by.

"I would have killed you both last night, but my supplier wants a word with you. Forced me to trade the two of you for more elixir, so I'm stuck until he gets here."

Well, that was slightly interesting. "Oh? When might that be?"

"As if I would tell you."

"Why not? You seem to think that we're not escaping alive. Just two lads chatting."

"And Brigid." He glanced over his shoulder. "So you bagged Brigid. Really, who can blame you? She's marvelous. But that probably means you don't want her hurt." Jack cocked his head. "Of course, I don't want her to light up either, so it appears we're both stuck for the time being."

Carwyn could hear a low snap. Then another. Jack didn't seem to notice, so intent he was on taunting his captive.

"Of course." He studied Carwyn like an animal in a cage. "You're still quite dangerous."

Carwyn could feel the low snarl that was building in his chest. He heard another snap. Brigid was escaping from her restraints. He held Jack's eyes, determined to give her time to work. "More dangerous than you can imagine."

"And I'm bored. So… I think I'll shoot you." Jack pulled a pistol from the small of his back in a blink, aimed through the bars, and shot. "Weren't expecting that, were you? The old ones never do."

He heard Brigid scream as the bullet tore into him. He felt it ricochet in his chest, spreading and shredding his insides until it hit one of his ribs, cracked the bone, and stopped. Then the blood, the blood he'd shared with his beloved, began to pool where he sat.

She screamed and raged, her throat harsh from the wire that wrapped around her neck. Despite the moisture in the room, her skin began to heat. She had both her hands and one leg free, and Brigid lifted blistering fingers to her neck, trying to grab the metal that still held her. She felt it heat, and the smell of burning hair filled the room.

Jack's eyes darted toward her. "Axel, you idiot! Keep that prod on her!" Jack stood and turned. "Steady now, Brigid. Lose it in this little room and your man is as likely to die as we will. That bullet won't kill him, just slow him down a bit so my associate has time to arrive."

Axel reached out and the cattle prod dug into her neck. She stilled, her heart racing as her eyes followed the blood that streamed from Carwyn's chest. He hadn't fallen. Hadn't even moved much. He was still crouched in the corner of the cage, motionless as he bled on the floor.

His eyes met hers.

She mouthed, *I love you.*

CHAPTER THIRTY-TWO

"Aren't you two sweet?" Jack said. "Who knew Brigid had it in her to be more than the Ice Queen?"

Carwyn held her eyes for a moment before he looked back at Jack, who had knelt down level with him.

"Those are hollow point bullets, by the way. Best thing on a ship if you don't want things piercing through. They're designed to spread out, create the most damage quickly, and stop." Jack leaned closer and gripped the bars, his fangs falling as he curled his lips. "You know, my associate only insisted on meeting you. Brigid is pretty, but expendable. Imagine what those bullets would do to that soft, white neck... What do you think, Father? Think that might shred her spine? Should we find out?"

With a roar that surprised even his jaded captor, Carwyn leapt, bursting from his silent crouch as he tore the bars apart like wet paper. In one blurring motion, the two guards with swords rushed forward and Jack fell back. Carwyn reached out, ignoring the pain in his chest, and pulled the first guard into the cage, twisting off his head as he kicked the bars away. The roof of the cage fell in, trapping him for a moment before he knocked it to the side.

He saw Brigid free of the wires—she must have snapped the last ones during the commotion—and fighting the vampire with a gun. Within seconds, she had disarmed him and was bashing the side of his face in with the butt of the weapon.

He grinned. Oh, she was lovely when she was in a bloodlust. He turned, suddenly suspicious of the stillness.

"Where's Jack?" he called out.

"Behind you," said the vampire as he slashed at Carwyn's neck. Carwyn ducked down and rolled across the room, tossing the guards into Jack's way as he moved toward Brigid. He rolled past Axel, who was crouched in the corner, still holding the cattle prod.

Carwyn eyed it with interest.

Cattle prod... explosion... leaky rusting ship...

"Oh, she's going to kill me..."

Good thing they were already married, and he'd have an eternity to grovel.

He rolled over to Brigid, smashing in the head of the vampire she was punching and spraying them both with gore.

She curled her lip and yelled, "That's disgusting!"

"Beating him bloody wasn't?"

"You were shot. Are you hurt?"

"I'm *desperately* hurt—"

"You are?" Her eyes were panicked.

"—by your lack of confidence, my darling." He laughed and tossed two vampires to the side as they attacked. Then he snatched the cattle prod from a quivering Axel, and grabbed Brigid in his other arm. He swooped down on her mouth for a quick kiss before he winced. "But this bullet *is* taking its toll, love. We need to get out of here."

"Well—" She stopped to grab the sword of the vampire who was attacking them, slicing her hand, but grabbing the blade in the process. "If you have any ideas, let me know. They're blocking the door, and we have no way of knowing how many others he has with him, so—"

"Obviously, we need to make a new door."

She glanced at him, confused. "What?"

Carwyn looked up, winked at Jack from across the room, then grabbed Brigid and darted toward the cage in the corner. The cocky water vampire's eyes moved from the steel sheet metal to Carwyn to Brigid. He yelled something unintelligible, but it was too late.

Carwyn dragged her, kicking the vampire who lunged at them out of the way.

"Brigid, darling?"

"Yes?" Her eyes were racing around the room, evaluating it, taking in all their options to kill the remaining three vampires who blocked them. The one with the Taser was standing near Jack, eyeing Brigid nervously.

"Please remember just how much you love me."

Her eyes widened. "Wha—"

He stopped her mouth with a kiss a second before he pulled the steel roof from the cage in front of himself, braced his back against the rusting hull, and turned the cattle prod on Brigid.

Oh yes, she was going to be furious.

His finger squeezed once. Just once. He hoped it would be enough.

It happened in the space of a heartbeat. A spark. The zing of the current as it connected. Then the explosion knocked him back into the hull, ripping it open as Brigid's fire tore through the room. The rush of energy was astonishing, enough to suck the air from his lungs as he let the room fill with fire. In a split-second, every vampire in the chamber was incinerated.

Except for Carwyn behind his steel shield.

Just a slight push...

His massive shoulders tore through the weakened hull, feeling the water flood from the broken seam as it rushed into the chamber, dousing

Brigid's pale body and quenching the flames around her. The vessel groaned and tilted as he swam back to retrieve her.

Nothing but bones remained. But Brigid was still alive, her mysterious internal shields protecting her from the force of her own fire. He could feel his blood moving within her and hers in him, their energy humming together even as she drifted in unconsciousness. Carwyn grabbed her, tucked her under his arm, then swam through the dark water. He broke the surface to see the ship angle into the black as crewmembers desperately tried to escape.

"Well, that's a mess," he said to his passed-out mate. "Best exit the scene here and sort it out later. Brigid?" He patted her cheek. "Love?"

Nothing. He could feel her energy, but it was coming in short bursts. He wondered whether his blood might help. He bit into his wrist and held it to her lips, tilting her head back as he kicked away from the wreck. He held her on his chest as he swam, cradling her body and humming a happy tune. Still nothing.

"Brigid?"

He could feel her begin to stir. She suddenly latched on to his wrist with a fury, sharp fangs digging into his arm as she sucked down his ancient blood.

He let out a low moan. "Oh… that probably should *not* feel as good as it does considering we just escaped a life-threatening situation."

She growled low in her throat and bit harder.

"You're mad at me, aren't you?" He halted, treading water as he pulled her closer. "I'm still wounded. Do I get any sympathy for that?"

After one final deep pull, she lifted her head, her eyes glittering in the light of the moon over them. Then Brigid launched herself at him, wrapping her arms around his neck and cutting his lip as she pulled him into a passionate kiss.

She wrapped her legs around his waist and held him tightly as he groaned into her mouth and drank her in. She cut her tongue on his fangs and her blood trickled into his mouth as he struggled to remain above water.

"Mmm, Brigid…" he mumbled against her mouth. "I love—"

Just as suddenly, she pulled back, narrowed her eyes, and punched him square in the jaw. "You bastard!"

He only shook his head, laughing as he tried to pull her closer. "I love you."

"You fecking ass! You shocked me! *Shocked me.*"

"Well, I needed to sink the ship and it seemed like the thing to do."

Her eyes widened and went to the nape of her neck. "Did I burn my hair?"

He bit his lip, trying not to laugh again. "Maybe… just a little behind your ear, but—ooh!" He ducked away from another punch, swimming toward the shore as she chased him.

"I cannot believe you shocked me, Carwyn! You are going to pay for —"

He turned suddenly and caught her, stopping her furious words with another kiss. She gave a little sigh then sank into him for a moment before she pulled back. "You don't fight fair."

"Absolutely not." His lips touched her collarbone as he held her, running his hands up and down her sides to reassure himself. "Besides, I can't help myself. You're naked again."

"Please tell me that wasn't your ulterior motive for turning me into a human firecracker."

He reached down and cupped her delicious backside, pulling her against his hips. "It wasn't, but it is a nice bonus."

They stopped talking for a few moments, lost in relief. He kissed her mouth tenderly and she offered her vein for him to drink. His fangs slid in and he held her close as he felt his chest knit together. Finally, Brigid pulled him away with a stern look on her face.

"If you ever use me as a weapon in a fight again—"

"I'd say I won't, but I probably will. That was fantastic, my very talented wife."

"Oh, I forgot I *married* you!" She curled her lip in irritation as he hooted in laughter, ignoring the ache as his muscle and bone continued to heal.

"You didn't forget."

"I did. Is there any getting out of it at this point?"

"None at all." He grinned and pulled on her hand, leading them toward the shore. "Married before God. We're stuck with each other, Brigid."

She tried to look irritated, but he could see the smile teasing her mouth. He poked and prodded, teasing her until she started to laugh.

And that, Carwyn decided, was exactly as it should be.

CHAPTER THIRTY-THREE

Howth, Ireland
January 2013

When she remembered that night, Brigid Connor remembered Carwyn's hand as he held hers and swam toward the lights of the fishing harbor north of Dublin. She remembered the cries of the crew they didn't try to save. She also remembered the Coast Rescue boats sent from shore that they passed as they swam toward the glittering lights that dotted North Dublin Bay. Most of all, she remembered Murphy's stone-set face as he reached a hand out to lift her from the water.

"It was Jack," she panted.

"I know."

That was all he said as immortals and humans clustered around him. Tom gave grim orders to the humans while Declan spoke into a speakerphone with a quietly devastated face. In the hubbub surrounding them, Carwyn grabbed a woolen blanket from someone and covered Brigid with it. Her skin still prickled with hot energy, but her husband wrapped his arms around her and held tight, drawing her away from the crowd.

"They had no idea," he said in her ear as he drew her down to the ground and into his lap.

"Did you think they did?" She could feel him connect with the earth as he held her and his amnis grew stronger by the moment.

"I didn't know. And I wouldn't have trusted one of them if I hadn't seen the Dubliner's face just now."

"Jack was his." She sniffed. "They never spoke of it—none of them—but Murphy is their sire."

"Tom and Declan, too?" He paused. Nodded. "Yes, I see it now. No wonder they're… Well, it's no wonder."

The three vampires moved with quiet efficiency and bleak expressions around the dock where they had come ashore. Brigid wanted to comfort her friends. Wanted to be there for them, but she had no idea what to say. "How could he betray them like that?"

"Not all families are like ours, Brigid."

Our family.

Her family. Brigid realized in that moment how truly extraordinary her husband was. Over a thousand years, he had created a vast network of humans and immortals held together, not by fear, but by love. Grounded by faith and devotion, her clan chose to be guided by the immortal who held her, not because they were afraid to act without him, but because they simply didn't want to.

Brigid stared at Carwyn over her shoulder as he watched the activity that spread through the harbor. "I love you so much."

A smile crossed his uncharacteristically serious face. "I love you, too."

"I'm very honored to be your wife, Carwyn ap Bryn. I hope I'm a good one."

He looked down, and Brigid saw sudden tears touch his eyes. "I hope I'm a good husband. I'm a bit out of practice, so you'll have to be patient."

"I think we both will. Lucky for us we have an eternity to get it right."

He chuckled and pulled her closer. "I imagine I'll annoy the piss out of you at times."

"I imagine you're right. And I'll probably try to run away once or twice if things get difficult."

"That's fine. As long as you understand that I'll catch you."

"Every time?"

"Every time."

A bubble of joy rose in her chest and she bit her lip to hold in the laugh. "I'll count on it, then."

Carwyn looked down and kissed her forehead. Then he hung his head over her shoulder and pressed his cheek to hers, inhaling deeply. "That contraption they shocked me with drained me, woman. I'm hungry again."

"You're always hungry."

"For you... Yes."

"I'm starving, too, but you'll have to be patient. Declan is coming this way."

Her friend was approaching with a carefully blank expression. He shooed away the human who followed him and hooked his hands in the pockets of his trousers.

"Connor," he said. "How are you?"

"I'm fine, Declan. Carwyn's fine. They used a stun gun on him at the house, I think."

Declan nodded. "That would explain it."

A knot grew in the pit of her stomach. "Explain what, exactly?"

The tall water vampire rubbed the back of his neck in a nervous gesture. "Well... there was a bit of damage, Brigid."

She stood up, forgetting her bare skin until she felt Carwyn throw the blanket over her and saw Declan avert his eyes. "What do you mean 'damage?'"

"We've explained it to the city as a sink hole."

Carwyn must have stripped off his shirt because a soggy rag smelling of earth and seawater was quickly pulled over her shoulders. She wrapped the blanket more securely around her waist. "A sink hole?"

"Remember when Jack—" He broke off suddenly at the mention of the brother who had betrayed them all. "Remember what the Taser does. It knocks us out, but it also releases massive elemental energy. So when they hit Carwyn—"

"Oooh," she groaned. "The earth really does move. My house is rubble, isn't it?"

"There was an unexpected class four earthquake in your neighborhood very early this morning that triggered a sink hole that… swallowed your house. But no one was hurt and we'll be happily paying for all the damage to your neighbors."

Carwyn muttered, "I suppose I'll contribute."

A sudden thought set Brigid's heart racing. "Madoc!"

"Found him in the garden hiding behind some hydrangeas. He's fine."

She saw Carwyn wipe a relieved hand over his face. "Thank God for his cowardice. I let him out when we came inside to call Gio. Whoever came in the back must not have seen him."

"Who was it that shot you?" Declan asked. "Did you recognize any of them?"

"No. I wasn't paying attention, and they must have moved quickly. Someone was at the front…" Carwyn shook his head in disgust. "I was distracted. I'm sorry, Brigid."

"Don't apologize," she said, putting a hand on his shoulder. "We were all surprised. It was Jack at the door. None of us expected…" She glanced at Declan. "Well, none of us suspected him."

Declan suddenly found something on the ground to be very interesting. Carwyn squeezed her fingers and Brigid caught sight of Murphy, standing on the edge of the dock, looking out to sea.

She stood on her toes to whisper in Carwyn's ear before she walked over to her boss. She stood next to Murphy, watching the Coast Rescue boats in the distance.

There was a moment of silence before he finally spoke. "You're well?"

"I am."

"And Carwyn?"

"Fine."

Another long pause. "I didn't know he was back in town," Murphy said.

"Just back. He came to see me. I mean… he came back. For me. You know, we're… he's… we're married now!" she blurted. "I mean… yes. We're married. It was sudden."

"A bit." Murphy snorted. "But not entirely unexpected, considering last March. So you're content being a *priest's* wife, are you? Not the most conventional of matches, but—"

"He's not in the church anymore."

Murphy spun toward her with a sharp look in his eye. His fangs had fallen. "He's not?" He stepped toward her.

Brigid stepped back, blinking in surprise, until she realized why he felt threatened. "I can't imagine he has any interest in ruling Dublin, Murphy. If Deirdre has stayed out of your way all these years, what makes you think he has any ambition for it?"

He cocked his head. "Do you?"

"Do I what?"

"Have ambition for it." Murphy crossed his arms and eyed her cautiously. "I don't see your man wanting the rule of my city for his own. But if you wanted it, Brigid Conner, he'd hand it to you on a silver platter, along with my head. You're too young to be a very good liar, so I'll just ask you. Do you have ambition or are you still my ally?"

She frowned. "Murphy—"

"Answer the question, love." Carwyn's voice came from behind her. "Do you want Dublin?"

She spun around, staring at Carwyn, whose eyes were locked with Murphy's. Brigid finally threw her hands up in exasperation. "Look at you two! Why on earth would I want Dublin? I can hardly stand sitting through trade meetings with you when I have to go, Murphy. And Carwyn, you'd be miserable being a politician's husband. Why are we even having this conversation?"

The tension in the still night air dissipated, and Murphy cautiously relaxed. After a few more minutes, she saw him nod respectfully to Carwyn, then to Brigid before he backed away. When he was a few meters down the dock, Brigid said, "I'll be in the office tomorrow night for a debriefing, boss."

Murphy stopped and turned. His face wore the bleak look she remembered when she first came ashore. "I'm very sorry. About Jack."

She shrugged. "You couldn't have known."

"Oh yes, I could have." She saw the raw combination of fury and pain in his eyes. "And I should have. Carwyn"— he tipped his head toward the older immortal—"would you join us tomorrow evening? Dublin would be grateful for your assistance."

Carwyn's voice was still tense and formal. "Depend on it."

They both watched as Murphy melted into the black night. Finally, Carwyn tugged on her hand. "Let's go."

"Would you really have killed him and given me the city?"

He paused. "If you really wanted it. Murphy has become lax. This will either teach him a lesson, or Deirdre and I will put someone more dependable in his place. We'll have to see how it goes."

"So we're settling in Dublin?"

He frowned. "Of course, love. This is where you work. And I'm currently… unemployed." She laughed at the grin that broke across his face. "I'm unemployed!"

"So, you're just going to lay about and watch wrestling now, aren't you? Drink beer. Make a mess in the kitchen."

"That sounds splendid! And I may even cook dinner for you now and then like a good house-husband."

She pulled his neck down and bared her fangs to scrape along his neck as he shivered. "Or just *be* the dinner. That's fine, too."

"I knew you were a smart girl. Can we leave now?"

"Yes, please."

He pulled her to his side, and they walked past the boats and trailers. Past the car park and through the streets of the deserted suburb north of the city. They finally crossed a road that led to an empty field where Carwyn stopped.

"Where are we going?" Brigid asked. "It's getting close to dawn, Carwyn, and we're miles from—"

"Remember I told you I was rather rich?" He pulled the blanket from her and tossed it into a hedge. "I have a somewhat large house on the outskirts of town where we can go. Nowhere *near* water."

"How are we…?" She looked around at the empty field, then down at her feet. "Oh, no."

"Oh yes."

She glared as he grinned and flexed his massive arms. "No."

"Yes."

Carwyn grabbed her and tossed her onto his back. "I was hoping you had an alternate form of transport," she whined. "There's rocks and leafy bits and dirt *everywhere*. I'll be even more filthy than I am now."

He pulled her legs tighter around his waist and squeezed her right knee. "I'll just have to clean you up later. Consider it my reward for doing all the hard work getting us home."

"I'll never understand why you like to travel like this."

"Just hold tight and close your eyes," he said with a grin. "This gets dirty."

Brigid squeezed her eyes shut and ducked down as the ground opened up beneath them.

The following night, Carwyn tried to pull her to sit on his lap in Murphy's office, but Brigid remained irritatingly professional. He winked at her, subtly licking his lips to remind her of how she'd woken at twilight. Then he laughed internally as she kicked his shin and scowled at him. He tried to rein in his good humor—it really wasn't appropriate considering the circumstances—but ever since the woman had married him, he felt as if he'd been floating.

Well, that and he remembered how much he *really* enjoyed sex.

Murphy called the meeting to order with a quiet voice. "I'm sure we've all figured out the basics at this point, but let's have some specifics. Tom?"

"Jack, needless to say, didn't keep records. And most of his people were burned in that boat when Brigid went up in flames."

Declan coughed and muttered, "Well done, Welshman."

There was a smattering of amused grunts as Brigid elbowed him. Carwyn thought he might like the serious Irishman after all. "Thank you, Declan. It's nice to be recognized for my—"

"Idiocy?" Brigid said. "Recklessness?"

"I was going to say 'strategic brilliance,' my love."

Tom continued. "We did find a rather princely cache of gold at his house early yesterday morning after we recovered what we could from the ship."

Brigid asked, "Did he have stockpiles of Elixir?"

Tom shook his head. "No. There were a few boxes that we've already destroyed according to the directions that Carwyn gave us, but nothing substantial. We can assume, as grandiose as Jack's ambitions were, he was a middleman. He'd already distributed his supplies. Was probably waiting for more."

"That's what he said on the boat. That his 'associate' was going to trade us for more Elixir." Carwyn said, "Could have been lying. But we knew the drug wasn't being produced here. So far, the locations we have discovered are Bulgaria, which has been shut down, and Brigid suspects Germany. There may be a connection in India, as well."

"Why?" Declan asked. "Germany, I mean? Why do you think German?"

"Emily," said Brigid. "She said that Axel was speaking German on the phone with someone."

Tom asked, "Did she speak the language?"

"No, but she recognized it. It was the only thing that stood out to her."

"She could have been mistaken, as well," Murphy said. "I'm not saying she was lying, Brigid, but she could have misheard. Especially if she'd been taking Elixir for some time."

She nodded. "That's true. We'll have to investigate more."

"We'll have to investigate a lot more if we're going to get any kind of control over this."

"This is bigger than Dublin," Carwyn said quietly. "Bigger than Ireland." The whole room fell silent, and Carwyn took a deep breath.

"I know sharing information does not come easily to any of us." He paused until every eye was focused on him. "But I have lived a thousand years and have not seen a threat to our way of life like this in all that time."

Murphy's eyes narrowed, watching him.

Carwyn continued. "I have contacts, friends. A thousand years of favors owed to me. And I now have time that I didn't before. My son was killed because he knew something about this drug. My friends have risked their lives. My own wife has been attacked and is losing a friend to this disease. I *know*," he repeated, "that sharing information does not come easily to any of us, but if we have any chance of controlling this, we must begin to coordinate our efforts."

Declan and Tom's eyes were riveted on their sire, and Brigid glanced between all of them.

Murphy crossed his arms and leaned back in his chair. "What do you propose?"

"I spoke to Terrance Ramsey in London early this evening. He asked that I share some information with you and requested that I keep him informed about things going on here, as well. With your permission."

Carwyn eyed the Dubliner. Terry and Gemma had their own spies in Ireland, just like they did in most major cities in Europe. Just as Murphy did for his own intelligence gathering. But coordination could not come from spies. Coordination could only come from allies. Would Murphy's pride allow him to accept the help? The vampire was charming, but wasn't known as a team player, except for a very few, one of whom had just proven to be a traitor.

Would he be willing to trust again?

After a long tension-filled minute, Murphy nodded. "What do Terry and Gemma know?"

He heard Brigid let out a long breath, and he smiled. The first bridge had been built. "We know quite a bit. Brigid?"

Brigid launched into what they had found two nights before. "Most important right now, we think we know how to detect it in humans who have taken the drug. There's a distinctive scent that more than one vampire has noticed…"

Carwyn leaned back and let her lead. He would share the knowledge that he'd gleaned from the Vatican and from his daughter. And he and Brigid would find more. The Father might have given up the collar, but he felt the stirring of a new mission in his heart. And that night, the first stones were laid in a foundation that he hoped would rise to meet this new threat.

Hundreds of allies around the world. Years of friendship and favors. What else had it prepared him for but to protect those he cared about? To protect the woman he loved and the family he had nurtured? And in doing so, Carwyn knew that he and Brigid could protect innocent humans and vampires everywhere from falling prey to this madness.

Looking at the passionate woman next to him—who had already thrown herself into the struggle—Carwyn knew he could not have chosen a more perfect mate.

Wicklow Mountains
June 2013

Brigid ran her hands along the spines of the books. Some were familiar. Most were new. A few had been recovered from Ioan's original library, shielded by the falling rocks that had collapsed in on them when Carwyn had pulled the mountain over her. She saw a few she remembered from childhood that remained curiously unmarred.

"Those were sent from Lucien," Carwyn said.

She turned to see him leaning against the doorframe. "Ioan's friend?"

"Yes. He's somewhere in Africa right now, but I received a package from him several months ago with all the papers and books on vampire blood that Ioan had sent him to look over."

"Anything helpful in there?"

Carwyn shrugged. "It'll take someone more scientifically minded than me to tell you that. B's friend, Dez, has been looking into a few human scientists in the States who she'd like to consult. It's just a matter of finding the right person."

Brigid shook her head and continued walking around the cozy room. "I'll leave that one for the academics."

"And I'll agree with you. I've been told by my daughter that it's always the right thing to do, agreeing with one's wife."

She laughed as he sat on the plush sofa in front of the fire. After a few more minutes of wandering, Brigid came to sit next to him. He wrapped an arm around her and quickly pulled her into his lap.

"You're always dragging me about, Carwyn."

"Well, you fit better on my lap than next to me."

She smiled. "Because I'm so much smaller?"

"No." He ducked down. "Because I can use you as a shield should someone try to attack me. You're far more frightening than this old man, love."

Brigid giggled as she grabbed his hands and wrapped them around her waist. Then she laid against his chest and nestled under the scruff of his jaw where he hadn't shaved in months. Some things never did change.

"I love you, crazy man."

"I love to hear you laugh," he said quietly. "It's my own addiction. I fall in love again every time you laugh."

"Sweet man," she murmured as she kissed his cheek. "I can't laugh at that."

She fell quiet for a moment as she reveled in the memories of Ioan's library. Many were sad, like the night she had woken in pain as a new vampire, but most were happy. Memories of jokes by the fire and books shared by lamplight. Cookies stolen and eaten in the company of a good story. A safe place to rest when sleep eluded her.

"When I was a girl," she said, "this was the safest place in the world. Nothing bad could happen here. It was magic." She felt his arms tighten around her, but she continued. "But then, inevitably, life *does* happen. And you realize one day that no place is truly safe. And no one is truly untouchable."

"And even things you love can burn you," he whispered.

"But then..." Brigid began to smile. "You grow up a little more and realize that whatever happens, if you have love and love has you, you can build again."

Carwyn rested his chin on her shoulder and they both looked into the fire. "And we did." He glanced around at the walls of books. The wall where a painting of his lost son hung next to a picture they'd taken one Christmas with Tavish and Max. "I told you we'd build again, Brigid. It's not exactly the same, but almost."

Brigid smiled. "No, it's not the same. It's better."

Epilogue

Dublin, Ireland
October 2013

Brigid walked through the door of the carriage house around midnight, waving at the human driver who lived in the small village near the estate. She wouldn't see him until nightfall on Monday when he came to pick her up for the eighteen-mile trek back to Murphy's offices in the city. After a long week, and an even more exhausting evening, the weekend was her own to spend at home. Their home. As her husband would say with a teasing laugh, Carwyn and Brigid's little country cottage.

When Carwyn had said 'fairly large house,' what he actually meant was an estate won from a drunk baron in a game of cards sometime in the 1890s.

"Details," she muttered, tossing her purse on the table and kicking the uncomfortable heels into the laundry room near the kitchen door. "Very sketchy on the details, that man."

Carwyn had asked her if she wanted to live in the main house, but Brigid refused. The one maid that kept up the small carriage house was enough domestic help for her. There was a full-time staff that kept up the main house, but she didn't want to be tripping over them in her bathrobe.

"Carwyn?" she called into the silence. "Hmm…"

She wandered through the rooms, but he was nowhere to be found. She heard Madoc lope down the stairs. "Where's the man, Madoc? Upstairs?" But her senses told her he wasn't anywhere near. She could only feel a trace of old energy in the usually lively rooms. Suddenly, she smiled softly. Brigid knew exactly where he was. She gave the dog a pat and slipped on some boots before she wandered out into the pebbled courtyard between the carriage house and the main.

The estate may have been too grand for either Carwyn or Brigid, but the main house did have one feature that had become dear to them both. Tucked into the back corner was a private chapel that the previous owners —a family of questionable devotion, but abundant funds—had built.

BUILDING FROM ASHES

Covered in ivy, its windows were lit with a warm glow that called her as she walked through the misty night. She pulled open the door to see her husband kneeling at the front of the chapel, his head bent in prayer before the two lit candles. She walked toward him, lifting her own small votive to light and place next to his. Then she knelt down beside him and Carwyn put his arm around her waist.

"How was the service?" he asked quietly.

She sighed and stared into the three flames. "It was nice. Sad, of course, but the mass was well said. The music was lovely."

"She'd have liked that?"

"Yes, Emily always liked music. Went to concerts all the time."

He pulled her a little closer into his side and she laid her head against his shoulder. "I'm glad they had it at night so you could go. Was Murphy there? And the boys?"

She nodded. "Angie, too. Even though they didn't know her."

"They knew her parents. They knew you. She was under their aegis. It was right. I'm sorry I couldn't go with you." He pulled her up and they both quickly crossed themselves before they sat in the old wooden pews that filled the chapel.

"It's fine. How was the meeting in Wicklow?"

He put an arm around her shoulders as Brigid continued to stare at the small altar in the front of the room. "Productive. Gemma and I discussed what she and Terry are doing in London. Deirdre received another letter from Lucien. He seems to be much improved after drinking his sire's blood, so that cure seems to work as well as we'd hoped. Still no progress on any cure for humans who've taken it, but that seems to be where he's turning his attention next."

"Any news from Russia?"

"Not yet. We may have to send someone. We'll see."

They both fell silent as they watched the candles flicker. An intricately painted depiction of the Good Shepherd decorated the back wall and warm brass sconces lit the room. The chapel was one of the most peaceful places on the grounds, and she often found Carwyn sitting in it, praying, reading, or writing in his journal. She was glad he had it; she knew he missed his church in Wales, no matter how often he claimed he didn't.

"Was Anne at the meeting?"

"Yes. Drove me home, as a matter of fact. She's staying with some friends in town before she goes North. Said she'd come by tomorrow night."

"Good." Anne, as well as being a good friend, was also a close associate of Mary Hamilton, the water vampire who ran Belfast. And since Carwyn and Brigid's first priority was stopping any further distribution or importation of Elixir into Ireland, Belfast was a place they needed to be.

"And I've a meeting with Gio later tonight," Carwyn said casually.

"Oh?" Her ears perked as they always did when his American friends were mentioned. Brigid still hadn't met them, but had spoken with both several times since their first conversation, usually to find the answer to some obscure fact, but sometimes, just to talk. She liked them both. A lot. The couple had begged Carwyn and Brigid to come for a visit, and they were considering a trip around the New Year.

"What are you two meeting about?" she asked. "Have there been any signs of Elixir in America? Has Beatrice found that scientist who—"

Carwyn cleared his throat. "It's not—strictly speaking—about Elixir. The meeting, I mean. It's more of a… personal kind of meeting. About other things."

She frowned. "What things?"

He shrugged. "Nothing major. Just… things."

She narrowed her eyes. "You two have a date to watch some wrestling match, don't you?"

Carwyn opened his mouth, but no sound escaped.

"That's it, isn't it?" She tried to suppress the smile. "You were going to hide in the library, put some wrestling program on the television, and you and Gio were going to gossip on the speakerphone."

He squirmed. "You make it sound so illicit when you put it that way."

Brigid burst into laughter and hugged him around the waist. "You're still such a bachelor sometimes."

"I've sacrificed for married life, woman."

"How?"

"I've given up… the Hawaiian shirts during mass—"

"No you haven't!"

"Well, I don't wear them *during* mass anymore."

"You don't *say* mass anymore. At least, not for a congregation."

"Details. And I've cut down on beer consumption."

"That is a lie, Carwyn, plain and simple."

"I shave more regularly?"

"That's true." She snorted. "You poor man; you're almost a martyr. Those sacrifices practically qualify you for sainthood."

He whispered in her ear, "I do entertain very lustful thoughts on a regular basis, but only about my wife."

The warm scrape of his fangs against her ear made her shiver, so she whispered back, "When was that meeting again?"

"Not for some time."

Brigid gave him a wicked grin as she rose and took both his hands in hers. "But is it enough time?"

"Never." He stood up, darting down for a kiss that quickly grew heated. "It's never enough time with you."

"You say that now."

"I'll say it always." Carwyn rose and cast one last look at the sputtering candles before he flicked off the lights of the chapel and led Brigid away.

The three candles continued to light the small chapel, filling the room with a faint glow. Darkness surrounded them, but they shone even brighter for it. The small building remained an oasis of peace in the gathering dark, and faint laughter rang through the still night air.

THE END

"We can build again. Even from ashes."

1.800.656.HOPE
Free. Confidential. 24/7
Or visit www.rainn.org for help or more information.

It's never too late for hope.
Love, Elizabeth

Building From Ashes

Continue reading for the first chapter of the highly anticipated Cambio Springs series from Elizabeth Hunter, due in Winter 2013...

***

Welcome to Cambio Springs. Population? Well, you could say that it... varies.

In this small desert town, secrets bubble up from the desert floor, and history is written on the canyon walls. Seven friends will gather at the crossroads, because in Cambio Springs, everything—and everyone—changes.

In a town populated by shape shifters, tradition and loyalty hold the community together, but when change comes from the outside, secrets are revealed, friendship is tested, and more than a few claws come out.

Cambio Springs is the new paranormal romance series from the author of the best-selling Elemental Mysteries series, Elizabeth Hunter.

***

CHAPTER ONE

Jena Crowe narrowed her gaze at the old man, whose eyes were twinkling with mischief. The corner of his silver mustache twitched a moment before the air around him began to shimmer like asphalt on an August day.

"Joe Quinn, you better not." She lunged a hand toward him, but only caught the edge of an empty shirt before it fell onto the tired red barstool where Old Quinn's pants had already pooled. An empty straw hat was the last thing to fall to the ground. "Quinn!" Jena darted out from behind the counter.

The bell on the diner door rang, and a scurrying shadow darted toward it. Jena's grandmother almost tripped over the tiny creature as she made her way into the air-conditioning with four pies balanced in her hands.

"Goodness! Was that Joe Quinn?"

Jena ignored her for the moment, leaning down to swipe up the empty hat and charge out the door, her brown eyes locked on an old red pickup parked under the shade of a Palo Verde tree on the far edge of the parking lot. She raised the hat and shook it into the dusty air.

"Quinn, I am keeping this hat until you settle your damn bill!"

She saw the telltale shimmer on the far side of the truck, then Old Quinn appeared again, buck naked, sliding into the passenger seat and scooting over to roll down the window. "Aw now, Jena, don't be hard on me. I'll pay you next week, I promise. Throw an old man his pants, will you?"

"Not on your life. I hope the highway patrol gives you a ticket on the way home!"

Jena spun around and pulled the door closed to seal in the precious cool air. The temperature in the Mojave desert was already in the 90s at breakfast time, and the radio said it would reach a sizzling 120 at the height of the day. She brushed the damp brown hair off her forehead and stomped behind the counter, reaching under the cash register for the hammer.

"That old snake," she muttered as she searched a drawer for a nail.

Devin Moon looked up from his coffee. "I always thought his natural form looked more like a horny toad than a snake."

"Shut up, Dev." She glanced up with a scowl. "And can't you arrest him for driving naked or something?"

"I probably could…" Dev glanced down at the sheriff's star on the front of his shirt. "But I just got my eggs." He went back to sipping his coffee and glancing at the messages on his phone.

"Why is there a pile of clothes here?" Jena's grandmother, Alma Crowe, had set the pies on the counter and unboxed them. "Did Joe shift at the counter?"

"Yup." Jena finally found a nail. "Right after I handed him his check."

"He still hasn't paid that tab? Sometimes, I think that man has forgotten any manners his mother ever tried to teach him. Shifting at the counter and running out on his check? Does he have any sense?"

"Nope." Jena raised a hand and aimed the nail right through the front brim of Old Quinn's favorite hat. With a sharp tap, it was nailed up behind the register, right next to his nephew's favorite Jimmy Hendrix T-shirt. "Typical Quinns," she muttered, eyeing the T-shirt that had hung there since Sean Quinn had abandoned it—and the town—shortly after high school graduation.

Jena turned to the diner that was still half-full from the breakfast crowd. "The hat's mine until he pays his bill. Someone want to toss those clothes out to the parking lot?"

She saw Dev snicker from the corner of her eye as he sent a text to someone. Alma opened up the pie rack and slid her latest creations in. And the youngest Campbell boy, who was busing tables for her until he left for college in the fall, quietly picked up the pile of clothes that Joe left and took them somewhere out of her sight.

The boy's grandfather, Ben Campbell, lifted an eyebrow and stared at the hat. "Remind me to pay my tab later, Jena."

"I'm not worried about you, Mr. Campbell." The worst of her anger taken out on the unsuspecting hat, Jena leaned over and refilled Ben's coffee. "I doubt you've run from a debt in your entire life."

He winked at her before turning his attention to Jena's grandmother. "Now Alma, what did you bring to spoil my lunch today?" The familiar chatter of her regulars began again, and Jena put the coffee pot back to start the iced tea brewing for the day.

When Jena had moved back to the Springs after her husband passed three years before, the last thing she had expected was to be running her dad's diner full time. Cooking at it? Sure. After all, she was a trained chef and this was the only restaurant in town besides The Cave, her friend Ollie's roadside bar that sat on the edge of the highway. She expected to be cooking, but not running the place. Unfortunately, a year after she'd moved back, her mother and father decided to answer the call of the road in their old Airstream and Jena had to take over. Now, her parents came back every few months for a quick visit while Jena ran the place and took care of the two boys she and Lowell had produced.

Was it the life she had planned for? No. But then, if Jena knew anything from growing up in a town full of shapeshifters it was this: Everything changed.

Dev finally glanced up from his phone. His mouth curled in amusement as he looked at the old hat hanging on the wall. "Remind me not to piss you off. God knows what you'd nail up for everyone to see."

"Since you don't actually live here, Sheriff Moon, that's a tough call. But I'm gonna say those red silk boxers I saw hanging off of Mary Lindsay's line would be the first thing."

"Is that so?" She might have been imagining it, but she thought a red tinge colored Dev's high cheekbones. It was hard to tell. Unlike Jena, who was only part Native American and still burned in the intense desert sun, Dev was full-blooded. His dark skin, black eyes, and lazy grin had charmed half the female population of Cambio Springs, including one of Jena's best friends. But then, Dev had charm to spare, even though he knew better than to try it on her.

She said, "I think Ted's coming in for lunch today. You sticking around?"

"And risk pissing off that wildcat? Nope. But I might go to The Cave tonight."

"Off duty?"

"Yup. You working?"

"Sure am." She heard the cook ring the bell and slide two *huevos rancheros* over the pass. Jena pulled them over and slid them in front of the pair of old farmers who were gossiping at the end of the counter. "Ollie asked me to help out this whole week. Tracey's on vacation with Jim and the boys."

"I'll see you there, then. What are you doing with the boys if you're working all week? Your parents in town?"

"No. Christy's still home from college." Christy McCann was her late husband's youngest sister and her boys' favorite aunt. "She's hanging out this week while I'm working."

The free babysitting would only last a few more weeks. It was August, and though the boys' school had just started, the state colleges hadn't. Jena would take advantage of the extra hand that family provided as long as she could. It was the reason she'd moved back, after all.

Well, one of the reasons. The other one had just slithered out the door a few minutes ago.

Tucked into an isolated canyon in the middle of the Mojave Desert, miles away from the state highway that the tourists drove, was the little town of Cambio Springs. It was a close community, made of the descendants of seven families who had made their way west over a hundred years before. Seven families that discovered something very unusual about the mineral springs that gave the town its name.

Dev stood up and walked to the counter. "Well, I'm outta here, Jen. Hey, did you see that Alex was back in town?"

"Really?" Jena looked up from the ketchup containers she was filling and walked over to the cash register. "Have you seen him?"

"Just saw his Lexus out at Willow's." Alex McCann was one of her late husband's many cousins and one of her closest friends in high school. He'd moved, like so many of the younger people, when he went to college. Still, as the oldest McCann of his generation, she'd suspected he'd be back sooner or later.

"At Willow's, huh?" She gave Dev a sly smile. Willow McCann, Alex's sister, was one of the few girls that Dev hadn't bagged, and not for lack of trying. "He's probably just out for a visit."

"He still doing the real estate thing in LA?"

"As far as I know. There's some kind of town meeting tomorrow night. He's the oldest in his family. His dad probably asked him to show up."

"Anything I need to be there for?"

Jena shrugged. Monthly town meetings were a tradition in the Springs and the oldest members of the seven families made up the council. It was an archaic kind of government, but when you were running a town full of various shapeshifters, normal rules of city government didn't always apply. They did have a mayor… but he pretty much did whatever the elders asked him to do.

Alma Crowe, Jena's grandmother and a member of the town council, poked into Dev and Jena's conversation. "Nothing the tribes need to be concerned about."

"You know we're always available, Alma."

She leaned down to kiss his handsome cheek. "I know. You're a good friend for asking."

The various tribes along the Colorado River had known about Cambio Springs for ages. But sharing a history of wanting to be left alone, they'd tacitly helped to keep the Springs a secret. And it really wasn't that hard. What did the outside world care about a dusty desert town in the middle of nowhere? If you weren't a resident or a friend of one, you were sure to receive a cold shoulder. Visitors, if they happened to come around, didn't stay long.

Jena's voice dropped so she couldn't be overheard by the ears that sat at the counter. "It's probably just Mayor Matt pushing another plan to create jobs since the airfield shut down."

Dev said, "Well, it would be nice if one of them worked."

The military air base that had provided half the town with jobs had shut down in the latest round of federal budget cuts, and more and more families were having to move away. Moving away meant hiding. Though Jena and the rest of the town could shift at will, the myths were true. Come the full moon, the urge to change was almost overwhelming, except for the oldest and strongest of them and any women who happened to be pregnant, the mothering instinct even stronger than the urge to change. That meant that families who moved were forced to keep secrets. And as someone who had lived 'away,' Jena knew just how hard that was. For her, there was no place like the Springs. It was the one place where people understood you. The only place you didn't have to hide.

"It'll all work out," Alma reassured them. "It always does."

Dev paid his bill, still glancing at Old Joe Quinn's hat hanging on the wall behind her, and whistled as he made his way out the door. The continuous hum of conversation flowed around her as Jena went about her tasks for the day. Old men argued. Young moms fed mischievous children. Silverware clattered and the kitchen bell rang. Just a normal day in the Springs.

She heard the door slam just as she slipped off her shoes.
"We're home, Mom!"

Building From Ashes

Aaron, her youngest and most cheerful, thundered like a small elephant down the hall. He was the picture of her late husband, Lowell. His sandy-brown hair was mussed from his bike helmet and his shirt was sweaty. The small town school was only a few blocks from the house she'd taken over from her parents, but a few blocks was enough to drench an eight-year-old in sweat in 115 degree heat.

"Is Low home, too?" she asked, wondering why she only heard one child. But then Low, Jr. was almost twelve and in the full swing of hormones.

Aaron nodded as he gave her a quick, sweaty hug. Ugh. It was a good thing she hadn't showered from the diner yet. The Blackbird Diner closed down at 3:00, which meant she got home from work right about the time the boys came home from school. Usually, her evenings would be devoted to homework, more cooking, and wrangling two active brothers, but since Ollie had asked her to help out at The Cave, her evenings had become much more hectic.

Jena finally heard the door to Low's room close.

Not a word of greeting to her. Jena frowned. It was typical recently. With shifter kids, who usually had their first change in puberty, adolescence took on a whole new hairy, feathery, or scaly dimension. Low was coming up on his change; she could feel it. Or, it was just wishful thinking, because for the small percentage of kids who didn't shift, a far harsher fate was in front of them.

"Aaron, homework out on the kitchen table. I'll make you a snack as soon as I get out of the shower." *And wash the diner grime off.* She walked down the hall to Low's door, which was closed. She gave a quick knock and heard shuffling inside.

"What?" Her eyebrows lifted at the haughty tone. Jena cleared her throat and knocked again, a little louder. Finally, Low came to the door.

"What was that?" she asked.

Low had the manners to look embarrassed. "Sorry, I thought you were Bear. He's been bugging me all day."

"You shouldn't be rude to either of us. Do you have homework?"

"Finished it in study hall. I just have a book report to do."

"Anything interesting happen today?"

Low shrugged.

"What does that mean?" Why did her son have to be so much like... her? Jena frowned. He was, too. From the dark hair and olive skin to the sullen expression. Her mother had enjoyed that one. Jena knew she hadn't been the easiest teenager, so it was fair. Rotten, but fair.

Low gave a tortured sigh. "Kevin shifted last night. He wasn't in school today."

"He did?" Her face broke into a grin. Kevin Smith was her friend Allie's oldest son and she knew Allie had been worried sick. He was older than Low by a year and his shift was beginning to seem uncertain. Allie and Joe had been a wreck about it. "What did he—"

"Fox, like his mom."

"Aww." She melted. Allie would love that. She'd married another canine shifter, so her kids would always be furry, but it was nice when a child's natural form took after one of his parents. In time, Kevin would be able to shift into any canid he focused on, but his natural form, his first shift, would always be his most comfortable. It was hard to explain, but then, Jena rarely shifted out of her natural form.

Low still had a sullen expression on his face. "I'm never going to shift."

Ignoring the flutter of fear in her heart, Jena patted her son's shoulder and reassured him. "Yes, you will. Just be patient."

Low had a familiar, mournful look in his eyes. "Dad didn't."

She swallowed the lump in her throat. "That doesn't mean it will happen to you, Low. You know how rare that is."

Rare it may have been, but for the descendants of the seven families who didn't shift, life was short. Heart attack. Premature stroke. Lowell Sr., Jena's childhood sweetheart, had been lucky to make it to his late twenties before a mysterious brain cancer had attacked him and cut his life short, leaving Jena with two small boys and an aching hollow in her heart that still echoed on the loneliest nights.

Low just shrugged his thin shoulders and grabbed a book out of his backpack. "I'll help Aaron with his homework. I know you have to get ready."

"Thanks, kiddo."

"Is Aunt Christy coming for dinner?"

"Yep. She'll be here around five."

"Cool."

Low walked down the hall. Jena called out to him. "Low?" He turned. "I know she lets you stay up late, and I'm okay with it for you, but make sure that Bear's getting enough sleep, okay? You're his big brother."

He rolled his eyes. "I know, Mom."

She winked. "Good kid. I'm gonna get clean; then I'll come out and get you guys a snack."

"Thanks."

Hours later after a rushed dinner, Jena was primped and ready for another night of work at the bar. Her long runner's legs were encased in skintight jeans that showed off a trim figure. She'd put on a halter top that Ted, her other best friend, had convinced her to buy on a girls' weekend in Palm Springs. It was snug in all the right places and even gave the illusion that Jena had breasts, which hadn't really been true since the last time she'd breastfed, but then, illusion was everything when it came to good tips.

Building From Ashes

Plus, it was just fun to get out every now and then. She never minded helping Oliver Campbell run his family's old roadhouse on the edge of town. The Cave was an institution and drew some of the best business in the desert. It was also the unofficial boundary of the Springs's territory. Few outsiders ever got past Ollie. They were welcome to the cold drinks and the good music, but if you weren't one of the regulars from the Springs, the Tribes, or one of the motorcycle clubs that made The Cave their home, then don't linger. And don't get too familiar with the staff.

But please tip your waitress, because Mama needs to buy two growing boys shoes before their toes poke out of the old ones.

Jena did all right. The diner was steady business and she didn't need much to get by. The house was family property and didn't have a mortgage. Her car was paid for. But keeping up with everything that two kids needed was still a challenge some months. And that was another reason that Jena was dolled up and headed out to Ollie's. A few good tips wouldn't hurt the bank account.

She pulled into the back and could hear the band warming up. Despite the isolated location, The Cave had become known for some of the best music in the desert. Rock, blues, old-fashioned country. If you were an independent musician looking for a gig, then The Cave was the place to play. Ollie paid the bands decent, but the money wasn't really the draw. Saying that you'd survived the tough-as-nails crowd at The Cave without bottles being thrown at you was the real prize. More than one famous musician or group had a picture on the wall that led to the bathrooms.

Not behind the bar, though. Nothing was behind the bar besides beer, liquor bottles, and the hulking form of Ollie Campbell.

"Hey, honey." Jena slipped into Ollie's office and put her purse on the bookcase behind his desk. Ollie's office was very much like the man himself. Solid furniture, an eclectic mix of decor, and quiet, soundproofed walls.

"How was your day, Jena?"

He had a pencil in his mouth and he was chewing on it. He'd been doing that ever since the year before when he stopped smoking.

"It was fine. You gotta stop that, Ollie, you're going to ruin your teeth."

He chuckled. "Doubtful. You know what these teeth tear up on a regular basis?"

"I'm not talking Bear Ollie; I'm talking Regular Ollie, and you *will* ruin your teeth if you keep doing that. Try some gum."

"Yes, Mom."

She whacked the back of his head. "Shut up. You're two months older than me."

He just gave her a quiet smile. Quiet smile. Quiet man. If you didn't know him, Ollie Campbell might seem like a hard case. He was well over six feet tall, had dark curly hair that was trimmed short and a full beard that hid his dimples. His suntanned skin was covered in black-and-grey tattoo work that decorated most of his arms and a lot of his back.

And Ollie was a giant teddy bear.

"Hey, Kevin shifted! Fox, just like Allie. Low told me he wasn't in school today."

Ollie's face softened at the mention of Allie. But then, it always had. Ever since they were kids. "Good." He nodded. "That's really good. She was worried about that. I'm sure Joe's relieved, too."

"Yep." Ignoring the sorrowful tinge to his eyes, Jena fluffed her hair and put her hands on her hips. "How do I look, boss?"

He whistled. "If you weren't like my sister, I'd hit on you. Between the band tonight and those jeans, we should both make out pretty good."

"Good to know."

Ollie rose from his desk and ushered her down the hall. "Hey, did Old Joe Quinn really run out of the diner buck-naked today?"

"He shifted and ran when I handed him the bill. His favorite hat's nailed behind the cash register."

Ollie chuckled and shook his head as they walked down the hall and into the bar that was growing louder by the minute.

"He won't forget that one."

"I'm counting on it."

Want to read more? The first short story in the Cambio Springs series, _Long Ride Home: A Cambio Springs Short Story_, is now available in e-book edition from Amazon and Barnes & Noble.

ABOUT THE AUTHOR

Elizabeth Hunter is a contemporary fantasy and romance author. She is a graduate of the University of Houston Honors College in the Department of English (Linguistics) and a former English teacher.

She currently lives in Central California with a seven-year-old ninja who claims to be her child. She enjoys reading, writing, travel, and bowling (despite the fact that she's not very good at it.) Someday, she plans to learn how to scuba dive. And maybe hang glide. But that looks like a lot of running.

She is the author of the Elemental Mysteries and Elemental World series, the Cambio Springs series, and other works of fiction.

Learn more about her writing at
ElizabethHunterWrites.com
Or visit the Elemental Mysteries fan site at
ElementalMysteries.com.

She may be contacted by e-mail at
elizabethhunterwrites@gmail.com.
Twitter: @E__Hunter
Official Facebook page: Elizabeth Hunter

Made in the USA
Coppell, TX
13 September 2020